THE

DELTA

ALSO BY MARSHALL HARRISON

A Lonely Kind of War: Forward Air Controller, Vietnam

Cadillac Flight: A Novel

THE DELTA

A Novel

Marshall Harrison

LYFORD
Books

This is a novel. The characters and military organizations are an invention of the author, except where they can be identified historically, and are intended to depict no real persons or organizations. Any resemblance to actual persons, living or dead, is purely coincidental. Likewise, names, dialogue, and opinions expressed are products of the author's imagination and should not be interpreted as real.

Copyright © 1992 by Marshall Harrison

LYFORD Books
Published by Presidio Press
505 B San Marin Dr., Suite 300
Novato, CA 94945-1340

Library of Congress Cataloging-in-Publication Data

Harrison, Marshall, 1933–
    The delta : a novel / Marshall Harrison.
      p. cm.
    ISBN 0-89141-436-3
     1. Vietnamese Conflict, 1961-1975—Fiction. I. Title.
PS3558.A6715D4 1992   91-45203
813'.54—dc20   CIP

Typography by ProImage

Printed in the United States of America

This book is dedicated to those combat advisers who were in Vietnam long before most Americans even knew where to look for it on a map. They made do with second-rate equipment, weapons, and even food, often commuting to a day's combat aboard an ancient helicopter with a World War II submachine-gun, and carrying their lunch in a brown-paper sack. Half were probably fast-burners, promoted before their contemporaries; the remainder were likely to have been passed over for their next rank a few times and at the end of their military careers. It was difficult to distinguish between the two groups in the field. There was one other thing they had in common: they bled and died together in obscurity.

And, as always,
to Mary Ann

"This is what extremely grieves us, that a
man who never fought
Should contrive our fees to pilfer, one
who for his native land
Never to this day had oar, or lance, or
blister in his hand."
Aristophanes,
Wasps, 422 B.C.

"Among other evils which being unarmed brings you,
it causes you to be despised."
Niccolo Machiavelli
The Prince, Chapter 14

THE
DELTA

CHAPTER 1

Sam Brooks glowered at the disinterested sergeant. He could feel the sweat dribbling down the back of his khaki shirt, and his armpits were sticky. His eyes burned from lack of sleep and his anger was just barely in check. He was in no mood for unpleasant NCOs. Sam shoved his flight cap forward over his closely sheared head until it almost rested on the bridge of his nose, then removed his fogged sunglasses to let the sergeant have the full benefit of the reddened eyes. He glowered some more. The sergeant was not impressed.

"Look, Major," the sergeant said, bending to his small desk to resume shuffling papers, "I don't have anything on your arrival. See?" He displayed the stack of orders collected from the other new arrivals as proof. "If you were supposed to be coming to 2d Air Division, we'd have a set of confirming orders. But, as you can see, we don't."

"Nevertheless," Sam grated, "as *you* can see, I am here. All I want from you is the location of where I can go to straighten this out."

"Jeez, sir. I dunno. I guess the personnel office at 2d Air Division. They oughta be able to help if anyone could."

"And just where does a person find this particular place?"

"It's 'bout a mile down the road in front of the terminal. Big wooden building. You can't miss it."

"I don't suppose," Sam said slowly, "that in the frantic press of your duties it would be possible to drop me off there while you're delivering these other men wherever the hell they're supposed to go."

"Jeez, Major, I don't know. I'm not supposed to give rides to anybody unless they're authorized by—"

He stopped talking abruptly as Sam's big hand rested gently on his shoulder. He flinched from the hard, staring, bloodshot eyes and the

1

fetid breath enveloping him, as much as from the unexpected touch. The tall major leaned in until their faces were only inches apart. A chill thrilled the sergeant as he realized he might have gone too far with this one. Most of the new officers arriving at Tan Son Nhut airfield in Saigon were so hammered by the trip that, except for a few sour looks, they submitted docilely to the sergeant as he alternately ignored them or bossed them around. The sergeant normally enjoyed the exchange, figuring it helped even a career of grievances against the officer class. It was also a matter of pride. They had to be kept in their place or they'd forget who really ran the air force. He might have a problem with this one, though.

"Sarge," the major breathed at him gently, "I've been on and off that airplane for the last thirty-four hours. During that time I've been served five fucking breakfasts, all of them soggy pancakes and fatty ham. I've been drooled on by sleeping men and ignored by hostesses. I've seen one-hour waits turn into five hours at tiny little dots all over the Pacific Ocean—places where they wouldn't even give you a cup of coffee, places where the flight crew of the airplane disappeared for hours on end to do God knows what.

"Sergeant, I'm not a happy man. In fact, I'm downright cranky. Please believe me when I say this because it comes from the heart. If I get one more ration of shit out of you, I'm not only gonna see that those five stripes get ripped off your arm, I'm going to kick you so hard in the low-hangers that they'll end up someplace around your spleen. Now, I'm usually a reasonable man. I don't expect a ride to 2d Air Division headquarters if it's far out of your way, but I better never find out that you've been jerking my chain and that the truck actually goes by it or real close to it. In that event I'd be forced to hunt you down and hurt you real bad. Sarge, I feel like I'm about to become violent and you don't want to be around me when that happens."

The sergeant considered this briefly. It was language he could understand. "Do you need any help with your bag, sir?" Anything to get away from that breath. Jesus! You could almost see it.

"No, Sergeant. I can handle it just fine," the major said. "You just wait right here until I collect everything. And if you move, I'll hunt you down and rip off your damned face."

The guy looked just pissed off enough to do it. The sergeant stood fast until the major returned.

The blue air force truck pulled to a halt in front of the Tan Son Nhut officers' open mess. Sam crawled from the cab, where he had ignored attempts at conversation by the newly solicitous sergeant, and waited for the men seated on the hard benches in the rear to pass him his two bags. He glared once more at the sergeant, who saluted him nervously from the driver's seat. Sam lifted his bags and headed toward the door of the club, knowing he was being flipped a bird behind his back. It didn't help his mood.

The front door was propped open, and two small Vietnamese women were on their hands and knees scrubbing the hardwood floor. Sam surveyed the club as he walked down the entrance hall, trying to find a place to safely stow his bags. At the entrance to the bar he found a cloakroom with another Viet female in attendance. This one wore the traditional *ao dai* costume—loose trousers and a tight tunic with a long flowing split skirt that billowed out from her tiny waist. She reminded Sam of an inverted tulip or an exotic butterfly.

"Uh, pardon me, miss, but could I stow these bags here for a while? I don't really have any other place to put them."

"Of course, sir," she replied. Her vowels were a little slurred but she seemed to have an excellent grasp of the English language.

Sam noticed that she shrank away as he moved the bags into the small vestibule. God! His breath would probably gag a maggot. Body odor too, undoubtedly. The butterfly gave him a numbered claim check, trying hard to avoid physical contact. He pocketed it and walked into the bar. It was empty save for two Vietnamese men stacking glasses. He returned to the long hall and followed it to the rear of the ramshackle building. There, a dining room opened onto a screened porch, also set with tables. A few of them were occupied by men in various uniforms: khakis, fatigues, and flight suits. Worn linoleum covered the floors except where wood peeked through irregular holes.

Sam sat at one of the tables and stared moodily through the screen at the dusty patio. A small thicket of brownish bamboo drooped limply in the heat behind the small square of concrete, a haven for buzzing insects. Large black flies dotted the screen. They looked dusty too. A waitress materialized beside him and looked at him questioningly.

"Order, sah?"

"Anything but breakfast," Sam replied. At her look of confusion he realized he had exceeded the limits of her English. "Bring me a hamburger with everything on it and a bottle of San Miguel beer."

She padded away quietly on small bare feet. The flies stirred lethargically for a moment, driven by some unseen force into a communal shifting before resuming their positions on the screen. Just off the concrete was a large dead rat lying on its back, which Sam had not noticed before.

He went back to his brooding. He really should try to get his orders straightened out, but hell, he had a year to do that. They read simply that he was assigned to Headquarters, 2d Air Division, Republic of South Vietnam. About as noncommittal as they could get. Nearly every air force type in the country was assigned to 2d Air Division except for the few working directly with the embryonic Military Assistance Command, Vietnam, or MACV. Only a couple of years ago it was upgraded from the old Military Assistance Advisory Group, or MAAG, and had since grown like a weed. At the present time, January 1964, Sam knew that most of the 11,000-plus Americans in country were assigned to MACV. Half appeared to be here on the Vietnamese airfield of Tan Son Nhut.

The burger and beer arrived and the waitress left them and the check on the table. Sam wondered if the club accepted American money, since he'd done no in-processing yet and hadn't changed any of his greenbacks for local currency. Hell, he didn't even know what the local currency was.

Laughter drifted toward him from one of the other tables, but Sam continued to chew methodically and stare woodenly out the screen, watching a small bird pick halfheartedly at the dead rat. Why in hell had 2d Air Division even requested a tactical jet fighter pilot for assignment? There were only a couple of squadrons of jet fighters in the entire country, and should he be destined for one of them his orders would have stated it. Surely it couldn't be a staff job, not after sixteen years of flying almost every tactical jet fighter in the air force inventory. Anyway, the commander of 2d Air Division, the only outfit in the air force fighting a shooting war, wouldn't want a staff major who'd already been passed over once for lieutenant colonel. Not with all the hotshots and fast movers fighting for a chance to get into the action.

Sam continued to chomp the overcooked sandwich without tasting it and thought bleakly of his future. One more passover for promotion and that would be it. Sixteen years of service, make it nearly seventeen when the board met, down the toilet. Released from active duty due to failure to attain promotion.

The burger and beer quieted his roiling stomach, which had seen too many sodden pieces of dough over the Pacific. He checked the date in his mind. The promotion board would meet in August. Realistically, that meant he had about seven months before the ax fell. There was damned little reason for optimism—consideration after a first failure almost certainly meant being passed over again. Then what? Too old for the airlines, and flying fighters was the only thing he'd done in his entire adult life. How the hell could it have come to this? Admittedly, there had been few opportunities along the way in so-called career-broadening activities, except for insignificant jobs at the squadron level, which had been offered as a reward for some flying achievement. The plums had never been offered, and there was no doubting the reason. Idly, he wondered if the air force would send him home after the next passover or insist that he complete the full year's tour. What difference did it make?

"Sam? Sam Brooks?"

One of a small group of men leaving the porch had stopped and was looking quizzically at him. Sam knew him immediately. They'd been classmates in gunnery school after graduating from the pilot training course together, and then had flown Sabres in the same outfit in Korea. They'd been reunited after the war in a bent-wing F-84 squadron in California. He was now a lieutenant colonel, Sam noted.

"Cal Upshaw! How the hell are you? Have a seat and tell me some lies." They shook hands and sat grinning at each other. Sam raised his beer bottle questioningly and the other man made shooing motions with a hand.

"Sorry, I've got a takeoff in an hour. From the looks and smell of you, I'd say you just got off the boat."

Sam looked down and surveyed his sodden and wrinkled khakis. "You'd be right. Got in about an hour ago. Congratulations on the silver leaf."

Cal looked embarrassed, having noticed that Sam's collars sported the gold leaf emblem of major. "Hey, no sweat, man. You'll get 'em next time."

"Sure. No problem. You got a takeoff coming up, huh? What are you flying? I saw the F-100s and RF-101s on the flight line. You kicking one of those dudes around now?"

Cal really looked embarrassed now. "Naw, believe it or not, I'm an aircraft commander on a C-123."

Sam stared at him in disbelief, as if he'd just confessed to carnal encounters with a close relative. The C-123 was a *cargo* plane. Not only that, but probably the ugliest cargo plane ever built. Designed originally as a heavy glider, some entrepreneurial engineer had mounted huge radial engines on it and sold it to the air force as a short-haul freighter.

"How did this happen?" asked Sam quietly, as though inquiring about the death of a loved one. Actually, it might be as tragic, being forced from a jet fighter into one of those multiengined monstrosities.

Cal looked as though he'd been caught peering up his grandmother's dress. "Well, I had just gotten out of command and staff school last spring and the USAF personnel people came down to Maxwell field to talk to us about assignments. They strongly recommended that some many-motored time might be career broadening for me."

There was that fucking phrase again, thought Sam with irritation.

Cal continued. "So, I figured if it would help me make bird colonel, when the time came I'd give it a shot for a while. We do get to fly all over the country, and we get to live off base here in Saigon. It's really pretty interesting to see how the other half lives."

"How is it really?" Sam asked gently.

Cal thought for a long moment before answering. "It's the shits," he said with a sigh. "I'd rather be driving a damned bus. I don't know how these people stand it for twenty years. I'd give my left one to get back into a fighter again. I mean, it's downright embarrassing to even walk by those fighter and recce jocks in base ops and have them see me in my little fatigue suit, then go out and crawl into that big tub of crap. Hell! That's not flying. It's just like driving around in your old man's pickup. But, in any event, I'll be through with it in another three months. I've already told the personnel pukes here that if I don't get back into a fighter wing, when I head home they're gonna be in deep kimchi. How about you, though? What do they have in mind for the world's best fighter pilot?"

"Beats me. I'm assigned to Headquarters, 2d Air Division. But it looks as though they weren't even expecting me. I might just skip checking in and take the next bird out heading stateside."

"Well, it could be any assignment with orders like that," Cal said, looking at his watch. "There's all kinds of rumors floating around about a big American buildup, but who knows. Maybe they'll put you on a staff somewhere. That'd help when the selection board meets again. Look, I gotta run to make this takeoff. We wouldn't want Long Vinh to run out of toilet paper, would we? Look me up in the bar tonight if you're still here and we'll burn a Christian or something. Air Division is right up the block to the left. A big rambling wooden building with the CO's and his senior staff's living trailers parked next to it. They can straighten you out. Good to see you again, Sam. Hope we can connect tonight."

They shook hands. Sam watched the fatigue-clad figure until he left the room, then resumed his contemplation of the dead rat on the patio. He felt saddened by his friend's fall from grace. Jesus! C-123s. That had to be the pits. He cocked a finger and deftly flicked a fly from the table. A gecko on the wall watched with professional interest, the lizard's padded toes looking like tiny fingers as they suctioned it firmly in place. The bird had given up on the dead rat, which had begun to swell in the gathering heat.

Sam knew he might as well get it over with. He left his bags in the club, promising the Vietnamese girl that he would return for them. She still seemed wary about getting too close to him. His body odor had obviously not improved with time.

The 2d Air Division building was easy to find. There was even a sign on the front of the two-story structure. As Cal had mentioned, the living trailers for the commander and his immediate staff were parked in the side yard. The trailers were air-conditioned, as the bar in the club had been. All the other buildings in sight had louvered windows. The road in front of the headquarters building was paved, and a steady stream of jeeps and trucks passed by. Most were driven by Americans; fewer by Vietnamese. Singles and groups of the small brown-skinned people crowded the dusty border of the road, seemingly oblivious to the heat that had Sam almost comatose.

A sudden roar engulfed Sam, and he turned toward the flight line to watch a pair of F-100s launch. They were close enough for him to see the full bomb racks beneath their wings. Watching the flight speed away, he felt disoriented and alone, filled with a sudden, almost desperate yearning to be sitting in one of the fast jets. Shrugging mentally, he turned back to the headquarters building and entered.

It was good to get out of the sun, and he stopped in the hallway for a few moments to allow his eyes to adjust to the gloom. When he was able to read the sandwich board on the wall, he saw that the personnel section was up one flight. He realized just how whacked-out he was as he negotiated the wooden stairs. He'd been awake for almost forty-eight hours and it was beginning to show. At the top of the stairs he had to stop and catch his breath before trudging down another hall to the personnel shop.

Typewriters chattered away, and clerks in a variety of khaki and green fatigue uniforms bustled around, acting as though they knew exactly what they were doing. All the busy efficiency depressed Sam even further. A wall clock above his head showed that the time was either 1130 or 0430, depending on which set of hands the observer chose to believe. Those pointing at 0430 had to be set for Greenwich mean time, but Sam couldn't verify that with his own watch, which had lost all side-real meaning for him somewhere around Wake Island, as he was being served his fourth consecutive breakfast. There had also been the crossing of the international date line, which apparently meant it was either tomorrow or yesterday. Sam's exhausted frontal lobe was in serious danger of overloading. Only the primitive brain stem remained active, keeping him alert to the dangers lurking in a headquarters building.

He tacked toward a bespectacled lieutenant sitting at a desk in the corner with his head bowed to a sheaf of papers. Sam executed a sluggish veronica to avoid a collision with a stoutly built staff sergeant, and finally came to a stop in front of the lieutenant's desk. Sam stared at his bent head for a moment before clearing his throat. The lieutenant looked up with irritation at the noise, then came slowly to his feet as he took in the red-eyed wraith before him.

"May I help you, sir?"

"I sure as hell hope so," said Sam, holding out a copy of his orders. "These things tell me I'm supposed to be here, but the sergeant meeting the new troops at the terminal said there was no record of my having been assigned."

The lieutenant took the orders and waved at a chair by the desk. Sam sank wearily into it. He saw to his disgust that he had sweated completely through his shirt front, adding yet another layer of perspiration to ripen on his body. The younger officer excused himself and walked to the far corner of the large room, where he began opening and closing file drawers. Sam fanned himself with his cap to little effect. The lieutenant returned with a large manila folder.

"Here we go, Major. It says here that you're to be assigned to IV Corps. That's down in the Mekong Delta, by the way. Headquarters is at Can Tho, but you may not stay there. You could be farmed out to one of their subordinate units. That's what they usually do. Wait. It says you have a directed duty assignment as a FAC, a forward air controller, so that means you'll have to interview personally with the director of operations right here before you head on down. And I know he's in Danang today, so I guess you'll have to hang around until tomorrow. Anyway, that'll give you a chance to do some in-processing and draw your field gear. Besides, you look like you could do with a few hours of sleep. That flight over here is a real killer, isn't it?"

Sam's fogged mind finally assimilated what he'd just heard. "Just a minute. Did you say forward air controller?"

The lieutenant nodded.

"Hey, hold on," said Sam. "Let's get this thing straightened out before it goes any further. I'm not a FAC. I don't have any FAC training or qualifications. I've flown fighters for sixteen years and I've never even *worked* with a FAC. Now you're trying to tell me I am one?"

"Guess so, sir. As they say over here, 'sorry 'bout that!'" He grinned at the large major until he saw the huge hands clenching into fists. The face was darkening under its tan, and the obvious broken nose seemed to throb with a life of its own. Quickly, he tried to mollify him.

"That's just the way things work over here, sir. Things are so screwed up that if anybody shows up who's halfway qualified to fill a slot, then he's slapped into it before he knows what hit him. It's really not so bad, though. Look at my situation. I came over as a communications officer. But they had plenty of them and they needed a paper shuffler—so, here I am. It's actually kinda interesting finding out about all this crap. There's stuff in these regs I'd never even heard of before. Why—"

Sam cut him off with a curt wave of his hand. "Look. I'm too tired to even think straight about all of this. If I've got to talk with the DO tomorrow anyway, I'll just bitch to him and try to get it straightened out. Who can set me up with an appointment and tell me where I can bed down?"

"Let me call his office for you. It's right down the hall, and there's a visiting officers' quarters in a barracks right across from the officers' club. You know where that is?"

Sam nodded wearily and listened as the young officer made a 1000 appointment the next day for his interview with the director of operations, 2d Air Division. A FAC, he thought. What the hell did he know about being a FAC? This didn't sound good. If he could make enough of a case against it tomorrow during the interview, then maybe there'd be a good chance he could slide out of it and into something more in his line of work. If the DO was a reasonable man he might approve of moving Sam into one of the fighter squadrons that were just coming into the country. Hell, he'd take a job flying A-1 Skyraiders even if they were recips and damned near twenty years old at that. Suddenly, he felt almost optimistic.

The light was almost gone when Sam woke. Rather than sleeping it had been more like he'd been knocked unconscious. If he hadn't been completely whacked-out, he might not have gotten any rest, for the VOQ abutted the busy main road through the air base, and a never-ending stream of vehicles roared by no more than a few feet from his iron GI cot. A miasma of exhaust fumes blanketed the long room. The open bay of the old wooden barracks building contained at least thirty cots identical to the one he was sprawled on in his underwear. Transient officers had clomped in and out throughout the day, often bringing Sam almost to consciousness before his exhaustion pulled him into darkness once again. The shrill voices of Vietnamese vied with the roaring trucks as the maids strolled through the ranks of sleeping Americans, casually flicking the floor with long dusters made of straw. Their tonal language made it seem as if they were forever screaming at one another.

Sam found the community shower room and felt almost fresh after he emerged cleaned and shaven. His soiled uniform had disappeared while he slept. Probably one of the maids had taken it to be washed. Or maybe they had just taken it. He wasn't going to worry about it now. He dressed in clean but wrinkled khakis and began to notice the void in his stomach. A couple of drinks and a slab of whatever kind of meat was available would fix that. Then, maybe another ten hours' sleep and perhaps he'd be ready to plead his case to the DO.

The officers' club had undergone a metamorphosis. The bar was now three deep with drinking men, and a blue pall of cigarette smoke hung in a stratus over the room. His experienced eye soon sorted the herd into distinctive groups that a civilian would never have noticed. At the far end of the bar, the fighter and recce pilots congregated, some wearing flight suits, others garish civilian clothing. The transport pilots were mostly seated around tables or standing next to them in small groups. Most wore green fatigues, but some had on civilian clothing. They were older than the fighter pilots and their demeanor was more sedate. The staff pukes gathered at the near end of the bar and wore either khakis or fatigue uniforms. They were the most serious of the lot, often looking up with irritation as a particularly loud noise would come from the fighter pilots. Army officers and a few conservatively dressed civilians, distinguished by their longer hair, fit in at odd intervals. Sam was drawn instinctively toward the group of fighter pilots, but he stayed away. He was no longer one of the fraternity and knew with certainty that any advances he made toward the group would be rejected. He didn't know anymore where the hell he did belong. He was turning to leave when he heard Cal call him.

"Hey, Sam! Over here!"

He peered into the smoky dimness and saw an arm waving from one of the far tables. He gave a small wave in return and began making his way through the mob. There were three other men seated with Cal at the table. One of them got up as Sam arrived.

"Here," the man said, "take my chair. I've got to leave anyway."

There were introductions and handshakes from the remainder of the men. That formality completed they all sat again. Both of the men with Cal were in their late thirties. One was a major, the other a lieutenant colonel. As it turned out, not surprisingly, they were all from the same squadron.

"Well," said Cal, grinning at Sam after he'd ordered his scotch and water, "how did your first day go? Find out what you're going to be doing?"

Sam shrugged. "They've got me down to be a forward air controller somewhere in the delta, but I've got to interview with the DO of 2d Air Division tomorrow morning and I'm going to try to get that changed. When I tell him I know from strictly nothing about FACs, maybe he'll slide me into an F-100 or even an A-1 squadron."

"Well, it'd probably be best if you could get the orders switched. A FAC's rough duty anywhere in the country. And the living can really be crappy down delta way. I didn't know you had FAC training."

Sam laughed. "Hell, I don't. That's why I think I can get it changed. I know they started assigning fighter pilots to army brigades a few years ago, but they only took volunteers, which I never did, of course. I mean, who wants to go play soldier and crap in the woods like a bear? The assignment then was just for a year, and the guys who did it and came back to the squadron said they didn't do dick the whole time except ride around in a jeep in the boondocks and act like they knew what the hell was going on. The army would give 'em a radio jeep and a sergeant, and about once a month they'd all drive out in the country to play soldier for a few days. They thought the whole thing was a big joke."

"Well," Cal said slowly, "I think they do a little more over here. I don't know all the fine points, but I know they fly Bird Dogs—you know, those little Cessnas the army calls L-19s and the air force calls O-1s? And I know they're assigned to an area or an army unit or something like that. They're responsible for finding and marking targets for attack aircraft. The FACs get a lot of respect from all the fighter jocks, and you know how hard that is to come by from one of us egotistical assholes."

Even though Cal was now directing traffic on the flight deck of a transport aircraft, he obviously still considered himself a fighter pilot. The same way I do, Sam thought.

"Anyway," Cal continued, "it might not be a bad idea if you did try to get your assignment switched. I understand you can get your ass shot off real easylike in that business. If that was the job they had in mind for you all along, surely they'd have sent you through school. They've got one going now, I know, back at Hurlburt Field in Florida. I know 'cause that's the same base where we went through transition on the C-123."

"Well," Sam said, "that's why I'm really not too worried about it. I don't think there's much chance that the DO will let the assignment go through when he finds out I don't know squat about it. That wouldn't make sense. Who is the DO for 2d, anyway?"

"You might know him. He's an old fighter jock but we were never stationed together. A real hardass, from everything I hear. Name's Colonel Jackson Jones."

A blow to the head would have stunned Sam less. Jesus! Jack Jones! He was a dead man. He looked quickly over his shoulder as though expecting to find the enraged Colonel Jones bearing down on him.

"What's the matter, Sam? You're looking a little peaked. Want another drink?"

"Yeah," Sam said slowly. "Make this one a double."

The hard, straight chair outside Colonel Jones's office was getting uncomfortable and Sam was beginning to squirm. Actually, he'd been squirming most of the night as his mind incessantly replayed the scene of Colonel Jones's humiliation and the beginning of his own slide into oblivion. It had been Major Jones and Captain Brooks then.

Sarah Jones's gentle flirtation had begun early the night of the squadron party. She had arrived before her husband, who as ops officer had been delayed by some mundane squadron matter. As one of the few bachelors, Sam had intended only to make a brief appearance at the party before cutting out in search of some of the more interesting diversions of Tampa. After an hour of drinking, there was still no appearance by Major Jones. Sarah's manner had become subtly predatory. Sam watched with fascination as with each new drink her decolletage crept lower on her magnificent bosom.

It was unfortunate that Major Jones had been accompanied by the squadron commander and the maintenance officer as he made his way across the patio surrounding the pool, avoiding the long walk from the crowded parking lot. Had he been alone, perhaps Major Jones would have been satisfied with an apology and, after a few threats, the incident would have ended. Instead, as the three men walked around the pool, they saw a couple entwined behind the lifeguard's chair. The lady appeared to be nude from the waist up and her partner was clutching her breasts with both hands. The lovers might never have been identified had not the maintenance officer, with all the boorishness of that breed, switched on his flashlight and illuminated the panting Mrs. Jones and the slathering Sam.

There was a dreadful moment of silence in which there was absolutely no movement. Finally, the squadron commander said in quite a reasonable tone: "Sam, you really should let go of Sarah's breasts now."

The Joneses, of course, left immediately amid sobs and threats. The squadron commander had counseled Sam intensively and sworn the maintenance officer to eternal silence. That lasted until the elevated grease monkey joined the crowd inside the officers' club.

Sam was an instant celebrity. Until his transfer to Arizona the following week, he had successfully avoided contact with Major Jones, but there was no way to avoid the remainder of the squadron. He was pointed out proudly by his pilot mates to those from other squadrons, and the story was related, embellished with each rehash. Wherever he went, a lapse in conversation was sure to be filled with some wag's: "Sam, you really should let go of Sarah's breasts now."

The story of his exploit had followed Sam to Arizona, and even in

a community not particularly known for its decorum, it influenced his
effectiveness reports. No one doubted Sam's flying skills or his abil-
ity as a flight leader, but neither was anyone willing to lay his career
on the line in order to give Sam positions of increased responsibility.
Always waiting unseen in the organizational background of the Tactical Air Command (TAC) was the specter of Jackson Jones and the
probability that some day he would become a general officer. No one
wanted to be identified as the friend of the sworn enemy of a general
officer. Careers had been destroyed over much less.

Sam's career had languished. Only innocuous little jobs that led nowhere
had been offered; soon, with increasing bitterness, Sam had refused
even those tentative offers. Who the hell needed to be the squadron
scheduling officer?

Sam had felt badly for Sarah, and there was little doubt the incident was a major cause of the Jones'es divorce within the year. Still,
he reckoned, if there had been a real victim it was Sam Brooks. It was
at the lady's insistence that they had moved away from the party and
into the fresh air. It had even been Sarah who had pulled down the
bodice of her dress. He would admit that he'd needed little incentive
to begin grappling her, though, and the consequence of that action was
the blame that could be placed nowhere except on his own head. In
the final analysis, Sam knew quite well who had cooked this particular goose.

"Colonel Jones will see you now." The sergeant's voice brought him
back to the real world and to the imminent meeting with a man who
had threatened to kill him more than a decade ago.

Sam nodded and stood, checking his appearance in the wall mirror. A tall, lean man with a crew cut stared back. There wasn't
anything very pretty about him. It was a hard-looking face, and the
broken nose that curved slightly to the left gave him a sinister air. The
face was sharp. Someone had once told him that it looked as if he could
chop wood with it. In the dimness of the anteroom, he looked almost
bald, for although he retained a full head of hair, it was so short as to
appear nonexistent.

Sam took a deep breath and squared his shoulders. He walked to
the closed door and rapped twice in the approved military manner, then
opened the door and stepped into the air-conditioned office. Four brisk
steps put him squarely in front of the large wooden desk. He kept his
eyes straight ahead and well over the figure seated there. He came to

the position of attention and saluted, hand to his forehead in a manner that would have brought tears of joy to a West Point graduate. "Sir," he snapped, "Major Brooks reporting to the director of operations, as ordered. Sir!"

Sam's peripheral vision caught the movement of the returned salute. The voice was just as he remembered from his nightmares. Low and tight.

"Stand at ease, Major."

Sam came to "parade rest," spreading his feet apart and grasping his hands behind his back in the approved manner. He dropped his gaze to stare directly into the unblinking pale blue eyes of Col. Jackson Jones. The long silence made the hair prickle on the back of Sam's neck. Finally, the man spoke.

"I won't bother asking you to sit down, Major, for this meeting is going to be extremely brief. I'm required by the commander, 2d Air Division, to interview all personnel who will be working directly with the Vietnamese in any capacity. Usually I enjoy that duty and I've met some fine men with whom I'd be proud to serve anywhere. That is not the case in this instance, however. I had hoped never to see you again. In spite of everything I could do, I see that you have attained your majority. I assure you that I did everything in my power to stop that promotion, just as I've pulled every string and called in every marker I have out to ensure that you'll never wear the silver leaf of a lieutenant colonel. Of course, my pull isn't as strong as it might have been had I made general officer. But that was hardly likely for someone who is known to nearly every member of the officer corps as one who was cuckolded by a subordinate."

"That's hardly fair, sir," Sam murmured. "You know very well that little happened that night, and that I was certainly not the instigator."

"Be that as it may, Major, you were one of the main players. Since your little assignation with my wife, I've spent every day of my life trying to regain my reputation and get myself back on track—"

"As have I, Colonel," said Sam with some heat. He was getting angry himself, losing the nervousness that had been with him since the prior night. After all, what else could this jerk do to him?

Colonel Jones stood, clasping his hands behind his back, and looked from his window at the passing traffic. Sam noticed that the man kept himself in good condition. His stomach was flat and the biceps were clearly defined. Jones had to be forty-five, but he looked as if he could still run the mile relay, as he had done at the Point. Sam was delighted to see, however, that he was losing his hair.

"My initial impulse, Major Brooks, when I found that you were coming to us, was simply to get rid of you. It would have been easy enough to do, but we're desperately short of pilots right now and will remain so until the pipeline from the States gets cranked up. Even so, I could have shuttled you off to Thailand or someplace where I would never have had to see you again."

Here was his chance! "Sir, I'd like you to know that I'm still current in the F-100 and have more than a thousand hours in them. I've instructed gunnery in the two seater and I was the Top Gun in both of my last two squadrons. I'd like very much to be assigned to one of your fighter squadrons as a pilot."

Colonel Jones gave him a frosty smile. "I'm sure you would like that, Major Brooks. But I have something a little different in mind for you." He leaned forward, both hands on his desk, and stared into Sam's eyes. "I do need pilots, but which pilot goes where is entirely up to me. And I've spent a considerable amount of time that I can't really spare just to find the very best place for you."

He smiled with relish as he continued to stare at Sam. The smile looked genuine now. "Major Brooks, you are to report to the air liaison officer at IV Corps headquarters in Can Tho. From there, I have directed Lieutenant Colonel Robinson to see to your checkout in the O-1 aircraft and to further deploy you as one of the sector FACs to the Cau Mau peninsula. Specifically," he turned to a large map of South Vietnam, "right here."

Sam leaned forward and peered where the finger was pointing. He could barely make it out. It was about as far south as you could get and remain out of the South China Sea.

"Bac Lieu," said Jones, showing his teeth for the first time.

CHAPTER 2

Sam sat on the wooden bench in the shade of the in-country flight-scheduling building, surrounded by his baggage and recently issued equipment. The new jungle boots hurt his feet and felt cumbersome because of the hinged metal insoles designed to deflect *punji* stakes. Inside the building, the sergeant at the desk had promised to alert Sam if any aircraft came through with Can Tho scheduled as an en route stop.

Being in a flight suit again felt much better than wearing the sodden khakis. He looked down at the cloth command pilot wings sewn to the left breast of the green coveralls. On the right side was the emblem of the Tactical Air Command. On his shoulders were his old squadron patch and one showing him to be a graduate of the Fighter Weapons School. The emblems of his past should have been removed, but something in him resisted doing so. Hell! He knew exactly why he hadn't done it. He wanted to wear them into the club to separate himself from the staff people and transport crew members. In that, they had been successful; he'd been given cheerful admittance into the group of drinking fighter pilots. As a result there was a dull throb in the front of his head and a mouth that felt as if he'd been gargling sump oil.

Colonel Jackson Jones had made a one-martini visit to the club bar the previous night. Sam thought he was going to tell him to get rid of the unauthorized patches or get the hell out of the club, but the DO said nothing. Sam gave the colonel a cheerful grin, as though becoming a FAC and going to the Mekong Delta was the one thing he'd needed to make his life complete.

After the session in the DO's office, Sam had spent the remainder of the day doing the usual base check-in. Most of his records would remain with the headquarters at Tan Son Nhut airfield. He had drawn the standard load of field equipment for a forward air controller, including a .38 Special revolver and an AR-15 assault rifle with folding stock. There was a flak jacket and a steel pot, K-BAR sheath knife and web gear, poncho and liner, canteens, rucksack, and what appeared to be everything else the supply sergeant wanted to get rid of. And he still had his own two bags to wrestle with. Shit! They should have issued him a batman as well just to take care of all this crap.

A jeep pulled in front of the ATCO building and a tall Special Forces captain unfolded from the passenger side. He pulled a small musette bag and an M16 from the rear of the covered vehicle, gave a quick nod to the sergeant behind the wheel, and walked into the building. The jeep slung gravel as it departed. Sam checked his watch—almost 1000 and getting very hot. The Special Forces officer came out of the building and walked over to where Sam sat. His eyes flickered over him once, then he too sat on the bench and leaned back against the wall of the building. Sam noted that the man was a good two inches taller than his own six-two, and that he was very tan. The jungle fatigues beneath the web gear were bleached almost white from repeated washings. Sam recognized the flash on his green beret as that of the 5th Special Forces. The captain had an air of patience about him, as though he could sit, stand, or squat for as long as necessary. Sam thought he looked like a college quarterback who would prefer to play defensive tackle.

Sam shut his eyes and tried to ignore the heat and the company. He had little use for people who went around eating perfectly good snakes. People who were interested in that sort of thing were inevitably weird, and almost never showed any enthusiasm for talk about important things, such as fighter flying techniques. Maybe it would be cooler inside. At least they had an old fan going in there. Jesus! It had to be a hundred frigging degrees and the same humidity.

"Major." The sergeant was at the door. "Just got an inbound that ought to do you. It estimates here in fifteen with no more than half an hour ground time. It's an Otter and they say they've got enough room for you and the captain here. It stops at My Tho before going on to Can Tho. You'd better grab it 'cause I don't know when another one's going to come along."

Sam nodded without speaking and glanced at the guy in the green beanie. So, we're going to be neighbors. The captain looked over at him and then at all his gear but said nothing. Sam knew that the

Otter was a big single-engine, high-wing aircraft flown by army aviators. It was just one step above driving a truck, he thought, then grimaced as he remembered what his own mount was going to be.

The time passed slowly and the heat increased disproportionally. Sam amused himself by watching the various aircraft taxiing by for take-off. Pairs of F-100s and A-1 prop attack aircraft went by at regular intervals. Probably going out on preplanned strikes. C-123 cargo birds waddled by in a constant parade. Army Caribous and Navy EC-121s. A single RF-101 recce bird sharked by, its long nose containing myriad cameras and sensors. He heard the unmistakable clatter of a large radial engine before he actually identified the olive-drab Otter taxiing in to park in front of their building. The engine clanged to a stop and a sergeant and two army officers in nicely pressed fatigues climbed to the tarmac and walked toward the building. The sergeant looked pissed off about something, but then most sergeants always looked pissed off about something. The trio disappeared into the building.

One of the pilots of the aircraft sauntered toward them while the other peered suspiciously into the bowels of the engine. An army fuel truck drove to the aircraft and began to replenish the bird's tanks. The pilot had a lighted cigarette dangling from his mouth as he tinkered with the engine. Sam could smell the high-octane avgas from his bench more than fifty yards away. He averted his eyes, having no desire to witness the incineration. But the fuel pumper completed his business and pulled away. Sam let out his breath.

The transportation sergeant came to the door. "OK, gentlemen. Y'all can move your stuff on out to the aircraft now and get ready to load."

Sam stood and began picking up bundles and bags. It was obviously going to take two trips. The Special Forces captain glanced at him, then slung his rifle and grabbed one of the largest bags, the muscles cording in his forearms as if he was hiding two large boas under his skin. Without looking back he started for the aircraft, striding briskly in the heat. Sam followed at a more moderate pace.

The pilot had the bag stowed when Sam arrived with his load. It, too, went into the cargo hold. He nodded his thanks to the captain and stepped back to get a better look at the aircraft. He decided that it was not only the ugliest aircraft he'd ever seen, but possibly the dirtiest as well. It reminded him of a farmer's pickup—utilitarian but beaten, with a not-so-fine coating of mud and dirt. He walked back to the hatch and started to climb in but was stopped as his fellow passenger finally spoke.

"It may be a little while yet and we'll roast in there." He looked at Sam's flight suit, now soaked through front and back. The captain's own face looked completely dry and the creases were still sharp on his fatigues.

Sam nodded and walked under the wing to get out of the sun. The captain joined him there and lit a cigarette. Sam started to mention that it probably wasn't too good an idea to be smoking this close to a standing aircraft, but he remembered the pilot during the refueling operation and decided to hell with it. An air force safety officer would have gone into shock had he witnessed either incident, but the army obviously didn't care.

Sam stuck out a hand. "Name's Brooks. Thanks for the help."

"No sweat," the captain answered. "Jim Christian. Heard the sergeant say you were heading for Can Tho. Going to be stationed there?"

"Naw, just long enough to check out in the Bird Dog and then on to someplace called Bac Lieu."

Christian looked at him with more interest. "Bac Lieu, huh? Going to be on the sector team there?"

"Beats hell outta me. All I know is that I'm supposed to be a forward air controller down there. I guess I'll get more of a briefing at IV Corps headquarters. Are you at Can Tho?"

"Hell no!" Captain Christian's face broke into a huge grin, which somehow softened the hard features. "Too much brass there, and besides, they make you play volleyball. Naw, I've got a lovely little A-Team camp at Ba Xoai. Just north of the U Minh Forest."

"Sorry. Afraid I don't know much about the countryside yet or where anything is."

"Well, Major, if you're going to be a FAC I imagine you'll know a whole lot more before you get much older. We'll probably run into each other from time to time. There really aren't that many round eyes in IV Corps. Here comes the pilot; I guess it's time for us to get on board."

The flight to My Tho was an eye-opener for Sam, quickly dispelling myths he'd built in his own mind about towering rain forests covering the land. Indeed, after takeoff from Tan Son Nhut there was one jungle-looking area with thick tree growth and waterways cutting through it. Noting his interest in the terrain, Captain Christian yelled above the noisy radial engine: "That's the Rung Sat Special Zone. The Vietnamese marines operate there, but the VC own it. It's mostly mangroves and snakes." He then pushed his beret down over his eyes and was apparently soon asleep.

Sam continued to stare from the little window. The mangroves were soon behind them and the Mekong Delta stretched as far as he could see. There were no jungles here, just miles and miles of flat paddy land with wooded dikes. The canals were the surprise. There seemed to be literally hundreds of them—some straight as a die and obviously constructed by man, others following the paths of natural streams. Small villages were everywhere but always on a canal. There were dozens of small boats in the waterways. Some of the canals and all of the paddy fields looked dry and barren.

Sam wasn't sure what he had expected, but it was not this peaceful, pastoral scene flowing beneath the lumbering aircraft. Where could Viet Cong hide in an area such as this? Or perhaps he should ask where could they not hide. How in heaven's name could anyone keep track of such a scattered population? How could anyone even move down there except by boat? Sam saw very few roads. Evidently, most of the traffic did move by sampan, or whatever they called their boats. There was one road the pilots had obviously been following all the way out of Saigon; from their altitude, which Sam estimated to be about two thousand feet, the roadway appeared to have been built above the level of the rice fields.

Sam's body sensed the slight nose-down shift of the aircraft before his ears picked up the decrease in power as the pilot throttled back. Sam leaned into the aisle so he could look through the forward windscreen between the two pilots. Both of them were young warrant officers and looked to be about eighteen. They were laughing and snickering at each other like a couple of high school kids. They were just a little younger than he had been when he downed his first MiG south of the Yalu River in Korea.

The pilot took the Otter down fast, and Sam had time for only a quick glimpse of a good-sized town before the aircraft turned onto the final approach for the My Tho airport. There was a flash of a large muddy river under the wing and the kid up front greased the aircraft onto the pierced-steel planking (PSP) runway.

As they were taxiing back, the copilot left his seat and crawled back into the cabin. "Gents, if you'll just sit tight, we're not even going to shut down. I gotta throw out a couple of boxes and we've got to pick up one soul and we'll be on our way again."

It was a fact. Before the aircraft had stopped moving, the warrant officer had the door open and was heaving out boxes and bags. Completed, he waved toward an American soldier, who headed for them at a gallop. He mounted on the move, the door was shut, and the large radial engine belched as the pilot increased power for the taxi back to the takeoff position. The new arrival sprawled in a seat and grinned at the officers.

"How's it going, Sarge?" asked Captain Christian.

"Can't complain, I guess. At least, I don't know what good it'd do me."

"Going back to the team?"

"Yes, sir. They say I'm all healed up nice and neat. And then the dumb quack said to be sure and not get any contaminated water in it." The sergeant seemed to think this highly amusing.

"Sergeant Bowman," Christian said to Sam, "is with a subsector team over at Rach Gia. He managed to get himself shot in the ass awhile back." Christian grinned at Sergeant Bowman before sliding down into the seat once more to resume his nap. The sergeant did the same. Sam suddenly did not feel drowsy at all. This was as close to shooting as he had been in thirteen years.

Back at the window he saw that the country seemed unchanged—more canals and rice paddies with villages perched back beneath what looked to be banana trees. Most of the dwellings were built right along a canal or stream to give everyone access to the water. The tree lines along some of the waterways looked very dense, hinting at what the original foliage must have been before the Vietnamese cleared it to plant their rice fields.

Another twenty minutes and the aircraft began to descend again. Sam could see another large, muddy river to their front with a sizable town hugging its southern bank. The river was filled with sampans, some with simple sails, others propelled by a single sweep oarsman. Some boats appeared to be motorized. The plane lurched into a left bank and positioned itself for the final approach into Can Tho.

It was another PSP runway, Sam noted after the warrant officer greased it on again. The edges of the steel matting had warped in places, leaving sharp steel spikes protruding. Pools of stagnant water stretched on either side of the runway.

The aircraft's engine complained as the pilot cut the fuel mixture control to the idle-cutoff position, then the engine ticked sullenly as the hot metal cooled. The copilot scampered down the aisle, flung open the door, and stepped outside. He stood by the hatch grinning like an idiot, acting as though he was a hostess. Lugging his carbine, Sam stepped into the sauna.

"Thank you for flying TWA today," said the grinning copilot; noting Sam's cocked eyebrow, he expanded: "That's Teeny Weeny Airline."

Sam gave him an exasperated look and began collecting his bags. There was a small stucco operations building, painted an offensive yellow, and several smaller outbuildings. Captain Christian brought the remainder of Sam's load.

"You going to the MACV compound, Major?" the Special Forces officer asked.

"I reckon," Sam answered. "I really don't have any idea. They weren't too specific at Tan Son Nhut."

"Well, if you're checking in with Colonel Robinson, the air force ALO, I expect that's where you'll find him. Either there or at the DASC. If he's not there now, he will be later this afternoon. You'll need to get set up with someplace to bunk anyway. If you want, I can give you a ride in. I've got to call for transportation anyway."

"Yeah, that'd be great."

Christian walked into the building and Sam squinted at his surroundings. Christ, it was hotter here than it was in Saigon. The air felt saturated yet there wasn't a cloud in the sky. Three Vietnamese men in flight suits and colored baseball caps hunkered on the ground by the corner of the building. One held a leash securing a small monkey, which had mounted a scruffy-looking mongrel lying on its belly. The monkey was doing its best to screw the dog, and it screeched hysterically as its tiny hindquarters thrust back and forth in an obscene frenzy. The dog looked backwards with a bored expression, as if this was not the first attempt by the monkey to have carnal knowledge. The Vietnamese giggled at the performance and called encouragement to the primate. Sam felt that he would like to see how far he could drop-kick the lot, but turned away.

Other than the Otter, there were only three other aircraft parked on the ramp of the airfield. One was a C-47 with Vietnamese markings; the other two were both Cessna O-1 Bird Dogs. One had Vietnamese markings painted on its olive-drab fuselage. The other was painted a light gray with USAF markings; without the rocket racks beneath each wing, it wouldn't have looked out of place in any little airport in the United States. Sam started to walk out and inspect it more closely, but Christian came out the door.

"The jeep's already on the way. I had 'em check. Lieutenant Colonel Robinson is at the DASC, which is about a mile or so from the compound. We'll drop you there, if you like, and take your bags to the compound and have somebody put 'em in your quarters. I'd hold onto your weapon, though. They're mighty touchy about 'em being stolen."

"That's fine," Sam replied. "I've got my pistol in my bag. Do you think that's all right?"

"Better take it out to be safe. If you don't want to wear it, I'll leave it at the first sergeant's desk."

"What's the deal? Are we supposed to wear them around here?"

"Well," the tall captain answered, "most people don't if they're staying in the compound or work close to it. If you stick your head out of town, even for a trip here to the airfield, I'd strongly suggest wearing it. It's about a three-mile ride, so better safe than sorry."

Sam nodded and began rummaging through his bag for the weapon. He found it and awkwardly strapped the web belt around his waist, feeling slightly foolish. As he straightened, he saw Captain Christian watching the monkey's efforts with a slight smile. Then the captain walked to the squatting Vietnamese and spoke rapidly to them in their language. They answered without raising their eyes from their sport. Christian leaned forward, and one large hand fastened around the scuff of the Viet holding the leash. He straightened, still holding onto the neck, and spoke to the man once more. Their eyes were level, but the smaller man's feet dangled at least a foot off the ground. The monkey kept humping away until Christian's jungle boot sent it through the air like a furry football. The dog scurried around the building, and the Vietnamese men, at least the two with traction, backed away from the tall American who still held one of their number aloft. Christian spoke again quietly to the man and lowered him gently to the dusty ground. They all fled toward the C-47 as Christian walked back to Sam.

He acted as though nothing unusual had happened, but Sam noticed him unholster his .45 automatic and insert a clip, even jacking a round into the chamber before safing and replacing it.

"You think they'll try something?" Sam asked.

"Naw," Christian said, grinning. "This isn't for them. Those assholes would run if you made a face at them. This is for the ride to town. An empty weapon doesn't do you much good."

"Well, I guess I wouldn't be much use then, 'cause they gave me this rifle and pistol without any ammo."

"No problem. You can get all you want here. That's probably our jeep."

The short ride into Can Tho was exotic even by Sam's standards, and he had been stationed in many parts of the world. Through the dust kicked up by the jeep on the unpaved road, he saw that the road-way was indeed elevated three to four feet above the surrounding paddies. Water buffalo pulling ploughs stepped ponderously through the dry, cracked fields. Small scrawny boys in conical hats perched atop them like birds. Some lay full length on their mounts, riding the undula-tions like seasoned sailors in heavy seas. Dusty nipa palms and elephant grasses grew along the dikes, where an occasional goat or a skinny cow grazed forlornly.

One moment their jeep was in the countryside and the next it had entered Can Tho, the major city in the delta. Sam thought it didn't look so much like a city as it did a teeming slum. Buildings were constructed of whatever happened to be handy, including beer cans and cardboard boxes. Vendors hawked their wares to crowds wearing the traditional black pajamas and conical straw hats. Interspersed among them, an occasional woman in an ao dai stepped delicately through the mobs. Vietnamese soldiers mounted guard at irregular intervals, and pairs of white-uniformed national police strolled or leaned against buildings.

Christian pointed them out to Sam. "Americans call them 'White Mice.' They're mostly useless," he explained. "The real control over the town comes from the army."

The jeep pulled in front of a two-story building with a pair of Viet-namese soldiers leaning languorously against a sandbagged barricade. They appeared to be extremely uninterested in the jeep.

"Here's IV DASC." Christian pointed out the building to Sam. "I'll make sure your gear gets to the compound safe and sound. Maybe I'll see you at the club tonight."

They shook hands. The captain nodded to the Vietnamese driver and the jeep lurched away. Sam looked at the soldiers guarding the build-ing. They eyed him without curiosity and went back to staring into space. He walked through the door and looked for help. A U.S. Army staff sergeant sat at a desk just inside the room rustling papers. He looked up at Sam's approach.

"Can I help you, sir?"

"If you know where Lieutenant Colonel Robinson is, you can."

"His office is up the stairs and just before you get to the double doors." He went back to his papers and Sam headed for the stairwell.

The air liaison officer's door was marked "USAF ALO." Sam knocked and entered. A U.S. Air Force sergeant and a Vietnamese Air Force man sat at desks facing each other from either side of the room. The American looked at him with inquiring eyes. Sam stared back and won.

"Can I help you, Major?"

"Major Brooks to see Colonel Robinson."

"What's the nature of your business, sir?"

"I don't know that it's any of your fucking concern."

The sergeant flushed, and rose to walk toward another door. It opened before he got there. A large black man in a flight suit stared at Sam. On his shoulders were the silver oak leaves of a lieutenant colonel. Cloth command pilot wings were sewn to the left chest of his gray flight suit.

"You've *got* to be Major Brooks," he said. "Colonel Jones said to expect you. With a nasty temper like that, I can see why you aren't too popular with him. Come on in."

Inside, the light colonel turned and stared at Sam, then looked as if he'd come to a conclusion. He stuck out his hand and Sam shook it. "We're going to be working together for quite a spell, Major. I don't know what your problem is with the DO except he sure doesn't like you very much. What do you say we try to start off on the right foot with each other, because whatever's going on, it's got nothing to do with me and you."

"Yes, sir, Colonel."

"And I think we can dispense with the rank as well. We're a pretty casual group down here in the delta. There aren't that many round eyes in IV Corps. You thought I was going to say 'white men,' didn't you?" He waggled his eyebrows like Groucho Marx. "Call me Bill."

Sam couldn't keep from grinning. There was a warmth in the man that was hard to ignore. "I'm Sam. I'm sorry I jumped down your sergeant's throat. I'll apologize to him on the way out."

"Tell me a little bit about your background, Sam. I'm not being nosy. Just want to know what kind of wild man I'm going to be dealing with. I mean, you pay dues to the KKK or anything like that? Something I ought to know before I turn my back on you?"

"No, Bill. I've got no problems like that."

"Just wanted to be sure," the big man rumbled. "I had a FAC down south of here awhile back from Pascagoula who made me so damned nervous every time he came up here I'd almost choke on my watermelon."

Sam laughed. "What happened to him?"

The smile disappeared from Bill's face. "Sent his ass home in a rubber bag. The Cong put three .51s through his gizzard when he got to thinking he was too smart to get hurt. Only had three weeks before his rotation. Remember that. These people don't care if you have a rotation date or not. The only time you're going to have it made is when you get on that bird that takes you home. Any other time, old Charley is just sitting there, waiting for you to make one screwup. Even if you do things right, you can still get hurt. Do it wrong and I'll guarantee it. Now, tell me all the sordid details. We don't even get your personnel file down here for me to root around in and find out all the juicy stuff."

"Well, I don't want to go into details, so let's just say that Colonel Jones and I go back a long time. He hates my guts for something he thinks I did to him. And our Colonel Jones is not the type to forget about it."

"Wouldn't have anything to do with his ex-wife, would it?" Bill's roguish eyebrows semaphored at Sam again. He giggled. It sounded high and slightly girlish for a man of his girth and deep voice. He shook his head at Sam's surprised look. "Hell, man. I've been in fighters all my life, until they snagged me for this job. I heard that story back when I was a captain, but I never knew who the other man was. I'm right honored to make your acquaintance." He folded his hands across his ample stomach before continuing. "Just think of that! We've got a real celebrity in our midst. Man, you're famous in half the fighter squadrons in TAC."

Sam's face was screwed up as if he was being given an enema. "Yeah, and famous with promotion boards as well. I had two passovers to major and one to light colonel. It's something I could just as easily have done without."

Bill's face became instantly serious. "Passed over once for light colonel, huh? That's rough."

Sam nodded. "And a second one guaranteed by the good Colonel Jones. He told me so himself."

Bill rubbed his chin slowly as he looked at the other officer thoughtfully. "Maybe we can figure out something, Sam. There's usually a way. The main thing is not to screw up big-time while you're down here. It's awful easy for a FAC to do. You didn't get a chance to go through the school, did you?"

"Nope. I suspect that's some more of Jackson Jones's work. Fill-

ing a forward air controller slot was the last thing on my mind when
I got orders for 2d Air Division. I think he wanted me to have the least
possible preparation for whatever job I had."

"Maybe so, but I'd prefer that we think positive about this situation. With your flying time and experience, I know you won't have
any trouble learning the job. We'll start on the checkout tomorrow. Also,
I'll try to give you a quick run-through here at the DASC and then
get you on to the compound and get you set up in some quarters. How's
that sound?"

"Good enough."

Lieutenant Colonel Robinson led Sam through another door into a
large room next to his office. There was a languid current of activity. Several Vietnamese and Americans, both officers and enlisted
men, seemed to be occupied but not at a frantic pace. Each national-
ity was paired with a counterpart from the other. Robinson introduced
Sam to all of them as they made their tour of the room. Sam gave up
trying to remember the names, especially the Vietnamese. A large map
of IV Corps hung on a wall, covered with acetate. An American enlisted man was writing something on it. The American duty officers,
Sam was told, came to their jobs after six months in the field as forward air controllers.

"The way we get air strikes down here," Bill explained, "is through
what I'd guess you'd call a weeding-out process. That is, the request
originates, say, from the 43d Ranger Battalion. Their commander or
his American adviser calls to the province or sector, where it's either
approved or disapproved. If it's approved, it goes up from there to
division—in the case of the Rangers, to the 9th Division headquarters at Sadec. From there, it comes here to IV Corps DASC. That stands
for Direct Air Support Center and is what you're standing in right now.
If the request is approved here, the duty officers, Vietnamese and American,
can send aircraft from our allocation of TACAIR. In an emergency,
the duty officers can call on the TACC at Tan Son Nhut in Saigon for
additional allocations.

"The Vietnamese need American approval before they can get U.S.
aircraft. They don't need it to use their own resources. That's the main
job of the advisers down at battalion level. He's the guy with the radio
to American fighters and helicopters. Let's face it, that Vietnamese battalion
commander sure doesn't feel as though he needs an American lieutenant advising him on anything. But, he sure does like to have that
entry into the U.S. tactical air net."

"It all sounds a little awkward," Sam said.

Robinson roared with laughter. "Of course it's awkward. It's the most awkward goddamned thing I've ever worked with. Particularly when you've got a troops in contact—what we call a TIC—and the province chief or the division commander is out screwing around and can't be found and the Vietnamese duty officer won't make a decision on his own. Then, too, either one of those worthies or a dozen or so in the loop just like them may have promised all of IV Corps air to a friend over in the next province for the entire day so he can blow away someone he's got a grudge against, or somebody who's holding out on their taxes or some shit like that. Remember that you're in the delta and it's strictly a Vietnamese show."

He led Sam away from the working men. Sam wondered if the Vietnamese understood sufficient English to catch the derision in Bill Robinson's voice when he spoke about their senior officers. If so, it didn't seem to concern the large black man.

"Sam," he continued, "the main thing to remember down here is that we assist the Viets all we can. But the American advisers in the field are our first priority. If they say they're hurtin', then we pull everything we have to get them out of trouble. VNAF almost never flies at night, and there are Special Forces A-Team camps that could be dead meat without U.S. night scrambles or helicopter gun teams. There's nothing written down about that, but every American down here knows it. That's the only way any of us get to sleep at night. At first, it may feel a little trashy to pull a flight of U.S. F-100s off a troops-in-contact situation where there's no Americans, just to put them in another place where there are. But it's their war still, even though the rumors say the big buildups are coming. . . . That's enough of this crap for the morning. Let's get on over to the MACV compound and let you get squared away. It's about time for lunch anyway."

It was only a few minutes by jeep to the compound. About two dozen buildings were contained within the rectangular cement and stone walls. Guard towers manned by Vietnamese sentries defined each corner. Other strongpoints were sandbagged at intervals along the walls. Concertina wire formed two parallel barriers, straddling either side of a dried-up moat. Most of the buildings were low and louvered to catch any breeze. A large Roman IV was painted on a wall of the largest structure. The South Vietnamese flag hung listlessly from a pole in the center of the large courtyard. There were at least three dozen jeeps parked in front of the buildings. The outer gate was open; a small Vietnamese soldier opened the inner one. Bill pulled the jeep in front of the first building.

"We can find you a bunk from these folks," he said.

Sam followed him into the building. A Vietnamese woman in a white ao dai sat behind a dark green government desk. A slow-moving overhead fan created enough breeze to stir tendrils of hair around her face. She brushed them away with a graceful hand as she smiled at the approaching officers. An army master sergeant sat in regal isolation in the far corner of the big room. He did not look up from the sheaf of papers before him.

"Ah, Co Tan," Bill said to her, "you get more lovely every day. Major Brooks will be with us for three or four days. I need you to find a place for him to sleep. Preferably in one of the buildings away from the perimeter, in case your relatives in the elusive Cong decide to descend upon us while we slumber. Remember, my dear, that we are air force officers, and as such could hardly be expected to participate in anything as crude and uncivilized as ground combat. Such pursuits should be left to those who enjoy debasing themselves in such childlike activities. For example, fools and army sergeants."

Without raising his eyes from the papers, the master sergeant spoke. "And good morning to you, too, Colonel Robinson. Didn't you leave the game a little early last night? I needed more of your money for my R and R."

Lieutenant Colonel Robinson turned back to the Vietnamese girl. "Knaves and cheats, my dear. They couldn't touch me without a collusion amongst them. That's the only explanation. You do understand, don't you?"

The girl laughed and covered her mouth with her hand. "Boo' shit, Coronel. Boo' shit."

Bill gave his high-pitched giggle. "Charming, absolutely charming!"

She bent to a ledger and traced a long painted fingernail down a list, pausing often before continuing the search for a satisfactory bed. Sam glanced under the desk and was fascinated to discover that the toenails on her tiny feet were long and shaped exactly like her fingernails. She obviously never wore stockings with those daggers.

She found a vacancy she liked and looked up at Lieutenant Colonel Robinson. "He be sleb' in teeny-one wit' Captain Chrisen." She appeared to be pleased with her efforts.

"Well done, dear," said Bill. "And with the good Captain Christian. One of our formidable snake eaters. A good man."

"I know him. Rode down from Saigon with him today. He's the one who dropped me off at the DASC."

Sam followed his boss down a long covered walkway after getting promises from the first sergeant that his gear would be forwarded to him. Rooms flanked the walkway on one side. In their approximate middle was a community shower room and latrine. Number 21 was a spartan cell with two iron cots and two metal lockers. Sam chose the one that was obviously unoccupied and noticed that the locker had a bare electric bulb burning inside. He looked questioningly at Robinson.

"It's a hot locker. Things mildew so damned quick down here that you have to keep the light burning all the time, unless you like everything you own to turn a pukey green. The heat helps create a little dry zone to store your lingerie. You notice it's got a lock. Use it to store your weapons at night or whenever you don't want to keep them on you. Most of us don't wear 'em in the compound. Ready to eat?"

Sam realized suddenly that he was exhausted. Jet lag from the many time zones he'd overflown, coupled with the lack of sleep at Tan Son Nhut, left him feeling wobbly and disoriented. "If it's OK with you, I think I'll skip it. I'm not really hungry and I'm about to crash. Think I'll try to grab a few z's."

"Not a bad idea. Matter of fact, take the rest of the afternoon off and get a good rest. I remember what it feels like when you first get in country. Take it easy and I'll see you at the club tonight."

He clapped Sam on the shoulder and spun on his heel, walking through the screen door more gracefully than would be expected of a man his size. Sam sank wearily onto the bed and unlaced the new jungle boots. His feet felt as if they'd been chewed by rats. He lay back and watched the slowly revolving overhead fan, feeling the sweat oozing from his pores. God! He hated this place already. He tried to remember how cool it had been the day he left California. Before he succeeded, his exhaustion had claimed him.

Little clicking noises awakened him. He lay still and tried to place them. Through the screen door he saw that it was late afternoon.

"Sorry," a voice said. "I was trying to be quiet but I needed to get this done before dark. That twelve-watt bulb we have is just about enough to find your bed. And I'm leaving before first light in the morning."

Sam raised onto his elbows and saw that Capt. Jim Christian had his M16 disassembled and spread about his bed. His .45 automatic lay on the pillow. The odor of gun oil hung in the air.

"No problem," Sam said. "I need to get cranking anyway." He shook his head to clear the fuzz. "Leaving in the morning, huh?"

"Yeah, got to get back to the camp. I really just stopped by to get some money."

"You mean pay for your troops?"

"Naw. This is intelligence money—we use it to pay our informants." He grinned at Sam. "Some of 'em are pretty good. Some we pay just to hear the wild-ass stories they make up to get it. Like last week one told me with a straight face that he personally had observed a North Vietnamese submarine in the Bo Chu canal—regardless of the fact that the canal is about twenty feet across and two hundred feet long. When we asked him how it made the sharp ninety-degree bend at Hau Chai, he said it appeared that they had some sort of device that made it fold completely around. I figured, what the hell! I gave him twenty piasters and told him to be sure and let me know if he spotted any others."

Sam smiled and shook his head. He noticed that his gear had been brought in and stacked in the corner. His own carbine sat on top of the duffel bag. He looked at Christian's quick hands reassembling his weapon. It struck him that he didn't have the foggiest idea how to take apart his weapon.

"Uh, listen Jim. Do you suppose you have a couple of minutes to show me how to field-strip that thing?" He motioned toward the corner.

Jim Christian looked at him closely, to see whether his leg was being pulled. A look of incredulity came over his face as he realized that Sam was serious. It was as though he couldn't imagine anyone incapable of so ordinary a task. He didn't speak but walked to the corner and palmed the weapon. He looked at it disdainfully. "This piece of shit'll jam on you, you know."

Sam shrugged. "It's what they gave me. What would you suggest I ought to have?"

"For a FAC? Probably a shotgun."

Sam smiled at the joke, then realized that Jim was not joking. "Why a shotgun?"

"It's reliable, and if you're ever put into a position where you need a weapon, it's probably going to be at mighty close range. Five loads of double-aught buckshot might be the handiest thing you could come up with."

Sam pondered this before he asked: "Where could I get a shotgun? Would they issue me one here?"

"Not a chance. Next time I'm in, I could bring you one. Oh yeah, you're going on to Bac Lieu. Guess you could drop in and see me someday. Until then, here's what you do to take this little toy apart."

Within half an hour Sam felt confident that he could take the carbine down to its major components and reassemble them without having any spare parts leftover. It was growing dark quickly. He'd noticed that the sun had a way of dropping more rapidly than it did in the more temperate climes. It was light, and suddenly it was dark. Disconcerting to someone who liked to watch the sunset over the frosted rim of a martini glass. Or maybe a scotch. Maybe both.

"You know where the club is?" he asked Christian.

"Yeah," said Jim. "I was about to head that way myself. Got a date for cocktails and dinner." He smiled at Sam's puzzled look. "Strange deal. In the middle of the Mekong Delta, Republic of South Vietnam, I'm meeting my sister-in-law for drinks and dinner. How about that?"

Sam shook his head. "I don't get it."

"Yeah, it's a little weird. She's a widow. Her husband was killed in a helicopter five or six years ago. He was an SF man too. She tried a couple of things but there really wasn't anything she liked. No kids or anything like that, so she just upped and joined AID; that's Agency for International Development. The branch over here is called USOM, or U.S. Operational Mission. They have a variety of projects going all over the country. Like trying to get the farmers to convert to that new 'miracle rice' that's supposed to double their yield. Stuff like that. She's been over here about six months. Says she likes being around soldiers. Makes her feel at home again. I married her sister about three years ago, so I look her up whenever I'm through Can Tho. Come on. I'll introduce you, but I warn you, every man from the senior adviser on down is sniffing after her."

The club was on the far side of the compound and as they walked over Sam noticed an absence of Vietnamese in the camp. He asked Jim about it.

"They all go out at night. Even the sentries are outside the wire. They leave at sundown except for the barmaid and waitresses; they're escorted out after the lights are turned off at the club, which is at eleven o'clock. Down here you really never know who to trust except other Americans. Yet you'll notice that it's the Vietnamese flag they fly on the pole. Quite a deal, huh?"

The bar in the club was short, with room for only five or six drinkers. A dozen or so tables dotted the concrete floor. One, the largest, was filled with field-grade officers. There were majors and a few light colonels. A full colonel sat at the head chair; the others flanking him were seated by rank. Bill Robinson's high-pitched giggle came from a corner table. He motioned for Sam, who excused himself from Christian. The tall Special Forces officer was peering around for his sister-in-law, but the only females in the place were two waitresses and a bar-maid.

The two younger officers talking with Robinson stood as Sam approached the table. Sam looked at them quizzically. Anyone other than a commander was normally treated as just another one of the boys in air force messes. They shook hands as Bill made the introductions. The first lieutenant, Gary Maeghan, wore an air force flight suit with pilot wings. Captain Frank Godneau was in army fatigues. He wore the army aviator's badge.

"Gary, here," said Bill Robinson, "is in for the night from Tam Kien. He's a province FAC over there. Old Frank," he continued, indicating the army pilot, "lives right here in Can Tho. He flies a Bird Dog too and does most of the artillery adjustment missions. How about a drink?"

Sam agreed and the waitress was dispatched. He noticed that food was being served at the large table. The drinks came and Sam rolled the smoky taste of scotch around in his mouth before swallowing. The cost was twenty-five cents per drink, payable in either greenbacks or piasters. Or it could be tabbed.

"Major, do you . . . ," Gary Maeghan began, but his voice trailed off. A subtle hush came over the room and Sam looked over his shoulder to see the cause.

The cause was tall, at least five-eight, and she had short dark hair. Small neat ears peaked out below the boyish cut. She wore jeans and a khaki shirt and sneakers that had once been white but now were covered with dark mud. In the dim light Sam couldn't see whether she wore makeup, but he thought not. Her hips were full but trim beneath the denim, and the blouse was filled nicely. Early thirties, thought Sam. She might never be called beautiful, for the mouth was perhaps a shade too generous, and her small nose seemed to wander a bit to the left. But she would always be described as a good-looking woman. It was a face that would age well.

The senior adviser rose quickly from his place at the head of his table and advanced toward her as she scanned the crowd. She spotted

Jim Christian's tall frame across the room and angled toward him just as the colonel completed his interception. She stopped and faced him, flashing a radiant smile made even more so by the contrast of her white teeth against the very tanned face. They talked quietly for a few moments before she placed a hand on his arm, then made her way to where her brother-in-law stood waiting. They hugged briefly, then sat alone at a table and began an animated conversation. Jim signaled for drinks. The Vietnamese girls, Sam noticed, were staring at the American woman as if she had suddenly dropped in from the moon.

The dinner over, Sam tried to decide if he wanted a brandy as he listened to the nonstop conversation of his three companions. He decided not. The two scotches had already made him a little woozy as they compounded his exhaustion. He needed sleep. Christian and his sister-in-law had stopped at the command table and were seated on either side of the senior adviser, who immediately began focusing considerable attention on her. Christian looked bored. Sam saw him fidgeting, and soon the tall captain rose. The colonel obviously didn't want them to leave but was mollified when the woman put a hand to his shoulder. They were walking toward the door when Jim noticed the fliers at their table in the corner. He steered her toward them.

Close up, Sam revised his estimate. She was prettier than he had first thought. Probably in her mid-thirties, she had a mature face, and small crinkles showed at the corners of her eyes. They were large, very green eyes. The generous mouth smiled impartially at all except Bill Robinson. She leaned forward for a quick buss to his heavy cheek. Her voice was low and had a hint of the South as she spoke.

"Bill, it's good to see you again. How's the family?"

"Good, Lee, so far as I know. Sarah wrote that you two had a nice visit in Arlington when you were in Washington last month. I appreciate it, and she was delighted to hear from an eyewitness that my black butt was still in one piece. Thank you, babe. I owe you."

She held his hand. "Not as much as I'll ever owe you," she said softly. "Colonel Robinson here pulled my favorite and only brother-in-law's bacon out of the fire a few months ago when his camp was very nearly overrun," she told the others at the table. "He launched in the middle of a monsoon to bring in fighters—"

"Hey," broke in Bill, "just doing my job." He seemed genuinely embarrassed by the attention. "Let me introduce you to the folks you

don't know. You've already met young Gary here. Meet Captain Frank
Godneau and Major Sam Brooks. Gents, this is Lee Roget." He pro-
nounced it Ro-Shay. "Lee, Sam's going to be a FAC down in the Cau
Mau peninsula and a few other places. Just got in, so he'll be around
for a while."

The green eyes raked him broadside. He became acutely conscious
of his sweated-through flight suit. Her clothing was dirty, he noticed,
but her face was dry. Jesus! Was he the only goddamned person in the
delta who sweated? The hand she offered was compact and had short
fingernails. A very competent-looking hand. Her eyes circled his face
as though she was classifying it. He felt a gentle tug. Embarrassed, he dropped her hand—he realized he'd been holding it after
the handshake.

Her smile widened slightly. She turned to Jim Christian. "You'd better
get me on back to my compound. I know you've got an early go in
the morning." She turned back to the table. "Nice meeting you all and
seeing you and Gary again. I hate to dash, but Jim's borrowed a jeep
and a shotgun guard to get me home safely. He needs his beauty rest.
I'll see you guys again."

Sam watched them go, then felt foolish as he realized that he was
the only one who had not sat down. Bill grinned at him but said nothing.

CHAPTER 3

Sam sat in front of Bill Robinson's desk in the IV Corps ALO's office, grateful for the current of air the old standing fan was pushing toward him. The air liaison officer stood before the wall map that showed the entire corps area. The large black man cut his eyes at his newest forward air controller and scowled. Sam was thinking that the briefing was boring but told himself that he needed the information.

"This is boring, but you need the information," Bill Robinson confirmed, "although the American ambassador to South Vietnam, Mister Henry Cabot Lodge his own self, has said that he expects the Viet Cong will be eliminated from the Mekong Delta by 1965. And you know that a politician wouldn't lie about something like that. Now, just where the ambassador gets the information to make such a statement, I ain't really quite sure. But it didn't come from anybody down here in IV Corps. Let me give you kinda an overview of just what's what in the delta."

Sam made himself as comfortable as possible. He wondered if he should take notes.

"Don't take notes," said Robinson, "just listen. First of all, IV Corps takes in all of the Mekong River delta south of Saigon. You notice here on the map that that big sucker of a river has three major mouths emptying into the South China Sea. Here at Can Tho we're on the lower branch the Vietnamese call the Song Hau Gian and also the Bassac. Don't ask me why they can't decide on one name for the mutha. Like I said, we got the IV Corps headquarters located here. The major town on the center branch of the Mekong is Sadec. ARVN 9th Division is there along with the independent 43d Ranger Battalion. On the northernmost branch the major town is My Tho. That's where the ARVN 7th

Division is. Now, all the way down here on the Cau Mau peninsula, right next to the South China Sea, is where Colonel Jones wants your sorry ass. Bac Lieu. They also call it Vinh Loi sometimes—again, don't ask me why. I hate to say it but it's a sorry place to be. If old Jack Jones wanted you to live in a crapper, he sure has done put you in the right place."

Sam noticed that Bill Robinson could talk like a field hand or an English don, as he chose. Just now, his speech wouldn't have been out of place had he a cotton sack strapped to his large back.

"Bac Lieu," the big man continued, "is about six feet below sea level, and I'm not joking about that. When the monsoon starts in May you'll be landing and taking off in the bes' part of a foot of water. Technically, your AO, or area of operations, will be Bac Lieu province. Same name as the town. But I got sixteen provinces to cover down here with exactly seven USAF forward air controllers, and that includes my sorry ass. What I'm telling you is that you're going to have to go wherever you're needed.

"As for Bac Lieu town proper, for more than thirty years the Viet Cong have controlled everything outside the city limits sign, if they had one. Just between us girls it don't look like ole Marvin the ARVN is about to push 'em out either. The delta used to be able to feed just about all of Asia with its rice crops, but now Uncle Sammie has to bring in rice to keep the people down there from starving. Kinda like taking oil from New York City and piping it to Texas. But it gives you an idea of how much damage old Charley is really doing down that way. They still grow the same amount of rice but it's just going in a different direction now. Like to old Charley's depots in Cambodia.

"Here's the bare bones setup. Each province has a province chief who's supposed to run the political side of things. He answers directly to the premier. He's usually an ARVN light colonel. Kinda superimposed over that structure is an organization called a sector. Its size depends on the amount of military activity and a lot of other things. It's generally a little smaller than a province but not always. It's supposed to be the military side of the government. They got their own internal resources but they don't necessarily call on one of the ARVN units that happen to be stationed in the sector because they get their orders from Saigon." Bill's eyes sparkled and he moved around in his eagerness to share the information. His enthusiasm was infectious.

"The thing is," he was positively gleeful, "they're usually the same dudes running each side of the picture. Now, ain't that some shit? Do you start to see the problem?" He looked encouragingly at Sam as though he were a slow student.

Sam wanted to please his teacher but he didn't really see the problem. He slowly shook his head.

"The U.S. advisory teams," Bill continued rapidly, "help make plans for operations with the Vietnamese army folks they work with. They'll get it cleared all the way up through the sector commander. Remember, that's the military side. They get it all ready to go and the sector commander's growling like a tiger to Saigon that he's going to the field and kick ass and take names. But, before it happens, the *province* chief turns down the operation for some piddly-ass reason. He turns that fucker *down*! Don't you get it? It's the same fucking man who approved it as *sector* chief! Ain't it beautiful? They can plan all kinds of elaborate shit and get supplied for the operation, but they never have to *do* anything! The sector boss is always assured that his doppelganger is gonna turn it down!"

Sam felt as if he were in a barrel tumbling over a waterfall. "You mean, nobody questions the province chief or the sector commander, who's the same man, when this happens?"

"Hell, no! 'Cause that's the way it's done all over the country. Their only problem is that old Charley doesn't want to play their little game. And just to fuck things up even more, the Viet Cong have got a *parallel* government that matches the one from Saigon, right up the line from village to capital. And just to make it really interesting for all the folks down here, there's three of the weirdest religions in the entire world, all of which are semiautonomous and have their own governmental hierarchies and even their own private armies." Bill was positively radiant as he gave Sam more bad news.

"First, you got your basic An Quang Buddhists. Then, there are the Hoa Haos. And last, but certainly not least, there's a real large population of Cao Dais. Man! I love those Cao Dais. They combine *all* the religions of the others and throw in a pinch of this and a peck of that. They've come up with a group of saints that includes Joan of Arc and Charlie Chaplin and Victor Hugo! How's that for a saintly triple? They worship Jesus Christ and Buddha and God knows who else. We are definitely not talking Southern Baptists down here, my friend.

"Lemme get back to the Viet Cong. Down here, most of the folks don't even know who their government *is*. But old Charley knows and he's the one in the countryside telling everybody who it is. It's him! We've got two VC regiments in the delta, each of which has three main force battalions. They almost never fight in regimental strength but these are the hardcore boys. There's the DT-1 south of Saigon and the D-2 in the southern U Minh Forest. That's one badassed area and you'll be doing a lot of work over it. The six battalions that belong to the two regiments operate anywhere in the delta, and the local VC supply 'em.

"Then, each province has its own VC provincial mobile battalion, which operates just in its home province. They reinforce the main force troops when they do a big attack. Usually, though, most of the action comes from the DCU, or district concentrated units. They have up to about a hundred men who cut roads, snipe, and that kinda shit. They're the ones you hear about that farm by day and soldier by night—them and the VC village squads. Each vill has its own squad that operates just in the vicinity of that village. Usually ten or twelve men.

"You see, Sam, the entire VC structure is geared for mobility. Strike quick and hard with small units. Even their battalions break their component companies down into separate operating units. But, just to make sure that the ARVN stays in place and doesn't stray too far from base camp, they can muster damned quick for a battalion-sized attack, which will be supported by all the local help.

"Now, to counter this threat we've got all these South Vietnamese divisions I was talking about, plus a bunch of Regional Forces/Popular Forces, who the Americans call the Ruff-Puffs. They correspond roughly to the VC district concentrated units and the village squads. Only they ain't as good most of the time. Their main job is to defend their village, but they get damned little support and damned little pay and a bunch of them probably work for Charley as well. Unfortunately, we've got American advisers with some of their larger units who stand a better than even chance of getting their shit blown away."

"How about the South Vietnamese regular army?" Sam broke in. "It looks as if there ought to be enough of them to keep the VC from doing anything they want to do."

Bill clapped his hands and chortled, looking like a big happy bear. He drew his words out lovingly, as though he'd found a screwup of such proportions that it could make them all proud. He looked gratefully at Sam for bringing it up.

"Yes, the Vietnamese army," Bill relished the words. "First, push any conceptions out of your mind concerning what you might think you know about an army. They'll only confuse you unless you happen to be an expert on Central America and its politics. You see, the Viet Cong are not a direct threat to the Vietnamese army so long as they continue to conform to their present practices. If the ARVN doesn't go into the field on operations, or the operations are so well publicized that the VC know about them almost as fast as the subordinate ARVN commanders, then there's little chance of any serious bloodletting. And if the VC get too audacious, then there's always your friendly U.S. Air Force and artillery to make him repent.

"No, you have to see that the major threat to the ARVN commanders from battalion level on up is strictly political. First of all, he got his job through politics, not merit. Next, he keeps his job through politics, not merit. Sometimes a maverick comes along who actually pursues the Viet Cong, but if he takes losses, then he falls out of favor and his supplies and monies stop. A Vietnamese commander's worth is determined not by how many of the enemy he destroys but by his loyalty to whoever pulled the latest coup and is in charge in Saigon at the moment. The more loyal the general, the closer he'll be stationed to Saigon. The most loyal are *in* Saigon, and that's the ultimate goal of ninety percent of the ARVN general officers. Once he's made it, his primary job is to protect the current premier."

Sam thought a moment. "Looks like my new outfit, the 21st Division, must not be so loyal then, if they're stuck way the hell down in Bac Lieu."

"Ah," said Bill, "not necessarily all true, only partly. The commander of the 21st is General Tranh, who at one time commanded troops in the Bien Hoa area, just outside Saigon. He had the bad luck to be a fairly competent officer, and the current premier needs a modicum of professionalism to keep the VC from coming outta the U Minh Forest and completely overrunning the southern delta. Like I said, that's where the D-2 Main Force Regiment is holed up, and they must be tough if they can stand to live in there. It's a thick mangrove swamp and jungle, most of it subject to tidal flow from the Gulf of Thailand, with only small lumps of firm land. It's as bad as it can get. The ARVN do not, under any circumstances, go into the U Minh Forest. Before the D-2 set up their base camp in there, the only Vietnamese who did go in were a particularly hardy band of woodcutters. So, the premier needs someone fairly competent just to contain these tough nuts, and General Tranh is paying his dues until he can move to Saigon with the rest of the dilettantes. Even so, it's not the ARVN division but American air, fighters and helicopters, that keep the VC hiding out in that pest hole."

Sam thought over what Robinson had said. "What you're telling me is that the countryside is terrible, the army won't fight, the people don't care, and the generals and politicians are, for the most part, all corrupt."

Bill beamed at him. "That's about it."

"Just one question then. What the hell are we doing over here?"

Bill drove and Sam rode shotgun as they made their way through the crowded streets of Can Tho before hitting the more open road to the airfield. Sam handled his AR-15 carbine with delicate motions since he'd inserted the loaded clip. Bill continued the brief as he drove the jeep with the aplomb and elan of a born fighter pilot. His meaty hand steered the jeep from certain collision with an errant pedestrian at the last moment. He didn't seem to notice the near miss, but Sam's hands white-knuckled around the carbine and side of the seat. He wasn't sure he wanted to fly with this maniac.

"Remember," Robinson was saying, "that FACs are *the* prime source of American intelligence. We provide to the advisory teams in the field just about the only information they can really trust, other than their own. For that reason, we make sure that what we pass to them is good, not just speculation or opinion, unless they ask for it. This part of your job is secondary only to putting in the air strikes. To do it properly you have to really learn your AO and be able to tell when something unusual is going on. Not an easy job sitting fifteen hundred feet over the top of it, but not impossible either. Pay attention to the small things. Are the water buffalo out in the fields? If they're not, then it might mean that the VC have moved in and papa-san is protecting his investment in his water boo by putting it in the family bunker to keep it from getting dinged in a possible firefight. What are the people doing? Are there more of them in the fields than there should be? Maybe Charley is helping out with the rice harvest.

"That's the sort of thing you have to always be looking for. Don't expect a VC to shoot at you if he doesn't think he's been spotted. He knows very well that you can bring the wrath of God down on him quicker than a blue jay eating a June bug. You can have five-hundred-pound bombs falling all around his scrawny ass before he's got time to get his sampan halfway to a hidey-hole. But, if he thinks you've seen him, whoa! He knows he's got to blow your little ole airplane outta the sky real quick before you can start directing those A-1s or F-100s onto him."

Bill Robinson pulled the jeep to a halt in front of the stucco building at the airfield. Carefully, he locked a large chain between the clutch and the steering wheel. He turned to Sam and continued. "Today, we're just gonna let you get used to flying the airplane. Tomorrow, we'll work on FAC procedures. It looks like you're going to have to learn an awful lot of it on your own, since you didn't go to school and we don't have time to do it all here. We gotta get your sorry ass on down to Bac Lieu before ole Jack Jones decides to send me in your place. Good thing you're a fighter pilot or you could be hurtin'. Grab your stuff and let's us go look at this marvelous machine."

Sam followed his ALO around the aircraft while Robinson gave a running commentary on the preflight inspection he was conducting. "The O-1 is a tandem two seater, as you can see, with a high wing for best ground observation. It was first built for our army starting way back in the early fifties. They called it an L-19. Main difference between their early ones and ours is the constant-pitch prop on ours. Also, a little better avionics. The air force took it over for the forward air control mission a coupla years ago. Till then, the FAC was supposed to ride around with the crunchies in a radio jeep or walk his silly ass off with those young studs carrying the rifles. Sam, it was a terrible way to make a living. Couldn't see shit, of course, so now we go in style, baby. But, back to this terrific piece of machinery.

"What does it have, you ask me? Well, it's got a mighty 213-horse-power Continental engine that'll turn this ninety-inch prop. It's s'posed to have a maximum gross weight of twenty-one hundred pounds, but with you and me, four rockets under the wing, full fuel, and 'bout two hundred pounds of delta mud, we'll exceed that for sure. It'll carry it, though. It's got a tail wheel rather than the nose gear that just about every other military plane in the world uses. Makes it hard to handle on the ground until you get used to it, but you won't break off the gear in a rough field. Some of our young fools try it, but it's usually even too tough for them to do too much damage.

"There's sixty degrees of flaps to help you get in and out of short fields, and if you pull the power back until you're just hanging in the air by your prop, you can get more than five hours of flying time out of it. So it don't hurt your head, I'll figure it for you. That works out to about five hundred miles. I never claimed it was fast, did I?

"Now, what ain't it got? Just about everything that you're used to. There's no guns, no armor, no self-sealing tanks, and no gunsight except for a grease pencil mark on the front windscreen. It's got no air-conditioning, no pressurized fuel system, no ejection seat. Instead, we have these two old moth-eaten, rotting parachutes, one for each seat, that we never use except as back cushions."

Sam looked at him with a raised eyebrow.

"No point in it," Bill said. "We almost never get over fifteen hundred feet and are usually somewhere around a thousand. Get hit there and there's not much chance of bailing out anyway. Besides, wearing those things in the cockpit is just too confining. There's not that much room for a big man like me and you, and with all the squirming around you have to do putting in a strike, well, it just ain't worth it.

"Here's something that's more important than that parachute," Bill continued. "You'll notice that your flak jacket folds up like this and fits real neatly into the seat rack. We use it that way instead of a cushion. You gotta get your priorities straight when you fly the O-1. Would you rather protect your chest or the family jewels?"

Sam folded his flak jacket into the front seat, copying the procedure Bill used in the rear. He let the large man crawl into the rear before contorting his own body to get through the side door into the front seat. He plugged in his newly acquired army crash helmet, which was equipped with an adjustable boom mike, and placed the helmet in his lap as he let his eyes wander over the gauges and knobs in the cockpit. There weren't many; most would have fit on one side panel of a Century series fighter.

"You ever done any light-plane flying?" Bill asked from the rear seat.

Sam nodded. He had owned his own small aircraft, a Beechcraft Bonanza, for several years. It had served him well as transportation to the larger cities when he felt the desire to absent himself from some of his more isolated stateside assignments. Sam's hand caressed the control stick of the O-1. It had a fighter-style handle with a single button on the head rather than the half dozen or so that could normally festoon a fighter stick. He assumed it was used for firing the rockets.

"Well," Bill continued, "since we don't have time to go through a regular checkout program, you're just going to have to learn a lot of this stuff yourself. Start the O-1 the way you start any light airplane. Mixture rich; throttle opened 'bout an inch or so. You won't need any prime down here, but with all the moisture you do get quite a problem with carb icing. Go ahead when you're ready to start her up. On the takeoff roll, as soon as the tail starts to come up, put a little back pressure on the stick and she'll fly right off. We'll go out and do a spin or two and a few stalls in different configurations; then come on back in and shoot a few landings. You've flown tail-wheeled aircraft before, haven't you?"

Sam acknowledged that he had and that he understood the instructions. He slipped on the helmet and adjusted the boom mike until it was just brushing his lips. He switched the radio selector box to the intercom position so he could talk easily to Bill. Giving the instruments another quick scan, he adjusted the throttle, prop, and mixture, switched the magneto switch to the "both" position, and hit thc starter. He watched four blades rotate past the windscreen as the engine fired and settled into a contented clatter. Sam carefully adjusted the throttle until it was idling at 1,200 RPMs for the warm-up. Oil pressure was good and the oil temperature was coming up. The cylinder head temperature was starting to show a slight rise. Things looked normal.

"I'll handle the radios for this flight and you can just listen and learn the procedures," said Bill. "There's not too much to it normally. You don't have many control towers to talk to unless you go to Tan Son Nhut or Bien Hoa. Before we're airborne we check in with arty to see if they're firing and, if they are, where it is heading so we can stay clear. After we're airborne, we check with our control room to let 'em know we're up. We make periodic checks with them to keep 'em up on our location. Course, we do a lot of talking to the fighters and the folks on the ground around the area we're bombing, but we won't do that on this flight. Like I say, we don't have a tower to talk to down here, but that doesn't mean you can just go out and take off without looking around real good. You never know when a stick of Hueys will try to land square on your ass. Let's move whenever you're ready. Just do it like you want to and don't worry about me back here."

Sam pulled the control stick back to keep the tail wheel anchored firmly to the pierced-steel ramp and advanced the throttle. The little aircraft surged forward almost gratefully. A flight of four Huey helicopters clattered overhead, bound for some place farther south. An American air force sergeant alerted by the noise of the O-1's engine strolled out of the stucco building and leaned against the wall, watching them taxi by. The man lifted his hand in a casual wave. Sam returned it.

"On the first takeoff," Bill said over the intercom, "try a no-flapper. The tail will start coming up about the time you've got full throttle in, unless you hold quite a bit of back pressure on the eleva-tors. Keep it in a slightly nose-high attitude and it'll fly off before you're really expecting it to. It'll seem pretty odd at first, 'cause flying fighters you develop a kind of mind-set about how long it's supposed to take for an airplane to get off the ground. You just naturally expect an aircraft to eat up a mile of concrete before it decides to fly. This little hum-mer will do it in five hundred feet. Though it's hard to imagine that a pilot can get behind an airplane that's flying less than a hundred knots, you sure as hell can."

Sam scanned the checklist and made certain that he knew where most things were located in the cockpit. The magnetos checked out, and he cycled the prop from high to low pitch and back again. He checked the flaps and turned on the booster pump. "Ready?" he asked.

"Try not to black me out" was the response, followed by a high-pitched snigger.

Sam wiggled all the controls once more to make sure that they were not binding, then moved out onto the runway.

"Better make sure your gyro is set," Bill suggested.

Gyro set? Christ on a crutch! He hadn't flown anything that had a vacuum-driven gyro since his earliest training days. He aligned the aircraft with the runway and let the magnetic compass stop swirling around and settle down, then read his magnetic heading. He caged the gyro and set the heading into it, then uncaged it again.

"We'd better move our ass," said Bill. "There's an Army Beaver turning final about two miles out."

Sam nodded and began advancing the power. The response was immediate. The little aircraft leapt forward with a snarl in all its 213 horses. As Bill had predicted, the nose began to lower quickly as the tail came off the runway with the increasing airspeed. Sam stopped it with a rearward movement of the control stick. His toes made delicate nudges to the rudder pedals to keep the Bird Dog aligned with the center of the metal runway.

The airplane *was* off the ground before he expected it to be. He'd been advancing the throttle slowly and suddenly he was airborne. Even Sam's own light aircraft had needed much more takeoff roll.

"Pull it back to about 2,300 RPMs and climb out at eighty," said Robinson. "Let's work southwest of town at three thousand feet. Go ahead and play with it for a while."

The air was marginally cooler at altitude but Sam could still feel the sweat dribbling down his neck and forehead from under the tight-fitting helmet. He leveled and trimmed the aircraft, then looked around to get his bearings. There was flat, flat, and more flat. Through the distant mist and perpetual haze to the northwest, he thought he could make out the irregular shapes of mountains. He squinted but couldn't be sure. He twisted his map in an effort to make sense of the myriad canals, trying to keep himself oriented to the airport. It would be humiliating to have to ask Robinson where it was hiding in the haze. A solitary road curved south from Can Tho and a major canal ran southwest from the river west of town. Sam thought he could see the South China Sea to the east, but it could have been a low-lying cloud layer.

He made a few turns, beginning with a moderate bank of thirty degrees, gradually increasing the bank until the aircraft seemed to be pivoting around the down wing at a seventy-degree angle. The little observation aircraft could literally turn on a dime and give back change. He reversed the steep turn and decided he might as well find out about its stall characteristics. Gradually, he increased the back pressure on the stick until he felt the shudders that warned that the wings were losing their lift-versus-drag battle and were rapidly approaching a full stall. He kept the pressure in as the buffeting increased until the nose pitched downward. Sam let the airspeed increase and returned to level flight.

He tried stalls in different configurations—some with flaps down and power off, others with flaps up and full throttle. Always, there was the strong shudder before the nose would drop abruptly. It was a well-mannered airplane.

Finally, he pulled back the throttle and raised the nose of the Bird Dog until it was high above the horizon. As the stall grabbed it and the nose fell through the horizon, Sam shoved in full left rudder and held the stick back in his lap. The aircraft flung itself inverted and, with its nose down near the vertical, began the typical corkscrewing motions of the spin. Sam let it go through three full turns before he reversed the rudders and shoved the stick forward to break the spin. He added power to regain his altitude and tried it twice more.

"If you're about through trying to make me sick, we ought to head on back and get in a few landings" came the voice from the backseat.

Sam couldn't erase the grin from his face. If there was anything more fun than flying in the three-dimensional world of the fighter pilot, it had to be flinging a small uncomplicated aircraft around the skies. No power-boosted control systems, no spoilers, no slats. It was flying in the most basic sense. Sam's good mood lasted through the series of landings, each one better than the one before.

Too soon the flight was over. His lightweight flight suit was wet through as he crawled from the aircraft. Bill had been a good instructor, offering only an occasional comment. He'd let Sam make his mistakes, then work out the solution for himself, ensuring that he wouldn't forget it.

"What do ya think?" Bill asked Sam as they climbed into the jeep and he unlocked the chain around the wheel.

"It was fun but it won't replace tactical fighters. I already miss 'em."

"Yeah, me too. But if you gotta spend a year over here and you can't have fighters, then this is the next best thing."

Sam looked doubtful. Robinson persisted. "It's gonna be an uncomfortable way for you to live a year of your life, but I'll guaran-damn-tee that you aren't going to be bored outta your gourd like you would be behind a desk. You'll get to come up here to Can Tho pretty often to clean the mud outta your system and get dewormed. Another guarantee. You sure as hell won't see Colonel Jackson Jones down there at Bac Lieu!"

Sam agreed silently that being at Bac Lieu might have a silver lining.

In his room in the MACV compound Sam debated whether to take a quick shower. His flight suit was dark with sweat and his hair was matted from his helmet. It was also nearly time for lunch and he felt hungry for the first time since he'd been in country, so he opted for a quick washup and a clean flight suit. He still didn't feel comfortable wearing jungle fatigues, whereas the light green coveralls fit him like an old friend.

Shouts from the open area by the club made him peer through the wire mesh that made up a wall of his room. A volleyball match had just begun. Two dozen men clad only in athletic shorts and jungle boots bounced around the dusty court, hammering at the ball like deranged teens. It was at least a hundred degrees in the sun and the humidity was high. A tidal wave of sweat poured down the thrashing bodies— some bronzed and muscular, others pink and rotund. Some were athletic and agile; others were not and they stumbled, fell, and rolled in the thick red dust in vain attempts to keep the ball in the air. A tall, wiry man with a graying crew cut shouted encouragement to the more hapless. The forced camaraderie made Sam, who loathed all team sports, shake his head in disgust. The tall man playing the role of team captain looked vaguely familiar, reminding Sam of a camp counselor he'd found particularly revolting as a youth.

Sam patted the many pockets of the flight suit to ensure he had everything. If asked, he couldn't have said exactly what was in each pocket; however, a missing or misplaced item was immediately noted and he didn't feel comfortable until it was restored to its rightful place. When he was sure that all was accounted for, Sam secured the hot locker and stepped into the broiling sunshine spilling onto the partially covered walkway. He fumbled with his aviator sunglasses and felt new wetness begin to form on his body and under his arms.

He tried to stay in the shade of the long building as he made his way to the mess, past the volleyball players. The enthusiasm of some seemed to have waned as the red dust clung to their drenched skin. Sam averted his eyes, feeling that it was ill-mannered to stare at the insane. He had always felt that, among other precautions, a person should avoid direct eye contact with madmen and strangers in bars with unexplained scars.

"Join us, Major!" a voice shouted from near the net. It was the tall man with the crew cut. Sam waved a cheerful negative and continued slouching toward the dining room, intent on a shadowy passage.

The voice followed him, this time with a hint of steel in it. "Come along, Major. It's PT time for all hands."

Sam glanced at the perspiring mob and shook his head mutely. He continued steering for the cooler recesses of the officers' mess. He had a grimace on his face, anticipating what was coming. It came like a cannon shot across his bow.

"Major!"

That, Sam reasoned, was a definite hold-it-right-there-mister, West Point–type voice. Suddenly, Sam's reservoir of good humor, created by the flight with Bill Robinson, was badly leaking.

He stopped, turned slowly, and faced the group, placing his hands on his hips. The round pink figure closest to Sam started screwing his face around like a mime having a seizure. He seemed to have some sort of affliction. Sam stared at him with fascination. The man seemed to have no angles. He was round everywhere—head, torso, buttocks, legs. His rounded belly hung precariously over his gym shorts. Sweat trails made rivulets down his face and body; they looked like patterns drawn for some ancient, exotic ritual. Sam saw that the man was trying to say something without the others hearing it. He watched the man's mouth and leaned closer, trying to be helpful. Damned clever. The command-type voice suddenly supplied the sound, perfectly matched to what the rounded man was lip-synchronizing.

"I'm Colonel Chastain, in the event you can't decipher what Major Bunch is trying to get across to you. I'm senior IV Corps adviser." That certainly explained why he looked familiar, thought Sam. "In that capacity I require that all my officers and staff participate in physical training, regardless of branch or service. Since you are unknown to me and obviously new to this corps, I will pass this message to you one time. Volleyball at noon is a mandatory formation for all officers. Major whatever your name is, you have exactly five minutes to get into proper uniform and join us."

Sam couldn't believe it. How did he get into the clutches of these lunatics? Where was Bill Robinson, and why the hell wasn't he out here if it was mandatory? Sam looked at the staring mob. Some were grinning. Others looked happy for the respite. Most just looked away as though there was something of great interest happening in other parts of the compound. Sam saw the first sergeant standing in a doorway out of sight of the others, shaking his head slowly in disgust. It could hardly match his own. The resentment flared quick and hard within him. Just what did all these fuckers want from him? He'd done a damned credible job his entire career. There weren't that many people, after all, who had three MiGs to their credit before they were twenty-one. Suddenly, he was furious. It was assholes like this who had passed him over for promotion, sent him to Vietnam to fly toy airplanes, and would probably get his butt killed. They'd taken him away from the one thing he'd truly loved and were going to send him to some frigging humid swamp no civilized person had ever heard of. And now, *this*! To be ridiculed in front of a group of officers—*army* officers at that. Just what the hell did everyone want from him? Play volleyball, huh?

"I'm afraid I don't have the proper uniform, Colonel. Just where do you want me?" Sam asked in a flat voice.

"That's the spirit! Just step in anywhere. Serve it up, Charley!"

Sam carefully removed his sunglasses and secured them in a leg pocket before stepping onto the dusty arena. Slowly he spread his legs and folded his arms, facing not the attacking team but the senior adviser. His face was impassive and his eyes didn't blink or waver as they stared directly into the lean face of Colonel Chastain.

The served ball went to the far side of the court from Sam, and his teammates shifted into return positions. Sam held his ground and his stare. A lean young officer made the first setup toward Sam, who ignored the ball even after it ricocheted from his left shoulder into the dust. The opposing team cheered lustily. The senior adviser gave Sam a sharp look before turning back to the net to await the next serve.

The return setup was once more toward Sam. He was aware of a body pulling up sharply just before it collided with him. The ball fell into the dust. Sam raised a hand to wipe sweat from his forehead before refolding his arms.

It was soon apparent that Sam's teammates were setting the ball to him on every occasion to see whether he would break. He didn't, even though the ball struck him twice more. Both teams became silent.

Colonel Chastain's face matched Sam's—expressionless under the coating of red dust. Chastain looked at his watch and spoke quietly: "That's it, gentlemen." He walked toward his air-conditioned trailer without looking back.

Sam held his position until the other officers walked silently away from the dusty court. Several gave him wry smiles as they passed. Alone, he reached into his leg pocket, pulled out his sunglasses, and adjusted them to his lean, bent nose, then walked to the mess.

Inside, Sam removed his cap and hung it on a peg, then, turning, saw Bill Robinson standing where he could have watched the entire episode through the screened side of the building. He motioned Sam to a table on which there were two large glasses of iced tea. Bill pushed one toward him, shaking his head and frowning, before giving way to his high-pitched giggle. "Man," he said, "you are some piece of work. Is there anybody you don't plan on pissing off while you're over here?"

"Pretty childish, wasn't it?" Sam asked with a rueful smile.

"Who? You or the colonel?"

"Both, I guess. Anyway, how come you weren't out there sweating like a pig like everybody else?"

"Same's you, except I'm smarter. That's probably why I'm a lieutenant colonel and they made you stay a pissant major."

The big man giggled loudly again. "When I first got down here and saw what kind of craziness they expected outta their officers, well, I just got myself assigned on a ground operation real quicklike. While I was out there I just made sure I stepped on one of them punji stakes. Just a little, mind you. I got this tame air force doctor at Bien Hoa to give me a medical profile that says I don't have to do any of that shit. That's the smart way to do it. Not you, though. Oh, no! Not you! But I will say one thing for you, baby. You sure do have your very own style!"

CHAPTER 4

"There it is," Bill Robinson said from the front seat of the O-1 Bird Dog. "Beautiful, scenic Bac Lieu. Kinda gets you all choked up just seeing it, doesn't it? That's the airstrip 'bout two klicks southwest of town, and that's the advisers' compound a klick south of there. I tole Carl Markham to keep his young ass available to meet us today, but we'll just buzz the compound to let 'em know we're here."

Sam Brooks, riding in the rear seat, could just manage to get a glimpse of his new home over the mounds of his baggage that filled the cockpit to nearly overflowing. The small PSP runway was surrounded by rolls of concertina wire, and a small building sat isolated on the southern end adjacent to the runway. What he initially picked out to be the MACV compound turned out to be, on closer inspection, a small cluster of thatched-roof huts surrounded by banana trees. His eyes finally came to rest on the compound, and he was only mildly surprised to find it to be much smaller than he had anticipated. There didn't appear to be more than four or five buildings within the four walls.

The aircraft tilted. Bill Robinson rolled and let the nose sag downward until it was pointing directly at the compound, much like he'd been doing for the past hour, as he directed two pairs of A-1 aircraft against a set of preplanned targets. Sam's mind still reeled from that experience. He admitted to himself that he hadn't known what the hell had been going on most of the time. In truth, he'd even had trouble *seeing* the slow-moving, chunkily built attack aircraft as they dropped nearly vertical to release their weapons. It was depressing. Christ, if he'd had trouble seeing *them,* he'd never be able to pick up an F-100 going down the chute at six hundred knots.

Bill Robinson apparently had no such problem, for he had their tiny aircraft in position for every pass, placed so that he could check the run-in headings before he issued the attack pilots their final clearance to drop their ordnance. There had been one American pilot in each of the flights who talked over the radio. Bill told him that was common, but working with all-Vietnamese flights was far from unusual. Then communications could get to be quite a problem. Most FACs, if they knew that it was going to be an all-Viet show, attempted to have their Vietnamese counterpart in the aircraft to handle the radio chores. This was not always easy, since the Viet FACs hated to fly and were particularly leery of getting into situations where their VC brethren might fight back. At one time, their presence in the aircraft was a requirement rigidly adhered to, but recent relaxation of the rule now meant that most of the American FACs flew alone. Bill had chuckled as he told Sam that when a FAC did get his counterpart to join him in a flight, he was often surprised to find that the man had never been in an O-1 and often had never been in *any* aircraft before that trip. Robinson had laughed aloud as he recounted his own story of landing at a small dirt strip, only to have his indigenous observer, a low-ranking enlisted man, bolt from the backseat of the aircraft and scamper into the woods, never to be seen again.

Bill took them over the walled compound so low that he had to tip the Bird Dog on its wing to avoid losing one to the tall radio antenna atop one of the buildings. He chuckled over the intercom as they saw a figure burst from a building and jab an erect middle finger into the air. The figure ran to a jeep and raised a dust cloud as the vehicle shot through the gate in the wall.

"That'd be Carl," said Bill. "Carl Markham. He's a first lieutenant and the other FAC down here. Between the two of you you're gonna get to cover a goodly part of southern IV Corps. This is his airplane we're flying. It's been up in Bien Hoa going through a hundred-hour inspection. A chopper outta Soc Trang is gonna pick me up in fifteen or twenty minutes. I'll have you an airplane down here in a coupla days."

As he talked, Bill maneuvered the aircraft onto a final approach to the short airstrip. To Sam, it didn't look to be a thousand feet in length. He barely felt the tires touch and the plane rolled to a stop by the small building. In front of it a stenciled sign had been stuck into the ground: Welcome to Bac Lieu International Airport. Elevation Six Feet Below Sea Level.

The two officers crawled stiffly from the aircraft and Sam passed his baggage to Bill, who threw it into an untidy pile. There was a small mountain of it by the time the aircraft had been emptied.

The chore completed, Sam took stock of his surroundings. Large, deep ditches paralleled the runway, put there to drain the water, Sam decided. Large dikes or levies, banked on the far side of the ditches, mostly cut off the view of the adjacent rice paddies. The fields he could see had dried, cracked surfaces or were freshly plowed. Large white birds wandered through the newly turned earth and picked halfheartedly at insects. Trees, surprisingly thick, covered dikes farther from the airfield. A small group of thatched huts studded the bank of a canal about a klick to the west. The water in the canal didn't appear to be moving and was an unwholesome-looking brown.

Sam felt as though he was going to melt. Only a few fair-weather cumulus dotted the piercing blue sky over the South China Sea a few klicks to the east. The remaining sky quadrants were clear, although a heavy haze leached the blue from it. A scrawny mongrel wandered from the shade of the building to listlessly hoist a leg and direct a thin yellow stream against the left wheel of the aircraft. Bill frowned at the dog but made no move to stop him.

"Poor devil's lucky nobody's eaten his scrawny ass yet," he muttered, turning to Sam. "This airstrip we're standing on. That compound." He pointed as the jeep thrashed toward them. "That town over there that you can't see. That's all that either we or the ARVN own. Everything else," he gestured with both arms to describe a circle, "belongs to the Viet Cong. Always has and probably always will. Don't ever forget that down here. And at night we don't even own this airstrip. It's gotta be swept for mines each day and the aircraft checked for booby traps before you fly. They keep an ARVN guard down here at night but that don't mean nothing. Americans just have to take care of themselves, 'cause nobody else is going to do it for them. Here's ole Carl now."

The jeep slid up to them in a cloud of dust. As it cleared Sam saw a Norman Rockwell portrait of small-town America sitting, grinning, behind the wheel. Carl threw them a quick, airy salute that he didn't wait for the two field-grade officers to return before he popped from the jeep. He stood a couple of inches shorter than Sam's six feet two, and would probably weigh in as a middleweight. Freckles that had taken on a dark pink hue in the tropical sun covered his face and arms. Bright

red hair grew a uniform half inch around a squarish head. He had small
neat ears, a pugged nose, and a bright white grin that exposed more
teeth than most people seemed to have. He wore baggy green jungle
fatigues bleached almost white by repeated washings. First-lieutenant
bars of cloth were sewn to his collars, and his last name was printed
in indelible black ink on a cloth tab over his left breast pocket. He
wore the new-style jungle boots, which were obviously well broken-
in. The lieutenant pumped Robinson's hand while keeping his bright
green eyes and white teeth turned toward Sam.

"Sam Brooks, meet Carl Markham," Robinson said. Markham's hand
relinquished Bill's and darted instantly toward Sam, intercepting his
hand before it was halfway to the horizontal, and pumping it with equal
vigor.

"Glad to meet you, sir," he said, still pumping and grinning. The
voice went with his Huck Finn appearance—animated and southern.

"Just call me Sam. It looks like we're going to be living and working together for a while."

"You bet, Sam." The enthusiasm was contagious. "Sure glad to get
my bird back," he said, turning back to Robinson. "The A-Team camp
at Quan Long got hit before dawn this morning. I could have been there
in fifteen minutes, but with no airplane the DASC had to call in Charley
Duff up at Rach Gia. Took him the best part of an hour to get cranked
up and get all the way down here. We *are* going to get another Bird
Dog for Sam, aren't we? I mean, y'all don't expect us to share one
airplane." He squinted suspiciously at Robinson.

Robinson laughed. "Naw, Carl. I wouldn't do that to you. His'll be
down in a day or two, but there's no real rush 'cause I want him to
fly with you for a while. Sam didn't get to go through the school before
they sent him over, and I want you to show him the ropes before he
goes solo. Luckily, he's a fighter pilot so there shouldn't be much problem.
I got a chance to give him a contact ride yesterday and he did real
good, but he only got to watch me put in a couple of sets of A-1s against
some preplanned stuff on the way down. That's the sum total of his
FACing experience. I need you to get him broken in. And just to make
sure that you can handle that rank of his, here, I brought you something." Robinson handed him a small brown paper sack, then folded
his arms and smiled.

Carl Markham looked at him curiously, green eyes flashing, then
took the sack, unfolded the top, and peered in. A wide grin creased

his freckled face. "Hey! Is this for real? I wasn't expecting it for another nine, ten months!" He held up two sets of twin-track captain's bars.

"Sure enough," said Robinson. "You deserve it and more. I heard some scuttlebutt that 2d Air Division is looking with favor at that award application for a Silver Star that the green beanies sent in on you after that fight down in Cau Mau. Man, just think! Going home with tracks *and* a Silver Star. No woman around gonna be safe from you."

"Hey!" Carl repeated, beaming like a cherub.

Just don't feel up some senior officer's wife and you might make another promotion, thought Sam sourly.

"Sounds like my chopper," said Robinson, twisting and looking to the northeast. They all stared with their heads cocked, listening. The whop-whop sound was soon definite, echoing off the flat paddies as the Huey turned into the wind for its approach. The helicopter settled politely, some distance away, to keep from overturning the small aircraft.

Bill shook their hands and clapped them on the back, then broke into a shambling gallop for the helicopter, ducking instinctively as he neared the slowly moving blades. Aboard, he waved as the pilot immediately pulled pitch and began a nose-low takeoff. Sam and Carl watched silently until the chopper faded from sight over the low horizon.

Carl gave another quick grin as he hurled Sam's gear aboard the jeep. As he bent over Sam noticed the tip of a holster peeking from the bottom of his fatigue blouse.

"Do we wear those things all the time?" Sam asked, pointing to the gun.

"You durned betcha," said Carl. "Nobody goes anywhere around here unless he's packing. And that means even into town. Maybe I ought to say especially into town. Half the people there are VC in one form or another. We try to stay away from there as much as possible, but most of the ARVN offices are there, so we do have to make an occasional trip in. There's not much to see there anyway. Hop in and let's get you to the compound. We need to find out if there's still anything going on over at that Special Forces camp that got hit this morning. Soon as we do that, we'll get you squared away with a place to bunk. You probably won't get a chance to meet the others until tonight. Most of 'em stay out with their assigned units or with their counterparts during the day. Damn! I *am* glad to get my airplane back."

They were silent during the short ride back to the MACV compound. Two Vietnamese in black pajamas guarded the gate and exchanged grins and parodies of a salute with Carl as the jeep pulled through the wire without slowing down. One of the guards had an old American M-1 Garand rifle slung over his shoulder. The other loosely carried an M-2 carbine. Each wore a web belt that had several grenades hanging precariously from it.

"Regional Force troops," Carl offered in response to Sam's raised eyebrows. "They're from a unit formed in this province. Kinda like the National Guard back home, but not really. Some are pretty good and others aren't. The RF/PF, or Ruff-Puffs, as we call 'em, have an American adviser who lives here in the compound. He tries to make sure that we get the best ones available. Course, we don't allow any of 'em into the compound at night. For that matter, we don't let the 21st ARVN Division soldiers in at night either. There aren't any around right now. They usually come just before dusk to reinforce the Ruff-Puffs during the night.

"That's another thing. They are only twenty-odd round eyes here and we're all scheduled for perimeter patrol. Doesn't matter if you're quartermaster or artillery, or even air force," he added with another grin. "We take it for two-hour shifts from 1800 until 0600. Everybody takes a turn, even the senior adviser. If we get visitors, even they have to take a turn."

Inside the compound, Sam looked with curiosity, and then with some dismay, at his new home. Low, thatched-roof buildings surrounded a small open area. He was relieved to see that there was no volleyball net in sight. Elevated wooden walkways stretched between the doorways of buildings, obviously designed to keep users out of the mud, although the ground was dry and covered with an inch of fine reddish dust. Sandbags and ammo boxes of dirt were leaned against the wooden flanks of each building to chest height. Above them heavy-gauge metal screens continued to the roof beneath the overhang. A large bunker with four entrances was centered in the opening in front of the buildings just behind a flagpole, from which a South Vietnamese flag drooped in the oppressive heat. The surrounding wall was head high and constructed of cement and stone. Guard towers thrust twenty feet into the air at each corner of the wall.

"Let's get your stuff to your room," said Carl, hoisting two of the larger bags.

Sam gathered the remainder and followed the new captain, who identified the different buildings. "That's the team house," said Carl. "It's where we spend most of our off-duty time, if there is such a thing down here. It's also got a small briefing room and the offices of a couple of the civilian advisers—police and economic. They actually live in their own compound downtown, though. They do most of their work down there too, so I don't know why they keep an office in here, unless they're working with the spooks as well. Yeah, there's a CIA guy here but he spends most of his time out lurking around, doing whatever it is they do. Over there is where the province senior adviser works. He's actually our boss. And, let's see, we have a medical adviser and an agricultural guy. We don't have much to do with them except when Charley starts giving us some trouble, then they all start hauling ass back here to the compound.

"That's the operations building and that's the cookhouse and mess hall. Intelligence shares with ops. And these are our living quarters. Not too bad when you get used to them."

Sam followed the young officer along a palm-thatched covered walkway that had individual cubicles opening onto it. Again he noted that sandbags covered the wall to chest height and a heavy screen went from there to the ceiling. Louvered panels covered the bottom of screen doors, none of which appeared to be locked. Carl stopped in front of one of the doors and set the bags down, then pushed the screen open for Sam to enter.

Inside, the concrete floor was bare and irregular, as though it had been poured by someone who didn't know a great deal about working with concrete. On one side of the room was the familiar iron cot with mosquito net. Opposite, a hulking metal wall locker squatted on three legs and a cinder block, leaning toward the door as though it planned a break at the first opportunity. A two-foot by two-foot field desk, a GI gooseneck lamp, and a folding metal chair completed the furnishings. Sam thought his new quarters looked like a chicken coop, a not unreasonable comparison considering the miasma filling the room. Sam sought its source and found it by peering through the warped boards that made up the rear wall of his room. A large odoriferous ditch half-filled with stagnant water lay less than two yards from the head of his cot. He turned to Carl. "Charming," he said. "Tell me, does it ever cool off?"

"Not really," the redhead answered cheerfully. "Not at night and not even during the rains. Turns into a pressure cooker then. Naw, it just stays hotter than hell all the time. Tell you what, I've got a few chores to get done so I'm going to leave you to unpack. Why don't you meet me in the mess hall in about half an hour? There might be a chance we could get a flight in this afternoon if there's still anything going on over at Quan Long camp."

After Carl left, Sam sat on the hard bunk and listened to his pores. He was sure he could hear them channeling the life fluids from his body. He listened carefully, interested, for he'd never noticed it before. It was a raspy little buzz ending with a small bumping noise as his heart contracted. He suddenly realized that he was listening to a fly trapped in the clothes locker. Slowly, he bent to unlace the stiff jungle boots and eased them from his feet with a sigh of relief. He thought longingly of his old flight boots, worn but with supple, expensive leather that conformed perfectly to his feet. He sighed heavily and looked around his new room. Two of the walls were made of concrete and stone where they abutted the rooms on either side of his. Warped wooden planks covered the wall by the ditch except for the lower portion, which was made of more concrete and stone—they seemed to be much in favor as building materials in the delta. What the hell were they expecting to attack? Tanks?

The rough concrete floor snagged at his socks as he walked to the leaning clothes locker and opened it, freeing a fly about the size of a turkey buzzard. His heart leapt! Wonder of wonders! Inside sat a rusted four-bladed fan some eight inches in diameter. If only it worked. He looked at the rusted plug with some consternation. It certainly didn't look like 110 volts. He found a receptacle in the wall under the desk and immediately the blades began a whirring grind. Sam held the little beauty inches from his nose and let the moving air dry the moisture on his face before reluctantly placing the fan on the field desk.

He sat on the bed with his chin cupped in his hands and stared at the rough floor. A drop of sweat fell from his face. A pair of panicked ants circled rapidly in confusion at the unexpected deluge. Like the ants, Sam felt disoriented and off center, out of his natural element. And he felt apprehensive.

Carl sat at one of the four long tables in the mess building, exchanging pidgin talk with a Vietnamese man in a filthy off-white apron. Only he didn't look Vietnamese.

"Major Brooks, this is Choy, our cook. He's such a terrible cook that we're almost sure he works for the Viet Cong and is trying to slowly poison us all. Choy's Chinese and originally came from the area around Vinh, up in North Vietnam. Seems like the benevolent Uncle Ho didn't particularly want any Chinese in his country, especially any Roman Catholic ones, so one day Choy got on his fishing boat and began sailing south. Sailed until he couldn't see land in front of him anymore and turned into shore. Turned out he was at Bac Lieu and he's been here ever since. Swears he's fathered more children down here than any mandarin in China. Here's a typed list of what he can cook or already has made up. Just point to the number of the item you want."

The Chinese cook shook with laughter at Carl's speech, revealing teeth with the reddish black stain of a betel nut chewer. Sam quickly scanned the dirty paper and pointed at bacon and eggs with toast. He really didn't feel hungry but thought he could drink gallons of any liquid available. That brought his attention to a metal pitcher on the table, beaded with moisture. It was cold to the touch. He looked inquiringly at Carl.

"Iced tea," Carl said and pushed him a glass from a stack at the end of the table. "Best thing in the world for putting out a thirst, except for cold beer of course. But I figured we'd better skip that since we're flying in an hour or so. I talked to Charley Duff on the land line; he's the FAC who covered the attack at Quan Long I was telling Colonel Robinson about, and he says that the camp is still taking a few rounds. So I figured we might as well head on over there in case things pick up again. OK?"

Sam nodded and poured another glass of iced tea. "Just tell me what I'm supposed to do."

Carl thought silently for a moment as he gnawed a hunk of French bread, trying to get his thoughts in proper order. "You know already, basically, what a FAC's supposed to do. I don't want to get too simple, but I don't want to leave you guessing about anything either."

Sam nodded again. "Just tell me from the beginning."

"OK, then. A forward air controller and a radioman are normally assigned to an army unit to coordinate air force resources with the ground commander in the close air support role. That is, the direct support of crunchies on the ground. In theory, we're supposed to walk with 'em if they're an infantry unit or ride in a tank if they're armored folks. It works a little differently over here, although the theory is the same.

First of all, they've found that the FAC can see the target a hell of a lot better from an aircraft than he can if he's up to his ass in mud or got his carcass stuffed into a tank. Course, it's gotta be a slow-moving aircraft or you might as well let the fighters find their own targets. But that's a situation that the army and everybody else has found to be totally unacceptable, 'cause, as you know, at five hundred knots you ain't going to see much from an F-100 cockpit unless the VC start riding to work in a train.

"Another thing that works a little different over here is that we're supposed to be primarily advisers to the Vietnamese. Although I haven't *seen* my Vietnamese counterpart for more than two months, I'm still supposed to be an adviser. The theory is the same, though, 'cause except in areas designated as free strike zones every American bomb that's dropped in country has to be cleared by either a ground or an airborne FAC. This is to make sure that the attack aircraft don't put their bombs on friendly troops or civilians by mistake. Of course, sometimes the Vietnamese send their aircraft out to bomb a village in some province where they're pissed off at the mayor or somebody for not paying their taxes on time or something like that, but we make sure that American aircraft aren't involved in that bullshit.

"Where the FAC really comes into play, though, is when there's a TIC, or troops in contact. Sometimes you have to get the ordnance real close to the friendlies to do any good. As I said before, most of the attack birds are moving so fast they can't even *see* anybody on the ground, much less distinguish between friendlies and enemy. Also, they don't even have the communications gear to talk to the ground commander, so the FAC acts as the go-between.

"So, your friendly forward air controller talks to the American adviser on the ground 'cause he's the one who's got the radio, which is probably why the Vietnamese put up with him in the first place. The Vietnamese commander can call for his own air support through his side of the DASC, but he never knows if it'll show up or not. Usually it doesn't, because their airplanes are out bombing a friendly village because the chief of the VNAF thinks that commander cheats at canasta or something else real important. Then, too, they simply don't fly at night.

"But the Vietnamese fighting the war know that American-led aircraft *will* show up, so it's real important to them to keep the American adviser reasonably happy, even if it means that they have to be a little aggressive occasionally.

"We'll work with a Vietnamese unit without an American being there but it's difficult, mainly because we have a hell of a time understanding what they say. You've probably noticed that their language is extremely tonal, and they really have to shout to reach all the right notes over the radio, which distorts everything anyway. When they get excited over the airways, it sounds like a cat being castrated."

"Wouldn't it help to have a Vietnamese FAC in the aircraft with you?" asked Sam.

"Sure it would," said Carl with a grin, "but like I said, first, you've got to find the rascal and then persuade him to go flying with you. It ain't that easy. In any event, as soon as we make contact with the friendly force that requested the air support, we get the target from them, either by map coordinates or a combination of pointee-talkee and their marking it somehow. Then, we do our damnedest to verify that it's a legitimate target and we haven't been called in just to settle an old grudge. This is usually no problem if there's an American on the ground with them. He'll confirm that they're really taking fire or whatever. If there isn't an adviser, then all I can suggest is that you proceed with real caution before you start dropping bombs on somebody.

"So, let's assume we got a legit target and we do get fighter support. We pass the local info on the situation to them, just a local sitrep as best we know it. It doesn't have to be too detailed, 'cause as you know most fighter pilots ain't bright enough to comprehend anything too complicated. They usually just want to know where to put their bombs and which way it is to the local whorehouse if they go down."

Sam grinned and shrugged at the none-too-gentle jab, and Carl continued his lesson.

"But we insist on telling 'em target elevation and where the best bailout area is if they are hit hard—stuff like that. Then we mark the target for them with one of our four smoke rockets or with smoke grenades, which, if you're smart, you'll carry plenty. Just chuck 'em out the window and use the smoke as reference for directing the strikes. Tell 'em what direction and distance the target is from the smoke.

"When they do start their runs we have to make damned sure they're lined up right and aren't about to wipe out the 43d Ranger Battalion. When we are sure, we give 'em final clearance to drop. After it's all over we give 'em their BDA, or bomb damage assessment. That is, we grade their ass, so they've got to be pretty nice to us."

"Sounds fairly simple," said Sam, knowing there had to be more to it than that.

"Yeah, doesn't it?" answered Carl with that wide grin that seemed to show more than two hundred gleaming teeth. "Unfortunately, it usually doesn't happen that smoothly. Either the troops won't be where they're supposed to be, or the fighters can't bomb worth sour owl shit, or something. Then, too, the guy on the ground will be screaming at you 'cause he thinks you're bombing too close or too far away or the wrong target or some such shit, and the guys in the attack birds are screaming at you because they're taking ground fire or don't like the run-in heading. Or all your damned radios quit working. Or the VC suddenly decide to open up with a quad .51 and it's making your asshole try to chew through the seat. You can bet there's always going to be something to make it interesting.

"Incidentally," Carl continued, "we try to mark above a thousand feet if we can. You're not always safe there, but it's a hell of a lot better than trying to do it down at five hundred and a heavy-caliber gun suddenly cuts loose. Remember, you're not going to outrun it at a hundred miles per hour. You've got to learn to be cagey and always try to keep something between you and the guns. This little ole bird might fly pretty good with holes punched in it but *you* won't."

"What do you do when there isn't any—what did you call it—troops in contact?"

"Why, we just putt around the countryside like we're charter members of a private flying club. Only we call it VR—visual reconnaissance. We try to overfly every part of our AO just about every day. We pay attention to what's going on, on the ground. Are there new road cuts? Is canal traffic backed up? It might mean there's a VC tax-collecting team at work. How many people are working in the fields? More or fewer than normal? Is there a reason for that? There's lots of things to look for after you've learned your AO. Well, that's it in a nutshell. You got any questions?"

"A million," said Sam. "But I don't know enough to ask any good ones yet."

Carl glanced at his watch, then back at Sam, who was just finishing his lunch. "Why don't we go flying?"

Sam eased in a little back pressure on the stick and the aircraft smoothly departed the PSP-matted runway. He trimmed for a climb and adjusted the power, all the time in a gentle turn to the west. The South China Sea shimmered brightly a few kilometers to the east until his turn put it behind them. The air flowing through the open window felt good on his sunburned face and neck.

"This is about the right heading," Carl said over the intercom from the rear seat. "Why don't you level at about fifteen hundred feet? Don't keep it there, though, because there's always people on the ground watching you and a lot of them have weapons. If they think they can get a free shot at you without being seen, they'll do it. Just let it sag up and down and try to keep it in a constant turn and sorta average out the desired heading. That's enough to complicate the problem for anybody who wants to take a crack at you."

Sam tried to orient his 1:50,000 scale map to the countryside below him. Map reading was a skill that had been neglected during his jet flying years, but it began to come back to him. He felt pleased that he was able to plot their position with some accuracy. He was also helped by the fact that they were doing only about a hundred miles per hour, which gave him time to confirm their location.

The town of Quan Long quickly appeared to their front, although the afternoon haze had reduced forward visibility to about two miles. Looking straight down, however, Sam found he could see the ground clearly. He checked his map. Before takeoff he had plotted the position of the Special Forces camp with a grease pencil mark on the acetate covering of the map. It was located about five kilometers southwest of the small town.

"Lemme give them a call," said Carl. Sam nodded his understanding. "Goldfinger, Goldfinger, this is Blackjack One Two. How do you copy?"

There was a lengthy pause before an answering voice, obviously American, came over the FM radio. "Good afternoon, Blackjack One Two. This is Goldfinger Six. You're running late today, Carl. I figured you'd be over here about dawn. You have something hot going last night?"

"Naw, Six. No airplane. Just got this one back. Did ole Blackjack One Five treat you folks right?"

"You bet! He called in old Puff, who put a whipping on them just as they got through the first line of wire. You'd better look out or we'll start giving him all our business."

"That'll be the day! You people still taking any incoming?"

"Not right at the moment," the voice said from someplace within the star-shaped camp below. "We expect 'em back tonight for a repeat performance, though. There's no indication they've moved out of the area. We'd appreciate it if you could check in with Blackjack One Five. Think he's got another set or two of fighters inbound to put into that swampy area to the southwest. Likely, that's where they've holed up. Maybe y'all can stall ole Charley's party before he gets it cranked up for the evening performance."

"OK, Goldfinger Six. I'm going to talk to him on uniform, but we'll listen out on your frequency. Talk to you later.

"OK," said Carl on intercom. "Let's switch to 261.4. That's Blackjack common frequency on UHF radio." Almost without pause, Carl was keying his mike button.

Sam looked at the Special Forces A-Team camp as he drifted around it in a lazy left turn. The fighting positions were filled with troops; others strode purposefully across the open area to and from mortar and machine-gun pits. The taller frames of the Americans were easy to pick out. One waved casually at the aircraft. Sam returned it. Several bodies lay tangled in the concertina wire surrounding the camp. They had achieved that loose-limbed posture that only the dead do so well. Sam had trouble shifting his eyes from them. He was no stranger to combat, but what he had experienced seemed to have little relation to what he was looking at below. His had been the freewheeling, three-dimensional world of the Sabre pilot in MiG Alley around Korea's Yalu River. To the best of his recollection, he'd never seen a body outside a coffin. He wasn't sure he liked it.

"Blackjack One Five, this is One Two," said Carl over the radio.

The reply came back instantly. "Go Twelve, this is Fifteen."

"Hey, Charley! How they hanging?"

"One behind the other for speed, Carl. How 'bout you?"

"You know me. No sweat. I got the new Blackjack One One in the front chair today for an area checkout. Sorry I couldn't make it this morning but my bird was in inspection up at Bien Hoa. What's happening?"

"A reinforced company is what Goldfinger Six figures. Tried to come over the wire just before dawn. They pulled back after Puff started to work out on 'em. Estimate we got over thirty but you know how that goes. I could only see about ten or fifteen by the time I got here and damned if some more of 'em haven't disappeared while I've been overhead. Shifty little devils. Anyway, I also worked Puff out in that swampy area about five klicks to the southwest and then put in four sets of fighters. Got two more coming up in fifteen. Kilroy Flight is F-100s outta Tan Son Nhut and Milo Flight is a pair of A-1s out of Bien Hoa. I hope you can handle them because I'm getting real skoshi on fuel. I need to be heading on back to the barn about ten minutes ago."

"No sweat, we can do 'em. Where'd you plan on putting 'em?"

"You see that swampy finger about twenty-five meters wide that points right at the camp?"

"Rog."

"Well, follow it for about a hundred meters past those scrawny palms until you get to an open area. Then go due south about two hundred meters into that real thick bush. If they're still here I think that's where they are. Course, that probably means they'll be on the other side of the camp."

"OK, Charley, I see where you're talking about. Looks like a pretty good place for 'em. We'll take over and let you go on home. Come over and see us sometime."

"I'll do that. Rendezvous point is the camp. Take her easy, y'all."

"Did you copy that down?" asked Carl.

Sam shook his head, angry with himself for not doing so. Carl passed him a grease pencil and repeated the call signs of the fighter flights for him to scrawl onto the Plexiglas of his windscreen.

"How does he know they'll be down there?" asked Sam.

"He doesn't. You just start getting hunches about things after awhile. Often there's no real rhyme or reason to it. I guess you just start thinking like a VC. Now, let's review what we're going to say to the fighters. You might as well start getting your feet wet."

The two of them went over the radio and operational procedures in more detail than they had done back in Bac Lieu. Sam felt a seed of anxiety growing in the pit of his stomach as they circled the camp well away from the target area. There was no sense in giving away their interest should the VC actually be hiding in the swamp. Nervously he checked the arming switches for the rockets and made sure he could reach the colored smoke grenades hanging on wire on the rear of his seat. Fuel was OK; readjust the boom mike until it was just brushing his lips; check all the radios and ensure he had the proper frequencies set. He removed his leather flight gloves and dried his sweaty palms on his flight suit. Sweat was pouring in a steady stream down his forehead from beneath his helmet.

A new voice suddenly came over the radio. "Blackjack, this is Milo Lead. How do you read?"

Sam took a deep breath before he answered. It was the pair of A-1s from Bien Hoa. "Roger, Milo Lead. This is Blackjack One One. I'll be directing your strike today and I'm real new at this so please bear with me."

"No sweat, One One. We were all virgins not too long ago. Do we have a real target today or are we just moving mud?"

"Milo Lead, this is Blackjack One One. Looks like you might have a real one. The camp that we're using for the rendezvous point got hit this morning, and another FAC thinks he knows where they might be hiding. Go ahead with your lineup but do it slowly please."

"OK, Blackjack. Milo Flight is a pair of A-1s with a load of eight Mark-82s and four napes each, plus guns. Milo Two is Vietnamese. We're about twenty klicks out from the camp at this time, descending through six grand."

Sam hurriedly scribbled the information onto the side windscreen using large numbers, which would be easily seen, then tried to remember exactly what he was supposed to pass to them in turn. "Roger, Milo Lead, Blackjack copied your lineup. The target is . . ." What the hell was the target anyway?

"Lightly dug-in troops beneath a tree canopy," prompted Carl from the rear seat.

". . . lightly dug-in troops beneath the tree canopy. Target elevation is about fifty feet and best bailout area is back toward the camp." Sam paused and thought furiously. What had he forgotten to tell them?

"Which way do you want us to run in and off?" asked Milo Lead.

Carl whispered over the intercom and Sam radioed: "Run-in can be at your discretion, only do not overfly the camp. Expect ground fire up to .51 caliber on each pass. Call FAC in sight on each pass and go through dry if you don't get positive drop clearance from me. Call coming off target with direction after each pass." Sam thought some more. "Oh, yeah. I want your bombs first, dropped in pairs; then the nape in pairs. Any questions?"

"Nope," replied Milo Lead with a chuckle. "I think we managed to finally get everything covered. I've got the camp in sight. Where are you, Blackjack?"

Smartass, thought Sam. "We're in a right orbit, just over the eastern side of the camp." Carl whispered and Sam continued. "As soon as you have us in sight, we'll depart the camp and head toward the target."

"Milo Lead has you in sight over the camp. Milo Two, take your interval and green 'em up. Blackjack, we're at your three, going four o'clock."

"Rajah, gren 'em op," said a heavily accented voice.

Sam rolled wings level and peered at the horizon over his right shoulder. He immediately picked up the bulky shapes of the two Skyraiders. He twisted his head to look back at Carl, who nodded that he had spotted them as well. He also pointed south without speaking. Hundreds of white teeth seemed to flash at Sam as the younger man grinned encouragement. Sam turned the aircraft until it was aimed at the heavy tree growth to the southwest of the camp and with his left hand again nervously rechecked the arming switches for the rockets.

"Do it just the way you'd shoot a rocket from a fighter," said Carl over the intercom, "except this time you don't have a real sight to use. Just point the nose where you want the rocket to impact and try not to make your pullouts too hard. Remember, you're not in a one hundred now and you can definitely pull the wings off this little Tinkertoy if you try to yank six or seven g's on it. Try to put your first rocket square in the middle of the heaviest tree growth."

Sam turned the aircraft to the right so the target area was on his left shoulder, then glanced back to make sure the pair of attack aircraft were following him. He eased the throttle back just a bit and firmly rolled the Cessna nearly inverted, keeping his eyes glued to the point he'd selected. It was one of the taller trees visible high above the tangled growth. As the nose of the little aircraft pointed below the tree, Sam brought in opposite aileron and rudder pressure to bring it into an upright dive. He glanced quickly at the altimeter and airspeed indicator. Twelve hundred feet and one hundred twenty miles per hour. He nudged the left rudder and aileron to correct for the wind drift. The black grease pencil marks he used for a sight were steady just beneath the large tree. At a thousand feet he punched the button on the stick, then jumped with a start as a rocket on the left wing ignited and sped toward the ground. Sam figured he must have fired at least a thousand rockets during his flying career, but never one six feet from his head by an open window. Christ, this was really back to basics. Open windows and a gunsight that would have made the Red Baron laugh outright.

Sam pulled the small aircraft from the dive, carefully trying to keep from loading it up with g forces, and banked to watch the smoke rise from the white phosphorous rocket. The rising column stood out starkly against the verdant tree canopy.

"Next time," Carl said, "tell 'em before you roll in to mark. They have to keep track of you too, just the same as you do with them."

Sam nodded, accepting the gentle rebuke in silence as he watched the lead attack aircraft pull onto its dive perch. "Milo Lead," he called, "hit my smoke."

"Rog. Milo Lead is in hot from the west. FAC and target in sight."

"Try to position yourself so that you can check his run-in heading," said Carl quietly.

Sam was trying to do exactly that but found he was too far out of position to adjust before Milo Lead was beyond his drop point.

"Milo Lead is off to the north. Dry."

The aircraft had followed instructions and had not dropped any of its ordnance. Sam was furious with himself, determined that it would not happen again. Savagely, he racked the small aircraft into a steep bank and pulled back hard on the stick. The result was an incredibly tight turn. He picked up Milo Two just as the wingman was rolling into his dive. The Vietnamese pilot said something over the radio but Sam didn't understand.

"Milo Two," he called, "hit my smoke." Sam pointed his aircraft directly at the diving Skyraider until he was certain that its run-in heading was correct. It was aimed directly at the smoke ball on the ground; its flight path shouldn't cross the Special Forces camp, where an inadvertent drop of ordnance could be devastating. The aircraft dove from the south. "Milo Two, you're cleared in hot," Sam said over the radio.

There was no acknowledgment, but Sam clearly saw the two heavy bombs leave the A-1. Both impacted only a few meters short of the target. Sam had been dive-bombing most of his adult life and he was impressed with the accuracy of the delivery. The twin explosions were awesome. Trunks of large trees were hurled yards into the air. Sam could actually see the concussion wave of the blasts in the moist air as it hurtled toward him. The O-1 gave a convulsive leap as it passed. Sam grabbed the reins more firmly and tried to quiet his startled mount. Accomplished, he peered toward the new clearings in the jungle.

"Why don't you move Lead's bombs about fifty meters to the south?" Carl suggested.

Sam nodded. "Lead, this is Blackjack One One. Put your pair about fifty south of the new craters. I'll try to stay on top of things on this pass."

"No sweat, partner. You're doing fine. Lead is in from the northeast. FAC and target in sight."

Sam nailed it this time. Using the incredibly tight turning radius of the O-1, he found he could orbit almost directly over the target and still whirl rapidly in another direction to face the oncoming attacker. The A-1 was right where he should have been, directly in front of Sam.

"Milo Lead, this is Blackjack. You're cleared in hot."

"Rog, cleared hot," the leader acknowledged.

The two bombs exploded almost exactly in the place Sam had directed. He was becoming more and more impressed with Skyraider pilots in general. After he rode out the concussion wave he let the aircraft sag to a thousand feet and watched the smoke from the blasts roil away from the new openings in the tree cover. He glanced curiously out the open window to the wing, where he'd picked up an unusual sound. He listened carefully but didn't hear it again. He had turned his attention back to Milo Lead's strained call off target when he heard it again. Curiously, he peered at the low wing. The airplane was definitely making strange noises that he couldn't identify. It sounded like the supersonic tip of a cracking bullwhip. Definitely odd, but there didn't seem to be anything wrong. Sam directed his attention back to the ground. Carl gave him no new instructions, so he decided to move the next pair of bombs to the east of the new craters.

He relayed his decision to Milo Flight and was not a little surprised that the Vietnamese wingman understood his instructions; once more the bombs fell as directed. Sam hauled the O-1 into a hard right turn and again became conscious of the cracking sound around the high wing. Startled, he peered closely at the offending wing tip but could see nothing unusual. He was diverted once more by Milo Lead.

"Lead's in from the southwest. FAC and target in sight. Where do you want 'em this time, One One?"

"Put 'em about thirty south of Two's last craters. I'll re-mark after this pass." Sam was starting to feel pretty comfortable in his new role.

A sudden "spoing!" from the left wing made him jerk his head toward the noise. Something was definitely wrong. He hadn't imagined that sound. He moved his eyes rapidly over the undersurface of the wing but once again could find nothing unusual. Then he saw a three-inch scar on the metal wing strut. He stared at it, puzzled, then glanced over his left shoulder at Carl. The young captain was looking at him curiously.

Sam thumbed the intercom: "Looks like something hit the left strut. At least I'm pretty sure it wasn't there when we took off."

Carl laughed. "I thought you were just being cool. Didn't you know they were shooting at us?"

The hair prickled on the back of Sam's neck. He faced forward, eyes wide and staring, wanting to crawl up inside his helmet. A violent twitch began jerking on his left buttock. Shooting! Jesus! That's what those cracks outside the window had been. What the hell was he supposed to do now?

Carl sounded almost nonchalant. "Guess there was somebody home after all. The way you're moving the bombs around is good; ought to put a real hurting on 'em. You're doing fine, Sam, but it's always a good idea to tell the fighters that they're taking ground fire. Not that they or us can do a hell of a lot more about it than we're already doing. I mean, you're letting them attack from the direction of their choice and pull off any way they want to go. Sometimes everybody just has to take their lumps. But I wouldn't go much lower than we are right now. This is just AK-47 fire, but they may be holding back something bigger and nastier. Naw, just go ahead. You're doing fine."

Sam felt like screaming. Didn't that dumb fucker realize that someone was trying to kill them? He heard the cracks outside the open window again, only this time he flinched. He knew what they were now. He glanced stealthily over his shoulder to see if Carl had noticed and was relieved to find him staring intently at the ground. Well, now he had to let Milo Flight know about the ground fire. Maybe they'd want to leave or something.

"Uh, Milo Lead, this is Blackjack. Thought I ought to let you know we're taking some ground fire."

"Yeah," came the laconic response, "I saw some awhile back. You going to put in another smoke now?"

"Roger, rolling in now." To hell with it! If everybody wanted to die, there wasn't much he could do except die with them.

He watched the rocket all the way to the ground. As he began the dive recovery he saw twinkling coming from a number of locations beneath the trees. Simultaneously, the cracking began outside the window. Sam shut his eyes but they popped open of their own accord as another "spoing!" came from somewhere in the aft part of the fuselage. He peered over his shoulder to find Carl doing the same. The green eyes flashed as the redhead turned back. There came the teeth again. Jesus. A person could go snow-blind around this guy. Carl shrugged his shoulders to indicate he didn't know where the round had impacted either. Sam thought everyone was being just a little too damned casual about the situation.

"You might want to try to work some nape under the tree line where that heaviest fire is coming from," suggested Carl.

Sam nodded and pressed the mike button. "Milo Lead, do you think you could get some nape up under the trees where that heaviest fire is coming from?"

"This is Lead. Yeah, if we run in from the south. Two, set it up for nape. We'll run from south to north with a left pull off target."

"Rajah," replied his wingman.

Sam watched the large piston-engine aircraft lumber around the half-orbit until they had their target almost perpendicular at their nine o'clock position. The left wing of the lead ship began to dip and the right wing came up as the pilot rolled, then righted the aircraft into a shallow dive. The large, blunt, rounded nose of the Skyraider was no more than ten degrees below the horizon, perfect for the spread of the jellied napalm mixture, which would ignite into a blazing inferno as it struck the ground. Sam had done it many times on the gunnery range in jet fighters. Two silver canisters tumbled from beneath the wings of the attacking aircraft, hitting the ground just as the pilot pulled the nose hard over the tree line. Small, rapid flashes like a child's holiday sparkler blinked at the belly of the aircraft until the twin flaming tracks of napalm disappeared beneath the trees.

"Lead's off left," the pilot grunted over the radio, straining against the heavy g forces he was experiencing during the dive recovery.

The Vietnamese wingman called something unintelligible; Sam took it to mean he was in for his pass and cleared him to drop. The second A-1 followed the track of his leader toward the smoke coming from the trees. His fiery spume closely paralleled the one already burning there.

"Let's go down and take a quick look before they get their brains back in gear," said Carl. "Just one quick peek beneath the trees and then right back up. OK?" Sam didn't answer but put the stick hard over into a left bank and shoved the nose toward the ground. "I'll be on the controls following you up," said Carl quietly, gently vibrating the stick to let the other pilot know he had his hand on it.

Sam opened his mouth to ask why Carl would want to do such a thing when the answer hit him with frightening clarity. Carl was putting himself in position to recover the aircraft in the event Sam's life was suddenly snuffed out or he was wounded sufficiently that he'd be unable to recover the aircraft so close to the ground. This shit was suddenly getting very serious.

Sam bumped the rudders to get an approach parallel to the scarred wood line. Carl didn't tell him how low to go, so he ignored the altimeter and leveled the aircraft when he figured he'd have an unrestricted view beneath the trees. He glanced quickly at the instrument as he stabilized the descent. A little over four hundred feet. Damn! That was too low, but he was already there and the opening was coming up quickly.

The napalm continued to burn brightly beneath the scorched trees. A lone line of greenish tracer lifted toward them, then fell away as though the gunner had decided to hell with it. Fear seemed to heighten Sam's perception, allowing him to see with more clarity and color. Bushes and trees had a newer, sharper definition than he'd ever seen. Even individual tree branches and vines were discernible with his newfound powers of observation. It was like examining a specimen under a microscope.

To their eleven o'clock position, a flaming figure emerged from the forest edge, its blackened skin worn like the fur of a forest animal. The apparition took several faltering steps into the newly blasted clearing and then, as though paying homage to the aircraft, sank slowly to its knees, arms raised in supplication. The traumatized muscles could not sustain it and the form slowly sank down upon itself, drawing into the fetal position from whence it began, and toppled slowly onto its side. The entire performance took no more than five or six seconds, but Sam's focused intensity made it seem much longer. He stared in horrified fascination at the creature that had fallen almost directly in his flight path, the hostile fire momentarily forgotten. He'd killed years before in Korea, but the sight before him immediately brought up all of man's ancient fears—they flooded into his brain like a tidal wave. Before him was the real truth of man's mortality. Then they were by it and climbing into the clean sky again. Sam breathed rapidly through his mouth, not trusting his nostrils to cleanse the smell of the burning flesh through which they had flown.

"Jesus!" he muttered over the intercom. It was more of a prayer than a curse.

"Yeah, I know," Carl said quietly. "You just fucking never get used to it. At least I haven't. I don't think I could live with myself if I did. But you do have to learn to live with it."

Sam nodded. "I'm afraid I didn't even look under the trees."

"I did. We got quite a few of them. I think if we finish up with this flight and that flight of F-100s that are inbound, it oughta pretty well take care of things. That nape takes the fight out of folks pretty quickly if you're in a position to use it. I'm sure that the camp will want to send some people to check it out, but they'll probably wait until tomorrow just to make sure we hurt 'em enough to stall any attack they might have had planned for tonight. We might as well get back to work."

The remainder of Milo Flight's strike was anticlimactic as far as Sam was concerned. It was as though watching the Viet burn had caused him to put everything into perspective. The mechanics of the strike assumed less importance; so he relaxed and was better able to do his job. He knew that nothing he could say or do could possibly overshadow the trauma or significance of watching a human being burn to death. His mind had already tucked the incident away in one of the dark recesses of his memory where, at his leisure, it could be brought out and studied more dispassionately. He realized that he'd scarcely given a thought to those MiG pilots he'd downed over Korea. If he thought about them at all, it had been as extensions of the aircraft he'd been fighting. But this had been nothing like that. His thoughts on combat had changed completely in those few seconds, and the empty feeling in his belly was a vivid reminder of lost innocence.

CHAPTER 5

"And how's our newest *dai uy* and all the members of the junior armed service this evening?"

Carl smiled and bent his head for a quick glance at the new captain's insignia sewn to the collar tabs of his jungle fatigues. He looked back to the pleasant face of the trim army lieutenant colonel, recently named the province senior adviser (PSA). It was a position normally filled by a full colonel, indicating the confidence the United States Army placed in the abilities of Lt. Col. David Whitehead. Carl had risen courteously to his feet when the PSA approached and spoke to them. Sam did not. He considered Lt. Col. David Whitehead a royal pain in the ass.

"Doing just fine, sir," replied Carl, with an anxious glance toward Sam, who seemed suddenly obsessed with the completion of a task he had set for himself—finishing a chain of connecting rings made from the damp bottom of his Ba Muoi Ba beer bottle. He marched the intricate pattern toward the edge of the table, ignoring the PSA. Carl glanced back quickly to Lieutenant Colonel Whitehead, catching the way the frosty blue eyes hardened at the deliberate snub by Sam.

"I really wasn't expecting it this early for sure," Carl said desperately, "but I'm very pleased."

The blue eyes switched back to the young FAC like the turret of the tank the PSA had once commanded. The handsome face softened once more. "Yes, of course. And we're all pleased for you, Carl." The small smile stayed in place but the eyes gave Sam another broadside. Sam didn't notice, for he was now intent upon drawing the outline of an anatomically correct female form on the damp tabletop with his finger.

Lieutenant Colonel Whitehead spun abruptly on the heel of a well-polished jungle boot and made for his table in the team house. Others of his staff had already gathered there, awaiting his arrival before ordering their drinks.

Carl sat and looked mournfully at Sam, shaking his head slowly. "Sam," he began, "you've been in country less than two weeks and, if I understand things correctly, you've already pissed off the deputy for operations for 2d Air Division, the senior adviser for all of IV Corps, and now the province senior adviser for Bac Lieu province. If that ain't a record, it's gotta be a hell of an average."

Sam snorted. "The DO for 2d Air Division doesn't really count. He was pissed off at me before I ever got here."

"Look," Carl continued earnestly, "there's probably not more than seven or eight thousand of us round eyes in the entire damned country. Probably not more than three or four hundred scattered over the entire delta. Everybody knows everybody, if you know what I mean. They talk to each other. We gossip like old women 'cause we're almost like a family. Particularly, the PSAs talk to each other. I know that you figure you got a raw deal from the air force, but you really ought to give it another shot. If things worked out, and with the backing of some of the people down here, you could still have a chance at making light colonel on the next board. Besides, everybody and his brother knows this whole thing is aiming toward an American war. Christ! They'll be throwing people back into the service rather than out in a couple of years at the outside. But you're going to have to play ball with them or you'll end up getting cut off at the knees. There's not a full bull around who's going to take the kind of crap you've been dishing out, no matter how much they need good people. Besides, Colonel Whitehead is a pretty damned nice guy. He's also a damned good combat commander."

Sam snorted again. "They're all nice guys as long as they get their way. Besides, what do I care what they think of me? I'll tell you, bubba, when that board passed me over for light colonel, I finally figured out exactly where I stood with all these nice guys. They'll use your skills and what you can do for them as long as it takes for them to get their tickets punched; then it's 'thanks very much for everything but we have to move on to our new Pentagon assignment now. So sorry we couldn't help you get promoted.' Don't talk to me about playing ball with the fast shakers. I played until they finally stuck the bat up my ass. So, I personally don't care whether or not Lieutenant Colonel Whitehead finds my manners abrasive to his well-bred gentility. Like they say, what are they going to do? Pass me over and send me to Vietnam? Anyway, since when do junior officers start telling their betters what they should do? It's supposed to work the other way around."

"That's 'seniors,' not 'betters,'" Carl said, smiling.

"Whatever. Listen, puke, it's eager assholes like them who are causing most of the trouble here, not those poor simple VC." Sam jerked his head around, roughly indicating the direction of the PSA and his coterie. The group looked unstructured but, in truth, was as carefully choreographed as a Gower Champion musical extravaganza. Key staffers sat closest to the PSA, and the junior and less esoteric members, such as the facilities and messing officer, were almost out of earshot.

"I know I haven't been here long," Sam continued, "but I've seen enough to reach a few conclusions. If the Vietnamese people were left alone by both sides, this feud they've got going here would just rock along without too many folks getting hurt. But if you raise the stakes and get enough people killed, then the other side has no chance to draw in its horns and pull back. No, they have to kill an equal number of your folks. Before long, people forget what they're fighting about and the fight itself becomes the issue. The way it is now, we 'advisers' are dragging the side we support—which seems to be made up primarily of crooks and killers—into a major war with the other side supported by Hanoi, which is made up of villains and killers. How can the ordinary people possibly win?"

"I'll have to say, Major, sir, that you certainly have learned a lot in the short time you've been here. I mean, I've been in country for nearly nine months and I'll admit I don't know what the hell's going on. You've managed to grasp the situation immediately."

"That's because I'm not only smarter than you, but I'm also bigger, stronger, and better looking," Sam said smugly.

It was Carl's turn to snort. "Tell me, do you also include folks like Lieutenant Colonel Robinson as one of the bad guys?"

"You know better than that," Sam said, suddenly serious. "Bill is just like ninety percent of the guys over here. He wants to do a job and go home and get on with his life. Most of us aren't bad guys. But somebody topside is putting us in the position where we easily could be, whether we want to or not. How do you suppose the family of that dink we incinerated feels about us? And yet, either one of us would do it again because of the circumstances.

"But, to get back to *my* problem, as you call it. I know it looks like

I've been riding the rag all the time, but do you remember the night I got here and checked in with our leader over there?" Carl nodded dubiously.

"Well, though it wasn't mentioned in so many words, it got to be obvious as hell that Colonel Whitehead had already talked to somebody about me. And I don't think Bill Robinson would pass on any shit. But somebody sure as hell did, and it had to be a member of the club. Those shiners who are going to wear eagles and stars very soon if they can just promote the American presence over here into real combat commands. They're in all the services and it's a brotherhood without a roster. But you can pick 'em out. Whitehead's one. Robinson ain't. And it's not just his color that keeps him out either. He's just not on the fast track, not that he cares one way or the other. And me? I'm not even *on* the track. In any event, the PSA had his mind made up about me before we ever met. I was used goods and not fit to fill the role he's decided we all ought to play. Well, I'm not going to play. I'll do my job as I see it, but I'm not gonna help shape a career for some snuffy who's laying the groundwork for becoming chief of staff."

"Hey," Carl protested, "all the grunts aren't bad."

"Hell, I know that. Most of them are top rate, from what I've seen. The difference is that *they* have to listen to assholes like Whitehead; *I* don't. And there's nothing they can do to me that they haven't already done."

"It really wouldn't hurt your promotion chances if you played the game a little," said Carl sadly. He'd become quite fond of the sardonic major.

"What you can't seem to get through your head, Carl, is that I don't have any promotion chances. But I do know how to play. Against all kinds of folks. Did I ever tell you what they used to say in one of the fighter squadrons I served in? It was kinda the unofficial motto: 'We can beat any man in any land, at any game that he can name, for any amount that he can count!'"

"That pretty well takes care of everything, doesn't it?" said Carl softly.

Sam peered closely at his air force–issue watch in the waxing moonlight: 0325. Thirty-five more minutes before his relief showed. All officers did indeed pull the duty for the inner-wire security check, though it seemed to him that he had more than his share of the 0200 to 0400 shifts. This shift virtually assured that he would be unable to get back to sleep, since the compound was always alive and moving by 0500. His thoughts were black as suited the hour. Why indeed did everyone have to be up and moving so early? Why couldn't the military day start at 0900? Which ancient soldier had made it a virtue to be up and moving at an hour when only burglars and paid women of the night really felt comfortable? More specifically, just what the hell was Sam Brooks doing walking around this compound in the middle of the night, completely out of his element? He knew as much about overseeing the conduct of Vietnamese guards as he did about yak farming. Possibly a little less.

At this late hour not even the soft whispers and murmuring of the 21st ARVN Division soldiers and Popular Force militia could be heard coming from the fighting holes outside the wire. Those had faded shortly after his tour of duty began. He strongly suspected they had fallen asleep. He was at a loss as to how he was supposed to keep them alert when he couldn't even see them. He could chuck rocks through the wire in hopes one would fall into one of their invisible holes and stir them into retaliation by gunfire. Instead, he tried to walk as noisily as he could, until it began to make him feel a little too conspicuous. What if *real* dinks were out there? He settled on a compromise: He scuffled along noisily, but hunched forward until he was almost duck walking, trying to make as small a target as possible. He looked as if he were trying to find a bell tower. It all became too complicated and he finally decided to hell with it. He went back to sauntering along the path like a tourist.

Clouds uncovered their veil around the moon and he watched as they sailed briskly inland from the South China Sea. Over the water, far to the east of the compound, vertical lightning discharged in a showy display as a cumulonimbus seemed to try to balance its positive and negative charges. Sam began another slow circuit of the path inside the inner barrier of concertina wire. Between the wire and the wall was a moat half-filled with filthy water and trash. During the day it was usually occupied by a few diseased-looking ducks that screeched and fought over choicer morsels found in the water and mud. A pig would sometimes get inside the compound and happily gambol in the filth. It always disappeared before dusk, leading Sam to believe that the animal belonged to one of the Vietnamese day workers. Maybe it was somebody's pet.

On the far side of the moat was a chest-high mortar and rock wall, which could be reached by a series of slippery pole bridges. Sam had not tried them because he realized that a man of his size had every opportunity to make a fool of himself should he decide to attempt it. He had made an effort, once, to peer over the wall just to see what was there. He found another moat, though not quite so grand as the one inside the wall. It had been dry except for mud and stagnant puddles and was covered with tanglefoot barbwire strung in a random pattern at ankle height. Pointed heads of punji stakes broke the mud and scum on the water's surface, pointing away from the wall. More concertina coiled beyond the far bank of the outer moat. Between the wall and the outer moat were the fighting holes scattered about in seemingly haphazard fashion. Sam stood on tiptoe and tried to see the holes, but they were quiet and invisible in the darkness. Those assholes were asleep. They had to be.

His route took Sam past the gate, now closed and barricaded for the night. Twin guard towers on either side of it were occupied by ARVNs. At least one was awake, for Sam saw the momentary flash as a match was lit, and cigarette smoke shimmered against the light of the moon. Let him smoke if it'll keep him awake, thought Sam. He lowered the butt of his carbine to the ground and scratched his belly thoughtfully.

Standing in the shadows with the moonlight softening the compound made it a night for reflection. What the hell was he going to do when the air force gave him his walking papers? The airlines were out, even if they had been hiring; no-nonsense replies from all of the major carriers had informed him that his application for a position would be unacceptable due to age. He supposed that they needed more time to develop their pilots into their own corporate image. Perhaps he could get on with some nonsched outfit that paid little more than minimum wage and gave you the opportunity to leave unclaimed laundry all over the country. Probably not even they would hire him. They'd want someone with at least a couple of thousand hours of multiengine time. So much for being a good fighter pilot.

Sam didn't physically react to the first sharp crack, though every sense went to full alert. He remained crouched over the planted carbine, trying to recognize the sound. When an entire fusillade of gunfire burst from the darkness, it quickly cleared the vapor lock in his brain. The sharp crack of a supersonic bullet near his left ear spurred him toward the only close sanctuary—the scum-filled moat. His leap took him almost to the far side and he scrabbled at the sunbaked bank. The water turned out to be less than a foot deep, but his weight drove him down into the mud. He almost panicked as the sludge reached his navel, but then he seemed to hit bottom. Unconsciously, he had raised his rifle high to save it. He looked up at it, planted over his head like a ceremonial banner, as though he were trying to rally his brave band. Simultaneously, he heard the first smattering of return fire from the somnolent defenders.

Shit! What was he supposed to do now? He'd read the standing orders before coming on duty but the contents of the book had fled his mind. Wait! He was supposed to sound the siren. Hell, that was over in the ops hut. Screw that! Anybody who could sleep through this noise had to be dead anyway. OK. Forget that one. What was next? Right! He was to direct the defensive fire of the ARVN soldiers. Sam pondered that for a moment. They seemed to be doing OK without his direction, especially since he didn't have any idea where to direct it. Crap! Where was a grunt when you needed one?

First things first. He had to get out of this cesspool before he caught some vile disease. He wallowed closer to the side and ran his hand over the packed earthen bank until he found a small purchase. He began levering himself upward, his curses filling a void in the shooting, which had become quite enthusiastic. He paused, panting for breath, and watched the odious bubbles struggle to the surface beside him, pop open, and release their foul-smelling gases. It was, Sam decided, as though a tomb had been disturbed.

Spurred on by the noxious fumes, Sam lunged upward, using his CAR-15 as a lever on top of the bank. Success! He rolled over the top and lay full length upon it, gasping for breath. Two explosions, only seconds apart, lit the center of the compound. Sam could hear American voices shouting back and forth as someone tried to organize the defense.

The firing continued unabated from the other side of the wall. Sam rolled over on his back and stared at the stars until he was distracted by the automatic weapon fire from the guard towers by the gate. He tried to determine from the trajectory of their tracers just how far the VC might be from the wall. They seemed pretty close.

He rolled to the wall and sat up, back flush against it, looking with disgust at his lower extremities. So much glutinous mud clung to his boots that even in the darkness his feet looked as though they were wearing snowshoes. Damned lucky the boots were still with him. He hunched forward and tried to retrieve his weapon from the moat's edge. He could just see its outline, and he tried to stay low as he reached for it. After all, he thought giddily, what good was a warrior without a weapon. Not much, he decided morosely as he watched it skitter over the edge into the moat.

Sam edged his upper torso forward, leaning his head and shoulders into the dark void over the stagnant water and mud. The rifle was not visible, but a new series of malevolent bubbles approximating the length of the weapon were just beginning to surface. Some days it just didn't pay to get out of bed. He shook his head mournfully and reached to his waist to reaffirm that his .38 Special was still in its holster. It was there but covered with several inches of slimy mud. Just about what he expected.

Knee-walking, Sam regained the safety of the wall and methodically extracted the shells from the revolver. He wiped them down with his baseball cap and made sure that the chambers and barrel were clear by peering through them during the next explosion in the compound. He felt light-headed and found that he was humming a little song as he worked.

The chore completed, he sat back against the wall and watched the green tracers ricocheting from the metal roof of the ops building. Another explosion blew down the flagpole; Sam ducked his head as bits of earth pattered around him. Through the gloom he could see the shadowy figures of the American team running about, doing soldierly things. Mostly, they all seemed to be trying to give orders to the outnumbered American enlisted men. Sam sighed. Back to the wars.

The rough surface of the wall felt cool as he knelt and bellied up to it, pistol dangling from his right hand. He reversed his muddy ball cap to keep the wall from knocking it from his head, then, beginning from a crouch, he slowly began to inch himself upward. Something hit his leg and with a thudding heart he threw himself around, pistol thrust forward. Beady little red eyes blinked at him momentarily before they disappeared into the moat. The long naked tail was the last he saw of the rat.

Sam sat again next to what he had come to think of as *his* wall and tried to compose his jangled nerves. The weapon fire outside the wall slackened momentarily, then resumed with a heightened intensity. In the light of another explosion he could pick out the wrecked remains of a jeep lying on its side by the shattered flagpole. He flinched as something hard dinked into the wall beside him.

Once again he began to inch his way upward on the wall, not stopping until his eyes were just clear of the top. Slowly, his vision adjusted to the sporadic green sparkles coming in chains from the darkness beyond the wire. Someone in the compound had cranked up a mortar, and its outgoing rounds moaned as they peaked over his head to come crashing back to earth with spectacular explosions.

It was time to get into the old ball game, Sam decided. He brought his service revolver to the top of the wall and aimed it into the void beyond. He waited for some kind of a movement, but the wily devils weren't giving themselves away. Another chain of green balls sped toward the compound. Sam shifted his aim toward the likeliest source, cocked the hammer, and fired twice. He was startled at the recoil. It had been quite awhile since he'd fired a pistol. He quickly found that he was also semiblind from the muzzle flash. Eerie shapes swam into and out of focus until he could just make out the form of one of the ARVN soldiers about four feet to his front. He was very small and his American-style helmet engulfed his head. He also seemed to be terribly angry about something. The little soldier stood upright with his back to the enemy fire, shaking his fist directly at Sam, who hadn't realized he was there when he fired. The man seemed to be yelling something that sounded like dinky dau! Sam had no idea what that meant but admitted to himself that he might have been shooting just a tad close to the young man. He crept back down his side of the wall and sat again.

The weapon fire was dying quickly. There had been no explosions for several minutes within the compound, though the American tube continued to belch its projectiles and the ARVN troops continued their sustained firing. Eventually, it died away altogether and in the silence Sam could hear approaching helicopters. He watched as they circled the camp, then stood to see them zoom away and begin firing in the distance. Their rounds skipped and sparkled as they exploded against the ground.

As he looked over the wall, Sam saw the ARVN in front of him come erect and climb from his fighting hole. The little man stretched as though working kinks from his muscles and glanced casually over his shoulder. When he saw Sam, he immediately threw himself headlong back into his hole. Sam realized he still had his pistol in his hand. He holstered it and grinned at the small Viet. The man smiled back nervously. "Guess we kicked their asses, didn't we, Marvin?" The man continued to smile nervously until Sam left.

The entire team seemed to have gathered in the ops building. Lieutenant

Colonel Whitehead alternatively gave orders to his staff and talked over the radio. Sam watched them do army things for a while, then walked over and helped himself to a cup of coffee.

"Jim," the PSA was saying to one of his majors, "get me a damage assessment ASAP so we can get it to corps. Frank, get me a casualty report. Check with the ARVN and see if they had any people hurt, and if they did, see if we can help. Lieutenant Smith, get on the horn to the civilian compound and see if they got hit. Also, check—"

The PSA stopped in mid-sentence to stare wide-eyed at Sam, who was sipping his coffee and watching all the activity with interest. Sam suddenly became aware that he had left a trail of mud and excreta from the door to the table holding the coffeepot. He'd lived with it long enough to become mostly immune to its fruitful aroma. He pretended to ignore it, wishing that he'd cleaned himself before he made an appearance.

"What the hell happened to you?" asked Colonel Whitehead.

"Had to go into the ditch when the shooting started," Sam answered briefly, aware now that people were edging rapidly away from him.

"Get yourself cleaned up," the PSA said abruptly and turned away to continue his string of directives. "Who the hell was the duty officer and why didn't I hear a warning siren?"

As the S-3 scrambled to get the duty roster, Sam raised his hand to get the PSA's attention. His euphoria from the fight had vanished. "That was me, sir. I had the duty." To hell with all of 'em! "My fault that I didn't get a chance to run your checklist then. I'll take care of it now, though."

With that, Sam carefully sat his cup on the table and, trailing mud and pig shit, walked briskly to the counter and firmly closed the throw-type electrical switch activating the warning siren. Instantly, it began to moan, building to a whining crescendo. Sam saluted, then turned abruptly and walked from the room.

Carl sat on Sam's bunk and slowly shook his head. "Jesus Christ! I can't really believe you did that."

Sam continued to towel off the moisture from his recently washed body. He still believed he could smell the gunk from the moat in his nostrils, but it might only be that his recent immersion had resensitized him to the aroma seeping in through the wall. He glanced through the grenade screen and saw that dawn was just beginning to break.

"Have you got a death wish or something?" Carl continued. "You just don't treat a commanding officer in the United States Army like that. Hell! You don't treat anybody like that. I wouldn't be surprised if they didn't have you drawn and quartered. Or he may just get rid of you. Really, Sam, he's a straight shooter but he's also pretty strait-laced. There could be real trouble here for you if he decides to go to corps with it."

"Screw him," Sam said stubbornly. "If he didn't want to hear an explanation of why his damned siren didn't get turned on rather than that old 'no excuse, sir' horseshit, then he'd better take me off his duty roster. There was absolutely no way I could have gotten to that fucking siren without getting my ass blown away."

"He'd have listened to an explanation. He knew how much incoming there was. Like I say, he's a reasonable man. But what's a reasonable man supposed to do when some maniac turns on the siren because he got his feelings hurt? Well, what's done is done. I guess we'll just have to wait and see which way the wind blows."

Carl continued to shake his head sorrowfully, then stood. "We'd better hustle on down to the strip. Colonel Whitehead had the minesweeping team out almost as soon as the shooting stopped. It'll be light enough for us to see by the time we get the birds checked out. You feel OK about putting strikes in by yourself in case you have to? If the ground sweep turns up anything of that VC unit, we're almost certain to get TACAIR diverted to us. You really haven't had much practice at it yet."

"No sweat, I'll be OK." In truth, Sam felt an anxious tremor in his belly at the thought of handling a troops-in-contact situation by himself. He'd never even seen one accomplished and could claim only a single solo strike against a preplanned target. Nevertheless, he and Carl needed to split today to increase their coverage in the search for the raiders. They leaned over Sam's map spread out on his cot. "I'll head down the canal to Gia Rai," Sam said, "and you'll go south toward Dam Doi. Correct?"

"That's it. Let's stay on the common frequency unless one or the other of us has to work fighters. Whoever gets fighters first goes to Blackjack secondary with 'em. The other one will stay up primary. That way we'll always be able to get in touch with each other if we need help fast."

"No sweat," said Sam, sounding more confident than he felt. "By the way, is there anyone around here I could kinda quietly borrow a weapon from?"

"Where's yours?" asked Carl curiously.

"Uh, actually, I kinda lost it in the moat last night. Damned thing went completely out of sight in all that mud and pig shit. It didn't seem exactly the time or place to go pearl diving, so I guess I need a new one."

Carl started to snicker and it grew into a full-bellied guffaw. He laughed until there were tears streaming down his freckled cheeks. Sam looked at him sourly. Finally the laughter died to an occasional snort and the younger man wiped his eyes with a none-too-clean handkerchief.

"Jesus! When you do it, you do it all the way, don't you? Remember what I said about how strict they were about weapon control down here? It can actually mean a court-martial if Colonel Whitehead finds out about it. You'd be better off just keeping quiet. Let me check with a few of my sources and maybe they can come up with a replacement. The serial numbers won't match but at least it will be a weapon when it's time to turn it in. Meanwhile, take mine. I don't plan on getting in any trouble today, but given your temperament you'll probably challenge the local VC province chief to a duel, mano a mano."

"Naw," Sam said, "I won't do that, and I won't take your weapon. Just thought I'd ask you to see if you had any ideas. I'll come up with something eventually. Maybe borrow Whitehead's."

"Jeez, you'd probably do it, too. Well, let's get going, and Sam . . ." Sam looked at the other FAC. "Watch your ass."

"Huh!" he grated. "They better watch their asses before I have to whip all of them."

"I didn't mean the VC."

"Neither did I."

The air felt almost cool blowing through the open window of the aircraft. Carl flew formation with him briefly before departing with a wave of his hand to his search area to the south. Sam picked up the canal that led to Gia Rai and throttled back to best endurance power setting. The ARVN 21st Division soldiers were still loading onto the six slick Huey troop carriers dispatched to them from the American Aviation Battalion at Soc Trang.

Sam dropped to a thousand feet and peered closely at the canal banks, trying to think like a Viet Cong commander. Most movement in the Mekong Delta was by one of the canals. Chances were that the VC would move the same way rather than tie themselves to one of the few roads, where they'd become easy prey if discovered. But how fast could those big *ghes*—he'd recently found that was what the Viets called the sampans—move if they really wanted to haul ass? Probably pretty fast. They'd had about a three-hour head start, but surely they couldn't move at top speed at night. Or could they? Who was there to stop them? Carefully, he studied the banks holding the sluggish brown water in the channels. He stuck his head out the window into the slipstream but could see nothing in sight in either direction. Where were the wily rascals? Suddenly, the thought hit him solidly. Where was *anybody*? Where was the sampan traffic of a normal market day? Where were the farmers? Where were the water boos with their small drivers perched atop them like lanky birds? He'd never seen the normally teeming delta so quiet. It was spooky. Something was definitely amiss.

Sam flew another few minutes down the canal, wanting to be sure that what he was seeing did not have a natural cause. He worked both banks carefully, but the search revealed nothing. He decided he needed to talk to Carl and draw on the youngster's experience. Hopefully, he'd still be within radio range. "Blackjack One Two, this is Blackjack One One."

"Go ahead One One. This is One Two."

Jesus! Sam thought, disgusted with himself. He had been afraid that Carl was out of radio range and instead he sounded as if he were sitting in his rear cockpit. His navigational instincts, honed by years of jet flying, were still not geared to the reality of his present world. Fifteen minutes of flying meant that Carl was only about twenty miles or so away; if they'd been in jets, it would have been two hundred miles.

"Rog, One Two. I got a thing over here about fifteen or twenty klicks down the Gia Rai canal. There's absolutely nothing stirring. No boats, no people, no nothing."

Carl was silent for a long moment before he answered. "Roger, Sam. I understand. Sounds like there may be something going on, but on the other hand it may not be anything. Better let the TOC know and have 'em pass it to the chopper lead. They may want to change their LZ and check it. I'll be listening out unless you want some help."

"I ought to be able to handle it. Talk to you later."

Sam quickly changed the radio frequency to Blackjack Control, a grand title for a pimply-faced airman second class monitoring their calls from the 21st Division Tactical Operations Center (TOC). He would act as a conduit for Sam to pass information to the American S-3 adviser. In addition, he could forward requests for tactical air to the IV DASC in Can Tho.

"Blackjack Control, this is Blackjack One One."

"Go ahead, One One. This is Blackjack Control."

"Rog. Pass this info to the green suiters and request that they relay it to the slicks. All waterborne traffic and people in the rice paddies are absent along the Bac Lieu–Gia Rai canal to a point, uhh, . . ." Sam fumbled with his map, ". . . thirteen klicks southwest of Bac Lieu." He peered into the distance. "It looks as if the water traffic starts again about eighteen or nineteen klicks southwest. I'm going to investigate and if it's not too late they may want to put the choppers back on the ground to conserve fuel. Copy?"

"Roger. Good copy. Stand by."

As Sam waited for a reply from the S-3, he eased his aircraft down to eight hundred feet and began searching the canal banks yet one more time. There were dozens of minor canals and waterways joining the major canal. The countryside was made up of broad expanses of rice paddies and grassland savannahs, where the water table was seldom far beneath the earth's surface. Sam could see spots where it broke above the mud and created swampland. Heavy tree growth in these isolated spots divided the flat landscape into manageable proportions. Christ! The dinks could be anywhere.

"Blackjack One One, this is Control. Be advised, helicopters have been requested to return to home plate and await instructions. The S-3 requests that you advise him, soonest."

What the hell did they think he was going to do? Keep the information to himself? "Rog. I'll let you know if I scare up anything. I'm going back to primary strike frequency. Out."

Sam retarded the throttle and let the aircraft sink into a gentle glide toward the southern bank of the canal. Where would he hide if he were the little devils? Certainly not on the main canal, where they could be spotted by one of the South Vietnamese patrol boats. But motorized *ghes* would be hard to hide in one of the smaller waterways because of their bulk. He eased the throttle forward as he approached five hundred feet and leveled there. He overflew several of the more likely looking tributaries but saw nothing suspicious.

He tilted the Bird Dog up in a lazy turn to return to the main canal when he suddenly noticed an irregular protrusion from one of the banks. For twenty-five yards or so along the stretch of brown water the eastern bank extended farther into the channel. Sam maintained the turn, more curious than concerned about the irregularity, and drifted slowly over the smaller canal. Strange. What little current existed seemed to push the water directly under the bank rather than swirling around it. Another oddity. Several yards from the canal's banks swatches of reeds appeared to have been harvested. He would not have noticed had the reeds not been a dry season brown. An odd place to gather thatch for a new roof. He stared at the area through another 360-degree turn, then decided that if it walks like a duck, and squawks like a duck . . .

Sam pulled back hard on the stick and let the nose of the aircraft rise to forty-five degrees. Then, as the incipient stall began to make the plane shudder, he kicked hard left rudder and slammed the stick to the side of the cockpit. The combination of stall and control movements made the nose rapidly reverse direction. Quickly, he neutralized the stick and rudder pedals before a spin could develop and let the nose aim straight down at the odd protrusion in the canal bank.

As the aircraft bottomed from its dive at two hundred feet, he jammed the throttle forward and stood the aircraft on its tail. His head was almost out of the window as he pulled hard into a steep climbing turn. Nothing happened. If anyone was there they were being very cool. He circled at a thousand feet, reached behind his seat, and pulled one of the smoke grenades free from its wire catch. He noticed that it was yellow. He righted the aircraft and flew directly toward the curious protrusion. As he passed overhead, he clenched the control stick between his knees and, using both hands, pulled the pin from the grenade and tossed it away from the aircraft.

The thick yellow smoke rose reluctantly in the heavy, still air as Sam began a shallow dive toward the canal. Whoever was there forgot about being cool. First one, then another sharp crack could be heard through the open window. Then there was a flurry of the cracking sounds. The right side of the Bird Dog's canopy starred crazily as a round went through it and out the top of the cockpit. Sam's initial reaction was to turn to stone. He heard and felt another thunk somewhere behind him as another round scored. He turned hard away from the canal site, forcing himself to look at it over his shoulder. The gunfire chased him until he had put several hundred meters between him and the guns.

Clear, he found his fingers were shaking on the stick and his sphincter was clenched so tightly a straw couldn't have passed. Willing his fingers steady, he unscrewed the top of the canteen and took a heavy pull at the chlorinated water. He began a cautious circle outside the range of the gunners. Recycling the radio to the control room frequency, he pressed the transmit button. His voice sounded high pitched and off key. "Blackjack Control, this is One One. I've found at least some of them. Or maybe I ought to say somebody. Stand by for coordinates."

In the small cockpit Sam tusseled with his map. It seemed to have grown since takeoff. Again, he clenched the stick between his knees and used both hands to steady the map while he picked off the coordinates. "They're hiding on a small canal off the main one at about Xray Sierra 224307. Advise the ops folks please, and you might want to give the DASC a call and let 'em know we're probably going to need some TACAIR diverted to us. I'll be listening out on this frequency."

"Roger One One. I copy all. The Sierra Three is standing here beside me and also has your info. I'll get right on the air request. And stand by a moment please. The Six Actual wants to talk to you." Well, well. The Old Man himself.

Lieutenant Colonel Whitehead's voice was crisp and clear over the radio. "Blackjack One One. This is Goldfinger Six. Can you give me an estimate as to how many people you've found, and is there a suitable LZ close at hand?"

Sam could detect no animosity in the PSA's voice. Good. We'll both be pros, he thought. "Six, this is Blackjack. I'd estimate at least five automatic weapons were firing at me. Sounded like AKs. But I really can't give you a good estimate on numbers. What I think they've done is cut reeds and used 'em to cover their sampans, which are moored close to the bank of a fairly small canal. I was just lucky to find 'em 'cause they're really well hidden. Had to drop a smoke square on their heads before they gave themselves away. And there is an LZ nearby."

"Good work, Blackjack. Here's what we're going to do. I'm going to expedite your request for TACAIR through channels while I have them hold the troops in the helicopters on the ground here at Bac Lieu. We'll give you half an hour to get your fighters put in, and just before the last strike is over we'll launch the helicopter force. I'd appreciate it if you could remain on station after the strike and mark the LZ for them, since we have no C and C bird available at this time. Let's get the little bastards! Here's your control back on the horn."

"Roger, Six. I understand the plan. Control, can you give me an estimate on when and how many fighters we're going to get?"

"I'm on the land line with IV DASC now. They'll give us a set of F-100s within ten minutes on a divert from the Seven Mountains area, also a flight of A-1s coming off the alert pad at Bien Hoa. If you think you'll need more, I'll see what else they can crank up. Oh, yeah. The Sierra Three advises that there are four Charley model gunships parked with the slicks back here at the strip if you think you'll need 'em."

"Better have them wait to cover the combat assault. Let's see what we turn up first. I want you to advise Blackjack One Two that I'm going to work the fighters on the secondary strike frequency. Also advise the DASC about that. One Two can meet me there if he wants to talk. Have 'em tell the fighters to head for Bac Lieu and then go southwest down the canal to Gia Rai. I'll be about fifteen klicks down that way."

"Control. Roger."

Sam eased the stick back slightly and advanced the throttle to climb power. He leveled at four thousand feet, figuring that should put him well above any small-arms fire. He banked the aircraft into a turn that would place him squarely above the VC's location. From the dimness of the shadowed canal bank and the reeds jutting up to it, he watched green tracers snake up toward him, then break away and fall short. His heartbeat slowed slightly as he watched the spent rounds trail away. The staccato of their supersonic cracks was muffled by distance and altitude.

His hand jerked convulsively on the stick and his sense of security vanished instantly as the heavy, throaty cough of the .50-caliber gun destroyed any delusions of safety. Only the involuntary twitch of his hand sending the aircraft into an unexpected bank had saved him as the gunner tried to track him.

Sam didn't remember shoving the throttle forward against the stop, nor was he really conscious of rolling the Cessna inverted. He was acutely aware, however, that he was about to pull the wings off the little aircraft as he tried to haul it through a split-s maneuver. His initial reaction was to point the nose of the aircraft straight down until he was out of the gunner's cone of fire. The ground rushing to meet him jiggled enough synapses in his brain to make him realize that the gun wasn't his only problem. He was about to bury the Bird Dog in the boggy morass of the river mud. Christ! There wasn't even a g meter in this thing to guide him in his recovery from the vertical dive.

With the throttle at idle, the aircraft recovered—just. Sam found himself lifting his hips against the restraining belt in unconscious body English, trying to help the aircraft get its nose up. Finally, the nose blocked out the horizon and Sam screamed across the flat countryside at thirty feet. He refused to let his eyes move toward the airspeed indicator, for he knew it would tell him things he didn't want to know. He knew he had exceeded the aircraft's red line. He just didn't want to know by how much.

Considerably chastened, Sam climbed and maintained a wide, cautious orbit around the VC position. He watched it as well as he could from the wary distance. It looked as if they were throwing back some of the reeds covering the boats. They were! They were going to make a run for it! Probably planning to get back to the main canal and mingle with other river traffic, not knowing there was no other river traffic. They couldn't know that their presence had alerted the local people, who, in wisdom gained over centuries of dealing with armies, had decided to sit this one out inside their hootches.

Where the hell were those fighters? As though on cue, a voice rang in his helmet. "Blackjack One One. This is Beaver Lead. How ya copy?"

"Beaver Lead, this is Blackjack One One. Got you loud and clear. Give me your location and lineup. We gotta hurry. I've got some movers down here."

"Roger that. We're coming up on Bac Lieu from the northwest. Blackjack Control said you were down that canal going southwest out of town. Is that correct?"

"That's affirm. I'm about fifteen klicks down it, orbiting on the south side."

"OK, we're turning your way and descending to eight grand. Lineup follows: Beaver Flight is a pair of Huns on a divert with three zero minutes of loiter. We're wall-to-wall with snake eyes and a full load of twenty mike mike."

"Good deal, Beaver Lead. We've got VC in sampans located in a small canal and in the reeds back twenty meters or so from the canal bank. They look like they're getting ready to move, so be ready to go to work right away. Target elevation is about sea level. Best bailout area will be north of the canal. Expect automatic weapon fire, and there's at least one .50 caliber down there. They've been having at me for the last ten minutes. Run-in heading will be your choice, but be aware that the boats are nose to tail against the southernmost bank of the canal, so your chances of getting them are better with a north or south run-in. Pull-off direction is your choice. I want you to call FAC and target in sight and to go through dry if you don't get positive drop clearance from me. I'll want your bombs in pairs, then we'll work out with the guns if you have enough fuel. Any questions?"

"Beaver Lead. No questions. Two, let's arm 'em up and set 'em for pairs."

"Beaver Two, rog."

"Blackjack, Beaver Flight is heading down that canal going southwest out of Bac Lieu, passing through ten grand for eight."

Sam peered back to the northeast and picked up the glint of sun from the polished silver wings of the F-100s. They were rapidly approaching him. "OK, Beaver Lead, Blackjack has you. I'm at your ten o'clock low. Right over the main canal. I'm rocking my wings."

"Tallyho there, Blackjack. We'll set up a left-hand orbit around you. Let me know when you're going to mark."

"Wilco. I'll lead you to the target now." Sam put the Bird Dog into a steep turn back toward the sampans. The tiny seed of anxiety that had been incubating in his belly felt as if it were ready to bloom. He didn't relish getting within striking range of the .50 caliber again, but there was no other way he could think of to properly mark the target. He glanced at the altimeter and saw that it had moved upward past four thousand feet. Unconsciously, he'd been clawing for height in his dread of the big machine gun below. Already, he was over the target area and a glance told him that the lead sampan was moving. Time for a quick decision.

"Beaver Flight, this is Blackjack in for the mark. We've got one boat moving in the canal now, heading for the main water. It's still partially covered with reeds and appears to be trying to act like it's part of the canal bank."

"OK, go ahead with your mark. Beaver has you in sight."

Sam rolled the aircraft nearly inverted and pulled it into a steep dive. Simultaneously, he reduced the throttle to the idle position to prevent a repeat of his earlier maneuver when he'd almost overstressed the bird attempting to evade the heavy gun. He heard what he'd been expecting, albeit with little pleasure. The chuffing of the heavy machine gun disturbed the air outside the aircraft's window, accompanied by a burst of automatic weapon fire that Sam catalogued in an uninvolved part of his mind as belonging to an AK-47. He tried not to look at the lethal streams searching for him.

He tapped the right rudder until the homemade aiming marks were where he wanted them, then punched the firing button, loosing one of the white phosphorous rockets. He didn't wait to see it hit but pulled from the dive in a hard left break. There was another thudding sound somewhere aft in the fuselage as a round found the aircraft. Sam hunched his shoulders as if to protect his neck. His hair felt as though it were bristling.

"Jesus," he heard Beaver Lead say softly over the radio. "They're really mad down there, aren't they?"

"Yeah," Sam croaked, "they really are. Did you happen to see where that machine gun is located?"

"Rog. It's about twenty-five meters north of your smoke."

"Well, we're gonna have to get that thing before we do anything else. He's too damned good. I'm almost due west of the target. If you have me in sight you can start your run."

"Rog. Lead's in from the north with the FAC and target in sight."

Sam watched the swept-wing fighter begin its dive toward the target, wishing with all his heart that he was the one strapped into its cramped cockpit. The F-100 was on the right run-in line and there were no friendlies in the area. Sam cleared Beaver Lead for release. "You're cleared hot, Lead."

The Viet Cong troops may have been unaware of the presence of the fighters until that moment, but the explosion of the two 750-pound, Mark-82, drogue-retarded bombs undoubtedly made clear the true nature of their predicament. Sam had an excellent view of the folding fins, which acted as air brakes, pop open as the snake-eye bombs released, slowing their fall sufficiently for the F-100 to escape their lethal blast. The ground fire ceased immediately. Sam was quickly back onto the radio as soon as he heard Beaver Lead, grunting under heavy g forces as he recovered, call that he was off target to the east.

"Beaver Two, I want your bombs in the canal itself. About fifty meters north of where my smoke went. Those boats were below the canal bank and weren't hurt. They're still trying to move."

"Roger, understand. In the canal. Fifty north of Blackjack's smoke. Two is in from the south. FAC and target in sight."

"Cleared in hot, Two."

The bombing was good once again. The F-100 pilots were obviously not newcomers to the business. One of the snake eyes landed directly in the canal, sending a small tidal wave to swamp two of the sampans. The blasts ripped the reed cover from two others that were partly protected by an indentation in the canal bank. The rattling of the AK fire began quickly, indicating seasoned troops capable of functioning despite the bombardment. Green men might have panicked and hidden their heads;

seasoned veterans knew that their salvation lay in disposing of the threat from the air.

Sam surveyed his small war. Beaver Two's second bomb had hit the far bank of the canal, doing little damage to the enemy. It had been a miss of only thirty meters or so, an excellent drop really, but in this particular target configuration it had very little effect. The concussion of the blasts tossed Sam and his tiny aircraft two hundred feet into the air and then dropped them in a stomach-lurching fall. The concussion wave had also blown away his smoke marker.

"Hold high and dry, Beaver Flight. Blackjack is in for a new mark." Sam swung the Bird Dog into a savage left turn, then abruptly slammed the stick back to the other side of the cockpit and shoved the nose downward toward the canal. He punched another smoke rocket toward the ground and then corkscrewed back out of the area before looking over his shoulder to see if it ran true. It had.

"Beaver Lead, somebody is still shooting down there. I'm back to the west of the target again. Hit my smoke." Sam knew how difficult it was for the jet pilots orbiting at four hundred knots to pick out his small aircraft in the clutter below them, so he gave them all the help he could, leaving them free to concentrate on the target and their attack parameters. A midair collision was a good way to spoil everyone's day.

The bomb racks of the attack aircraft had finally been cleaned and even the sporadic ground fire had whimpered to a halt. Even so, Sam used one of his two remaining smoke rockets to direct the fighters' 20mm cannon fire up and down the bank. The heavy exploding slugs chewed up the reeds that had survived the bomb blasts and started several fires in the dry grasses. Nearly two dozen newly dug fighting holes lay exposed.

The flight of A-1s from the alert pad at Bien Hoa checked in with Sam. He didn't really feel he needed them but in the end he decided what the hell. What could it hurt? He moved their ordnance farther from the canal bank and was surprised to find another group of enemy soldiers that had moved away from the canal and hidden in the reeds. Once more there were the sharp cracks of the AK-47s and Sam felt another round strike his aircraft. The A-1 wingman complained loudly of a burst that had taken out the side panel of his canopy. Fortunately, except for slivers of Plexiglas embedded in his cheek, there were no serious injuries to the pilot.

Bombs expended, Sam quickly cleared the attack aircraft from his area and switched a radio back to the control room. "Blackjack Control, this is One One."

"Go ahead, One One, this is Control."

"Rog. I don't think I'm gonna be needing any more fighters at this time. If you've got some dedicated to us, release them back to corps. And you can inform the crunchies that it looks like they won't have too much trouble getting in. There's several real good LZs made by the bomb craters and some fires. I'd suggest that their gunships hose down the area all around the target before the slicks go in. I haven't received ground fire in ten minutes or so, but that'd be the prudent thing to do. I'll hang around and mark the LZs for them and in case they need any more TACAIR."

Another voice broke in on the frequency. Again, it was the PSA standing at Sam's radio operator's elbow. "Blackjack One One, this is Goldfinger Six. We're sending the word for the lift to begin now. We'd appreciate it if you could come up their frequency and guide them in. I listened to you conduct both your strikes. Sounded like all of you did a damned fine job. I'd like for you to pass my compliments to all the pilots involved."

"Roger, sir. Will do and thank you. Control, Blackjack One One is going to the lift frequency at this time. Out."

Sam was surprised and pleased at the PSA's graciousness, particularly after last night's activities. He fumbled one-handed through the signal operating instructions (SOI) and found the lift leader's call sign and frequency. He switched to them. "Dolphin Six, this is Blackjack One One."

"Blackjack One One, this is Dolphin Six. Good morning. You're loud and clear." The air commander's voice in the stick's lead helicopter had the usual vibration associated with being airborne in the clumsy-looking but useful aircraft. "Dolphin is airborne and proceeding down the canal. Understand you can guide us to the LZ, correct?"

"Affirm. I think we did a pretty good number on 'em but I can't guarantee that there aren't some still alive and kicking. You want me in close or away from the target area?"

"One One, this is Six. Let me talk briefly with the senior round-eye adviser who's gonna go in with them. I'll be back to you in one."

Sam used the interlude to drift down to five hundred feet over the bombed area. Small fires were burning in the reeds, and smoke from the red-hot shrapnel seeped to the surface of the disturbed mud. The bombs had devastated the area.

"Blackjack One One, this is Dolphin Six. We'd like you to stay close to the area if you can. What's the terrain like where we're going in?"

"It looks like mostly swampland with a thick covering of reeds growing about head high. I'm over the area now and am receiving no ground fire."

"OK, that's always good news. Can you direct us right into the heart of the strike zone? We oughta be about five klicks out at this time."

Sam peered back up the canal toward Bac Lieu. Movement caught his eye and he could soon distinguish the six slicks with their load of 21st Division troops. "Six, this is One One. I've got a tally on you. I'm gonna mark two LZs. Each ought to be big enough for three birds."

"Understood. We'll look for your smoke. Gunships are moving ahead now."

Sam studied the ground. He had several options, for the bombs had done a good job of opening up the terrain for his inspection. There were two blast circles nearly touching the small canal that would do nicely. The wrecked sampans were only fifty meters away. Figures in black pajamas sprawled outside the perimeter of the blasts. Throttled back, he flew slowly over the blast marks and threw a smoke grenade into each.

"Blackjack One One, this is Dolphin Six. I've got Goofy Grape and Raspberry."

"That's correct," said Sam, watching the purple and red smoke rise almost vertically in the still air. "I'm going up to about twenty-five hundred feet and get out of everyone's way."

Sam had a perfect view of helicopter force. It split into two sections, each approaching its own LZ with accompanying gunships, who ceased firing to escort the slick birds. The Charley models broke away and began more firing passes as the slicks waddled into the cold LZs.

Sam watched the Vietnamese infantry spill from the doors of the troop carriers and run rapidly to secure the perimeter. Small patrols immediately began tentative movements away from the LZs. The largest group walked slowly along the canal bank until they came to the wrecked sampans.

Sam stooged around for another hour until it became clear that the only living Viet Cong were a few badly wounded survivors of the bombing. Finally, a call came.

"Blackjack One One, this is Blackjack Control."

"Go."

"I've had a relay through the TOC from the American adviser with the insert. There's no point in you hanging around any longer. They've just about finished the sweep and are getting ready to call for their lift. Advise your intentions."

"Roger. I guess I'll head on back to home plate. I'm out of rockets anyway."

"Understand. You're RTB [return to base]. Uhh, One One, Goldfinger Six just asked me to relay to you that the sweep has turned up nearly forty KIAs. They were all KBA [killed by air]. He says 'way to go!'"

"Thank him for me," said Sam as he banked slowly to a heading that would take him back to the airfield. He was basking in a glow of satisfaction. Not because of the dead bodies he'd left in the beaten-up swamp; they had been only unfortunate chips in the game of war played by nations. The same as himself. The satisfaction came from knowing he'd done his job well, and he'd been publicly recognized for doing it well. In his mind he replayed the fight, making an effort to find and face the mistakes he'd made. There were still a few rough spots in his performance, but overall he felt he'd carried it off in a professional manner. Except for not expecting that damned .50 caliber. That was a mistake he'd never make again. Suddenly, Lieutenant Colonel Whitehead no longer seemed like so much of an asshole.

CHAPTER 6

"Sam! Hey, Sam! Wait up!"

Sam stopped and watched Carl jogging toward him from across the compound. Sam ambled slowly back under the thatched-roof overhang and leaned against the wall. Waiting, he looked down at the sodden front of his flight suit. Sweating like a damned pig, he thought with disgust. Carl was bareheaded; the noonday sun made his freckles seem even more prominent. Sam noted only the finest sheen of perspiration on the young man's brow.

"What's up, doofus?" he asked as the redhead skidded to a halt in front of him. Sam noticed that he didn't bother to step into the shade.

"Got a message for you from IV Corps. Just came in. Colonel Robinson wants you to meet him back there ASAP, or sooner. Got any idea what it's about? Maybe they're going to hang a gong on you for those air strikes you put in the other day." He looked at Sam with bright, curious eyes.

"That'll be the day," Sam grumbled. In truth, he still basked privately in the aura of the successful strikes. Fifty-odd enemy dead was hardly a major triumph when great armies locked together in combat. But the delta was a land of small-unit actions. War victims were more apt to be zippered into body bags two or three at a time. Sniper fire was more common than the battalion assault.

"He didn't say anything about what he wanted?" Sam asked, eyeing the young man suspiciously.

"Honest, Sam, not a word. In fact, I didn't even talk to him but to one of the air force controllers at the DASC. He just said that the IV Corps ALO wanted your behind in Can Tho as soon as you could get it there."

"Well, I guess I'd better do it then. I'll grab a shaving kit in case I have to RON [remain overnight] and you can run me down to the strip. That way you'll have the jeep in case I can't get back today. Oh yeah, you'd better let the PSA know I'm out of the area on orders from corps."

"My, we're certainly getting all military, aren't we?"

Sam glowered at him, then headed back to his room.

Sam did it the easy way and followed the road from Bac Lieu to Can Tho, enjoying not having to worry about navigating in a straight line. After takeoff he was able to coax the little aircraft to ten thousand feet, and wallowed in the pleasure of the cooler air there. It was the first time he'd felt really comfortable since moving south from Saigon. Marring his pleasure, however, was the urgent summons from Bill Robinson. It wasn't the sort of thing the IV Corps ALO was apt to do frivolously, and Sam knew from years of disappointments that the need to disseminate good news was seldom undertaken with such urgency.

Still, it was nice to get away from Bac Lieu for a bit. In the week since he'd put in the big air strike, the MACV compound had been mortared twice in retaliation. Only a few rounds had fallen on each occasion, but the apparent intent was to harass the Americans. If that indeed was the reason, the Viet Cong had been successful: The advisers had spent both nights in fighting positions, anticipating another attack that never came.

The days had been busy and full, and Sam had, in addition to his own work, undertaken a personal crusade to get his Vietnamese counterpart into an airplane. Politely rebuffed by Captain Trang on several occasions, Sam had become determined that the man would voluntarily fly a mission or he would personally tie him into the backseat of the aircraft and take it up. With great amusement Carl had wagered a bottle of scotch that it could not be done. The bet made Sam redouble his efforts. He spent hours pondering schemes.

Finally, he thought he had found a way. Sam noted that Captain Trang's eyes had come slightly unfocused and his bland facade cracked the tiniest bit when he found that Sam had unlimited access to PX goods in Saigon. Like a skilled interrogator, Sam probed the crack until he found that the Vietnamese captain was prepared to sell his soul or possibly his aircraft for a Japanese tape recorder. It would cost Sam more than fifty bucks but it would be worth it to take the scotch from that smartass Carl. The next time anyone went to Saigon they could pick one up for him to use as bait. He knew Trang would be unable to withstand its allure when he played it in his presence. He smiled at the thought.

Far below he noted that the VC had made a new series of cuts on the roadway. There were four deep ditches sliced perpendicularly across the dirt road. They appeared fresh; he didn't remember them from the situation map in the TOC. They'd probably been excavated the night before. He plotted their position on his map with a grease pencil. He'd report them to the G-2 after landing at Can Tho, although he was reasonably sure that the FAC for this sector would have already spotted them.

Sam squinted forward and could just make out Can Tho through the smoky haze. He reduced the power for the letdown and approach, although he hated to leave the cool, clean air at higher altitude. He gave a final check to his map and located the small district town of Thanh Hung just below him. Satisfied that he was right where he thought he was, he folded the map and stored it under his seat.

The haze thickened on descent and the Continental engine coughed as carburetor ice built, restricting the airflow that mixed with the fuel. Sam placed the carb heat momentarily to the full hot position until the engine cleared and began to run smoothly. The PSP runway of the Can Tho airfield shimmered into view and Sam aimed for its end as he made final preparations for landing. He banked sharply onto a short final approach and the tires squeaked onto the steel planking.

He secured the aircraft and walked into the yellow stucco building. No other aircraft were parked in front of it. A U.S. Air Force staff sergeant sat at an old metal desk; across the room his Vietnamese counterpart dozed behind another.

The sergeant looked up at Sam and smiled. He seemed glad to see a new face. "Can I help you sir?"

"Yeah, I need to get a ride over to the compound. Could I borrow your phone and try to find some transportation?"

"I'll do it for you, Major. Sometimes you really have to know the system to get through."

Sam became bored listening to the sergeant yell and swear into the phone; he wandered to the corner of the room where he hunkered down and scratched the head of the mutt he remembered from his last visit to Can Tho.

"Got 'em, sir!" the sergeant called in triumph. "They're sending a jeep out for you." When a man was sufficiently bored, it took very little to make him happy.

Sam thanked him and, becoming more bored himself, spent the next twenty minutes exchanging views with the sergeant on politics both domestic and foreign, the state of the world, the chances that the Yankees would repeat, the size and shape of Miss Marilyn Monroe's breasts, the odds on Chiang Kai-shek ever regaining control of the mainland, and how fucked up the current administration was. They agreed on the more important points.

When the jeep honked its arrival, Sam waved a hand at the sergeant and loaded himself into the passenger seat next to the driver, a grinning Vietnamese enlisted man. He apparently didn't speak English, or didn't want to, for his answer to all of Sam's questions was the same wide grin.

On the drive in Sam glanced at his watch and saw that it was after 1400. He'd missed lunch and Robinson was probably back in his office at the DASC. Using hand motions Sam steered the driver to the building. The same pair of Vietnamese guards, or their clones, drowsed behind the sandbagged emplacement in front of the door. Their eyes flickered over him in the same disinterested way they had done during his earlier visit.

The air force sergeant remembered Sam immediately and jumped quickly to his feet, answering the question before Sam could ask it. "Colonel Robinson isn't here, sir. He had to make an urgent trip to Tan Son Nhut to talk to 2d Air Division. It was an unexpected trip and he asked me to tell you to plan on spending the night. He'll try to get back as soon as he can tomorrow. Sir!"

Sam rubbed his face in simulated weariness to hide his smile. He'd forgotten to apologize to the sergeant for his abruptness and harsh words at their last meeting. "Thanks, Sarge. Listen, I'm sorry I jumped down your throat on my last trip. Please accept my apologies."

"No problem, sir," the sergeant answered with a poker face. *He* would be the one to decide when there was no longer bad blood.

Sam sighed and added Staff Sergeant Pirkle to the list of those pissed off at him. "Who's the acting ALO while Colonel Robinson's away?"

"That would be Major Tucker, sir. May I take you up?" The sergeant's expression told him that, should Sam accept his offer and make the man climb the stairs, Sam's paperwork and records would remain screwed up for the duration.

"That's not necessary. I know the way. Thank you." The sergeant's eyes gleamed in triumph.

Sam went up the stairs and into the large duty room of the DASC, the nerve center of the IV Corps air war. Vietnamese and American controllers busily allocated and coordinated air strikes for the different sectors and provinces of the corps. A short, stocky air force major sat behind a desk on an elevated stage, where he could observe the boards as they were updated. He was smoking a very large cigar. A Vietnamese officer sat at a desk next to him. Spread before both men was an impressive array of telephones. Major Tucker, identified by the nameplate on the desk, stroked his chin and stared at the situation board. He looked familiar. Then it came to Sam.

"Pardon me," said Sam as he approached the desk, "but would you be 'Filthy' Tucker, winner of the 2d Annual Projectile Vomiting Competition at Luke Field in 1960?"

"Actually," the major said modestly, turning to Sam, "I was only second runner-up. I won the fighter wing championship, but a maintenance officer who had studied under the great 'Guts' MacDonald took me in the semifinal barf-off. In the end, he was beaten out by that transient marine A-4 jock whose bird had broken down there at Luke. Fortunately, the crown reverted back to the air force when we found out he was a ringer planted by the Marine Air Wing at El Toro. Seems they had rigged up an airtight package of ripe oysters he could hide in his flight suit pocket and just at the right moment he could . . . well, no sense talking about what might have been."

"If it's any consolation, I think you could have been one of the great ones," Sam said.

"Thank you," Major Tucker said humbly. "I always gave it everything I had."

Pleasantries over, he looked at Sam's name tag. "I recognize the name, I think. Are you the Sam Brooks who . . . well, never mind," he said with a grin and stretched out a hand.

"Got any idea why Bill Robinson called me up here?" asked Sam, shaking the major's hand.

"Not really. I know he talked to 2d Air Division and left here mad as hell and in a big hurry. Don't know if it was about you or not, though. Stuck his head in the door and yelled that he had to get to Saigon immediately and when you showed you were supposed to keep yourself available until he got back. Said it would probably be tomorrow morning. If I were you I'd just head on over to the compound and get settled in for the night. You can take my jeep and I'll ride in with one of the other guys when the new shift arrives. Come on, I'll walk you down and show you which one it is."

Sam slept away the remainder of the afternoon in the same room he'd occupied nearly a month ago. Awakened by the noise of the corps staff as they returned from their offices, he felt refreshed and in good humor despite a slight foreboding about his visit with Bill Robinson. He showered and put on a clean flight suit, stuffing the soiled one in his bag to keep the hootch maid from grabbing and washing it. He probably wouldn't be here long enough to get it back. He tilted his baseball cap over his nose at a jaunty angle and started for the club. The sun looked huge as it sank below the horizon.

The room was thick with predinner drinkers. Sam scanned the mob from the doorway, looking for someone he knew. Having been acclimated to the social scene at Bac Lieu, he thought the room looked terribly crowded. What *did* all these people do? His eyes stopped at a smaller figure in the sea of brawn. It was an interesting form and certainly female. Her back was to him and Sam stared at the rounded hips, enthralled. Whoever it was listened attentively to animated talk from a middle-aged lieutenant colonel. A wave of tropical uniforms crested around her, seemingly vying for her attention. The light colonel had no intention of relinquishing it to them. The woman stood, leaning on the table with arms extended. One slim hand snaked to the back of her head to fluff her short hair. Sam recognized the gesture immediately. As though she could feel his eyes on her, the small, well-shaped head slowly pivoted, surveying the crowd until her eyes locked onto Sam's. He saw the look of instant recognition and his stomach flopped as a broad grin crinkled her features.

Lee Roget winked at Sam, then turned back to the crowd surrounding her. Whatever she told them made them all look very disappointed, especially the lieutenant colonel. Lee patted the two closest shoulders and turned to walk toward Sam. He thought it was like watching a large sleek cat glide across the floor.

"Hi," she said. "Remember me?"

Was she kidding? She knew damned well he remembered her. What he had forgotten was how tall she was. At least five eight or nine. She was dressed much as she had been the first time he'd seen her, in jeans and a simple blouse. Her teeth shone large and very white against the tanned skin. The denim-clad legs seemed to take a long time to reach the floor. Small muddy sneakers completed her ensemble. She was ravishing.

"Of course I do. How've you been doing, Lee?"

She moved a small hand back and forth. "Oh, so, so. You know, when you're pushing Bulgur wheat and miracle rice to people who just might starve if they miss a harvest . . . well, it's hard to work up a lot of enthusiasm among the locals to try your new products. How about you? What brings you to the city?"

"I have to see Bill Robinson, but it turns out he's in Saigon, so I have to stay the night. What do you hear from Jim Christian?"

"Oh, my beloved brother-in-law was forced to come in from his precious camp and leave his snake eaters for some reason or other a week or so ago. He hated every minute of it. I don't know if Sis will ever get that big gorgeous hunk completely tamed."

"Are you really sure you want her to?"

Lee looked at him for a long moment before she answered. "Nooo, I'm not really sure I do. He wouldn't be Jim Christian anymore, would he?" Sam nodded his agreement.

"On the other hand," continued Lee with a slight smile, "maybe a man shouldn't expect a woman he cared for to spend half her life alone while he's out playing cowboys and Viet Cong with the boys. How do you feel about that, Sam?"

"Uhh," Sam stammered, getting out of his depth.

Lee smiled at him mischievously. "Sam, I just know you're not one of those guys who feels that a woman's place is in the home, dropping a baby every year, while the man is off halfway around the world, having all the fun."

"Uhh."

She laughed, delighted at his discomfort, then patted him on the shoulder. "That's all right, Sam. I'll let you off the hook. Besides," she said, dropping her voice into a seductive whisper, "I've got something for you. You can have it tonight if you like."

Sam swallowed hard, heart fluttering rapidly beneath his flight suit. Oh, my God! Could it possibly be? Was this gorgeous creature so attracted to him that . . . Even as the flurry of wild thoughts bounced around in his superheated head, he knew he was wrong and that she was toying with him. She confirmed it.

"Jim gave me something to keep for you until you came to Can Tho again. I don't know if anybody else is supposed to know about it or

not. Are you OK?" she asked, putting a cool palm to his damp forehead. "You look all flushed."

"Naw, I'm OK," Sam mumbled, embarrassed at what he'd allowed
to flash through his mind. "What did Christian leave?"

"A shotgun! He said he'd promised you one." She leaned forward
to whisper conspiratorially. "He said to tell you that it's not on the
books anywhere. I can get it for you after dinner if you like."

"Sure. That'd be great. Uhh, would you like to have a drink or
something?"

The large green eyes roamed solemnly over his face for a moment
before the grin returned. "Let's find a place to sit," she said, grabbing
his arm to lead him to a corner of the room.

"So, how's everything in Bac Lieu?" she asked after they had settled
at a small table in the corner. "I've never been that far south."

"You haven't missed a hell of a lot. It's flat, dull, ugly, and sometimes pretty scary. But what it lacks in charm it makes up for in boredom.
Most of the time there's nothing to do and sometimes there's too much
to do. About the same as a military unit anywhere. Main problem is
that there just isn't anything to do when you're not busy."

As he talked his eyes had drifted unbidden to the deep opening of
Lee's blouse where an interesting expansion of smooth, swelling flesh
mesmerized him. He realized what he was doing with a start and glanced
up to find her watching him with a raised eyebrow and a small amused
smile. Feeling foolish, Sam glanced quickly toward the bar.

Lee patted his arm as if to say that everything was OK. Her fingers lingered there for a moment before she withdrew them. Sam could
feel his flesh tingling from her touch.

"Tell me about yourself, Sam. I pumped Jim but he couldn't tell me
very much about you."

This time it was Sam who raised an eyebrow and Lee who looked
quickly away. "That sounded pretty forward, didn't it?" she said, giving
him a half-glance from beneath the thickly lashed eyes. "That's pretty
much the way I am, you'll find out. That is, if I haven't frightened
you off yet. I really am interested in hearing about you, though. You
don't seem like most of the officers I've met over here. Matter of fact,
the first time I met you I thought you looked pretty mean and kind of
withdrawn. Are you?"

Sam smiled. "I didn't think it showed. I've had a little problem that
I'll tell you about one of these days. But for the basics, there's really
not much to tell. I've been a fighter pilot my entire adult life, stationed

in Korea, Germany, France, Japan. Also at a dozen stateside bases from one coast to the other. I was born and grew up in Santa Fe and got a degree in geology from the University of New Mexico. Went straight into the air force after graduation and I've been there ever since."

"Married? Engaged? Divorced?" she prompted.

"None of the above," he said with a laugh. "Engaged twice but neither of them took."

"Why not?"

"I guess they came to their senses in time." He glanced at her and saw that she really wanted to know. "One of them couldn't stand the thought of being a service wife, and at that time I had no intention of ever leaving the air force."

Lee picked up on that immediately. "Do you mean that you *are* thinking of getting out now?"

"May not have any choice," Sam said, and left it at that. He could tell that she was not satisfied with the answer but had decided not to push it.

"OK, that's number one. How about the other one?"

Sam sat back in his chair, eyes unfocused, for a few moments before he replied. "She was a winner; you remind me of her a lot." Lee nodded in friendly acknowledgment. "We were engaged before I left for Korea, right out of advanced gunnery. We wrote for the two years I was there. When I came back I found that she had decided to take the vows and become a nun."

Lee stared at him, wide-eyed. He watched her face go from disbelief to incredulity to jocularity, then make the trip again. Then she simply exploded. The laughter came in a sustained guffaw. Tears streamed down her cheeks as she doubled over, gasping for breath before launching into a new fury of cackling chortles. Sam sat quietly, not a little abashed at the looks they were getting as she shuddered into control. She wiped her eyes, looked at Sam, and had a relapse. Finally, with only an occasional tiny hiccup to mar her composure, she reached over and clasped Sam's left hand with both of hers.

"Oh, God! I'm sorry, Sam. I shouldn't have done that but it just came like a bolt out of the blue. I know how it must have hurt. What happened to her?" She tried unsuccessfully to suppress another set of giggles.

"I still hear from her. She sends me a Saint Christopher's medal every Christmas and I send her one of those bawdy greeting cards. I think she enjoys getting them."

"You do seem to have a strange effect on your women, Sam Brooks.

OK, you said you were in Korea. Was that during the war? My husband was over there then. He was in the ground forces, though. Did you shoot down any planes?"

He smiled at her. "I got a piece of a couple. That's enough about me, though. I'm afraid I'll cause you to go into cardiac arrest if I say something you find amusing. How about you?"

Lee sat back and folded her arms over her breasts. A small smile played over her lips. "Sam, I thought I had it all. A small-town Texas girl who married the greatest guy she'd ever met. And he adored her, too. I had a life that I loved. Lots of good friends. Travel. Plans to start a family. Then, bang! It ended very quickly with a nighttime visit by my husband's CO and the brigade chaplain. I found that life can turn on you pretty damned quickly. So I buried my husband and started trying to put things back together. I had a degree in finance so I tried working in a bank but found that even money can become boring very quickly. I tried opening my own business—a bookstore—and after a few months I figured out that I was earning about twenty cents an hour. Time just seemed to roll on and I found that I really didn't have any goals anymore. I was just getting through one day at a time and not doing a very good job of that. And the nights were worse. I forced myself back into what I thought was a sort of social life and found out that men actually believe most of those stories about divorcees and widows. Or maybe they were right."

The green eyes met Sam before she turned them to stare at her clenched hands resting stiffly in her lap. She sighed. "You know how the story goes. And if it hadn't been for my sister and Jim Christian, I'd have probably ended up as an alcoholic with a different stranger in my bed every night. The funny thing is that it wouldn't have been that way at all if I hadn't had such a great man and life and then had it snatched away from me like that. At least, that's what I keep telling myself. Pretty shocking, huh?"

Sam shook his head slowly and smiled. "It's a story I've heard before, though I know that doesn't make it any easier."

Lee leaned forward and spoke almost angrily. "I'll tell you another thing. It's a story people are going to be hearing a lot more often if somebody doesn't come to their senses about what's going on over here. All you hear these days is about the coming American buildup. In Saigon that's all anyone talks about, as if that's going to be the final salvation for this screwed-up little country. They don't seem to realize that most of these country folks don't even know where Saigon is. Their only connection to it is when the tax collector comes or their sons are drafted and never come back."

"I imagine a lot of Viet Cong and North Vietnamese families feel the same way," said Sam softly.

Lee stared at him for a moment before her smile returned. "Touché, Sam. They're both screwed-up little countries. But I honestly don't see how having a large American occupying force is going to help anything. That's just going to escalate matters."

"Not that I necessarily disagree with what you're saying, but do you think that a giveaway program like you're in is going to do all that much better than the military?"

Lee snorted delicately. "You have to be kidding! Do you know what the farmers do with the tons of wheat we give them? They feed it to their damned pigs! But you can't get it through the heads of those bureaucrats back in Washington that these are not wheat eaters. So they just keep sending tons of it over here, and the Vietnamese just keep feeding it to their pigs. If you want to give them some protein, send them some damned dogs! They love dog meat. But, since we don't eat it, we can't imagine that anyone else would."

"Uhh, speaking of dog meat, I'm getting a little hungry. I missed lunch today."

She laughed, good humor restored. It was a good laugh, Sam decided. Full, throaty, and enthusiastic. Boy, was it enthusiastic! Lee placed a hand on Sam's arm, which began to tingle again.

"You're right. Let's eat, then we'll go get that shotgun."

The dinner was not a huge success as far as Sam was concerned, since there was little opportunity for further talk with Lee. An uninterrupted stream of visitors stopped by the table to chat with her, many of them using the opportunity to stare down the open throat of her blouse. It irritated Sam, making him forget his own fascination with her chest. He hardly had any claims on Lee's time but nevertheless felt possessive and resented the attention she was receiving from the corps staff. In truth, he could hardly blame them. Lee would be considered stunning in San Francisco. In Can Tho, Republic of South Vietnam, she was a singular vision of loveliness.

Sam grew grumpy after the fourth visitor and took no pains to hide it. Colonel Chastain, the senior corps adviser, stopped to pay his respects and to chat about pigs and crops, subjects in which Sam was sure the man had minimal interest. Sam's irritation became apparent to Lee. She noted the speculative look he was giving to the full glass of water before him and then to the colonel's spit-shined jungle boots. Quickly, she placed a hand over his, which caused Colonel Chastain to look at Sam intently, as though he should know him from somewhere.

Try volleyball, you shithead, thought Sam as he idly wiggled his crooked nose with his free hand. He glared at the senior adviser.

Lee spoke with animation, her hands flying about as she described the status of her program to the colonel. The senior adviser attempted to give her his full attention, but Sam noted with glee that the man was becoming mired as she confidently tossed around statistics on tons of rice and wheat delivered, hectares of vegetables and animal feed planted, numbers of ducks and pigs allocated. Chastain's eyes began to glaze but Lee was ruthless. She delivered a left hook made up of the number of tilapia ponds needed for villages of one hundred or fewer peasants, more than a hundred but fewer than five hundred, and for small towns with a population between five hundred and a thousand. She right-crossed with a lengthy but beautifully organized explanation on the need for modernization of the traditional cottage industries of the region. Her coup de grace, the punch that neatly felled the colonel, was a triad of body blows that began with the foreign capital needed for further industrialization in the Delta region, followed by canal and road construction needs, and, finally, marginal land use.

Colonel Chastain was a beaten man. He straightened slowly and wearily rubbed his hands over his face. Lee continued to beam brightly at him, looking as though she was readying herself for the second round. Sam almost felt sympathetic for he, as well as Colonel Chastain, had just been bombarded by twenty minutes of uninterrupted talk by Lee Roget about possibly the most boring subjects in the world. Sam felt as though someone had trephined his brain and poured in a gallon or so of raw, dry information. Statistics dripped from his ears; figures clogged his sinuses; data clouded his corneas. Chastain was in worse shape for he had felt obliged to at least pretend he was listening attentively to the pretty woman. He looked as though he'd been lobotomized as he muttered a "good evening" and walked slowly from the table to rejoin his staff.

Sam squinted critically at Lee while she did her best to appear the innocent bureaucrat.

"Jesus Christ," he muttered. "I thought at first that you were just interested in your work, but you did that on purpose. I've never heard anyone talk for so long without breathing."

Lee smiled a little smugly. "It just takes a little practice. It's more feminine than carrying a blackjack, but just about as effective."

"I can see where it would be. It would take a really determined man to fight through that. Does it always work?"

"Usually. Of course, I don't do it unless I feel I have to. For example, I normally would be delighted to talk to Colonel Chastain, but I could tell you were getting a little upset."

It was Sam's turn to appear innocent. "I'm sure that I don't know what you're talking about." He was a little irritated at himself for becoming jealous of the senior adviser simply because he had access to Lee every night. No, he reconsidered. Not every night. *Tonight.*

The night air flowing through the open jeep felt almost cool to Sam as he followed Lee's directions to her compound. She seemed unconcerned about being outside the wire at night. It was nearly 2100 and he was surprised at the large numbers of Vietnamese still roaming the Can Tho streets. All the shops remained open and it appeared that the war had completely bypassed the city, until he had to slow for the military checkpoints. Lee stopped him at an intersection and he waited nervously as she crossed the street to purchase an armful of flowers.

Her hotel was located on a small block surrounded by barbwire and circled by defensive positions almost directly in the city's center. The usual sandbagged emplacement manned by national police in white shirts stood just in front of the hotel's entrance. The two Vietnamese guards ignored the Americans as Lee waved for Sam to follow her inside. A creaking elevator with a latticed wrought-iron door jerked them to the fourth floor after several false starts.

"Fix us a brandy while I try to find the shotgun and put up these flowers," she said as she walked through an inner door.

Sam found an array of bottles on a sideboard in a corner. He poured two generous portions of cognac, then looked around. The two-room suite had a tiny kitchen; no bed was visible, so he assumed that there was a bedroom on the other side of the door through which Lee had disappeared. The thought made him flush. Other than the clattering air conditioner in the window it could have been the apartment of a successful woman in the States. The Oriental-style furniture looked expensive. A rattan couch blended with the shiny black lacquered table and chairs. Ornamental porcelain elephants served as end tables, and matching easy chairs faced each other across the grouping. An elaborate high-fidelity system nearly covered one wall. In comparison, the MACV quarters at Bac Lieu or even Can Tho looked like flophouses.

"Here we go," Lee called as she returned with a long, wrapped package. In her other hand she carried a smaller bundle wrapped in newspaper and tied with a grass string. "This thing is heavier than I thought."

Sam took the bundles from her and leaned the long one against the wall. He tore an opening in the wrapper of the smaller one and saw that it contained shells for the shotgun. He placed them on the floor beside the gun and went to the sideboard for the cognac. Lee collapsed into a corner of the couch, kicked off her sneakers, and stretched her legs in front of her. She smiled her thanks as he handed her the snifter and patted the couch beside her. He sat, suddenly awkward and ill at ease again.

"Don't worry, Sam. Your virtue is safe with me," she teased. "Don't look as if I'm about to propose or anything. Just relax and enjoy your drink."

Sam smiled. "It's not that. It's this place. I didn't know anyone lived like this over here."

"This is nothing. You should see the suite the corps CIA adviser has." She glanced at him and frowned. "I know it must look strange to you, and I'll admit I've felt a little guilty about it when I see how some of the Americans live, but I finally decided what the hell. It's here for me to use and I'd be foolish not to take advantage of it. But you ought to hear the ration of crap I get from Jim Christian! He doesn't have to say a word. He just comes in, looks around real slowly, then smiles. The first time he did it I could have gone through the floor. Since then I've decided that if he wants to live in the jungle with his snake eaters, that's up to him. *I* didn't sign on for that. So, don't tell me you're going to give me problems too!"

Sam held up both hands in surrender. "Not me, lady. I just wish I had a place like it."

Mollified, she sipped her cognac, peering at Sam over the rim. "What happened to your nose?"

He tugged at the appendage. In truth, it did start its journey with a decided cast to the left before turning hard right, so the nostrils were almost ten degrees out of alignment with the vertical midline of his face. Sam had the habit of tugging at it in moments of stress, as though by straightening *it* out he could somehow straighten out the moment's problem as well. He had considered having it surgically corrected, but since it didn't interfere with his breathing the air force had declined to pay for the plastic surgery. Sam thought that unfair, since one of their aircraft had caused the damage.

"A small aircraft training accident," he said.

She frowned. "What kind of accident for God's sake? Do I have to draw everything out of you as though it was a military secret? How do you expect our relationship to grow more intimate . . . no, wait! That's not the word I want." Sam thought he could detect a rosy hue under the tan.

"How do you expect us to know each other *better*," she continued, "if you insist on acting like a cigar store Indian. Talk to me!"

Sam was getting a little uneasy. He wasn't that good with women under the best of conditions. Their thoughts seemed somehow alien and their perceptiveness was creepy at times. Then, too, most of them knew damned little about fighter aircraft and tactics—topics that dominated the conversations of Sam and most of his friends. He'd never been able to understand the stultified looks that would come over the faces of women at a party as he and his flight mates explained, in great detail, the events of the day's flying.

"Well," he began, determined not to get into a long-winded explanation and see *that* look slide over her lovely face, "I was on a low-level training mission in an old bent-wing F-84, and I had made a bet with another squadron pilot to see who could cross the bombing range at the lowest altitude. I got a little carried away and flew through a tree. Ended up having to eject and managed to land on my face."

"My gosh! What was the bet and who won?"

"Oh, as I recall, it was for a draft beer. And I won, of course. You can hardly fly lower than running into a tree. The guy I had the bet with was really steamed because he thought that was cheating."

"Let me get this straight," Lee said, a look of astonishment on her face. "You flew through a tree in order to win a glass of beer?"

"Well, uhh, yeah. I guess you could put it that way."

"Are you completely insane?" Her voice had become slightly higher pitched, overriding its usual pleasant huskiness. There was also a slight tremor detectable in it.

Sam thought she must be getting a little confused. Women seemed to do that around him. He tried again. "Well, no. I don't think so. I'm probably not saying this right. You see, I didn't *plan* on flying through that tree unless I absolutely had to. But the guy I had the bet with crossed the range so low that the safety officer in the scoring tower said that he was going to file a violation against him. Now, that safety officer was a guy from the fighter wing—the duty's rotated among the squadrons. So, here was one fighter pilot about to give a violation to another one because of how low he was flying. That got my attention. When I heard that over the radio I knew I was going to have to be pretty damned low if I wanted to win. And I really did, 'cause although the other guy was my friend, he was also a jerk, if you know what I mean. So, that's when I ended up flying through the tree." Sam sat back and sipped his cognac, satisfied that his succinct explanation had clarified things. He smiled brightly at Lee.

She gazed at him with a furrowed brow, then rubbed her face wearily. "So, to win a glass of beer you flew a jet fighter through a tree, destroyed it, had to parachute out, and landed on your face, breaking your nose. Is that about it?"

Sam nodded, smiling at her. She did understand. She really was different from most women.

"And your commander—he didn't say anything about what happened?"

"Well, when he came to see me in the hospital—you see, I also broke my leg when I hit the ground so they had to take me over there to get it set and everything—the colonel told me that, confidentially, he'd lost a lot of respect for George—the friend I had the bet with. Said he didn't really know if he wanted anybody in his squadron who always wanted to go *over* trees. He thought it might make some of the other outfits on the field think that we were kinda . . . I guess you'd say, tentative."

Lee slumped back into the sofa. She was quiet for a long time, and Sam thought she might have dozed off when she raised the snifter to her lips and took a large draught, then turned to look at him. She studied his face quietly for a long time before she spoke.

"Sam," she said softly, "there is either a great deal more or a great deal less to you than meets the eye. I'm not sure which right now. The first time I met you, when my brother-in-law introduced us, I thought you looked like you'd be a very interesting person to know. And tonight you've given me a great deal to think about." She reached a cool hand to cup his chin. "I have this feeling that we could become very,

very close friends. Or, on the other hand, I may never want to speak to you again after I've thought this through." She turned from him and drained her glass.

Sam thought he heard her mutter something. "I'm sorry. What did you say?" he asked.

"Oh, nothing really. I was just telling myself that I used to think the Special Forces were nuts. Listen, I think you'd better take your shotgun and go now."

Sam stood and placed the unfinished cognac on the lacquered coffee table. "Lee, if I've offended you I'm very sorry and I apologize." Sam was more than a little baffled. He quickly replayed their short conversation in his mind. He couldn't find anything there that seemed offensive.

"You haven't offended me," she said, standing with him and taking his arm to lead him to the door. "Maybe I'm just spending too much time around civilians these days and I've forgotten what it's like to be confronted with card-carrying insanity again."

Her lips were cool as she stood on tiptoe to press them lightly against Sam's. Instinctively, his arms wrapped around her. He could feel the firm muscle definition in her back as he clasped her. He tried to tighten the clinch but she gently pressed a hand to his chest, separating them.

"Let's leave it at that for now, Sam. Please do call me the next time you're in Can Tho. I mean it. Perhaps we can have dinner in one of the town restaurants or here in the apartment."

Sam bent to pick up the shotgun and shells and before he realized it was happening he was standing in the hallway watching Lee's door close firmly.

Sam sat on the bunk and unwrapped the shotgun. It was just after 0800 and already very hot. The MACV compound bustled with activity. He turned the gun over in his hands and looked at it intently. Though not a hunter he had frequently fired similar guns on the skeet range. This did not look like a skeet gun. The barrel was short, not more than twenty-two or twenty-three inches. And he'd never seen a shotgun with a carrying sling. He peered closely to read the small letters stamped in the top of the barrel: Stevens Arms Company, 12 gauge. He compared the bore size with that on the boxes of shells. Yup—twelve-gauge double-aught buckshot. He spilled a box of the shells onto the bed and began to load them singly into the magazine. He hesitated after sliding three of them into the gun, then tried another. It fit, as did one more. He was surprised, because the guns he'd used would take only three shells, limited by law to give the birds a sporting chance. He operated the slide and cleared the weapon, the shells ejecting back onto the bunk.

Christian had also sent along a bandolier-type belt with loops to hold the individual loads. It could be worn around the waist or slung around the neck and chest. Sam loaded the pouches, then put the remaining shells into his canvas bag. He ensured that the shotgun was indeed empty and that the safety switch was on, then practiced bringing it to his shoulder. It felt good. He placed the shotgun and bandolier of shells in the hot locker and secured the lock on the door. There was a quick rap on his door just as he straightened. Turning, he saw the bulk of Lt. Col. Bill Robinson standing just outside the screen door.

"Come on in, Bill." Sam stepped forward to shake hands with his air liaison officer. "Have a seat anywhere."

Robinson returned the grip in a perfunctory manner, and Sam saw that his brow was furrowed with deep lines. He didn't look like a jovial uncle anymore; he looked murderous.

"Let's walk, Sam" was all he said as he turned and started back through the door. Sam had to hurry to catch him before he rounded the corner of the building.

They walked in silence, side by side, around the path inside the wire of the compound. The Ruff-Puff guards outside the wire waved genial greetings that Robinson ignored.

The big man stopped at the rear of the compound where there were few buildings, pulled a large briar from his pocket, and began to fill it slowly with coarse-cut tobacco. Sam watched, fascinated with the intricate maneuvers necessary to get the pipe charged and ready for firing. Bill struck a large kitchen match with his thumbnail and set it to the open face of the pipe. Quickly, huge clouds of smoke were billowing around their heads. Sam decided it smelled kind of nice.

At last Robinson spoke in a low baritone. "Sam, there's some shit coming down that I don't like," he said without preamble. "That's why I had to make that quick trip to Saigon yesterday, to see if I could head it off or get it stopped altogether. It directly involves you," he said, turning large dark eyes directly onto Sam.

Sam remained quiet, waiting. But his stomach was already reacting to Bill's pronouncement. It was going to be something bad, and his stomach wanted no part of it. It felt as though there was something alive in his gut, scurrying around, trying to find a way out.

"Here's the story," Robinson continued, pausing a moment to blow out a huge cloud of smoke. "The word came down through back channels yesterday morning that Headquarters, MACV has approved a ground raid on a certain location where solid intelligence puts a VC prisoner-of-war camp. I know what that intelligence is but I can't tell you. Just take my word for it that it's good. Anyway, COMUSMACV saw it as a way of maybe getting four of our people back from the dinks. That's how many are supposed to be kept in this camp. It's in our area; the U Minh Forest over on the west side of the Cau Mau peninsula. A team of Special Forces people is going to try a raid on the thing. I don't know how much you know about that area, but I'll tell you the terrain is awful. Mostly mangrove swamp and shit like that, so it's gonna be awful tough for those green beanies to sneak up on the dinks without being compromised. But they figure it's worth the old college try."

"Hey! That's great," Sam broke in. "Hell, if they get any of them out it's better than doing nothing. At least the prisoners would have a fighting chance. That'd be better than the deal they've got now."

Bill Robinson stared at him with a grim expression. "Maybe you won't think it's so damned great when you hear the rest of it." He turned from Sam to look out over the wire. Sam looked too but didn't see anything of interest.

"It seems," Bill continued, "that the evidence points to one of the prisoners being an air force pilot. His name doesn't matter but we've had several good sources say that this man has had an injured arm amputated. Seems he was hurt bailing out of an A-1, and old Charley's doctor whacked that sucker right off. Who knows? Maybe he really had to. In any event, our intelligence says that one of the four prisoners in that camp is missing a right arm and is still wearing an air force flight suit. We're ninety percent sure who he is and that he's one of ours."

"Don't tell me that the U.S. Army has problems with springing somebody who doesn't belong to them. Some of 'em cheat at cards and a few are known to associate with women of loose moral character, but I will not believe that."

Bill smiled. "No, that's not it. The problem began when Colonel Jackson Jones, director of operations for 2d Air Division—your old friend, I believe—heard about the proposed snatch. He thought it would be an absolute dandy idea to add a member of the good ole USAF to that team. And guess who he volunteered?"

Sam swallowed hard. "Me?" he croaked.

"You got it, my friend. First guess and damned if you didn't get it right away. Anyway, knowing a little something about the background of you and the good colonel up there in Saigon, I thought it was necessary for me to get up there and personally find out what the fuck was going on. Well," he scratched the back of his neck and squinted at Sam, "old Jack Jones threw me the hell out of his office; told me the decision had been made and to stop bothering him or he'd have my ass going out there with you. I went over his head to the Old Man himself, who told me the exact same thing, only in much nicer language, of course. Told me he was proud of the job we all were doing down here, fighting them Cong and all that shit. When I alluded to the fact that there might just be something a little personal in you being volunteered for such a hairy mission, well, he threw my ass outta his office too. Seems he thought having an air force officer on the ground with the raiding party was a wonderful idea, in case one of the prisoners was indeed a pilot. He figured maybe you two could talk flying; exchange recipes. You know, that kinda shit."

"So, I'm lucky Pierre, huh?" Sam felt the animal in his stomach curl into a knot. Christ! The rawest infantry private knew more about that kind of job than he did. He would be completely out of his element.

"Looks like it, old son," said Robinson. "For your information I'm putting all this on paper and sending it up through channels. I'm gonna say that I think it was a personal vendetta by the 2d Air Division DO, seeking satisfaction for something that happened a long time ago. Course, it won't mean diddly if y'all manage to free those POWs. Then, it'd just be another example of good planning by the senior staff. Only time it'll matter is if they happen to kill your sorry ass."

"Don't do it, Bill," Sam said hastily. "I appreciate what you're trying to do, but I won't have you hanging your ass out any farther for me. Taking my side in this thing would mean the kiss of death for you, even if it did fix Jones's wagon. You'd never get promoted again, and the air force needs people like you. Besides, I don't need you on my conscience too. I've got enough problems with my own career without worrying about yours. Anyway, I'd still have to go. The government hired us to stand between the civilians and enemy bullets. They never specified that we had to do it in any certain way."

Robinson looked at him closely, brow still furrowed in thought. "Well," he said finally, "we both know there's no way of keeping you off this party, which, incidentally, takes place day after tomorrow. The group'll gather at Bac Lieu and chopper to the LZ on the west side of the U Minh. I promise you one thing, Sam. If anything happens to you, promotion or no promotion, I'm going after that sonofabitch Jones, regardless of consequences."

Bill turned practical, puffing away with enthusiasm on his pipe. "What do you need that I can get for you? I know there's nothing down there in the boondocks for you to resupply, but hell, man, we a corps headquarters." He laughed that strange, high-pitched giggle. "We got all kinda shit up here, so name your needs, my man."

"Hell, I don't know. I've never done anything like this before. I really just don't know."

"Not to worry. I'll turn the problem of outfitting you for your upcoming campaign to a grunt acquaintance of mine—that sorry-ass first sergeant who keeps taking all my money in his damned cheating poker game. He ain't worth much else, but he does seem to have mastered the grunt business. Come on, skippy! Let's go find his sorry ass and get you outfitted for your big adventure."

Sam nodded glumly and followed.

CHAPTER 7

Carl Markham admired the new shotgun as Sam tied down the aircraft wings to a pair of large rocks they used as anchors. Dripping wet, Sam swore at the younger pilot during the short ride back to the compound.

"I'm telling you that it just isn't natural for a man not to feel heat like this. Look at me! I'm wet clear down to my toes; you're sitting there without even a hat, looking like you don't even have sweat glands. You really piss me off."

Carl tried to look both sympathetic and apologetic without succeeding very well at either. He cut inquisitive green eyes toward Sam. "Did Colonel Robinson want anything special?" he asked casually.

Sam thought he looked like a curious cat. He knew Carl's mind was clicking, computing the pile of new acquisitions lying in an untidy bundle in the rear seat, trying to tie it all together. Sam had noted his thoughtful look when he saw the new jungle fatigues, knowing Sam's loathing for the uniform.

"I guess you could call it special," growled Sam, hanging on tightly to the front window frame and seat as Carl caromed into the compound with the panache of an Argentine racing car driver. They sat in the seats for a moment to allow the dust created by their arrival to clear. But it hung in the windless air, seemingly unaffected by gravity, attracted to Sam's sweating face and neck. He shook his head hopelessly at Carl, only to receive a wide grin in return. The redhead's freckles gleamed in the bright sunlight.

"Come on, Barney Oldfield," Sam told Carl when it became apparent that they could not out-wait the dust hovering around them. "I'll tell you a few things that are going to make your day, especially if you like to see old men suffer."

Sam gathered the gear from the rear of the jeep and staggered toward the shade of the palm-thatch overhang of his building. He followed the shadow to his room. Carl was right behind with the shotgun and ammunition, collecting the fallout of Sam's load. Inside the cubicle, he motioned Carl to the straight-backed chair while he dumped his load onto the cot and surveyed his living quarters. The tiny room seemed even seedier than it had before. Carl straddled the chair backwards, leaning on the back support with folded forearms.

"Wondrous things are afoot, my boy," Sam told him. "Wondrous things indeed. And this fool is caught in the middle of it all." He told Carl the entire story, even the background of the grudge held against him by Col. Jackson Jones. The young captain looked enthralled. The bright eyes never left Sam's face until he'd finished and had sunk wearily onto his back on top of his new gear. Keeping his eyes closed Sam reached for the GI towel he kept on the iron headwork of the bed. He was able to fetch it unerringly, even during the darkness, to wipe his sweaty face.

"Sam," the younger officer said tentatively, "why don't you see if they'll let me take your place on the raid? It sounds like they just want an air force body along. You know that those Special Force types aren't going to expect anything useful out of whoever goes. I mean, we're just not trained for that sort of thing. Whoever goes is just going to be extra weight for the team and I'm . . . ah . . ." Carl paused, knowing he was getting to dangerous ground, and tried to think of a diplomatic approach. "Well, I'm a little better acclimated to the heat than you are and—"

Sam opened his eyes and scowled. "Go ahead and say it. You're also ten years younger."

"Fifteen," Carl murmured absently, "but really, I wasn't going to say that. Damnit, Sam! You know it's true. Do you realize how hot it's going to be in that swamp, under that tree cover?"

"Hell, I know it's true too," Sam sighed as he lay back and closed his eyes again. "And I do appreciate you trying to take my place. Believe me, if it was up to me I'd let you. But it ain't up to me. Colonel Jack Jones wants my draggin' old ass out there in those weeds. Don't you see? Just think about it. What possible bit of difference could it make to drag an ignorant blue suiter out on this safari? Not a damned bit. They want just one particular blue suiter. So, thanks for asking, but don't give it another thought. I'm going whether I want to or not."

"Well, this explains one thing anyway." Sam raised his eyebrows in question.

"A gang of the toughest-looking hombres this side of Hollywood dropped in on us this morning. Didn't talk to anyone. Just marched in to see the PSA and then took up residence in a corner of the team house. Got spook business written all over 'em. They look like Zapata's bunch on the way to the revolution, ready for murder, rape, and pillage. If they're the bunch you're going in with, then I'd have to say you're in pretty good company. On the other hand, I wouldn't lend any of them any money if I were you. In fact, I don't think I'd even make eye contact if it could be avoided."

"Yeah, sounds as though that would be my group of jolly elves. I think I'll wait until tonight to introduce myself. Right now, they might take one look at these sweating old bones and decide to leave me in the U Minh."

"Yeah, there's always that to think about," Carl said, very seriously.

It was nearly dark when Sam walked to the mess hootch. Thankfully, his name hadn't appeared on the night's guard roster. He had a feeling he was going to need as much rest as he could get.

Inside, the Special Forces team was easy to spot. They had isolated themselves at a single table far from the door, and their low conversation was indecipherable. Sam recognized Jim Christian's blonde crew cut from across the room and walked toward him. All the faces at the table turned toward him, and conversation stopped when his destination became apparent to the men. Sam stuck out his hand.

"Howdy, Jim. Nice to see you again. I want to thank you for the shotgun."

"No problem, Major Brooks. Glad you could use it. Let me introduce you."

"Are you the group I'm going to be—"

"Why don't we talk about that later," Christian interrupted. Sam realized that Jim had no wish for the mission to become common knowledge. The large captain turned to the others at the table. "These are Sergeants Jake Jacoby, Mike Thornton, Dell Washington, and Jesus Carrasco. This is Major Brooks."

Sam felt the weight of their eyes upon him and knew this was not going to be an easy group to impress. His rank sure as hell wasn't going to do it. Only the fair-haired Thornton showed any expression at all.

He had a slight smile curling one side of his mouth. Sam would find soon that it was a pleasant, but permanent, feature resulting from the explosion of a B-40 rocket that had severed nerves in the sergeant's face. No berets were in sight; instead there was an assortment of flop hats styled to the individual's taste. All five men had bottles of Vietnamese beer in front of them.

"How about another beer all around?" Sam asked the table.

Christian spoke for all of them. "Better not." He lowered his voice. "I don't know if you got the word, but we're going in at first light tomorrow. Higher-ups are getting nervous about them moving the target. We'll brief in the PSA's office right after chow."

Sam nodded, his throat suddenly feeling very constricted.

Lieutenant Colonel Whitehead sat at his desk as the group filed in. No one saluted. Sam was surprised to see Carl Markham standing in a corner, leaning against the wall. He winked as Sam approached.

As Sam joined him he whispered, "The PSA just invited me to act as the radio relay for your little jaunt. I tell you, Sam, it makes me quiver with pride that I'm gonna be permitted to fly over you in all that nice clean air while you're thrashing around in that swamp helping to make the world safe for democracy, baseball, and the American way of life. I'm so proud of you that I could just shit!"

Sam growled low in his throat and gave him a venomous look. Carl beamed back at him.

"OK, Captain," the PSA said to Jim Christian. "Let's get started. Just give me a broad outline and save the details for the team brief."

"Yes, sir," said Christian, walking to the wall map of the IV Corps area. "The team is composed of Special Forces troopers from three different A Teams. We did this in order to not deplete any one team and also to get veterans of this type of operation." He turned to the map.

"One slick Huey and two gunships for escort from the detachment at Soc Trang will pick us up from your airstrip at 0530 tomorrow. We deliberately chose Bac Lieu for loading so as not to give any watchers the idea of where we'll be going. We'll fly directly to this point," he indicated a point on the western coast of the Cau Mau peninsula, "where, if we're unopposed, the team will insert onto the mudflats at low tide. The suspected camp is almost due east of this point at about five kilometers. Due to the nature of the terrain we expect to reach it on the second day."

Sam's ears perked up. Hey! Five klicks was only about three miles or so. More than a day to make that distance must mean they'd be moving really slow. Hell, he shouldn't have any problem keeping up on a march like that. Suddenly he felt much better about the mission.

"Due to the nature of the terrain and the unknown situation at the camp, we'll have to make final assault plans after we've seen the objective. If we do manage to secure the prisoners, we'll attempt to blow an LZ right there and come out on strings if we have to." He looked over to Sam. "That is, we'll be pulled out on ropes," he explained. Sam nodded.

"If we're in contact we may have to reverse course and go back the way we came to the original LZ. In any event, due to the nature of the expected terrain we'll need airborne guidance and a radio relay to help with orientation. That's why we requested one of the IV Corps FACs to be over us, since he has much more loiter time than the helicopters. I believe, sir, that you have dragooned one of the local FACs to help us out in that regard. We appear to have the other one with us," he said with a grin directed at Sam.

"Sergeant Washington," he continued, "will be our team medic and he'll carry sufficient supplies to hopefully be adequate for the short-term medical needs of the prisoners. With any luck, total time for the mission should be no more than four days. We're adequately equipped to spend several more should it become necessary. Recovery will again be at low tide. We'll carry two PRC-25 radios and spare batteries with us. Their range is limited but the FAC should be able to pick us up well enough."

"You're going to be high and dry at night when we can't keep an aircraft over you," mused the colonel.

"Yes, sir. But we're going to hole up before dark, and I think we should be fairly secure. In any event, I don't know what we could do about it."

"Neither do I," confessed the PSA. "Bac si," he addressed the muscular black sergeant as "Doc," "you sure you've got enough in the way of medical supplies? If you need anything we've got, get in touch with my S-4."

"Got everything I can carry now, Colonel," replied Sergeant Washington with a large grin.

"Good enough." Lieutenant Colonel Whitehead's eyes swept the group. Except for Sam the raiding party looked as relaxed as sunning cats. The eyes stopped on Sam. "Major Brooks, I wonder if I could see you for a moment after the captain is finished." Sam nodded, wondering what sort of additional trouble he could be in now.

"Is there any sort of assistance I can provide you?" asked the PSA.

Captain Christian surveyed his troops. All made small negative signs. "No, sir. I think we're in good shape."

Sam was tempted to ask if someone would at least show him how to put his web gear and rucksack together, but he kept silent.

"I'll see you on your return then. Good luck to all of you." The PSA stood and walked toward the door. Sam followed him into the compound yard. The air was moist and heavy as they faced each other in the darkness, arms folded across their chests. Whitehead's voice was low as he spoke.

"Major Brooks, we seem to have gotten off on the wrong foot together and I accept the responsibility for that. I'll admit that prior to your arrival word had come down to me that you had a real attitude problem and were not a team player. It was also said that your own organization, the 2d Air Division, was unhappy with you and that you carried a very large chip on your shoulder. Unfairly, I allowed those rumors to influence my judgment of your capabilities before I even knew you." He chuckled softly. "I must admit that when you turned on that damned siren in front of me and my entire staff, I thought the rumors must be valid. On reflection, however, I knew the fault had not been yours. Additionally, I've checked with your ALO, Bill Robinson—a man, I might add, whose judgment I trust implicitly, since he's gotten my ass out of a jam on more than one occasion in the past year. He thinks very highly of you. That, coupled with my own observations of your conduct and abilities since your arrival, has led me to believe that someone has made a very bad call on you.

"Then yesterday, when I found we'd been tasked to support this prisoner snatch and you were assigned to go with them, I knew that something, somewhere, was indeed wrong, and I doubt if it's with you. Quite frankly, you shouldn't be on this operation. Neither should any member of this advisory team. That's a very specialized business and I heartily dislike the idea of you making this trip. We both know it isn't right, but I do respect the fact that you've made no effort to get out of it. If there was a way I could relieve you I'd do so, but, as you know, the convoluted lines of authority in this advisory business make rapid action damned-near impossible. So, just let me say that I apologize for earlier behavior. All I can tell you is to keep your ass down and let those young bucks carry the load. They're good at it and it's what they're paid for."

Colonel Whitehead put out his hand and Sam shook it, then saluted as the PSA moved away in the darkness. He stood still for a moment, thinking, then remembered he hadn't said a damned word to Colonel Whitehead. Shaking his head he started back to the briefing. The NCOs and Carl were just getting to their feet and heading for the door as he stepped inside.

Jim Christian motioned him over and they stood silently until the others left the room. They sat and faced each other across the desk. Christian grinned. "What do you think, Major Brooks?"

"Call me Sam. I don't know what the hell to think. I suppose you and the rest of the world know that I was shanghaied for this trip. You also gotta know that I don't know squat about grunt stuff. I'm in pretty good shape but nothing compared to you guys. Hell, if I were you I'd leave me on the beach tomorrow so I don't screw things up for everybody."

"Well, I don't know the reason you've gotta go, Sam, but Colonel Whitehead said that neither you nor we have any choice in it. So, we'll do the best we can. Nobody can ask more than that. I had to tell the team, of course, that you didn't have any experience walking on the ground, and they accept it. We'll do what we can to look after you, but I'm afraid you're going to be pretty much on your own if we run into trouble."

"Do you expect trouble?" Sam's gut began lurching again.

"Of course. I don't know how much you know about the U Minh Forest. It's like your worst nightmare. Mangrove swamp that never ends— snakes, mosquitoes, saltwater crocodiles. Hell, if they're really there, they'll probably hear us coming a day away. And they know those swamps; we don't. About the only thing we've got going for us is that we've got as fine a team as ever stepped under a beret. I've served with all of them and they're damned good."

"And then there's me," Sam said with no little bitterness.

"And then there's you," Jim agreed with a smile.

Sam felt as though he could hardly move under the mountain of gear festooning his body. On his web belt, which was kept from sagging to his knees by suspenders, he carried four canteens of water, an empty canteen cover filled with shotgun shells, a first-aid pouch, a K-BAR knife, and another canteen cover holding two frag and two smoke grenades. In his rucksack were rations for five days, a mosquito net, a poncho and liner, mosquito repellent, a spare radio battery, a blivet of water, and a few odds and sods that Jim Christian had tossed in. In a shoulder holster he carried a long-barreled .22-caliber automatic pistol complete with bulbous silencer. He wore a flop hat and new jungle fatigues with the trousers tied tightly around the tops of his boots. Pockets were crammed with more insect repellent, a small flashlight, and waterproof matches. He had malaria pills, water purification tablets, and a Swiss army knife. A flashlight with a red-hooded lens was taped to one shoulder strap and a medical compress was taped to the other. Just thinking about all of it made him weary. Why would anybody in his right mind go into the grunt business?

He stood with Carl and watched the slick Huey and its two armed escorts swirl the dust of the Bac Lieu airstrip as they settled to the ground. Even the red-haired FAC seemed subdued in the predawn darkness. The others in the team got to their feet without a word and walked to the waiting slick. Sam could just hear Carl's shouted farewell over the engine noise.

"*Khong xau,* Boss. No sweat! I'll be over you as soon as those birds set you down, and you know no Cong are going to do anything if I'm up there. I'll kick their asses!"

Sam patted him clumsily on the shoulder, swaying under his equipment load. He gave him a wan smile and tottered off to the waiting helicopter, already sweating heavily. The door gunner pulled him aboard and he found a nest the others had left for him on the floor, well away from the doors. They all sat with their legs dangling outside as if they were on an amusement park ride.

The pilot pulled pitch and the Huey accelerated nose-low down the runway. The air flowing through the open doors felt cool and moist. Sam closed his eyes and tried to make his mind a blank. It was difficult to do. His thoughts ran together, melding into a diffused mess. He'd long since given up rehearsing the details given by Christian. He remembered his place in the column, number five, and he remembered he was to watch and keep his shotgun pointed in a nine o'clock to eleven o'clock arc to the left of their line of march. He figured he'd have to wing anything after that. Jim insisted that Sam retain the shotgun, believing it to be the perfect weapon for an untrained, unskilled marksman. The others, however, had threatened Sam with expulsion from the group should he be caught inadvertently aiming the scattergun in their direction.

The flat landscape flowed beneath them, showing a surprising number of lights. The Vietnamese seemed to sleep very little and get up early. Sam caught himself filling his lungs deeply on each breath and made a conscious effort to slow the rate to something close to normal to avoid hyperventilating. He tried to focus on anything that would take his mind off the coming mission. He concentrated on his inevitable second passover to lieutenant colonel, soon to occur. But suddenly that event, which had loomed so large in his thoughts for so long, seemed to lose importance. He looked between the shoulders of two of the men sitting in the right doorway and found that they'd begun to overfly a more densely wooded area. Sam glanced at his watch and noted that the false dawn was right on time.

The team began to refasten their gear and check weapons. Sam looked nervously at the safety catch on the shotgun. It was still on and he couldn't remember if he was supposed to leave it safe or not. He was glad he hadn't readied it to fire when Jim Christian leaned back to look at the weapon and nodded his approval. The team leader obviously didn't want to start the mission with an ass full of double-aught buckshot.

The foliage just below the dangling feet had thickened, looking dark green and ominous. There were no lights visible beneath the canopy. Sam detected a change in pitch and felt the helicopter's nose lower and the slight g force of a turn. Suddenly, he was staring over Christian's broad back at the Gulf of Thailand. The pilot flew them out over the water, then turned back in toward the narrow beach. Sam stretched his neck to look forward between the two pilots. The beach shimmered with the early light reflecting from the trapped water in the mud before it disappeared into a solid rank of low trees. The pilot didn't set the helicopter down but came to a hover a yard above the surface. Suddenly, the team was gone and Sam was alone in the troop compartment except for the door gunners. One of them waved his arm frantically at him. Sam scrambled for the door and jumped. The Huey was accelerating away even as he landed face first in the glutinous mud.

He pulled himself upright and scraped some of the slimy soil from his eyes. One eye focused on the other five team members scrambling for the tree line. Sam lurched into a rolling trot as the mud threatened to pull him off balance. The team had spread into a defensive half-circle before he wallowed into their midst. He sank to his knees by Christian, who didn't spare him a glance but concentrated instead on the sullen darkness beyond them. Carrasco and Thornton did look quickly at him as he blundered into the perimeter, noted his disheveled condition, and rolled their eyes at each other.

The noise from the helicopter faded, although Jacoby was obviously talking to it over a strange radio rig. The sergeant wore what looked to Sam like the earpieces of a stethoscope with a small microphone attached to it and positioned directly in front of his mouth. It left the sergeant's hands free as he talked.

Sam could feel his heart pounding beneath his new green fatigue blouse. After half an hour of staring into the trees, his heart rate had slowed almost to normal. Another fifteen minutes passed and Sam began to get bored. The others were motionless but he began to slowly clean some of the mud from his face and weapon. Another quarter hour passed.

Christian must have decided they'd landed unobserved, for he finally swiveled his head and looked at Sam fidgeting beside him. He grinned. "What the hell happened to you?" he whispered softly.

Sam could hardly hear him over the gentle waves slapping at the mud beach. "Had a little trouble getting out," he whispered back.

Christian nodded and stood erect, making a small hand motion to his men. He listened for a moment and moved cautiously into the gloom beneath the trees. Sam waited until four of them had filed by, then stepped into the line as they moved from the beach. Sam saw an immediate problem. The muddy flats didn't end at the trees.

Sam had never seen a mangrove tree and was not pleased with the introduction. Arm-sized roots sprang from unlikely locations on the tree and plunged into the mud below, creating a natural fortress. Branches grew thick and tangled, the lower ones covered with mud from high tides. As they moved beneath the trees a clammy heat enveloped Sam, permeating his skin. His lungs felt overburdened, as though the heat and moisture were more than that delicate organ could handle. His chest constricted and he found himself panting like a dog after only a few steps. He wondered if he was having a heart attack.

The gear weighted Sam down unmercifully, making each step a grueling effort. Every one or two steps he had to crawl over a buttress of slimy roots or sink to his knees and wallow underneath them. Within yards of the beach he had a new coating of the slick mud.

The mud coating had one benefit: It served as some protection against the hordes of mosquitoes that had sensed their presence and risen in a phalanx to attack. As Sam gasped for air, the insects were drawn into his open mouth. He tried to spit them out but lacked the necessary saliva. He tried to brush them away as they clogged his nostrils and wormed into the corners of his eyes, but soon he lacked the energy to do even that. He stumbled forward, the mud sucking at his every step, knowing that he was making as much noise as the entire team. The men began to turn and look at him with irritation. Sam didn't particularly give a shit what anyone thought of him at the moment. He was fighting for his life.

He fell over a slick root, going down to his knees, then levered himself erect and stood gasping. He turned to check their progress and was shocked to find they'd covered only fifty yards or so. The sea was still visible through the maze of protruding roots and branches. He rubbed the mud from his watch and found they'd been moving for nearly an hour. He started forward once more, only to run into the stationary form of Sergeant Washington. It was like hitting a redwood. Sam would have gone over except for the mud firmly clutching his feet. The sergeant had a hand raised, as did the other men in line. Sam felt the adrenaline begin to flow, and a fresh burst of energy coursed through his body. Cautiously, he moved the barrel of his pump shotgun, which had been pointing at the back of Sergeant Washington's head, and deflected it to his assigned arc of coverage.

A thick snake nearly six feet in length serpentined across their route of march and disappeared into one of the permanent semiliquid pools. The column moved forward again and Sam looked fearfully at the huge reptilian track in the mud. It had to be a foot across. Despite the heat he shivered mightily and for a few moments carefully watched where he placed his feet. The resolve lasted for only a few steps, until the adrenaline rush was gone and he became lax and wobbly once more.

An occasional hillock of firmer ground gave some respite. Formed by the tides that had swirled the mud around, most of these small islands were only a few yards in diameter. Christian used one of them to give the team its first break.

The men immediately formed a defensive perimeter. Sam found a place in the invisible circle and flopped. None of the others removed their gear, so neither did Sam. Anyway, he didn't think he'd be able to get it back on if he shucked it. He stared with unseeing eyes into the swamp, gasping painfully against the ache in his side.

Jim Christian oozed into position beside him as silently as the snake had moved. He put his mouth close to Sam's right ear and whispered. "How you doing? Having lots of fun?"

Sam was panting as though he was in labor. "Yeah, this is great. I just wish somebody had told me about it sooner. Think of what all I've been missing."

Christian grinned and held up the fingers on both hands, mouthing "ten minutes." Sam nodded an acknowledgment and watched the team leader slither over to one of the radiomen. He put on a headset, and his lips began to move. Although Sam couldn't hear a sound, he figured that Christian was talking to Carl, who'd be somewhere overhead in his Bird Dog. Sam knew that the FAC would stay well away so as to not compromise their position. He was filled with a desperate longing to be in that little aircraft, away from the mud and mosquitoes and goddamn snakes. Sam strained to hear the aircraft's engine, but Carl was probably revved way back to save fuel. God! He hated this.

It was nearly dark when Christian decided to halt for the night. They stood on a small hummock of nearly dry ground that felt strangely unsteady to Sam. The high tide had swirled past them almost an hour before, carrying the detritus of the swamp deeper into the darkness, where, Sam supposed, it waited until the ebb tide retrieved it. All but the highest points of land were inundated by the muddy froth. Sam stood with his head hanging down, swaying beneath his load, knowing that if he went down he was incapable of rising again. He stared in detachment at the water marks that came to his mid-thigh. For the past six hours he'd been moving simply because he had no other choice. He knew he would be left if he was unable to continue. Just now it didn't seem to matter much one way or the other. Perhaps he'd join the swamp's treasures that floated back and forth in perpetuity beneath the trees.

Christian came to him in the darkening gloom and grabbed his arm to get Sam's attention. "Home for the night," Jim said softly and pointed him toward a cluster of small trees that had taken root on the hummock. Like a dumb animal Sam staggered toward them. He leaned against one of the six-inch trunks and blinked at the sight of the others slipping out of their gear. The pain caused by his own had become a part of him and he could hardly remember being without it. Then Christian was behind him, helping to lift the load to the ground. Grudgingly, his aching muscles permitted him to raise his hands upward to scrub his face. Beneath the mud, his face was lumpy from mosquito bites; one eye was nearly closed. He'd long since stopped paying attention to the little devils, being more concerned with larger pains.

Three men were on guard, lying on their bellies around the night defensive position, facing the swamp. Christian and Carrasco were as busy as housewives, stringing jungle hammocks from the trees and laying out a meal of sorts. Numbly, Sam fumbled open his ruck and felt around in its unfamiliar interior. His rummaging hands found the plastic water blivet, and the terrible thirst from the last hours hit him full force. He quickly moved his hands away lest he devour its entire contents and be bereft for the return journey.

Sam tried to tie his hammock to the tree, but his numbed fingers simply would not cooperate. Strong black hands almost invisible in the gathering gloom pushed him aside and Sergeant Washington deftly completed the task. Giving the sergeant a wan smile, Sam was preparing to crawl inside the hammock when he saw Jim Christian waving him over. He staggered to him and was rewarded with a handful of stringy dried meat and a few dried apricots.

"These'll help the C rations go down," the captain whispered.

Sam shook his head. There was no way he could get anything solid down his throat. It felt raspy and swollen, and the thought of food almost made him retch. Christian insisted and he reluctantly took the proffered food. Putting a small piece of the dried fruit into his mouth and chewing slowly, he was surprised at the tart, fresh taste. He took a larger piece. It helped his thirst as well.

Christian leaned close to his ear to speak. "You did real good today, Sam. We didn't have to stop for you a single time."

"Would you if I couldn't have kept moving?" Christian smiled and patted his shoulder, then moved away to relieve Jacoby on the perimeter watch.

Sam tottered back to his hammock and crawled into it, still clutching the remainder of the fruit and the untasted meat. He unfurled the mosquito net, knowing he'd probably trapped dozens of them within it. There was little he could do about it, since in the briefing Christian had forbidden the use of bug spray. Instead, Sam dug out a small plastic vial of insect repellent and dabbed it on his swollen face and neck. He rolled down the sleeves of his blouse, then liberally doused his hands and the fabric. Curling on his side he watched the guard settling in for the first shift. He had no idea when his turn would come and preferred not to even think about it. Someone would wake him when it was his time. Sam chewed on another piece of dried fruit and wondered what tomorrow would bring. It was his last conscious thought.

There was a little light filtering through the tree canopy when Sam awoke. For a long moment he couldn't remember where he was and he stared in bewilderment at the dried fruit and meat he clutched. His hands, he noted, were covered with additional lumps where the mosquitoes had attacked him during the night. Either the repellent wasn't that good or he'd sweated it off. Strange birdcalls echoed in the forest canopy and the dusky ooze around him resonated with reptilian slithering and other goings-on. Movement attracted his attention and he turned with a start. The team had already taken their hammocks down and were preparing a meal of sorts. Remembrance came like a migraine. They'd let him sleep through the night, he realized, as he tried to manage a feeling of guilt. He could not. If he were to get through this day, he knew he'd needed that night's rest. They knew it as well.

Sam's entire body felt like one giant toothache as he eased from the hammock and rose to his feet, wobbling slightly. He felt as though he hadn't closed his eyes. Today was going to be bad. He tried to stretch his muscles, then urinated quietly into a bush. The stream was thick, yellow, and sparse. He needed more fluids, but damned if he knew where he was going to get them. He joined Jim Christian who was silent but winked at him.

The thought of food was repugnant, but Sam followed the example of the others and tried to force down a can of the C rations. He thought of burying the half-full can in the swamp when he saw Washington making encouraging motions to continue eating. The sergeant was right. He needed his strength. He swallowed more food but had to put the hard cracker in his pocket. It was beyond his capacity to swallow. After he was finished he realized he hadn't the slightest idea of what he'd just put into his stomach. Whatever it was lay there like a lump of lead.

Quickly, they were into their gear and moving at that mind-stultifying slow pace through the mud and mangroves. The tide was out and there was only the mud to suck at their boots. Crabs scuttled back and forth, pincers clacking defensively, to disappear down fresh holes or hide beneath the detritus of the high tide. There were thousands of them. The mosquitoes that had slackened their assault at dawn returned in force.

Sam's mind slipped into neutral. His entire focus ended at the next step: Complete one step, then shift his attention to the next. Time became meaningless, measured only by the infrequent rest breaks. The terrible agony in his legs and shoulders reduced to insignificance the mosquito attacks and the limbs slashing his face. He stopped only when a strange wall of green prevented him from thrusting his leg forward. Each time, he would stare at it, confused, until he could assimilate that the green wall was the broad back of Sergeant Washington.

During one short halt Sam regained consciousness long enough to observe the four men to his front. They reminded him of his grandfather's bird dogs. Their noses sniffed the air as though they were seeking out quail.

Then, he too smelled it. Wood smoke. Then he heard the ringing of an ax blade biting into wood. It was somewhere to their ten o'clock position. The adrenaline came pumping up again. Sam watched Jacoby talking quietly on one of the radios. The radioman looked up and nodded and Christian indicated with a wave of a hand their new path. The column slowly snaked behind him toward the source of the noise. The ax blows sounded very close, but Sam knew that they were farther away than he expected.

As they moved Sam realized he didn't feel as exhausted as he had before. He was almost alert. He also remembered all those things he should have checked before they started walking this morning. Was his shotgun barrel free of mud? Was there a round in the chamber of the .22 automatic? Did he still have his grenades in the canteen cover? Was he really in his right mind?

There was a slight rise to the ground now; the dry parts were coming more frequently and were larger. The smell of wood smoke was much stronger.

They walked another hour before Christian halted them in the cover of a particularly dense mass of mangrove. Sam's shot of adrenaline had turned to weak tea during the hard march, and he was only vaguely aware of his surroundings, becoming more interested again in the convolutions of his lungs and limbs. They formed a small semicircle around their leader. Christian slipped from his gear, retaining only his M16 and a bandolier of ammunition. He pointed wordlessly, assigning each man a position. When they spread to his satisfaction, he gave a small wave and slithered away on his belly. He was quickly out of sight.

Sam tried to fan the mosquitoes from his face and succeeded only in disturbing them. Sergeant Thornton looked toward him with some irritation, so he stopped and let the insects have a field day. His face was so numb from the bites of the previous day that he could hardly feel the new ones anyway. His right eye remained swollen, so that visibility from it was considerably reduced. He checked his watch. They'd been waiting for well over an hour. He thought he could hear muted voices in the distance, but it was difficult to be sure over the humming of the mosquitoes near his ears. He quietly spat out a mouthful that had been attracted to the blood-rich lining of his mouth as he panted in the suffocating heat. There was that sound again. Sam was almost sure it was voices.

He awoke from his reverie with a start as Christian slid back among them. The captain came up on one knee and motioned for the team to contract the defensive circle around him. He was covered with mud—only the whites of his eyes seemed clean.

"It's there," he whispered softly, deliberately slurring his consonants to prevent them from carrying beyond the small group. "But there's only one person in a cage. It looks like one of yours," he said, looking at Sam. "Right forearm is missing and looks like he's in pretty bad shape. Bac si," he switched his gaze to Sergeant Washington, "you'd better plan on taking him. He may have to be carried." Washington nodded, face sweaty and impassive.

"It's a small camp," Christian continued, drawing an outline in the mud with a stick, "only four hootches and the prisoner cage. There's a small rain-catch reservoir made out of plastic sheeting here on the south side. The cage is right next to it. Two main trails lead out of sight; one of 'em probably goes to the latrine. The other heads northeast. The only thing that worries me is that there are only four VC in the camp and the four hootches are big enough for at least five times that many. The others may be out on an operation or patrolling. In any event, I don't think we're going to get a better chance than right now. We'll take out the four with the silenced short guns. I'll assign one to each of you except the doc and the major when we deploy." They all nodded. Sam saw this and did likewise.

"I want you and your scattergun to be in place here." Christian drew Sam's position on the muddy earth. "We need you for cover."

Sam was not deluded that he was being given a role critical to the assault. He was not resentful, for he knew he'd only be in the way of the professionals. He remembered what Lieutenant Colonel Whitehead had told him about letting the team do their work without him. It was their business. Still, it did sort of hurt to be left out. He brought his mind back to Christian's instructions.

"I'll point out positions when we get there. Carrasco will fire first. As soon as he takes out his man, the rest of you do the same. When they're down we'll rush the camp, get our boy out, and move back to where we are now. If everything goes right we'll blow the LZ right here. If things fuck up and we get separated, take off on a bearing of two six five degrees and we'll rendezvous where we spent last night. Everyone remember where that is?"

Sam didn't, but it didn't seem to be the appropriate time to bring it up. He figured he could always follow someone's tracks.

"OK, let's do it." Christian slipped back into his gear, dropped down to his belly, and slid in the direction of the camp. They followed his trail.

Sam found they were making time as fast as they had when they were walking. The mud was slick and they scooted along at a good clip. They had spread from the column and he tried to match his movements to Jim Christian's. He was concentrating on keeping the shotgun from the mud, and was distinctly startled to hear voices speaking Vietnamese almost directly in front of him. They were very close, shielded by a low straggly line of saplings. Heavy undergrowth flourished beneath them.

Slowly, they inched forward until Christian turned and pointed at Sam and then to a spot in the foliage. Sam detached himself from the group and breaststroked into the undergrowth. His vision obscured by the foliage, he almost poked his head into the camp clearing. He shrank back until he was concealed again and froze for a moment, then cautiously parted the leaves in front of his face. Two Vietnamese men wearing only shorts sat opposite each other across a fire on the far side of the clearing. A pot hung from a metal bracket over the flames. Sam observed as one of the men leaned forward to stir the contents of the pot. The other watched with interest.

Sam let his eyes roam across the clearing. Just where Christian had said it would be was a stout wooden cage roofed with thatch. The door was roped shut and in the inner gloom Sam could just make out a shapeless bundle of rags. He held his breath as another Viet came from one of the hootches behind the cooking fire. He also wore shorts but had a black pajama top and wore thongs on his feet. His thick hair was tousled and he scrubbed it vigorously with both hands, as though he had just awakened.

Sam was slowly turning his head trying to find the rest of the team when the fourth Viet came into the camp on the trail Christian had said probably led to the latrine. It was a woman. She was barefoot and wore the traditional black pajamas. Her face was round with slightly flattened features. She looked identical to many of the country girls Sam had seen. The woman spoke to the man stirring the pot and snatched the wooden spoon from him. She leaned forward slightly to peer at the pot's contents. As the three men laughed at what she'd said, Sam watched a small black hole form in her right forehead.

He was still thinking about that odd hole when he became aware of a slight metallic cough from his right. It came again, several more times, as the woman fell into the fire, upsetting the cooking pot. Sam stared stupidly as the rice spilled onto the muddy ground.

All three men were down as well. One was completely still; the other two were thrashing and moaning. Suddenly, one jumped to his feet and dashed for the nearest hootch. Sergeant Thornton was only steps behind him through the door. There was a quick, loud burst of gunfire, then silence as its echo resonated through the swamp. Sam could barely hear a muffled cough through the thatched wall; then the team was into the camp, fanning out to peer through the hootches. Washington made directly for the cage and, using his K-BAR knife, slashed at the rope holding the door shut. He moved inside and knelt by the bag of rags.

Sergeant Thornton walked out of the hootch, his .22 automatic dangling at his side. Sam stood and walked slowly toward him, then faster when he saw the dark stain on the left front of the sergeant's jungle blouse. Thornton slowly sank until he was sitting on the muddy earth. His eyes flickered rapidly about the camp as though he'd taken a heightened interest in the activity. Christian walked quickly toward him while turning his head to call softly to Washington.

Thornton acted tired. He lay back against his rucksack. A trickle of blood wormed out of the corner of his mouth. His eyes were still bright and inquisitive. He smiled as Washington and Christian worked on his side.

Carrasco led the skinny white man from the cage. Sam saw that he indeed had an arm missing and wore the tatters of a lightweight USAF flight suit. His beard was long and matted and he was barefoot. Large jungle ulcers covered his thin arms and legs. He appeared confused but continued nodding at whatever Carrasco was saying to him.

At a low whistle Sam turned to see Christian motioning everyone to gather around him. He spoke low and rapidly. "If the dinks are anywhere around here, they had to have heard that AK. We're going to have to move. Can't risk getting ambushed trying to set up an LZ anywhere around here. We'll push off the same way we came in. Jake," he looked toward Sergeant Jacoby, "get on the horn and tell the FAC what's happening. We've got one serious WIA and . . . ," he turned to survey the one-armed prisoner, "one ex-POW who's in not too good a shape himself. Tell 'im which direction we're moving and that we'll try to blow an LZ as soon as we're certain we're not being tailed." He looked at the prisoner again. "Jesus, you'd better help our newest team member get ready to move."

Calmly and efficiently the Special Forces team made their preparations. Thornton could take small hobbling steps if he leaned one arm around the neck of Sergeant Washington. Carrasco supported the stumbling air force scarecrow. Sam suddenly realized that only Christian, Jacoby with the radio, and himself were left unencumbered. He saw Jim Christian eyeing him speculatively before walking his way.

"Sam," Christian said softly, "are you up to helping your air force compadre? I'm afraid I might need Carrasco."

Sam Brooks wasn't sure he could carry himself, much less help support another body through the swamp. But he nodded and walked to where Jesus Carrasco was trying to talk with his new charge. Sam squatted next to the pair, not at all certain he was going to be able to get back up, and looked into the bony face of the man with one arm. The face staring back at him had a vague and detached look. Sam lowered his eyes and saw that the arm had been amputated just above the elbow. There was suppuration where the skin flap had been crudely sewn over the wound. He looked back up at the lieutenant. Dull blue eyes stared at him suspiciously from the thin, hairy face. The single silver first-lieutenant bar still dangled from one shoulder of the tattered flight suit.

"What do ya' say, Lieutenant?" Sam asked. "Ready to go for a little walk in the woods?" There was no reaction. Sam tried again. "What do you fly? You wouldn't be an A-1 driver, would you?"

That seemed to strike a chord. At least the eyes blinked. The scarecrow seemed to think it over, then opened his mouth as if to speak. Sam noticed his front teeth, bottom and top, were jagged stumps. Probably broken off when he crashed or bailed out. The jaws worked up and down a few times as though trying to lubricate themselves. Finally, a hoarse sound came from the battered mouth. "Ahhh, who are you?" the voice croaked as though it hadn't been used for a long time.

"Just another air force weenie, like you, Lieutenant. Name's Brooks. Sam Brooks. We're gonna be walking out of here pretty quick and then meet a helicopter down the line. Think you can walk if I help you?"

The bag of bones thought it over for a while, then nodded. "Gotta, gotta get stuff. Gotta get my stuff."

He tried to rise but ended up scuttling on the ground until Carrasco, and Sam after he'd levered himself upright, helped with a hand under each armpit. The man smelled like a cesspool. He gestured with a single scrawny arm toward the cage. Sam and Carrasco helped him to the door, where he shook free, fell to his knees, then scratched among the filthy palm fronds in the corner of the cage. His search produced a white plastic spoon, like those found in C-ration parcels, and a rag that Sam immediately identified as the squadron scarf worn by most fighter pilots.

Sam felt his eyes fill and overflow as the one-armed lieutenant awkwardly wound the tattered flying scarf around his neck and regained his feet.

Sergeant Carrasco reached a brown hand forward to clasp the near-naked shoulder and squeezed it gently. "We're gonna get you home, man. I promise you."

Christian walked up to them. "We're moving," he said quietly. "Sam, you and the lieutenant will be directly behind me. Then, Washington helping Thornton, followed by Jacoby with the radio. Jesus, take the right flank. Let's go."

Their movement was painfully slow, but if it had been faster Sam knew he'd have been unable to keep up. When they moved back onto the swampy ground the lieutenant had been almost unable to pull his naked feet from the mud after each new step. Sam tugged at the skinny arm thrown over his neck, almost losing his own balance as he extricated the man. The lieutenant's dawning coherence in the camp had been lost in the torture of the march. Fortunately for Sam, he weighed no more than a hundred pounds after his captivity.

Sam choked and rasped out a mouthful of mosquitoes. He badly needed a break but knew it was senseless for Christian to call one until they'd reached firmer ground. Mindlessly, he concentrated on taking one faltering step after another, tugging the lieutenant in his wake. He saw that the frail flier was covered with two-inch-long leeches and knew that they had to cover his own body as well. Under normal circumstances the knowledge would have driven him into hysterics until they were removed. Now, he scarcely gave them a thought.

The lieutenant slipped and was almost completely immersed in the mud before Sam bent over and held his head free. He slid to his knees and tried to pry the man up but he appeared to be unconscious. He'd simply given everything he had left to give.

Christian loomed over them, then knelt to help Sam. "We've got to move," he whispered urgently into Sam's ear. "We're being tailed."

Sam listened to the active sounds of the swamp and could detect nothing alien, only his thudding heart. Then he heard it, a noise that was out of synch with the normal cacophony. Somewhere in the shimmering gloom beyond the mangrove barrier came the distinctive sound of other footsteps in the mud. By now, Sam was all too familiar with the noise of march through a swamp. That noise couldn't be anything else. He saw that Carrasco had positioned himself twenty yards to their right and had knelt and rested his M16 on a mangrove root. Sam could see the tension in the brown neck as the sergeant tracked the alien sound with his rifle.

"They're on both sides of us," Christian said softly. "We've got to pick up the pace or walk right into an ambush when they get ahead of us. Can you carry him?"

Hell, no! Sam wanted to scream. I can't even carry myself much longer. If they left the lieutenant maybe they'd have a chance. Otherwise, everyone would die on this godforsaken piece of shit. He turned and looked wildly behind them, hoping a solution might come forth. Maybe Jacoby could carry the unconscious man.

Sam saw Sergeant Washington shedding his rucksack and preparing to lift Thornton. Jacoby whispered urgently over the radio as he faced the rear, rifle at high port. It hit Sam then, and he was amazed at his calm reaction to it. They were all going to die here. Every mother's son is going to die right here in this mud! He looked into Christian's intense face and nodded. He didn't know how he was going to carry the man but he knew he had to try. Christian was obviously not going to leave the wounded. Under his mud covering, Sam flushed that such a thought had entered his mind.

He braced the lieutenant's head so that it wouldn't slip under the mud and wearily hauled himself to his feet. Christian helped him shuck his rucksack, allowing him to retain only the water and the shotgun and bandolier of shells, which he looped over his neck to dangle on his chest. He took a quick drink and turned to his task.

Sam knelt by the inert form and used a corner of the tattered flying scarf to wipe the thin face clear of mud. He slapped the cheeks gently. "Hey! Wake up! Can you hear me?"

It was useless. Sam pried the emaciated frame from the mud and, bending low, eased the slim figure over his shoulder. His eyes bulged as he pushed himself erect. He stood there for a moment, weaving, unwilling to try the first step. He was spurred into movement by the sudden crackle of M16 fire as Carrasco emptied a clip on their flank.

"Move!" Carrasco yelled. "We got people coming in." An AK-47 blast on full automatic punctuated the sentence. Carrasco answered it with another full clip and a grenade in the direction of the fire.

Sam stood, swaying and undecided. If he went to his belly, as all his instincts screamed that he should, he knew he'd be unable to get the lieutenant to his shoulder again unaided. No one seemed to be in the mood to assist him. Still trying to consider his options, he began a shambling jog in the direction of their march. His strides were those of a drunk. The weight was agony on his shoulders. There was more firing but he didn't turn to look.

A painful stitch developed quickly in Sam's left side and trying to ignore it was like trying to forget about a knife sticking into your flesh. He groaned to a tottering walk knowing that if he did not, there would be no way to continue. A grenade exploded and made him momentarily forget his pain. The thought came to him that he might be walking alone into the swamp; the others might have decided to stay and fight their ambushers. He picked out a small, dry hillock fifty yards to his front and promised himself that if he could reach it he would put down the lieutenant and try to readjust his load. Another burst of gunfire distracted him and made him pull harder toward his goal.

At twenty yards he didn't think he would make it. The mud was deeper and his burden was slowly slipping from his shoulder. Then he felt a different sensation in his thigh muscles as his feet began to find firmer purchase. Sam came to a halt and, heaving like a blown horse, peered through sweat-stinging, swollen red eyes at his island. Small mangroves had taken root and formed a fortress of sorts. Sam clambered over it and dropped his load. Somewhere along the line he'd stopped considering his load as another human being. He remembered in time to turn him on his back so he wouldn't suffocate with his face in the jellied soil. Clumsily, he pulled the shotgun strap from around his neck.

A great thrashing came from the swamp as Sergeant Washington, with Thornton slung over his shoulder like a feed bag, stumbled onto the dry land. Gently, he placed his unconscious charge on the ground next to the lieutenant and unslung his rifle. "Good work," he muttered to Sam as he sank to his belly and thrust his weapon forward. "And good thinking. They coulda pinned us down real easy back there. Now, we can give cover to the others. You did real good, Major." He grinned suddenly at Sam. "I don't know 'bout you, but I was expecting old Charles to put a B-40 RPG up my backside every step of the way over here. And you coulda knocked me over with a feather when I saw you walking off with that ole LT hanging over your shoulder while I was rooting around on my belly like I was tryin' to drill a hole with my navel. No, sir. That was quick thinking. They coulda hammered our asses real proper back there with these two wounded."

Washington came to his knees and looked around their small island before turning to Sam again. "Major, why don't you take a position on the other side of this dry land. We don't want nobody sneakin' up on us while our folks are trying to get in. 'Sides, with that ole scattergun there's no tellin' what kinda meat you'd get if you cut loose in this direction. Why don't you set up under those bushes over there."

Sam crawled wearily to where the sergeant had pointed, feeling that he should have corrected Washington's view of his behavior. He had done very little thinking when they were ambushed—certainly not about any defensive strategies. And he'd chosen this spot simply because there was nowhere else to go.

The bushes gave him an illusion of cover as he fell heavily to his stomach, then rolled onto his side to try to wipe the inner barrel of the shotgun. He cleaned out as much mud as he could, then rolled back on his stomach and shoved the gun forward.

Automatic weapon fire startled him, making him realize that they were not yet out of the woods. Then there was silence from the area of the firefight, and the mosquitoes found him and began to drill at the corner of his eyes. He buried his face in his folded arms, trying to keep them away. His eyes wanted to remain closed and he relaxed for just a moment.

He jerked back into consciousness, unsure how long he'd been asleep. Turning his head slightly he could see Washington's broad form in the same position and the two injured men lying quietly together. He couldn't have been out too long. As he reached for his last full canteen, he saw movement in the mangroves.

He froze, one hand on the snaps of the canteen cover. There it was again! He edged the barrel of the shotgun toward the movement and tried to slink farther back into the bushes. Had he given it any thought, he would have realized that, with his several coatings of mud, he was camouflaged as well as anything that had washed in on the tide. His eyes focused on something next to a large mangrove root, and he realized he was looking at a man. Sam was so astonished that he could only stare. How long had the man been there? He must have crept in while he dozed. He silently cursed himself. His stupidity was probably going to get them all killed. He could feel his pulse pounding in his temples.

The man was only fifteen yards away and standing perfectly still. Sam's shotgun was pointed almost directly at the figure. He could hardly miss at that range. It would scare the shit out of Washington when he unloaded but there was nothing he could do about that. It was a miracle that the guy hadn't seen him reaching for his canteen.

Sam studied the man he was about to kill. The Viet wore shorts and the now-familiar black pajama top, and stood calf-deep in the mud. His AK-47 was ready in his hands. Sam was close enough to see that the man's eyes were focused to the distance along the path that he and Washington had taken. He looked to be middle-aged; Sam thought he could see some gray in the thick hair hanging in lank, sweaty strands over the wide forehead. Certainly, he was older than his two companions who stepped into view behind him.

Sam felt the hair prickle on the back of his neck. It was too late to warn Washington. Also, he could hear the rest of the team making their way toward them through the swamp. Even trained men couldn't move quietly through this crud. But then, how did the Viets flank them without either he or Washington being aware of it? Perhaps they'd been to their front all the time. Irritated, he shoved the thought from his mind. It didn't matter how they got there. They were there and they were trouble. Under the noise of the approaching team, Sam clicked off the safety button on his shotgun. Then he waited.

The older Vietnamese man made a small hand motion and his companions began to deploy for ambush. Sam knew he could wait no longer. If the men separated there'd be no way he could take them. He took a deep breath and gripped the shotgun tightly. He tensed his muscles until his back began to ache. He felt sure that they could hear his heart pounding with such a ferocity that it actually shook sweat droplets loose from his crooked nose.

He sprang to his knees, simultaneously bringing the shotgun to his shoulder. The Vietnamese were shocked into statues. Sam aimed directly at the center of the cluster and pulled the trigger. The recoil kicked hard against his shoulder, but the movement assisted in quickly working the slide to eject the spent casing and replace it with a fresh one. Sam squeezed the trigger a second time and again worked the slide. He was firing blind now through the smoke, flying mud, and bits of wood chipped from the mangrove roots. He lost track of the shots but continued to pull the trigger and work the slide until he heard the click of the firing pin striking only an empty chamber.

His ears rang from the noise of the shotgun blasts as he peered through the maelstrom he'd created. All three were down. Two were unmoving and one lay on his back in the mud, one foot flopping back and forth aimlessly. Sam's hands trembled as they clutched the gun. The ringing left his ears and there was nothing but a delicious silence; even the swamp varmints were made mute by the gunfire. The Viet with the nervous foot twitched one last time. Sam stared at the bodies. Fifteen yards away he could plainly see the mangling effectiveness of the shotgun. Blood and bits of flesh colored the mud for yards around the bodies. The entire side of one man's head was missing; what remained leaked steadily onto the mud.

There was a rustling behind him and Sam whirled toward it, jacking the slide on the empty weapon. Washington gasped as he stared into the muzzle, then held up his free hand.

"Easy, man. Easy," he hissed, then relaxed as Sam lowered the barrel from his face. He low-crawled alongside Sam and peered at the bodies. The sergeant scanned the area for other signs of Viet Cong; finding none, he turned to Sam and muttered: "Man, you a natural-born *killer*!"

Sam graciously nodded his acknowledgment, then turned his head to vomit as Christian and the other two team members walked up cautiously to join them. Washington rose to meet them and spoke quietly. They turned to look at Sam, then at the dead men, then back to Sam again. Sam picked that moment to vomit again.

Christian motioned him to join them. They moved into the familiar circle, knelt, and leaned toward him—all except Washington, who looked warily at Sam. "Man, you're not gonna do any more throwing up, are you?" he asked. Sam shook his head with a weak smile.

"Listen up," Christian hissed. "We took care of those who were tailing us from the south, but they've obviously got our exit marked. That's why they had those three waiting for us." His hand swept toward Sam's carnage. "I don't think they're going to give us time to blow an LZ and get the pickup bird in here. And they're too damned close for fighter or gunship support. All we can do is keep moving toward the beach. How's Thornton and the lieutenant?"

"They're both bad," Washington replied. "Mike is bleeding internally and it's going to be tough on him if we have to keep carrying him like a piece of meat. Making a stretcher might help some. I don't know 'bout that zoomie lieutenant. Don't think there's anything specific wrong with him that shows; outside his amputated arm that's more than likely infected. He needs about six weeks of good living and medicine. He's dehydrated bad and needs to have an IV started as soon as possible."

Christian rubbed his muddy chin as he listened to the medic's report. None of his choices was a good one. "Sorry, Dell," he told the large man, "no stretchers and no IV. If you listen real careful you can hear Charley grouping out there to the north. Our little tussle crimped his style some but it sure as hell hasn't stopped him. If we don't get moving he'll be on our ass in about five minutes. We're gonna need every gun available if we expect to live to see the coast. So, we either carry 'em or stay behind and butt heads."

Leaving them never entered Christian's mind, thought Sam. He dreaded what he knew would be coming next.

The team leader looked at Sam for a moment before he spoke. "You did real good with that scattergun, Sam, but I need our people with their hands free. I'm gonna ask you to carry that lieutenant again. Can you hack it?"

What would he do if I said I couldn't? thought Sam, but he nodded wearily.

"Let's move!" said Christian.

Washington helped Sam lift the gaunt air force lieutenant before he pulled Thornton onto his own broad shoulders with no apparent strain. Christian was already moving, with Carrasco on the right flank and Jacoby walking backward as the rear security.

The tide was coming in and the brackish water pushed deeper into the U Minh Forest. As they trudged west Sam felt the water reaching above his thighs in places. Only the very tops of the dry-land hummocks were now visible above the muddy water. Day had turned to night without Sam being aware of the change. He was conscious only of the terrible burning in his lungs as he forced air through his parched throat. There was almost total darkness beneath the mangroves, with only faint illumination from random, muted spears of moonlight stabbing downward through the canopy. Sam used them as aiming points in his mindless trek. Each point became a goal to reach before he collapsed, unable to go farther. Just one more goal and he would slide the body from his shoulders and sit in the muddy water. Death would be welcomed with open arms if it could provide relief for his tortured legs and agonized back, a cool, dark oblivion in which he carried no burden. No burden at all.

Firing broke out on the flank. Bright sparkles from AK-47s swept toward the small column. Only the darkness saved them. Christian and Carrasco hurled grenades at the muzzle flashes so as not to give away their position. Again, a raking broadside as the ambushers fired at the sounds of the trudging men. More grenades and a scream from the darkness as fragments embedded in yielding flesh. Good! thought Sam in a moment of coherence. Let those little fuckers carry somebody for a while. He had continued plodding toward the sea throughout the exchange of gunfire—a mindless mule.

Sam's burden was still and quiet, a change from earlier when there had been occasional twitches and groans. It was as though with the loss of sunlight he too had become apathetic to their plight. They stopped briefly; Sam drank the last of his water and dropped the empty canteen in the mud, unwilling to carry its extra weight. Christian relieved him of the shotgun and shells and then they were moving again.

Sam made up a new game as he wallowed through the mud. He called it "take three steps and fall." He practiced it a lot as the long night wore on. He wondered if there was nourishment in mosquitoes. If so, he should be in great shape, since he figured he had swallowed several pounds of them since sundown. He decided to fall again. Even with all the practice he'd been getting, it was still more difficult to get to his feet each time. Large bats, seemingly ecstatic at the edibles being stirred up by the clumsy creatures below, flew about their heads in a frenzy. Sam stepped on something squishy that tried to escape from beneath his boot. He never paused; indeed, he scarcely gave it a thought.

He smelled the sea long before the synapse connected his brain to his nose. A slight breeze confirmed that indeed it was the sea. Suddenly, the stars were above him and most of the mosquitoes had drifted back into their swampy lair. Through swollen eyes, Sam could see the foaming breakers thrashing the mud flats. The tide was retreating and Christian urged them forward. The three soldiers providing security walked backward, their faces to the swamp, crouching with weapons ready as they stared into the malevolent forest.

At the water's edge, Christian immediately formed them into a defensive half-circle, giving Sam only moments to become coherent once more. His burden lay beside him in the same position that he had spilled him. Sam watched with dull interest as Christian dug a small hole and placed a light beacon in it. The light seemed blinding after having been accustomed to the stygian darkness beneath the mangroves. Christian moved to the radio and began to talk. Sam noted that there was a definite pinkness to the eastern sky.

Washington knelt by the lieutenant and examined him briefly, then stood and walked over to Christian. The team leader knelt by Sam. "The lieutenant's dead," he said. "Sorry, but it looks like you've been carrying a stiff all night." He patted Sam's shoulder and moved into the darkness.

Sam awaited a reaction from his mind but there wasn't one, so he began to dig a hole in the sand, scooping it out to form a barricade between him and the forest. There was a familiar sound and he squinted toward the brightening sky. Silhouetted against it was a Bird Dog and he knew it would be Carl. It flew directly over their position, drawn by the beacon, then turned back toward the tree line. Christian was still talking to the aircraft over the radio when it dipped a wing and rolled toward the ground. There was a whooshing sound and the light of a burning rocket motor. It exploded back into the trees and a ball of white smoke rose sullenly from the canopy.

"Heads down!" Christian yelled. It was the first time anyone had spoken above a whisper since they'd entered the forest and it sounded strange. "TACAIR coming in."

Sam crouched behind his mud and sand wall and waited, his mind blank with exhaustion. He didn't hear the jet's engine noise until after the explosion of the first pair of bombs. The mud trembled like gelatin beneath him as the jungle was blown apart. Time and again, the shadowy aircraft delivered their lethal loads until only shreds of the mangrove were visible through the smoke. The reduced visibility didn't bother Sam, for he had fallen fast asleep in his hole.

Christian shook him awake when the distinctive whap-whap of the pickup helicopter bore down on them. The accompanying gunships strafed and rocketed the tree line. The slick approached from sea side, and before Sam was really aware of what was happening, he found himself sitting on its floor in the same spot he'd occupied on the inbound trip. Christian was the last man to board, and as he squirmed into his seat in the doorway he turned and handed the shotgun and bandolier to Sam.

Sam leaned back and rested against the dead air force officer. The lieutenant didn't seem to mind. A helicopter medic worked on Sergeant Thornton as the pilot hovered, tucked the nose of the helicopter, and began his run down the beach. Sam had a fine view of the fighters' target area. The bomb craters were already filling with water and would probably disappear entirely with the next high tide.

Sam rubbed the sweat from his eyes and was preparing to take a nap while they flew back to Bac Lieu when he saw Jim Christian looking at him with a small smile on his rugged face. He gave Sam a thumbs-up and leaned over to clap him on the back hard enough to bring an audible protest from Sam. Another clap almost knocked him over and he turned in surprise to find Sergeant Washington grinning at him with his thumb stuck in the air. Jacoby and Carrasco beat him in turn, each giving him a big smile and the thumb signal. No more blows were forthcoming and Sam figured the unconscious Thornton and the dead lieutenant were going to give it a pass, so he shut his eyes with relief and snuggled against the familiar form of his dead comrade. These green beanies really are the strangest people, he thought, before sleep claimed him.

CHAPTER 8

"Major Samuel G. Brooks distinguished himself by gallantry in connection with military operations in An Xuyen province, Republic of South Vietnam, on 21 March 1964. On that date, Major Brooks, while acting as one of a six-man contingent intent upon securing the release of friendly POWs . . ."

Sam tuned out the flat, unemotional voice of the adjutant reading the citation and let his eyes focus on the silver-haired general standing at attention before him. The handsome face had only a few lines and he looked like the embodiment of a "soldier." The man's pressed jungle fatigues and shined boots made Sam feel like a seedy relation as he stood in his baggy short-sleeved khakis and dulled low-quarter black service shoes. He felt chilled in the air-conditioned room; for the first time in months there was not even a sheen of sweat on his face.

Looking over the general's shoulder to the row of dignitaries standing with a few of the MACV staff, his eyes locked with those of Col. Jackson Jones. The DO represented 2d Air Division at the awards ceremony being held in COMUSMACV's office. Jones's face was impassive as he and Sam stared at each other. Sam knew that the man hated the situation but had been ordered to attend by his commander. Sam's position on the raid, after all, had been at Jones's insistence. To the colonel's chagrin, Sam Brooks was ending up with a medal instead of coming home in a body bag. Tough beans, Jack, thought Sam. Yet, staring into those flat, hooded eyes made Sam nervous—about as much bluff there as with a rattlesnake. The eyes told him silently that Sam's tour still had a lot of months to run and Jack Jones had all the time in the world to deal with the situation.

". . . although under near-continuous hostile fire and with disregard for his own safety, Major Brooks continued to . . ."

Sam felt Sergeant Washington stirring restlessly beside him. It was, after all, the sixth time that variations of the same citation had been read. They were all there—the entire team, including Thornton sitting uneasily in his wheelchair. The ruddy face that had been so drained of color when he was taken from the helicopter more than three weeks ago, was once again alive and pugnacious. His stomach wound had required resectioning a bowel; the prognosis was that Mike Thornton could remain on active duty, although it was doubtful his medical profile would permit retention in the Special Forces. Sam smiled inwardly. He wouldn't bet against Thornton doing anything he set for himself to do. And if he decided he wanted to remain under a green beanie, he'd probably do exactly that.

It was good to see all of them again, Sam thought, surprising himself at the affection he felt for these men, though he'd known most of them for only a few hours. Jim Christian he felt he'd known forever.

". . . by his gallantry and devotion to duty, Major Brooks has reflected great credit upon himself, the Military Assistance Command, Vietnam, and the United States Air Force."

A major held the medal for the commander, who stepped forward and pinned it to Sam's shirt front, saying softly: "It's always a pleasure to present such an award as this. Particularly when the effort was directed toward saving another's life. The fact that it did not succeed lessens the effort not in the least."

The tall man with the stars stepped back and in a deep, commanding voice said: "Gentlemen, I salute your gallantry." He raised his hand to his forehead. The staff and onlookers followed suit.

At an almost invisible signal from the adjutant, the six bemedaled men responded to the salute and faced left, then stepped through the door to the outer office. Sergeant Carrasco pushed Thornton's wheelchair.

The men clustered together and talked animatedly as they removed the Silver Star medals from their shirts. Sam was not alone in giving the shiny metal star with the diamond chip in the center an admiring glance before he slipped it into the felt-lined storage box.

There was much handshaking, back clapping, and dire threats about what would occur if everyone didn't keep in touch before the group began to dissolve and go its individual ways. Jim Christian faced Sam just as the group from the commander's office trooped by. Colonel Jackson Jones didn't spare Sam a glance.

"Sam," Christian was saying, "if you can spend the night in town why don't we have dinner together? Unless you've got other plans."

Sam glanced at his watch. It was nearly 1600. By the time he got to his plane out at Tan Son Nhut, changed clothing, and got cranked up, it would be nearly dark. Why the hell not? He could do with a good meal. And maybe even find an air-conditioned place to sleep! The thought was very appealing. "Sounds good," he said. "Do we meet someplace or what?"

"Let's see. I've got a little business to do yet, so why don't we meet at the rooftop bar at the Rex and go from there."

"What's the Rex?"

"Man, you *have* been living in the boonies all the time, haven't you?" laughed Christian. "It's one of the officer BOQs here in Saigon. It's where all the staff weenies sip their drinks and eat their steaks and watch the war being fought outside town. Only ranking staff officers get to live there but the bar and restaurant are open to all officers. Why don't we meet there for drinks at 1800? Just ask any cabdriver to take you; they all know where it is. It's right by Tu Do Street so you can do a little shopping if you want to. Just stay outta the bars. Those B-girls can spot a country bumpkin like you at a hundred meters. They'd have you cleaned out by dark. Any plans on where you'll be staying?"

"I'll figure out something," Sam said vaguely and waved good-bye.

Sam wandered out of the old French villa that served as headquarters for MACV, returning the salute of two sharply dressed American MPs on station behind a sandbagged guard post. Two Vietnamese MPs, identifiable by the large "QC" stenciled onto their lacquered helmet liners, ignored him from another position. Sam stared about him undecided as several small blue-and-white taxis zoomed by on the tree-shadowed street.

"If you want a cab, sir," one of the American military policemen said, "you'll have to go to the end of the block to catch one. They're not allowed to stop here. Might be carrying explosives. They know we've got orders to shoot if they even slow down too much."

Sam nodded his thanks and walked beneath the towering trees to the corner. The traffic was heavy, and blue exhaust smoke hung in the sodden air. Motor scooters and small cars fought for a place on the wide avenue, just missing the cyclo drivers pedaling their carriages with little apparent concern for the automotive mayhem. Sam flinched at an inevitable collision, but both Renaults missed locking fenders by inches as the drivers flicked their steering wheels at the last moment.

The bases of the big trees flanking the busy street were whitewashed and had been there for a long time, remnants of a softer colonial time. Sam stopped at the corner and looked into the traffic. Immediately, a tiny blue-and-white Renault broke away from the main body of traffic and launched itself at him. After it screeched to a stop, Sam leaned down and peered through the open side window. "Rex Hotel?" he asked hopefully. The driver nodded vigorously and motioned him inside.

Several blocks down the road Sam decided it would be better not to watch the traffic to their front because he was becoming increasingly nervous. The driver, not content with darting back and forth between smoke-belching buses and trucks with apparent complete disregard for their lives, also insisted on steering onto the sidewalk when the traffic got too heavy for full acceleration. Sam looked away, deciding there was probably little merit in dying all tensed up.

Instead, he watched the pedestrians, who at times seemed to move faster than the traffic, and the occupants of the roadside stalls. Most of the stalls had latticed heavy steel doors that could be pulled down when the shop was closed. Solid doors in this climate seemed unnecessary. Shacks were springing up in areas not occupied by other buildings and were walled by a bewildering mixture of materials, the most noticeable being flattened Budweiser beer cans. Most people wore either the traditional pajamas and conical hat or western clothing. Here and there, delicate Vietnamese women seemed to float above the ground in their traditional ao dais. Most carried tiny parasols as protection against the burning sun. There were more Americans in the crowd than Sam expected. Their exotic hair colors and height made them stand out from the smaller brown people. Most were in civilian garb, usually slacks and open-collared sport shirts, and their hairstyles indicated that not all of them were military.

The cab squealed to a halt in front of a European-style open-air restaurant that took up the first floor of a hotel. Sam looked out the window at it but didn't see the customary guard post. The Viet driver tugged at his shirt sleeve and pointed across the street to another multistory building that did have the normal contingent of MPs watching the traffic from behind their sandbags. Sam understood. The cabbies weren't allowed to stop in front of the American billet.

Sam took his folded wad of Vietnamese piasters from his pocket and looked inquiringly at the driver, who hurled a barrage of Vietnamese at him. Sam handed over some of the money and realized he'd made a mistake when the cabbie smiled with great satisfaction. It was too late to do anything about it so he crawled out, lugging his canvas tote bag. The cab roared away belching blue exhaust. Probably going out to buy a farm with what I gave him, Sam thought in disgust.

Sam walked past the MPs, who didn't salute but kept warily observing the speeding traffic. A steady stream of Americans moved in and out the front door. Some were in uniform, others were not. He walked into the lobby and waited at the large wooden counter until a petite Vietnamese woman acknowledged his presence.

"I'm supposed to have a room here for the night," Sam lied. She looked doubtfully at the gold major's oak leaves on his shirt collars. "Colonel Jackson Jones of the 2d Air Division assured me that I would have the room for one night," he insisted confidently.

The girl turned to an American in civilian clothing writing in a ledger at the far end of the counter. At her call, he looked up and scowled, then closed the book and walked to them. "What's the problem, Major?"

"No problem that I know of. I'm supposed to have a room here for the night."

It was the man's turn to look doubtful. "We normally accept only lieutenant colonels and higher," he said, trying to sound like the night manager of the Royal Hawaiian being confronted by a drunken sailor and his waterfront whore. He frowned at Sam's golden oak leaves as though they were a personal affront. "What's your name?"

"Brooks. Samuel Brooks. The director of operations, 2d Air Division, Colonel Jackson Jones, told me they'd get the room for me. You can call him if you want," Sam bluffed. "I've got his number here somewhere if you don't have it. I'm up here for a one-day conference with COMUSMACV and his staff." Sam fumbled in his pocket, searching for the nonexistent telephone number.

The man gave Sam the eye again before conceding defeat. He was not about to call a senior officer and be sworn at if this guy was telling the truth. Besides, it was no skin off his nose. "Check him in, Co Van."

Sam gave the man a gracious nod and signed the proffered register.

The room was on the third floor and, though quite large, showed the ravages of the tropics on man-made objects. Rust stains smeared the wall under the small, wheezing air conditioner and marred the large French-style tub, commode, and bidet. The tile floor showed the abuse of years of wear with minimum maintenance. The whitewashed walls were peeling badly. A stenciled sign over the sink proclaimed: "Water Is Potable." Sam was a little disappointed that one of his theories on the luxury that senior officers claimed was not always true. Why the hell would anybody fight to stay in this place?

He stowed his bag in the lock closet and took the key. Glancing at his watch he saw he still had more than an hour before meeting Christian on the roof. Turning toward the door he caught a glimpse of himself in the full-length wall mirror and was shocked at how much weight he'd lost. Never a heavy man, he now looked almost gaunt. He ran his thumb inside the waistband of his trousers and realized he'd lost at least two inches around his middle. Small wonder that he looked like a scarecrow in his uniform. Perhaps he could find a store and buy some slacks and a civilian shirt before he met Jim. Hell, he had nothing else to do.

The tailors found him. Tu Do Street teemed with them, mostly Indian, jostling for space with the new bars built for the fast-growing American trade. Sam was literally pulled into a small shop. A little dazzled and protesting only feebly, he allowed the turbaned owner to take his measurements. The Indian ignored his protestations that he would not be in town long enough for custom-sewn clothing. Sam suddenly found himself sitting in his underwear in a curtained cubicle clutching his wallet in one hand and a bottle of icy Vietnamese beer in the other. A manual sewing machine whirred on the other side of the curtain.

In little more than half an hour Sam was encased in a spanking new safari suit, his uniform wrapped in paper tucked beneath his arm. Sam paid the proprietor the small amount for the clothing and was asked quietly if he would like to have his American monies traded at approximately three times the official exchange rate. Sam declined, not from high ethical standards but because he was afraid he'd get counterfeit Vietnamese money in return. Illegal money exchanges were common, for no one was willing to give up their greenbacks at the ridiculous rate set by the government. The only people who did were naive Americans who had been in country for only a few hours.

Sam admired his reflection in a shop window. He figured he'd paid the equivalent of seven U.S. dollars for his new outfit. And it fit his lean frame well.

It was past 1700 and the Tu Do bars were coming to life. GIs laughed and joked with the Vietnamese bar girls lounging in the doorways. The girls dressed in what they probably considered sexy American fashion. Sam felt a stirring in his groin but had no stomach for one of the overpainted young Vietnamese. Perhaps if they'd retained their traditional dress instead of making themselves parodies of American film actresses, he would have felt differently.

Hawkers and small stall owners crowded the street selling watches, pens, flowers, cigarettes, and other items from the American post exchange. National policemen, the White Mice, patrolled in pairs, and a bewildering array of vehicular traffic clogged the wide avenue. Scores of motorbikes surged among the automobiles, most with Vietnamese girls perched demurely sidesaddle behind sunglassed drivers. The din was deafening to one accustomed to the bucolic silence of Bac Lieu province.

Sam was glad to reach the air-conditioned comfort of his room; noting that he still had a quarter hour before meeting Christian, he decided on a hurried bath. The temptation to lie back and soak was strong but he was running late. He quickly climbed into fresh underwear and his new short-sleeved safari suit and left the room.

The old elevator creaked to a stop at the rooftop restaurant and discharged its cargo of American officers and civilians. The officers, identifiable by their haircuts though they wore civilian clothing, made up the bulk of the customers.

Clear of the elevator crowd Sam saw a large inside dining room and a larger outside bar area where prodigious quantities of drinks were being served by Vietnamese bar waitresses. A double row of slot machines clanged along one wall of the bar; the table occupants had a majestic view of the surrounding countryside. A low wall with a rail circled the entire table area. A swimming pool and sun deck dominated an elevated portion of the rooftop away from the bar. To the south, Sam saw flare ships already dropping their high-candlepower bundles in the gathering dusk.

"Hey, mister! Buy a girl a drink?"

Sam turned and found himself facing Lee Roget and Jim Christian. His mouth drooped in surprise. "Lee! This is great . . . I mean, what are you doing here? I didn't expect . . ." Sam was more than a little shocked at how pleased he was to see her. His stomach roiled as if he'd just taken a double shot of straight scotch.

She patted his arm while her eyes searched through the crowd.

Apparently finding what she'd been seeking, she hooked her hand inside
Sam's elbow and urged him toward a just-vacated table by the low wall.
They beat out two air force lieutenant colonels. Lee smiled sweetly
at the pair's disappointment; they nodded graciously and headed back
to the mob at the bar. Sam's arm felt warm where her hand had rested
on his biceps. He stepped behind her as they maneuvered between two
tables of bird colonels. There was unabashed admiration in their eyes
as she passed. He couldn't blame them, for she was ravishing in the
lightweight summer dress and sandals. He watched her twist in front
of him, avoiding yet another table of oglers, and realized it was the
first time he'd ever seen her legs. She'd always been in jeans before.
The sight was worth the wait. Her legs were long and firmly muscled,
not the skinny kind that women seem to think men preferred.

They gave their drink orders to the smiling waitress, who seemed
unable to keep her eyes off Lee. It was as though she was memoriz-
ing everything about her. She could have a worse model, Sam thought.

"By the way, Sam, it's nice to see you too," Jim Christian said with
a grin.

Sam turned to him with a guilty start, realizing he'd hardly registered that the Special Forces captain was with them. A difficult feat
considering the man was at least six feet four and weighed in excess
of 225 pounds.

"Umm, sorry, Jim. Didn't mean to ignore you. It's just that your
sister-in-law looks so . . . so . . ."

"Yeah, I think so, too," he laughed.

Lee raised a thick eyebrow and looked at each of them in turn. "If
you're going to talk about the lady, please don't exclude her from your
conversation."

"Sorry," Sam stammered. "What are you doing in Saigon? Getting
another load of Bulgur wheat for the villagers to feed to their pigs?"

"Something like that. I had some paperwork to get completed up
here, and then when Jim told me he was coming up for this awards
ceremony, it seemed like a good time to get it out of the way and to
have dinner with my favorite brother-in-law." She gave Jim an arch
look before turning back to Sam. "He didn't say anything about you
being along, not that I'm not delighted to see you again. In any event,
it seemed like a good opportunity to get out of my dungarees for a
night and put on my girlie things. Also, I always feel safer if I have
his big ugly mug along when I go out at night. What person in their
right mind would attack *that*." Christian smirked.

"But," Lee continued, "I don't want to crimp your style if you've got other plans. It's only fair to warn you, though, that if they include going to any of those sleazy bars on Tu Do Street, I've got a certain obligation to keep this big goof out of them, for my sister's sake."

Christian laughed. "Sam, if you could see her sister you'd know why there's damned little chance of me heading into one of those 'sleazy bars,' as she calls 'em. I want to tell you, Mary, my wife, makes Lee look like a boy! No way I'm gonna screw that up."

Lee patted his arm and smiled with affection. "Thank you. I'm sure there was a compliment for someone, somewhere in that. I think."

The drinks arrived and they held their gin and tonics together in a silent toast. Sam noticed that Christian's eyes strayed to the country-side before they drank. He sipped his cold drink and turned his own eyes to look outside the city. It was completely dark now with that suddenness found in the tropics.

The flareships were working an active target now. Strings of five and six floated slowly to the ground before the aircraft started another run. Tracers arced from one place on the dark ground to be returned from another. Sam figured they were seven or eight miles outside the city lights. Red rotating beacons identified helicopter gunships that joined the panorama, weaving a tapestry of multihued threads as they wheeled and fired. Greenish tracers licked the sky around them, giving the scene a holiday atmosphere. But it was no holiday. Someone was fighting for his life.

Except for low, muted conversations, the rooftop had become silent. Officers pointed out new sources of fire to one another but mostly they stared at the accelerating firefight in the night. Sam looked at their faces. There was no one unaware of the incongruity of the situation. One group sat in comfort, sipping their cocktails before dinner, while another fought and bled only a few thousand yards away. They may be staff weenies, Sam thought, but they're still military men and they do care. His respect for them went up a notch.

Sam watched the flickering flares make shadows dance on Lee's face, accentuating the high cheekbones and firm chin. Feeling the scrutiny she turned to capture his gaze. The rooftop was dark and the flare light reflected in her eyes as they stared at each other. Sam could almost feel something tangible passing between them. She smiled, nothing more than a small upward tugging at the corner of her lips, but Sam knew she'd felt the sensation too. She turned her gaze to Jim Christian and Sam's eyes moved with hers. The big man was staring intently at the night battle, identifying with those combatants slugging away at each other. He shook his head as though coming out of a dream and turned to them.

"Let's finish these and grab some chow," he said. "I know a little restaurant a few blocks off Le Loi Avenue that has never even *heard* of rice and *nuoc mam* sauce. They think noodles are something that ought to be used only as a bed for beef burgundy. Good wine, good bread, and some great, smelly, imported cheeses."

Sam was ready; his stomach had been complaining aloud for some time and had been hidden only by the blare of the jukebox and jangle of the slot machines. They drained their glasses and made for the exit, Lee clutching both of their arms tightly.

There were only ten tables in the small, dark restaurant and the elderly French maitre d' guided them to one of two not occupied. Candles provided the only illumination, and a Piaf song warbled softly from unseen speakers. The place could have been plucked intact from the Left Bank. Christian insisted on playing host, ordering for them: a green salad, onion soup, chateaubriand for three with fried potatoes, and two bottles of dry Algerian red wine. Their waiter, an elderly Vietnamese accustomed to American habits, brought their salads first.

Sam looked doubtfully at the crisp greens. "Is this stuff safe to eat? I mean, everybody says that we ought to stay away from vegetables unless they're from approved places."

Christian chuckled. "You can't tell me that after swallowing fourteen pounds of U Minh mud and damned near that many mosquitoes and other varmints that you're really concerned about this lettuce. Just try not to listen to the shrieks of the tortured caterpillars when you chew."

"Ugh!" said Lee. "Do you mind?"

"By the way," said Christian around a mouthful of salad, "did you have any problem getting a room? Or are you going on out to Tan Son Nhut tonight?"

"Naw, I got a room at the Rex."

Christian looked at him in astonishment. "How the hell did you do that?"

"Lied. Told 'em that 2d AD wanted me there for the night so I could attend a meeting with COMUSMACV. They bought it."

"Man, too bad you're in the junior service. You're a natural for the Forces."

The beef was tender and cooked to pink perfection. Sam dabbed a crusty piece of French bread onto the juices that remained on his plate, shoved it in his mouth, and reached for the wine bottle to top their glasses. It was their fourth bottle of a surprisingly good Algerian red. Lee gave a quiet, ladylike burp behind her fingers. Jim sat back in his chair and watched them finish. He'd gone through his meal quickly and efficiently. He put a morsel of cheese and apple into his mouth and sipped the rich coffee, smiling contentedly.

"You know," he said, "you two don't look too bad together." Lee and Sam looked at him in surprise, then at each other, then back to Christian.

"For Christ's sake," he said, noting their looks, "can't you take a joke? I'm not trying to announce your engagement or anything."

Lee smiled at him with deceptive sweetness and asked in a honeyed voice: "Jim, darling, didn't I tell you that if you tried to fix me up with any more of your crazed friends I would drop-kick you right in the . . . well, let's just say someplace that wouldn't make my sister happy?"

"Yeah," Jim said earnestly, "but those were all Forces people. Sam here is in the air force. I mean, it's not like they were in the real military. They're more like technicians. Pilots, you know. Computers. Stuff like that."

"Yes, I know," Lee said, the sweet smile becoming a bit strained, "wading around the U Minh Forest with you, flying through trees. Just a regular businessman."

Sam was taken aback that she knew he had been on the raid with Christian. He hadn't mentioned it, although the fresh scars on his face and arms were ample evidence that he had been doing something other than flying airplanes.

"Flying through what trees?" Christian wanted to know.

"Never mind what trees," Lee said, her voice turning a little brittle. "I know you want me to be happily married again, Jim. I want it too. Every happily married couple I know wants the same thing for me. I appreciate it but I am not going to jump into it just to make everyone happy. So please! Stop trying to shove me off on everyone you know."

Jim turned to Sam. "Did you really fly through a tree?" Sam shrugged and gave a brief nod. "Why did you do that?"

Sam shrugged again. Lee answered for him. "Why, to win a glass of beer. Doesn't that make perfect sense?"

"Really?" Jim beamed at him. "That's great!" He turned to Lee. "Honey, you'd better grab this one. I think he's gonna be a real winner. Imagine

that! Flying through a tree to win a glass of beer. Man, I knew you
came from good stock when you wouldn't put that old lieutenant down
out there in the U Minh." He chuckled. "Flew through a tree to win
a glass of beer. All right."

Lee made a small snorting noise and looked as if she was ready to
start hooking punches.

"Why don't we all head back to the Rex and have a nightcap?" Sam
asked, trying to defuse a potential family fight.

The air show was still going on: Jet fighters had joined the helicopter gunships and the flare bird, and large orange-red flashes lit the
sky before the spectators would hear the dull crump of the exploding
bombs. A silent crowd lined the rail of the rooftop bar and watched
as the defenders of some outpost fought to see another morning. Noise
interrupted the silence as two tables of older men who were drinking
heavily began to laugh. Their ages and hairstyles indicated that they
were not in the military service and they were too boisterous and crude
to be state or any other governmental agency. Sam turned to stare at
them as another loud burst of rowdy laughter filled the silence. Jim
glanced their way and turned to Sam in disgust.

"Those are RMK-BRJ construction people. It's a big conglomerate
that builds most of the bases and airfields in the country. Those guys
have never made so much money in their lives. Some of 'em have been
here for years and won't ever go back to the States if they can help
it. They've never had it so good. Mostly, they're drunks or dopers and
wouldn't even be able to get a job at home, but over here they're king
shits. All the booze and women that money can buy, and their company insists they be given honorary officer status while they're here.
Royal pains in the ass."

A large crumping noise brought their attention back to the distant
firefight. A spectacular explosion lighted the night sky. "Somebody
sure got something that time," Jim muttered. "Wonder whose side it
was on." He turned to Lee, who had been very silent since their return to the Rex. "Listen, babe. I'm sorry I got out of line before. You
know that Mary and I only want what's best for you. We're happy so
we want you to be happy, that's all. Now, I gotta move 'cause I've
got an early-morning flight back to the delta. You want me to walk
you back to the Caravelle?"

Lee was quiet in the shadows for a moment. "No, that's all right.

I'm sure that Sam is trustworthy enough to get me back to the hotel. I'm sorry I jumped down your throat. Guess I'm just getting a little overly sensitive about everything. Give Mary my love when you write her tonight." She rose on tiptoe to kiss his cheek, then wrapped her arms around him and squeezed tightly.

"You bet I will. Take care of yourself." He turned to Sam and thrust out a big hand. "Take care, partner. I enjoyed it. Drop in at camp sometime."

Sam shook his hand and smiled. He saw Lee's eyes glistening in the flare light. She grabbed Christian's arm and hugged it.

"You just take care of yourself," she said as he turned to leave. "Seriously, I don't think I could stand it if anything happened to you too." She laughed. "Anyway, Mary would kill me if I came home without you."

"You got it, sweetheart." He clapped Sam on the shoulder. "You remember not to fly any higher than you're willing to fall."

Christian turned and walked briskly away. Sam heard him chuckle and mumble something about flying through a damned tree. They turned back to stare at the distant flares. The fire from the large blast had subsided to a dull glow masked by the smoke hanging in the air. Lee shivered, though it had to be at least eighty-five degrees and humid.

"Cold?" he asked.

She shook her head. "Felt like a rabbit ran over my grave, as Gramps used to say." They watched the fire silently for a long time. The shooting appeared to have stopped.

"Did you ever decide?" he asked finally.

"Decide what?"

"Whether you wanted to see more or less of me." He reminded her of their last conversation in her Can Tho quarters.

Lee turned to stare at him, eyes wide and dark, then took his hand. "God help both of us, Sam Brooks."

The first light of dawn filtered through the filmy gauze curtains, not yet reaching their corner of the room. Sam lay in a half-sleep, one hand resting on Lee's satiny flank. Without thought his hand began to caress the warm skin in sensuous circles. He felt her stir, arching her bare back toward him, responding to his touch even in her sleep. Sam's dream state evaporated as he felt the awakening in his loins yet again.

He turned slightly until he was pressing spoon fashion against her back, his legs tucked beneath her bottom. She moved slowly against him and he draped an arm over her side until his left hand could reach her breast. His fingers traced its full outline, gently rubbing the erect nipple. He knew she was awake when he felt her shiver and her own hand cup his over the fullness before trailing back over her body in search of him. He pressed more tightly to her curved buttocks. Her fingers closed gently around his swelling organ and began a caressing motion that soon had him in full erection.

Lee opened her legs slightly and Sam moved forward between them until he was completely buried within her. He kissed her neck and felt her breath become ragged as she moved with him. It lasted longer this time and, because there was no urgency, it was better. He felt her shudder just before his own climax blotted everything else from his mind. He took a deep breath and rolled onto his back while Lee turned to face him. They lay in comfortable silence for a time. The room was getting lighter and the traffic sounds were more blatant outside the window.

"My God," he murmured, "I don't think I'm going to be able to walk."

Lee stroked his cheek. "That's what I like. You know exactly the sweet little things a girl likes to hear after she's given herself to you. Submitted to your horrible male desires and—"

"If I remember correctly," he interrupted, "there was more than just a little giving by the lady. There was some taking and grabbing by all parties involved."

"Only a complete beast would remind a lady of that," she said, smiling contentedly and snuggling into the hollow of his arm. Her fingers idly twisted the hair on his chest into ringlets. Suddenly, the fingers gave a sharp tug and she leaned up on an elbow to stare at him.

"Ow! What the hell was that for?"

"This didn't mean anything, you know."

"I know," he said, with a satisfied grin, eyes closed.

"I'm not trying to trap you into anything. This was just a . . . ," she cast about for the right words, "crazy fling. It doesn't mean a thing."

"I know," he said. His eyes were still closed and he continued to smile.

"This was just like . . . two ships passing in the night. Like a catharsis or a healing of sorts. Just two friends who were able to give comfort to each other in unusual circumstances."

Sam opened one eye to peer at her. "A catharsis?"

"You know what I mean," she said and pulled another handful of hair.

"Ow! Listen, I agree with you, OK? It didn't mean a thing to me either."

"Don't you dare say that, Sam Brooks! Last night was wonderful!" She looked at him with an arched eyebrow. "I just wonder if you're capable of being housebroken."

Sam lay back and closed his eyes again, a large smile on his face.

Sam leaned against the fuselage of his aircraft and scowled at the runway. Tanks had taken up positions along its center stripe about a hundred yards apart for its entire length. South Vietnamese flags flew from their whip antennas. A company of Vietnamese soldiers stared impassively at him from where they ringed the Tan Son Nhut terminal and transient aircraft parking area. A roar caused Sam to look up at one of the four circling Vietnamese A-1 Skyraiders as it began a low pass down the runway, barely missing the tanks' antennas. He watched the aircraft recover and rejoin its flight in their oval circuit of the airport. Another peeled from the formation and repeated the dive. What new kind of mischief had the Vietnamese decided to lay on him?

Sam had arrived at the airport still basking in the glow of his night with Lee. He found the base under a virtual siege. American military police no longer manned the gates; only the Vietnamese MPs with the familiar QC on their helmet liners were visible. More disturbing were the pair of tanks parked on either side of the entrance, their long cannons aiming down the avenue leading to the base. It was only after Sam was out of the taxi that he had noticed the Vietnamese soldiers deployed in fighting holes alongside the high wire fence surrounding the base proper.

Sam had been hesitant, but was admitted with only the usual impassivity shown by the Vietnamese. He carried his bag warily inside the wire and quickly noticed the complete absence of all U.S. military personnel. The place was normally teeming with them. Now, there were not even cars and trucks on the road inside the base perimeter. What the hell was going on? He trudged the mile to the flight-line terminal.

Sam watched the A-1 recover and, realizing he wasn't getting anywhere, he walked to the transient terminal and rattled the door again. It was still locked. He could think of only one other place that might be able to shed some light on the situation. He slung his shotgun over his shoulder, picked up his canvas tote bag, and began the walk back toward the 2d Air Division headquarters building. It was most of the way back to the gate. Another A-1 made a low pass down the runway, and Sam noticed that the machine guns on the tanks had begun to track the aircraft.

The big wooden building appeared to be occupied because there were lights in some of the windows, but the absence of normal traffic still made Sam feel uneasy. He went up the steps and pushed his way into the gloomy hallway. He found the stairs he'd climbed his first day in country and went up searching for signs of life.

At the same desk he found the same lieutenant he'd talked to on the day he arrived in Vietnam. The young man's feet were propped on the desk while he leaned back in his swivel chair and read the *Stars and Stripes*. He sipped from a steaming cup of coffee, unaware of Sam's approach.

"I could use a cup of that if you could spare it." Sam looked around as he spoke. Other than the lieutenant and himself there were only two others present in the big room, both sergeants.

The lieutenant looked up from his paper and swung his feet to the floor. A look of recognition creased his face into a grin as he looked at Sam. "Ah, Major . . . Brooks, I believe. Former fighter pilot and now forward air controller extraordinary. Good to see you again, Major. Saw some good-looking paperwork cross my desk a week or so ago. It was the PACAF endorsement for your Silver Star. Fastest I've ever seen it done. They usually sit on it for weeks, but I suppose when old COMUSMACV himself adds a personal handwritten note to expedite something, then it gets expedited. What brings you to Disneyland East?"

Sam accepted the coffee and sipped before answering. "They had the awards ceremony over at MACV headquarters yesterday and now I'm trying to get back to Bac Lieu. Only there's some ten-ton Tinkertoys keeping me from taking off. What the hell's going on and where are all the round eyes hiding?"

"Ah, there's always that ten percent who don't get the word. Presumably, living way down there in the delta, that word might be a trifle slow to filter through, so I will fill you in. We have what our intelligence folks like to call the beginning of the Coup Season. Since General Khanh decided to dispose of General 'Big' Minh earlier this year, who had incidentally just helped some other generals dispose of President Diem, the politics of our host nation have become, ah, shall we say a bit unsettled. As of this moment we're not really sure of the lineup and who's counting coup on whom; at least I don't have any idea, though presumably someone does. The only thing we're sure of is that the ARVN Airborne Division has occupied the base and General Ky's VNAF is opposing them. So far, no one has been shot, and eventually it'll all probably be settled with a golden handshake. One side or the other will get the payoff and get to be in charge, and the losers will be transferred to I Corps, as far away from Saigon as possible. In the meantime, COMUSMACV has ordered all American personnel off the streets and into their quarters until it's settled. I'm surprised you didn't get the word in your billet."

He looked curiously at Sam. Sam drank his coffee, not wanting to explore with the lieutenant where he had spent last night.

"Anyway," the lieutenant continued, disappointed that Sam wasn't going to be more forthcoming about his nocturnal habits, "me and my two trusty sergeants are the duty element for 2d Air Division and as such are prepared to stand in the way of any bullets fired by either side at our young American boys. It's a terrible responsibility for one so young, but I'm prepared to make any sacrifice. Want a refill?"

The master sergeant passing them on the way to the coffeepot snorted and muttered: "Bullshit!" He took Sam's cup, filled it, and handed it back.

"Do these rules about staying holed up apply everywhere or just here in Saigon?" Sam inquired of the lieutenant.

"Beats me. Probably the entire country, since I don't think anyone has the complete lineup of all the units and which are playing on whose team."

Sam drank his coffee and drummed his fingers on the desk. Perhaps he'd have a chance for more time with Lee if he could figure out how to get back downtown without being caught. A few more days in Saigon with her was certainly an appealing thought. If all American activities were curtailed at Bac Lieu, there wasn't a hell of a lot he could do down there. The more he thought about it the more he liked the idea of staying over. Hell! Maybe this thing would last a week or more!

His chain of thought was broken as the lieutenant leapt to his feet. Oh, shit! Colonel Jackson Jones was striding across the room toward them. Sam rose slowly and faced the director of operations.

The man's cold stare fixed on Sam and didn't waver even after he stopped three paces away. "What the hell are you doing here?" he demanded in greeting. "Who told you to stay in Saigon last night?"

"It was too late to get to Bac Lieu before dark," Sam said flatly.

"Are our FACs afraid to fly at night now?"

Sam ground his teeth and tried to wait, lest his temper get him into trouble again. It slipped out anyway. "I'd be glad to have you in the backseat anytime you'd care for a little night flying, Colonel."

Jackson stared at him for another moment before saying: "Get into my office." He turned his cold eyes to the lieutenant. "I'm sure you could be doing something more productive than bullshitting with transients and reading the paper, right?"

The lieutenant decided there was and scurried for a file cabinet. The two sergeants, Sam noticed, had become very occupied with their own work. He turned to follow Colonel Jones, who made immediately for his office. Inside, there were few excess words.

"Why did you not fly to Bac Lieu last night?"

"Because, sir, I would have arrived after dark and there's no runway lighting or even any way to find the airstrip."

"What happens if we have an emergency and need a FAC up at night down there?"

"Then we'll launch and try to recover where they do have runway lighting. If not, I suppose we'll crash."

Colonel Jones stared at him for a long moment. "Did you know about the general curfew on American personnel?"

"No, sir."

"You do now. Report to the transient officers' quarters and stay there except for meals. As soon as the restriction is removed I want you off this base within half an hour. Do you understand?"

"Yes, sir."

"You're dismissed."

Sam raised a languid hand to the lieutenant now frantically pushing papers around his desk, and received a wary wave in return. He thought of the hot, noisy, crowded, open-bay barracks awaiting him and then of the cool room in the Rex Hotel with Lee curled up on the wide bed. He sighed deeply and went down the stairs.

CHAPTER 9

"OK, Blade Flight, this is Blackjack One One. I'll want your bombs in pairs. We're going to spread 'em on both sides of the LZ. I'm in for the mark now."

Sam brought the nose of his aircraft high above the horizon and stared at the wooded tree lines stretching along both sides of the bare red earth that would shortly receive the helicopters. The trees were a dull green, muted by the dust at the end of the dry season. He picked his spot and coordinated left aileron and rudder pressure to roll the aircraft onto its wing, then shoved the nose down toward the ground.

The tree line quickly filled his windscreen and he risked a quick glance at the altimeter—eighteen hundred feet. He let the speed build up until the slipstream whistled loudly through the opened window. He pressed the firing button on the stick at fifteen hundred feet and heard, then saw, the rocket leave the wing, trailing a thin wisp of smoke from the ignited motor. At twelve hundred feet he began the dive recovery, ending with the aircraft in a hard, climbing turn. Sam glanced over his shoulder to find the white smoke ball billowing up from the trees. "There's your first target, Blade Lead. Hit my smoke."

"Roger, Lead is in from the north, FAC and target in sight. I'll be off target to the east."

Sam twisted his aircraft into a tight, level turn until he saw the sun glinting from the wings of the diving F-100 jet fighter-bomber. He quickly checked its run-in line, staying in the turn to keep the fighter on his nose. "You're cleared in hot, Blade Lead," Sam said.

The two five-hundred-pound bombs fell cleanly from the wings of the attacking jet as it passed Sam. Twin condensation trails burbled from each wing tip as the fighter began its pullout. The bombs, with drogue slabs extended to slow their flight, disappeared into the tree line, and near-simultaneous explosions cleared twin circular areas in the forest. The instantaneous fusing had caused the weapons to leave only shallow craters, but they did create havoc with the foliage.

"Lead's off to the east," the pilot grunted, fighting hard against the heavy g forces of the pullout.

"Good bombs, Lead," said Sam, already switching his attention to the other aircraft. "Blade Two, put yours about a hundred meters south of Lead's craters."

"Rog. Blade Two is in hot from the west. FAC and target in sight."

Sam eyed the roll-in of the sleek jet before he responded. "You're cleared in hot, Blade Two."

Two more explosions killed another hundred years of tree growth. Sam had shoved the nose of the Bird Dog down toward the smoldering jungle before Blade Two began his recovery. He leveled at five hundred feet, alternately kicking the rudders and moving the stick back and forth to prevent becoming a stable target for any potential gunners as he searched for movement beneath the trees. He didn't see a thing. He shoved the throttle full forward to begin a maximum climb back to a safer altitude. Just because he didn't see them didn't mean they weren't there.

Methodically, he worked the ordnance of the fighters along the dense growth surrounding the landing zone. Blade Flight was the second set of attack aircraft he'd used prepping the area for the helicopter assault, now already airborne. Smoke from the bombs and dust were beginning to obscure the clearing. Sam was satisfied with the bomb pattern he had laid around the LZ. He glanced at each wing to confirm he'd used all four of his marking rockets to put in the two flights of fighters, then lowered the aircraft's nose for a last assessment run.

The trees had been tumbled aside like giant matchsticks and he saw nothing moving among them. The area was far from pristine, however. The last pair of bombs had uncovered several irregularly spaced rectangular holes that he instantly recognized as reinforced bunkers. Sam hadn't a clue as to whether they were or had been occupied, for he could see no casualties. It was something for the helicopter gunships to check out before the main force went in.

"Blade Lead, this is Blackjack One One. Your BDA will have to be incomplete until we get some troops on the ground, but I'm going to give you a hundred percent of your ordnance in the target area. Looks like Blade Two uncovered some bunkers with his last bombs. I'll forward anything the crunchies turn up. You're cleared out of the area. See ya later."

"Roger, Blackjack. Thanks, and take care of yourself. Blade Two, let's go to company frequency."

"Two. Rog."

As soon as the two F-100s left Sam's radio frequency he heard another pilot calling him. This voice had the curious, vibrating quality readily identifiable as coming from a helicopter. "Blackjack One One," it warbled, "this is Red Lead."

"Go, Red Lead. Blackjack One One here."

"Rog. First stick is about five minutes out. What's the situation?"

"Red Lead, Blackjack. I've put in two sets of fighters along either side of the LZ. Negative movement seen. However, the last bombs uncovered bunkers on the eastern approach to the LZ. I can see five of them but they extend back under the trees. There's no confirmation as to whether they're occupied. You might want to send your gunnies on ahead to check 'em out before you come in."

"Roger that, Blackjack. That's what we'll do. Pink Lead, you want to take your gun elements on in and do like the man says while we do a slow three-sixty turn out here?"

"Roger that," a new voice said over the radio. "Let's go, Pinks."

Sam picked up the flight of four gunships as they approached from the south, then slammed into a tight turn in front of them and aimed for the bunker area. He'd been watching the bunkers from altitude and had almost convinced himself that they were old and no longer used. He descended to five hundred feet and flew directly at the bunkers visible in the blast-cleared area. He reached behind him and unhooked a smoke grenade from the wire behind his seat, pulling the pin but keeping the tongue depressed. When he was in the proper position, he straightened his arm out the window and released it. Leaning outside he watched the purple smoke trail to the ground and land squarely on the target area. "Pink Lead, this is Blackjack. Smoke's away."

"Rog. Pink Lead has Goofy Grape."

"That's it."

"We're on our way toward it."

Sam climbed up to two thousand feet to be sure he was out of everyone's way. The four gunships fell into a line astern, split into two elements as they approached the smoke, then began a counterclockwise wheel above the exposed bunkers. The leader dipped his nose and unleashed a high-explosive rocket toward the bunkers. There was no return fire or movement.

"Red Lead, this is Pink Lead," the gunship leader called the troop-carrying slicks' commander. "We've found the bunkers but it looks like nobody's home. I think it ought to be OK to bring 'em on in."

"Red Lead. Roger that."

Sam sat high and watched the first stick of slicks approach the barren LZ. They carried the elements of two companies of the 45th Ranger Battalion, one of the better fighting forces in the delta. Another stick of Hueys would be a couple of minutes behind the leader. A third would follow the second element. After they disgorged their initial loads, the birds would return to Soc Trang for the remainder of the troops. Things looked routine to Sam as the first stick approached the LZ. He opened his canteen and took a long drink of tepid water, shuddering at its chemical afterbite, then rescrewed the top and placed the canteen on the floor. Slightly bored now that his part in the operation was presumably completed, he rested his chin in his hand, arm propped on the window's ledge, and watched the show.

The four helicopters began to slow for their approach. A germ of uneasiness crept into Sam's mind as the leader disappeared into a red dust cloud kicked up by its own rotor. With true formation integrity the remainder of the slick flight followed their leader into the red murk.

"Red Flight, this is Red Lead! Abort! Abort! I'm instruments in the dust! Go around! Go arou—" His transmission was cut abruptly as the second Huey crashed down through his canopy, its skid breaking the air commander's neck and nearly severing the copilot's head from his body. Vietnamese Rangers tumbled from the opened doors, falling to their deaths beneath the flailing metal carcasses of the helicopters. Red Three and Four added to the carnage when they delayed an instant too long in responding to their flight commander's order to abort the landing. They unknowingly revenged his death by slamming unseen into Red Two. Sam watched in horrified silence as shards of blade, metal, and human body parts were tossed high above the red dust. He pressed the transmit button for the radio but found he couldn't speak, so he released it.

"Jesus Christ! Green and Purple Leaders, this is Pink Lead. Abort! I say again! Abort the approach!"

The next two sticks of troop carriers had arrived over the LZ but now broke away to circle aimlessly, their landing aborted by the gunship commander.

As the dust slowly cleared, the pattern of events became sickeningly clear. Red Two had landed squarely atop his leader's ship, and Three and Four had smashed onto it in turn. Two of the helicopters burned brightly, and Rangers were scattered about in the red dust as if sown by a giant hand. Some scrubbed angel wings into the loose dust; others lay very still.

The gunship commander took control. "Green Leader and Purple Leader, this is Pink Lead. All of Red Flight has dinged on the LZ, but I think it was because of the viz and not because the LZ's hot. Come on in but stay well clear of the center where Red Flight is down. It's a damned dust bowl there. You should be all right if Green takes the far right side and Purple the left. I say again, it's a cold LZ and Green Flight takes the extreme right, Purple the left."

The two sticks of helicopters touched down almost simultaneously at opposite sides of the wide LZ. The dust was still thick but nothing like Red Flight had tried to penetrate. The pilots gave each other more help by separating their individual touchdown points by a considerable distance. As they disgorged their troops another voice began to yell over the tactical net.

"Pink Lead! Pink Lead! This is Jolly Six! We're taking fire from the bunkers east of the LZ, back up into the tree line. We're taking fire from the bunkers to the east of the LZ."

"Jolly Six, Pink Lead. I heard you the first time" came the voice of the gunship leader. He sounded as though there could be few surprises left for him anywhere. A routine insertion had turned into tragedy right in front of him, and now this.

"Where's the heaviest source of fire, Jolly Six?" the gun team leader asked the American adviser on the ground with the Rangers.

"All along the eastern tree line, well back into the trees. There's also some from the northeast that's pretty heavy as well."

"I've got you, Jolly Six. Pinks, we're going to work out in the eastern tree line, starting where those bunkers are. Ah, Blackjack, do you think you could scare up some more TACAIR if we need it?"

"Rog, Pink Lead. I'll get some cranking," said Sam, watching the horror show unfold beneath him. Some of the small figures flung about by the helicopters' crash had gotten to their feet and were wandering aimlessly in circles; then they began to fall over again. Then Sam saw the bright sparkle of automatic weapons beneath the gloom of the tree line. The addled and injured ARVN Rangers were an easy target.

Sam switched his radio selector to his control room and placed an immediate request for additional fighters. He should be able to draw on the air assets of any preplanned strike in the delta, if the system operated properly. Should no fighters be immediately available, the Direct Air Support Center would forward the request to the Tactical Operations Center in Saigon, which would authorize birds from the alert pads at Tan Son Nhut and Bien Hoa. Unfortunately, that could take half an hour, and Sam didn't think the friendlies had that long. More and more of them were playing dead.

The helicopter gunships went right for the Viet Cong's throat and paid for it. Pink Two went in for the attack; it burst into a large ball of orange flame and fell into the trees, severing large branches all the way to the ground. The remnant burned for a while, then exploded, sending a greasy plume of black smoke drifting over the tree line, obscuring the target area for the remaining gunships. Where *had* all those dinks come from? Sam wondered.

"Blackjack One One, this is Blackjack Control."

"Go ahead."

"Roger. You've got a pair of A-1s coming up. ETA in zero five. Load is snake and nape."

"Thank you," said Sam. Nape was napalm, the soapy gaseous mixture that ignited on contact with the ground to spew along the flight direction of the aircraft, searing everything in its path. It also deprived any air breathers in its vicinity of oxygen. Bombs and nape were a lethal mixture.

"Control, this is One One. What's their call sign?"

"One One, call sign of the A-1 flight is Ramrod."

Sam stayed at altitude above the carnage and watched the three remaining gunships attack the tree line. Green tracer fire from the trees met each pass. The enemy troops had obviously rushed forward after the last of the bomb explosions to engage the infantry and helicopters they'd known would be coming. It was not the first LZ prep that this VC commander had seen. He obviously knew the pattern well, and Sam was forced to admire his ingenuity. The man had kept his troops well back until the most significant danger had passed, then pressed in close to his adversary for protection against air and artillery attacks while he inflicted maximum damage. Sam suspected that the enemy commander was prepared for a quick disengagement as well. He'd have to remember that when the fighters arrived.

Another gunship limped out of the fight to the south, a victim of the concentrated fire they were receiving on each pass. The fourth and last stick of troop-carrying slicks approached the LZ as far to the west as they could get from the ground fire. The door gunners raked the trees, their red tracers licking into the gloom in search of the enemy gunners.

Doubt was creeping unbidden into Sam's thoughts. Could he have prevented this? Should he have placed the bombs differently? He shook his head to clear his thoughts. No, he'd done it right. He'd put the ordnance where logic said to put it and if he'd missed the enemy it had been because they'd been lucky or better at this business than he.

The Rangers scrambled into a defensive perimeter around the mangled remains of Red Flight. The fire had spread to all of the broken helicopters and the troops worked hurriedly to pull the bodies from them. The two remaining gunships were still doggedly making firing passes against the tree line. Sam hoped the gunship leader was still there. He had to quickly find the most productive area in which to expend the approaching fighters.

"Pink Lead, this is Blackjack. I've got a pair of A-1s inbound. ETA in about two. Can you use them?"

"Hell, yes! We're getting the shit shot out of us. If you see where we're working, you can put them in anyplace in the trees. I don't know what we've got ahold of, but it sure ain't no VC local force platoon, like they briefed. You'd best tell your Spad drivers that there's a pair of fifties down there that are real good."

"Rog. I'll do that."

Sam continued a slow orbit over the fight. The Rangers were having a difficult time moving off the LZ toward the trees. A small group leapt to their feet and charged the wood line only to lose half their number to the withering fire. The survivors flopped prone and began inching back to the comparative safety of the defensive perimeter. Sam was concentrating so intently on the carnage below that he was startled when a new voice cut into the radio.

"Blackjack One One, this is Ramrod Lead. How do you read?"

Sam switched to his UHF radio. "Ramrod Lead, this is Blackjack One One. I've got you five by five. We don't have a lot of time for briefing so listen up. The situation is this: We've got friendlies pinned on an LZ. They're taking heavy fire from the trees to their east and northeast. There are five choppers down and one other has been shot out of the fight. There are at least two .50 calibers and numerous automatic weapons in the area. You'll have to make your run-in along a north-south line to keep from overflying the friendlies. You'll need an east break-off target. Elevation here is about fifty feet and the best bail-out area is as far to the west of the LZ as you can get. Go ahead with your lineup and your ETA."

"Sounds absolutely charming. OK, Ramrod is a flight of two A-1s. We're wall-to-wall with Mark-82s and a full load of .50s. If you're working where all that smoke is off our nose we ought to be with you in a couple of minutes. We're coming in from the east at five thou."

"I'm sure that's us. We're the only smoke in the area," said Sam, trying to match the languorous tones of the Spad pilot. "Incidentally, I'm out of marking rockets so we'll have to do with smoke grenades. Stand by one and I'll get the gunships cleared off."

Without waiting for a reply he quickly switched back to his VHF radio. "Pink Lead, Blackjack. If you folks can clear to the west and stay below a thousand feet I'm about ready to bring the A-1s in and go to work."

"Roger that. Pink Flight, if any of you are still left out there, let's clear to the west at five hundred feet. Get some, Blackjack!"

Sam was already switching back to the fighter frequency as he watched the remaining gunnies wheel abruptly away from the tree line and head west. He peered through the dust and rising smoke and picked up the blocky frames of the approaching A-1 flight. They looked to be a couple of thousand feet higher than his orbit. "Ramrod, this is Blackjack. Got you in sight. I should be at your two o'clock low."

The lead aircraft tilted up on one wing. "Got you, Blackjack. Is the target that big batch of woods east of where the choppers are burning?"

"Affirm. I'm heading that way now. I've got all sorts of colored smoke in here so don't be surprised if it changes on you."

"Roger. Two, let's arm 'em up and take position."

"Two. Roger."

Sam turned until he was east of the tree line, well back over the heavily forested area, figuring that there would be less opportunity for a gunner to track him through the thick foliage. He shoved the throttle forward to the stop and dropped the Bird Dog's nose below the horizon. All 213 horses of the Continental engine screamed in protest at such ham-handed treatment. He watched the airspeed indicator nudge the red line—115 miles per hour! Jesus! This was ridiculous! He'd had automobiles that could go faster than this.

He leveled at a thousand feet and reached behind the seat, groping for a smoke grenade. He picked one from the cluster. There was the clash of metal against metal as something struck the fuselage hard. He forced his eyes toward the trees and saw that he was almost to the bunker complex. He pulled the pin from the grenade, keeping the handle depressed. He altered course slightly, waited, and finally threw the grenade toward the ground. Simultaneously, he tromped heavily on the rudder, shoved the stick to the side to stand the Bird Dog on its wing, then sucked back hard on the stick. The aircraft responded with an unbelievably quick change in direction before the excessive forces caused the air flowing over the top of the wings to burble and the wings stalled. The aircraft pitched down nearly three hundred feet before Sam could release enough back pressure on the stick to let it regain flying speed.

Once out of the immediate danger area he climbed back to his perch at fifteen hundred feet and looked at the red smoke just beginning to boil through the tree canopy. "OK, Ramrod. That's your first target. Lead, hit my smoke."

"Rog. Hit the smoke. Lead is in hot from the north. FAC and target in sight."

Sam eyeballed the lead attack ship's run-in line before he spoke. "Cleared hot, Lead."

The Skyraider rolled nearly inverted, then plummeted toward the ground in a sixty-degree dive angle. Its speed brakes jutted into the wind to prevent excess speed from building during the dive. Sam imagined that he could hear the roar of the big radial engine as it wound up tightly. Two shapes fell from the wings and sped toward the jungle as the A-1 pulled agonizingly into its recovery. Streams of tracers followed as its nose slowly crept above the horizon.

"Lead's off east," the pilot grunted.

"Ramrod Two is in from the south. FAC and target in sight. Where do you want it, Blackjack?"

The southern accent told Sam that this was also an American pilot. Unusual. Normally there would be only one to a flight. "Put yours about thirty long on Lead's smoke."

"Rog. Thirty long."

"Cleared hot, Two."

Sam watched the new explosions with a critical eye. He'd requested them to be dropped thirty meters north of the lead ship's craters; they were. "Good bombs, Ramrod Flight. I'll re-mark and we'll do it some more. How are you two fixed on fuel?"

"Enough to take out homestead papers," Ramrod Lead said laconically.

Sam shoved the power up again and aimed toward the LZ, hoping that it was the last time he need mark for the flight. He steered toward an unsullied section of the woods and reached for another grenade. Resting his left elbow on the window ledge, forearm sticking into the slipstream, he waited to drop the grenade.

Sam never saw the .50-caliber stream of high-explosive shells. The little aircraft never had a chance. Sam watched with stunned eyes as the engine disintegrated, chewed apart by the shells. Before he had fully comprehended his situation, the aircraft was thrown on its side and engine components began to rain back through the Plexiglas of the windscreen. Several smaller metal pieces grooved Sam's face on their way to their final resting place in the rear cockpit bulkhead. Something large and solid caromed across the top of his helmet, momentarily dazing him. A smaller piece cracked the sun visor of his helmet, breaking off the bottom half over his left eye and cracking the remainder so badly that it was useless. He slowly became aware that he was taking deep rasping breaths, but doing nothing. He pulled his head up with a jerk as he gained rational thought. Sight was impossible through the mutilated sun visor, so he viciously slammed it up with the heel of his hand.

Odd. He still couldn't see. His immediate fear was that his eyes were injured, for a thick red haze constituted his entire forward field of vision. Suddenly, he realized that the smoke grenade had been jarred from his hand and had rolled somewhere beneath his seat when the aircraft went on its side. Red stinging smoke billowed through the cockpit, so dense that Sam had trouble seeing even his instrument panel. In truth, he realized as the smoke cleared momentarily, there was little to be seen, for the .50 caliber exploding shells had left holes the size of a large coffee can all through the panel.

Sam could hear the hissing of the smoke canister as it purged itself of its pressurized contents. He realized with a start that the only reason he could hear it through the cocoon of his helmet was a complete absence of engine noise. OK, he thought, trying to steady himself, let's just see if we can't get all of this into perspective. The engine is definitely out because he'd seen it go. Besides, pieces of its innards were lying in his lap. No chance of restarting that sucker. He didn't know whether he was right side up or inverted because some asshole had rolled a smoke grenade under the seat. Since he could hardly see the instrument panel, much less outside the cockpit, it was just possible he was coming down right on Charley's head. Besides that, all that fucking red smoke was making him sick to his stomach and he was sure he was going to puke.

Sam tried to get his head out the window but his fastidiousness only got him a lap full of vomit as the slipstream hurled it back into the cockpit. This is really not my day, he thought. And worst of all, he was embarrassed. He could imagine the spectacle he was making of himself to both the friendlies and the Viet Cong. A powerless airplane that couldn't hit 120 knots when it was well, floating down in a whimsical fashion, belching red smoke like an aerial circus entertainer.

He found that if he used cross-control pressures he could slip the aircraft and draw some of the smoke out of the cockpit through the open window. Unfortunately, that maneuver cleared only the portion of the windscreen that was scarred. It did show him to be approximately right side up, however.

In addition to his other problems, some fool was trying to talk to him over the radio. "Blackjack! Blackjack! This is Ramrod Lead."

"What?" he answered querulously.

"What's your status?"

Sam choked back a bitter laugh. "I'm going to crash, that's what my status is. What else do you want to know?"

There was a long moment of silence before the A-1 leader answered. "Well, if you've decided that's what you want to do, do you mind if we slide in and take some pictures? It's really quite a show."

Sam gave a tight little grin and shook his head at the mordant humor of the attack pilot. "Yeah, you can take your pictures, but it might be a little more helpful if you'd tell me where I'm heading. I can't see a thing."

"OK, come right about twenty and get your nose up a little if you can. You just might be able to stretch your glide to some rice paddies.

That's it. Just a little more. Perfect. OK, you're by the tallest trees. Too bad. That would have made a hell of a shot if you'd have straddled one of those babies. Well, not to worry. There's lots more chances to screw up before you crawl out of that thing. Crap! I think your smoke is going out. That *is* too bad. Now the scene won't be nearly as interesting. Can you see forward at all now?"

"Yeah, I can." What he saw was not encouraging. He estimated he was only two or three hundred feet above the ground. The attack pilot had been right. There were several large paddies just off the nose; with just a little luck . . .

He almost made it. The little aircraft stalled while he was still six or seven feet in the air, trying to milk it for distance. It fell to the earth like a rock only feet short of the rice paddy, then bounced back into the air only to crash down again, this time on its side, one wing folded under it.

Sam hung from the harness, dazed and unclear as to what had happened. When he smelled the gas dripping from the crumpled wing, he panicked and released his safety belts, only to fall through what had been a closed door. He lay beneath the aircraft on the door he'd taken with him and rubbed his shoulder, which had absorbed most of the fall. The smell of fuel was stronger and he struggled to his feet, realizing he must get away from the broken aircraft. He leaned back inside to turn off the ignition and battery and saw the stock of his shotgun in the rack in the rear cockpit. He grabbed it and a bandolier of shells and hurriedly crawled outside, then darted in again to pick up two of the smoke grenades now rolling loose on the inside of the cockpit. He slung the bandolier, put the grenades in the leg pocket of his flight suit, and began to survey the area.

The Skyraiders roared over his head, one in trail behind the other. He waved his shotgun at them before taking off in a stumbling lope for the nearest wood line. He gained the trees and belly flopped beneath some low bushes. His heart was racing; he could feel his pulse hammering away insanely in his ears. Several klicks away—to the south, he thought—he could hear the staccato of automatic weapons. He lay motionless, waiting. Waiting for what? He wasn't sure. Sweat began to sting the open gashes on his face. He found a dirty handkerchief in a breast pocket and tenderly wiped his face, then stared in horror at the bloody rag. Tentative fingers told him that the wounds were superficial. Hah! Superficial is when it happens to somebody else. He went back to waiting.

The earth suddenly shook beneath him as the double crump of detonating bombs showed that the A-1s had gone back to work by the LZ. What the hell did that mean? Were they just going to forget about him? Logic told him that the attack aircraft had gone where they were needed most; still, it disturbed him to be left alone. Warily, he stretched his neck up as far as he could and peered through the leaves of his bush. The fuel from the leaking tank must have seeped onto the hot exhaust stacks, for small flames had ignited and were building around the wrecked aircraft. Sam was torn between getting away from the flaming wreckage, knowing it would attract every unfriendly in the area, and staying close by, knowing it was also his sole source of contact with a rescue effort. He decided to stay, for the moment.

Sam's scrutiny had picked up a well-traveled trail that led into the darker recesses of the forest. That concerned him, since it lay roughly in the direction of the Viet Cong bunkers by the LZ some kilometers away to the southwest. If that were the case and the VC retreated, as inevitably they must when more and more firepower was deployed against them, odds were that Sam could soon find himself in the middle of a very cranky group of enemy soldiers.

He squatted and duck-walked out of the bushes, pausing often to listen for any unusual jungle noise. Hell! All the noises sounded unusual. He rose carefully to a crouch and slowly crept deeper into the gloom beneath the trees. Within fifty meters he found a small depression that was probably a jungle pool during the wet season. New growth crowded the edge, which was nearly thirty meters from the trail.

Sam crawled into the depression, wedging himself beneath the low bushes, and waited. His tongue stuck to the roof of his cottony mouth, seeking moisture. He cursed himself for not having the foresight to grab the canteen from his aircraft. He searched the pockets of his flight suit until he came up with half a pack of very old chewing gum. He tried a piece and, after overcoming an initial failure to work up enough saliva to keep it from sticking to his teeth, found that it helped a little. He chewed noisily and surveyed himself. The cuts on his face were still stinging but had stopped bleeding. Gently, he dabbed the arm of his flight suit against his face, trying to blot the moisture. He noticed the entire sleeve, no, the entire flight suit, was completely darkened with sweat. He'd have to get water somewhere if his wait was too long.

The roar of the huge radial engines of the Skyraiders almost caused him to go into cardiac arrest as they buzzed the tree line where his Bird Dog burned. Sam took a long look around, then got to his feet. There were more explosions from the area of the LZ. Other aircraft must have joined the fight.

Sam stealthily retraced his route to the edge of the jungle. The A-1s had departed after one pass, the sound of their engines fading into the distance. In their place came another sound—a familiar one. It could only be another Bird Dog. On his belly, Sam slid away from the comforting haven of trees, peering suspiciously over his shoulder. The engine noise was getting louder. The last pass by Ramrod Flight must have been to show his location to the pilot of the approaching aircraft. Then he saw it, heading directly for the smoke rising from the wrecked aircraft. The new aircraft was flying low, damned low.

After peering carefully back into the forest once more, Sam got to his knees and waved the shotgun. The aircraft was close enough that Sam could see its pilot, who had his head turned away from him, watching the fire consume the wrecked O-1. The new aircraft wore the olive-drab paint scheme of the army rather than air force gray.

It overflew the wreckage and turned toward the trees. Sam waved lustily and knew immediately he'd been sighted when the pilot enthusiastically rocked the wings of his aircraft before passing over just high enough to clear the tall trees. Sam could follow his turning flight path by listening to the engine noise. OK, he'd been spotted. But now what? Was the army pilot directing a rescue helicopter? Sam shook his head and tried to mentally quiet himself. For all practical purposes he was out of the loop on anything that was to happen. He'd just have to take what came and try to use his common sense. But, damnit! He really thought they ought to be in more of a hurry to get him out of here before the dinks came back.

Sam watched the aircraft reappear and begin a puzzling maneuver. It crisscrossed the field at fifty feet as though the pilot had lost something and was looking for it. At the edge of the paddy clearing the pilot pulled up sharply and reversed course. Sam watched the large flaps on the aircraft come down in a partial setting and heard the increased pitch as the pilot pushed on more RPMs. It came to him. No! The idiot was going to try a landing! Forgetting about any Viet Cong in the area,

Sam jumped to his feet and began waving both shotgun and his free arm back and forth desperately. The surface in the clearing around the paddies probably looked smooth from the air, but erosion had created deep trenches where the ground declined toward the trees. The ditches were concealed by matted grasses. The paddies were relatively smooth but were completely inadequate for a takeoff or a landing by anything other than a helicopter.

But a landing it was to be. Either the pilot had not seen Sam's frantic arm movements, had misinterpreted them, or had chosen to ignore them. Sam watched in dismay as the aircraft turned onto its final approach, flaps coming down full. The pilot sideslipped to lose altitude, then righted the aircraft just before it settled into a gentle, perfect, three-point landing.

There was a landing roll of a hundred feet or so before the inevitable disaster. The O-1's main gear dropped completely out of sight into a rain-carved gully, and the aircraft stood abruptly on its nose. It paused there, as if for dramatic effect, then slowly fell forward onto its back. It was enveloped in a cloud of dust.

Sam wasn't conscious of starting to run and was rather startled to find himself in full flight toward the stricken aircraft. The adrenaline pumping through his system seemed to allow him to float over obstacles, shotgun held in front at port arms to knock aside small bushes. He felt light as a feather and would not have been surprised to find that if he flapped his arms he could fly. He could see movement inside the inverted cockpit as the dust began to settle. Except for the bent prop and the crushed vertical stabilizer, the aircraft looked as though it could be righted and flown away.

He skidded to a halt, panting, beside the entry door in the fuselage. Wrenching it open, he stooped to help the plane's single occupant. The feet came first, and they were huge. Sam had never seen a pair of boots like those sticking into his face just now. The man's frame unfolded and as it eased through the opening Sam saw that the man matched the feet. Eventually, all of him was outside and standing upright.

Sam was not a little man. His friend, Jim Christian, at six feet four inches, was a big man. The helmeted figure now standing next to him had to be at least six feet seven inches tall. The visor of his helmet obscured the features from the nose up, but Sam could see a wide, goofy grin pasted onto the bottom of his face.

Sam couldn't believe it. This character stuck out his hand as if they were meeting socially. Even worse, Sam automatically accepted and shook it, all the time thinking of the incongruity of it all. An entire main force battalion may have them within their gunsights and here they were, shaking hands and smiling as though they were at a bridge party.

"How do you do? Name's Chief Warrant Officer Donald Lyle. Friends call me Stretch for obvious reasons." He removed his helmet and surveyed the dinged aircraft with sad blue eyes. "Really fucked that up, didn't I? Thought they'd probably give me a DFC if I pulled you out by myself," he said with amazing candor. "Well, easy come, easy go. What's your name, Major?"

With his mouth hanging open, Sam stared at the good-natured face. It was long and the ears protruded slightly. A straight, narrow nose and firm chin were balanced by a broad forehead. There was a full head of rusty brown hair. A good-looking kid. But, didn't CWO Donald Lyle realize there was a firefight going on two klicks away and that they were both now standing dehorsed in Charley's backyard?

"Later," Sam responded shortly to the request for his name. "Let's get anything outta the bird we can use and get the hell out of this clearing."

Without waiting for the warrant officer's agreement, Sam knelt and began rummaging in the cockpit. He passed out the pilot's M16 and a bandolier of ammunition, two more smoke grenades, a canteen of water, a six-pack of Pepsi, a bag of Cheetos, three C rations, a large Hershey bar soggy from the heat, and a small cluster of finger bananas. He decided to leave the box of crackers, the peanut butter—Skippy's Smooth, the bag of Oreos, more C rations, the paperback books, and the small watermelon. After a moment's consideration he went back for the melon.

Chief Warrant Officer Lyle methodically stowed the material Sam passed to him in the voluminous pockets of his jungle fatigues and in his helmet storage bag. He'd retrieved a baseball cap from a side pocket. Sam scrambled out of the aircraft and looked queerly at the lanky man; then he grabbed the six-pack of soft drinks and, without turning to see if he was being followed, started for the trees at a slow trot. Most of the adrenaline that had coursed through his body was beginning to wear off. His legs felt heavy and it was with a great deal of relief that he reached the shadows once more. Cautiously, he led the lanky aviator to his depression and crawled into it. Donald Lyle looked around at his new surroundings with interest, as though he might want to put in a bid on this piece of real estate.

Sam lay back with the shotgun over his chest and tried to get his breathing under control. His face felt hot and flushed, and somewhere in the chain of events he'd swallowed his gum and his mouth had dried out once again. He caught Lyle's eye and nodded at the canteen in the helmet bag. The army pilot smiled with delight as though he was the host of a dinner party and a guest had asked for seconds on the roast beef. He passed the canteen and Sam was hard-pressed not to empty it. Instead, he allowed himself a couple of quick gulps, then hastily screwed on the top and passed it back before he lost his willpower. His eyes inventoried CWO2c. Donald "Stretch" Lyle. The army pilot stared back with a good-natured smile.

"What the hell were you doing with a watermelon in your airplane?" It seemed to be the most important question Sam could come up with at the moment.

All seventy-nine or eighty inches of Stretch Lyle wriggled with delight. "Well, you see, I'm the army sector pilot over in Kien Long sector; that's in Chuong Thien province, you know."

Sam nodded that he understood the geography and whispered, "Better try to keep your voice down."

The warrant officer nodded and smiled, happy to participate in such a fun game. "Anyway, there's this one dink over there who likes to take a shot at me every time I take off. He's about a mile off the end of the strip and he's there every day, rain or shine. He takes just that one shot, that's all."

"Why don't you drop some arty on him if you know where he is?" asked Sam.

Lyle looked horrified. "Oh, no! I wouldn't do that! You see, this guy has got to be the worst shot in the world. I mean, he's been taking a crack at me every day for at least four months and he's never once scored a hit. If I were to zap him they might replace him with somebody who is a very good shot."

"So what has that got to do with the watermelon?"

"You see, I don't want to get rid of my dink but I can't just ignore him blasting away at me all the time either. So, I came up with the idea of chucking these melons at him. I don't really try to hit him and I think he knows that. But I don't think he really tries to hit me either. So, 'bout once a week I buy a dozen or so of these, about the size of a bowling ball. I stow 'em in the Bird Dog to use during the week. They don't cost hardly anything at the market in Kien Long."

"How about the rest of this chow?" Sam swept his hand at the pile of snacks.

"I sometimes get a little hungry between meals," Lyle confessed.

Sam let his eyes linger on the amiable face for a moment, then let them drift over the lanky frame. The man was a walking arsenal. He carried the standard army .45-caliber automatic on his web belt along with a K-BAR knife. There was an additional handgun—it looked to be a .38 Special—in a shoulder rig. Taped upside down on the rig's main strap was a double-edged fighting knife.

"How old are you?" Sam whispered.

"Durned near twenty-one," Lyle answered. He peered at Sam's face. "Want me to dress those cuts?"

"Later, maybe." Sam shut his eyes and sighed. He opened them and they focused on the melon. Saliva began flowing freely in his mouth as he began to think of what it would taste like. If they ate it, there would be less to carry if they had to move. Besides, he really wanted it. Sam eased back from the lip of the depression to sit closer to Lyle.

"Listen," he said, "why don't we cut that melon? I need to get some moisture back into my system, but we'll do it only if you want to. After all, it's your melon."

Lyle looked pained. "Shoot, Major, this ain't my stuff. It's *our* stuff. Let's cut that sucker right now."

It took all of Sam's determination not to jerk the melon from the warrant's hands as he measured, then remeasured, the point where he would make the slice. Then he inserted the tip of the K-BAR, made a neat circular slice, and popped it into two halves.

Sam swallowed the first mouthful of red flesh, seeds and all. The juice seemed to fill in the cracks and crevices in the lining of his mouth. He looked at Lyle methodically munching his portion and gazing at the treetops while his jaws worked. Sam wolfed down the rest of his portion, even chewing into the paleness just inside the tough skin. He wiped his mouth with the sweaty sleeve of his flight suit. He saw Donald Lyle cock his head like an inquisitive puppy.

"Somebody's coming," he announced in a normal speaking voice.

Sam froze, head pointing toward the gloomy forest to the southwest. He heard it too. Someone *was* coming. A lot of someones. He could distinctly hear the sound of rubber sandals slapping the earth. Then he could make out the muted voices. There *were* a lot of them!

Sam slunk to his belly and wormed back up to the lip of the depression, moving until his head was beneath the boughs of the low bushes. He thrust the shotgun forward and tried to quiet his pulse. There was a sharp clang behind him and he almost jumped erect before he checked himself. He rolled with the shotgun in front of him, finger desperately trying to find the safety catch. There were no Mongol hordes behind him, only Stretch Lyle, who had unholstered the pistol from his shoulder rig and struck its barrel against the handle of the fighting knife. The warrant officer stood upright and shielded his eyes from the nonexistent glare of the sun like a young Davy Crockett. Sam hissed at him and, getting his attention, made a down motion with his free hand. Lyle nodded and dropped to his knees, then crawled to the top of the depression to join Sam. Sam was sure that his heart was going to explode as he rolled back onto his belly.

The noises were getting louder very quickly and the voices were becoming distinct though no one was yet visible. Sam swallowed nervously and stared into the dark forest until his eyes began to tear over. He could hear the movements of individuals and the clanking of their equipment. They'd be in sight at any moment.

Lyle stage-whispered into his right ear. "We'll kick their asses, huh, Major? Kick ass and take names, right?"

Sam looked at him in horror. Was the man crazy? They were probably outmanned a hundred to one and this fool was talking about kicking ass and taking names. Sam wanted nothing to do with a firefight against those odds. He wanted only to be quietly rescued and flown someplace where there was a well-stocked bar.

With mounting concern he watched the young, outsized warrant officer place his weapons on the lip of the depression exactly like someone prepared to go down fighting. As a final measure, Lyle reversed the baseball cap on his head and thrust the M16 forward through the bushes. His jaw jutted forward aggressively.

If he wipes the front sight of his rifle with a wetted thumb or gobbles like a turkey like Gary Cooper playing Sergeant York, I'm going to kill him, thought Sam feverishly. Not a jury in the world would convict me. He turned his frightened eyes front once more. Whoever was coming was very close now but still obscured from view by the undergrowth. Sam could hear the distinctive slap of the sandals and the panting voices of the runners muttering to one another.

Sam found that he wasn't even surprised when Chief Warrant Officer Lyle suddenly ripped off a full clip from his M16. Sam found himself nodding and thinking, yeah, that just about ought to do it! Sometimes you get the bear and sometimes the bear gets you. Lyle had switched to his handgun now and the shots were evenly spaced. Sam looked over at him. He had laid aside the empty M16 and now had the government-issue .45 in his right hand and the .38 Special in his left. He alternated shots into the thick brush just the way Roy Rogers used to do it in the Saturday matinees.

What the hell? Glumly, Sam brought the shotgun to his shoulder and fired, pumped the slide, and fired again. He continued until the gun was empty, then rolled to his back and began to pluck new shells from the bandolier and cram them into the magazine. He caught Lyle's eye as he rolled back onto his belly. There was an excited grin on the younger man's face as he shoved a fresh magazine into the M16. He actually winked at Sam before he threw himself forward once more to fire on an ammunition-conserving semiautomatic rate.

The return fire was surprisingly light. Only an odd AK-47 burst ruffled the bushes over their heads. Between the explosions of his shotgun and the sharper cracks of Lyle's M16, Sam could hear muffled commands in Vietnamese. Time came to be measured only by the absence of gunfire as they reloaded. Sam's heart sank as he realized he was loading his last five shells into the shotgun. It was almost payback time. He realized that Lyle was no longer firing. Together, they peered over the lip of the depression into the shattered bushes. Sam's ears still rang from the gunfire, but he couldn't hear or see any movement. What were they up to? He whirled and crawled to the other side of the hole, thinking they were about to be flanked.

Nothing! Quiet as a grave. Make that quiet as a church. He turned back to find Lyle standing erect, M16 held casually with the barrel pointing toward the dark forest. The tall man turned to him and smiled. "Durned good thing they decided to cut out," he said, "'cause I was just about out of beebees."

Sam crawled to his feet and looked around cautiously, then directly at the lanky warrant officer. He started to speak but cut it off as he heard the distinctive sounds of approaching helicopters. That was likely the reason the VC had run. They were also probably out of ammo after the fight with the Rangers back at the LZ. Sam took a step toward the clearing on shaky legs, knowing how lucky they'd been. The choppers had almost certainly been steered to them by the A-1 flight. On the other hand, the opened area where the two Bird Dogs lay smashed was an obvious LZ for a blocking force when the VC had decided to flee.

He watched Lyle walk carelessly into the thicker jungle, bending over often to look at something. He turned and waved happily to Sam. "Hey, Major! We got a bunch of 'em."

Sam didn't answer but turned and walked toward the clearing, pulling a smoke grenade from the leg pocket of his flight suit. His aircraft was still burning. He walked until he was well clear of the wood line, then pulled the pin on the canister and tossed it in front of him.

The approaching stick of Hueys veered directly toward him. He raised the shotgun with both hands and held it over his head until the lead ship began to descend. Lyle joined him. He had four AK-47s slung over his shoulders. Sam refused to look at him. The stick touched down, and the Rangers spilled from the hatchways and sprinted for the trees. Their American adviser gave Sam a small wave before charging after the troops.

"We're heading back to Soc Trang," the door gunner yelled as the two pilots walked to the lead helicopter.

Sam nodded wearily and climbed into the cabin. Inside, he turned and placed a restraining hand on Lyle's chest, preventing him from entering. "You'd better ride on one of the other birds," he told the warrant officer, "because if you get on this one I'll probably shove your ass out somewhere about Cai Con."

He sank back onto one of the folding canvas benches and rested his head on the rear bulkhead. He shut his eyes and sighed deeply. The wide-eyed gunner gave the up sign to the aircraft commander and the Huey broke ground, leaving a bewildered CWO2c. Donald Lyle swaying in the rotor blast like a young palm tree.

CHAPTER 10

"Major Samuel G. Brooks distinguished himself by gallantry in connection with military operations against an opposing armed force, deep in hostile territory . . ."

Sam let his mind drift; his eyes focused on the tall, soldierly-looking general with the graying hair. The general gazed back benignly, looking like the perfect grandfather—one who was pleased as punch that his favorite grandson was receiving a 4-H award for raising the very best hog of the year. Sam's eyes shifted slightly to the left of COMUSMACV's shoulder and found that Col. Jackson Jones, director of operations, 2d Air Division, was staring at him. Their eyes locked briefly before Sam looked back to the general and tuned in again to the adjutant's flat voice.

". . . Major Brooks directed the air strikes with extreme accuracy before sustaining heavy battle damage and undoubtedly saved many allied lives . . ."

What a bunch of crap! Sam thought sourly. If they keep giving me medals I'm going to be the most highly decorated officer ever to be booted out of the air force due to nonpromotion. He felt CWO2c. Donald "Stretch" Lyle wriggling beside him. Without looking Sam knew that the idiot would have that goofy grin stretching over his face. Jesus! Here he was with the world's nuttiest warrant officer, getting medals for bravery when by all rights they should have been shipped out in a body bag or at least court-martialed for outright stupidity.

". . . He and Chief Warrant Officer Lyle, predicting that the enemy forces would withdraw toward their location, set an ambush that resulted in twelve enemy casualties and two captured wounded Viet Cong with no loss . . ."

What *bullshit*! Sam had fired at the fleeing enemy because Lyle had
let fly and only then in self-preservation. And Lyle had fired because
he was a fucking idiot. If those poor VC had not been nearly out of
ammo after their fight with the Rangers, he and Lyle would never have
crawled from that hole alive. It was always better to be lucky than good.
Sam had tried to give a straightforward account of the action, but everyone
thought he was becomingly modest. After all, he had made the gutsy
trip with the snake eaters after the captured American pilot, hadn't he?

". . . by his gallantry and devotion to duty Major Brooks has reflected
great credit upon himself, the United States Air Force, and the Military Assistance Command, Vietnam." The adjutant folded the plastic
case containing the citation, opened the box containing the Silver Star
medal, and passed it to the general, who took two exact steps forward,
stopping at the exact distance needed to extend his arms and pin on
the medal. He gently grasped Sam's soggy shirt front and pulled it out
so he could attach the award. He has a very winsome smile, Sam thought.

"Major," the distinguished-looking man said gently, "this seems to
be getting to be a habit. I hope you realize that you have to give this
one back to us. We'll give you a cluster to wear on the first one. If
you got to keep them all it appears you'd run us short."

The general stepped back and eyed Sam speculatively. "You know,
Major Brooks, it's not often that I present two such awards to the same
man during one tour. The thing that I find a bit amusing is that although you are a pilot, both of these decorations were presented for
ground actions." The general turned and gave a slight smile to Colonel Jackson, whose lips contracted at the corners, more of a grimace
than a smile, in response to the gentle jab by the commander.

You'd find it even more amusing if you knew I was soon getting
my ass busted out of the service, thought Sam. A few more months
and these little trinkets you've hung on me won't mean a thing.

"Although we're, of course, extremely proud of you men in the field
who face the dangers and take the chances and are too seldom recognized by ceremonies such as this," the general continued, "still, I must
ask you to make certain that you are taking no *unnecessary* risks. You
advisers are well known for your aggressive spirit, but you must not
allow it to lead you into unnecessary dangers. We need men like yourself
and Mister Lyle. You're the future of our armed forces officer corps."
Hah! thought Sam. "And soon, perhaps sooner than any of us realize,
the need for trained and experienced men may be critical. So, do your

job, gentlemen, as I know you will. But keep foremost in your mind that a bigger play may soon be auditioning and we'd like to have you around as players. You're brave men and I salute you."

Ramrod straight, the general slowly raised a hand to his forehead. Sam and Donald Lyle returned the salute and made a facing movement toward the door. At a nod from the adjutant they quick-stepped into the outer office. There was a restrained whoop behind Sam and when he turned, Donald Lyle grabbed his hand and began shaking it like a pump handle.

"How about them apples, Major?" the tall warrant officer bubbled. "I thought I'd get my ass really reamed when I broke my Bird Dog trying to get you outta that rice paddy. But here I am with a Silver, by-God, Star! The Lord and MACV sure do move in mysterious ways."

Sam freed his hand, which seemed in danger of being torn from his arm, and failed to suppress a smile. Lyle's unaffected good humor was contagious. He glanced down at his own chest and briefly admired the Silver Star and the Purple Heart medals hanging there. The adjutant walked over to them and took the star from Sam's chest with a smile.

"Like the boss said, we keep this one. Only one to a customer. We'll be glad to furnish you with an Oak-Leaf Cluster if you want to wait a few months, or you could spring for one in the PX if you don't mind shelling out ten cents or so. You can keep the Purple Heart, though, since it's your first award. How's your head doing, anyway?"

Sam raised a hand and tentatively felt the groove just above his left eye where one of the parts of the disintegrating engine had crashed through his helmet visor. The helmet had absorbed the blow, for the most part, but it had left a two-inch gash that needed eight stitches to close. Sweat seeped into the raw area and burned like crazy. Still, he reckoned himself very fortunate to have escaped with only minor lacerations. By rights, both he and Lyle should have been very dead.

"No problem," he answered. "It's 'bout healed up."

"Well," the adjutant said, "nice seeing you again, Brooks. And you too, Mister Lyle. You guys keep your butts down out there." He squinted at Sam. "You know, the Old Man meant what he said. A star is great. Two stars and people begin to wonder about your judgment. *Three* and they figure you're certifiable. In any event, congratulations to both of you. Damned fine work." He shook their hands and strode briskly back into the inner sanctum.

"Major," Lyle said, "I sure wish I could stay and chat for a while but I've got a ride waiting to take me out to the 118th Aviation Company at Tan Son Nhut. Gotta pick up a new bird from them. They're really pissed about losing the old one, so I've got to hurry before they find a way to get out of it. You take care now, and I'll see you somewhere around the delta." Lyle grabbed Sam's hand again and started pumping.

Sam broke off the handshake before he was physically maimed and watched the tall young man bound down the stairs, surprisingly graceful in his size-fourteen jungle boots. Sam shook his head as he watched Lyle disappear into the street. Whenever he thought about their earlier predicament, he still felt murderous. Yet, there was something so intrinsically likable about Lyle that it was difficult to remain angry. Some of Lyle's impulsive behavior had been due to youthful exuberance and the certainty that one is immortal. Sam had stood on the lip of the grave once too often to believe that. Staring at his own mortality was enough to drive him into complete melancholia and the need for strong drink.

"Well, Major Brooks, you seem to have come up smelling like the proverbial rose yet again."

Sam turned slowly, knowing the voice. "Yes, Colonel Jones. Sorry to disappoint you but I guess I'm just a natural survivor."

"Hmm. Yes, it appears that you are. Much more so than I would have given you credit for. Still, you do have a few more months left before your tour is completed. Maybe some enterprising young Viet Cong will get lucky. Get himself credit for bringing down the winner of two Silver Stars. Probably get promoted off the mine-laying detail to the night ambush squad."

"No doubt, sir. Still, that could bring him other problems. Like, what would his wife do while he was out shooting up government outposts all night. She just might get a little bored with old Nguyen the Ambusher and try to find a little nighttime activity of her own. Right?"

Sam felt only slightly sick to his stomach at the cheap shot, but the man had asked for it. Sam knew then that his mind-set had changed: He would no longer take constant sniping from Jack Jones. What did it matter anyway? This man standing close to him with the white tension lines etched into the corners of his eyes and mouth was as much his enemy as anyone he'd faced in the provinces. In the long run, perhaps more dangerous, for Jones could continue to place him in situations from which it would be difficult to recover. And what could Sam do about it? Complain to the inspector general? Jones knew he'd never do that. So the jab felt good. And it felt good to almost be able to hear the man's teeth grinding.

Abruptly, the colonel turned on his heel and started for the stairwell. He stopped and whirled toward Sam. His voice was almost gentle. "I forgot to tell you, Major Brooks. The lieutenant colonel selection board meets in three weeks. We've just been solicited by PACAF for final comments on all eligible. The commander of 2d Air Division has given me the job of compiling and forwarding these comments from our happy little group. Do try to not get yourself killed until after the board meets. It wouldn't be nearly as enjoyable laughing at a stiff."

Colonel Jones turned and skipped briskly out of sight down the stairwell. He could throw a pretty good jab himself, Sam thought.

Sam stared moodily through the fly-speckled screen of the dining room of the Tan Son Nhut officers' club and chewed his way through a tasteless hamburger. For more than two hours he'd been fighting the complicated military phone system hoping to get through to Lee Roget in Can Tho. Once, he'd forged ahead as far as My Tho, only to be cut off by a higher priority call. Since that dizzying moment he'd been unable to get out of the Saigon area. It had been a long shot at best but he'd hoped to get Lee to Saigon for a few days. Their separation had caused a pain that was almost physical. He'd found himself doodling her name during briefings just as he'd done in the eighth grade when Mary Jo Falkenberry had confided to a go-between that she thought he was kind of cute. Of course, Mary Jo had laughed in his face when he'd asked her to the class social, seeding in Sam's mind the first doubts regarding the opposite sex. The doubts had never left him; in fact, they had blossomed over the years. He never felt that he really understood their motives or drives as well as he did those of the men he flew with. Their deviousness drove him to distraction and, as he grew older, served to move him farther and farther from the orbit of eligible women.

Lee was different, though. Sam tried to objectively list her faults and could find none worthy of the name. That in itself worried him a bit. Perhaps in his ignorance of the other sex there was something he was overlooking. And perhaps she didn't share his intense feelings. She had said she loved him, but didn't women always say that to justify sharing a bed with someone? And assuming she was serious, what kind of life could he provide for them? He'd be out of the air force in just weeks with no marketable skills and damned few dollars in the bank. What kind of commitment could he expect from any woman under those circumstances?

Sam glanced up from his brooding to look at a pair of flight-suited figures strolling into the screened dining area. Their faces still showed the marks of oxygen masks, and the upper parts of their suits were darkened with sweat. Salt-encrusted circles stained their underarms. One of the men was Red Morgan.

The newcomers sat three tables away, never sparing Sam a glance. He gave them a moment to settle, then said: "God! I hate red hair. I especially hate red-haired people who are going bald. There's nothing uglier than those freckles on a bald head with those little bitty snatches of red hair around the fringes. Unless maybe it would be a bald red-haired man who's got all that disgusting body hair like a damned jungle ape that somehow got commissioned and blackmailed his way through flight school."

The two men looked at him calmly before the older, a lieutenant colonel, turned to the other and said in a normal speaking tone: "You know I had a wingman once who couldn't even find the ground on the bombing range. I mean, he was pitiful. We got so desperate to find out what the problem was that we put this concealed movie camera in his cockpit one day before a hop. And you know what? We found the problem was self-abuse. That's right, self-abuse. Right there on the damned range. He'd be unzipped by the time he was on downwind; going at it full speed on base leg. And he'd be completely finished in time to pickle the bomb. We tried to cure him of the habit but couldn't. Finally had to let the poor shit go. Last I heard of him he was over in Vietnam somewhere. Wonder what the hell happened to that old reprobate. Name of Sam Brooks, if I remember right."

Red Morgan rose from his table, walked to Sam, and began pummeling him, then pulled him from his chair to their table. Before they sat, Morgan introduced Sam to the other pilot, a young-looking major. "Sam Brooks, meet Stan Lewis. Stan's my ops officer. We just got diverted in here because Bien Hoa had a few mortar rounds drop in. We figured to grab a bite to eat while they refuel and rearm us, then we could get in another strike on the way back. That is if old Charley will stop shooting long enough for us to get back in."

"You got a squadron? Hey, that's great. Congratulations! F-100s?"

Red nodded. "What else? Seems like I've spent the best part of my life in the old Lead Sled. What the hell are you doing here?" He suddenly took in the wrinkled khakis Sam still wore from the ceremony. "My God! They haven't screwed up and put you on staff, have they?"

"Not yet," Sam said. "I'm a FAC down in Bac Lieu, and you can quit pretending not to see that I'm still wearing gold leaves. Got my first passover last year. Probably be kicked out after the light colonel's board meets again."

Red looked at him soberly. "Still that Jack Jones thing?" Sam nodded. "Well, shit! That's rough. Anyway, I didn't even know you had a FAC background."

Sam grinned. "I don't, but I'm a real quick study."

"You always were, boy. You always were. Stan," Red turned to the other pilot, "this old boy sitting across from you has probably got more flying time in dive-bombing runs than you have total flight time and more fighter time than any one of our entire flights added together. I'd sell the gold out of my dear old mother's teeth to have him and a couple more just like 'im in the outfit. But I don't understand, Sam. Did you actually request to get out of fighters?"

Sam snorted. "That'll be the day. Naw, just some more of Jack Jones's handiwork. But don't sweat it. I've got a handle on it."

The barefoot waitress padded over and took lunch orders from the fighter pilots, vanishing as silently as she had appeared.

"What the hell are you doing up here dressed like a staff puke anyway?" asked Red.

"Just getting a little gong over at MACV," Sam mumbled.

"What kinda little gong?" Red demanded.

"Silver Star and a Purple Heart," Sam said sheepishly.

Red stared at him for a few moments. "They don't give that sort of trash away, boy. What the hell happened?"

Briefly, Sam outlined the day in question, cutting it as short as he could. Red asked a few penetrating questions until he was sure that he had the entire story. "Sam," he said, "I've also heard some scuttlebutt about you hanging out with a group of green beanies. Even that you were on a little ground foray with them down in the U Minh. Is that right?" Sam nodded, looking down at his glass of ice tea.

"Well," Red said softly, "I just want to let you know how much we all appreciate it. Half the guys in my squadron knew that young fella you folks tried to drag outta there. He was a brand-new butterbar on his first operational assignment when he came to my squadron out at

Luke. One of the first to volunteer for A-1s. A real tiger. Thanks for
trying." Sam nodded again, eyes averted.

"Listen," Red said, excitedly. "What are you doing the rest of the
day? I mean, do you have to get back right away?"

"Naw," said Sam. "Bill Robinson, my ALO, told me to take as much
time as I wanted. Said he'd cover for me."

"Bill Robinson? That ole spook is down in the delta? He and I were
in the same flight in the 308th at Nellis back in, oh, '58 or '59. God,
I remember one time the both of us . . . well, I'm getting off the track.
What I was going to suggest was that you come over to Bien Hoa
and spend the night with us. We'll have a few drinks and introduce
you around. Hell, you probably know half the squadron anyway. How
about it?"

"Well," Sam toyed with the idea in his mind and liked it. "Sounds
good but I've got no way of getting over there unless I head to the
flight line and start trying to hitch a ride. And they're bringing
my Bird Dog *from* Bien Hoa late this afternoon. It's been getting a
hundred-hour inspection over there. I'm afraid with this military phone
system I'd never be able to contact them in time to stop the delivery."

"No problem!" Red said triumphantly. "Stan here is in a two holer.
He and I'll switch birds for the flight back to Bien Hoa and you can
ride with me. Ride? Hell! You can fly the front seat if you want to.
We'll borrow a mask and a chute from personal equipment over at the
54th—the sergeant who runs the shop used to work for me. We can
call over UHF after we're airborne and tell 'em to hold your Bird Dog
on the ground there at Bien Hoa and you can fly it on down to the
weeds tomorrow. How does that all sound?"

Sam had to admit it all sounded very good. It almost made up for
missing connections with Lee.

Sam eased in a tiny bit of throttle. It would have been unnotice-
able to a layman but it stopped the slight aft movement the F-100 had
begun and tucked it back precisely into position on the right wing of
Stan's lead aircraft. The boosted controls felt incredibly light and sensitive
after slamming the Bird Dog around for more than five hundred hours
of flying time. It was like a release from prison to feel the aircraft respond
to even the most delicate touch. The parachute straps and restraining
belts over his shoulders and hips gave him a well-remembered feeling of security, and the tightly fitting helmet blocked out all noise except

the calm, measured breathing of Red Morgan. The hot mike allowed the pilots in the two seater to monitor each other without depressing an intercom switch. To Sam, the stentorian rumblings from Red were as comforting as a mother's coos to a baby. To the uninitiated, they were maddening.

"Think you remember how to hit the ground with a bomb?" asked Red.

"So long as that's the only requirement, I could probably manage it. What's the briefed target?"

Red snorted. "Suspected bunkers. What else? That's what you FACs always call it when there's a particular batch of trees you don't especially like. But at least the target is up in real gomer country. Even if there ain't any bunkers, old Charley just might be walking by singing camping songs. It's about fifteen klicks this side of the border, near Bu Dop."

The name was unfamiliar to Sam, never having been north of Saigon. He watched the lead ship bump his rudders to move Sam into an attack spread. Sam twitched the stick slightly to the right, then recentered it. His aircraft drifted slowly away from the flight leader. Simultaneously, he cracked the throttle back a fraction to put nose-to-tail separation between the two aircraft. He listened to Stan make the initial radio call to the forward air controller somewhere ahead and below them.

"Rash Two, this is Banjo Lead. How do you read?"

"Banjo Lead, this is Rash Two Two. Got you five square. How me?"

The reply had been immediate. "Read you loud and clear as well. We're about zero two from the romeo papa. Ready for our lineup?"

"Yeah, go ahead, Lead."

"Rog. Banjo Flight is two Huns with a split load of five-hundred-pound snakes and nape. Also a full load of twenty mike mike. We've got approximately thirty minutes' loiter time. We're coming up to the rendezvous point at angels fourteen. Go ahead."

"Copy that, Banjo Lead. We've got a tree buster for you this afternoon; however, there's pretty good skinny that there's a new set of bunkers down beneath the trees. We just don't know if old Luke the Gook is in 'em or not, so let's all just act like he's there and expect ground fire. Local elevation is around a hundred and fifty feet. Best bailout area is to the south around the river, fifteen or twenty klicks from here. Even if you're hit hard, I'd suggest you try to stay with your bird as long as you can. You don't want to come down in this immediate area.

We know for sure that it's swarming with those little munchkins. You can make your run-ins from any direction so long as you don't stray too far. The Cambodian border is about ten klicks to the north and fifteen to the west, so let's not get the Buddha heads all excited by overflying their airspace. It might piss off all the NVA camped there. There are no friendlies within twenty klicks, so that ought to make 'em safe from you fighter pukes. I want your snake eyes first, in pairs. Then we'll work the nape after I BDA the area. If we stir up anything, I might want to expend your twenty mike mike last. I'm going to perch over the target at fifteen hundred. Call FAC and target in sight before each pass and drop only after you get positive clearance from me. Otherwise, go through dry. Any questions?"

"Banjo Lead, we're set. Where are you, Rash Two Two?"

"OK, I'm directly over the confluence of two dry streambeds, just north of that burn scar in the trees. In a left turn now. Hold it, I've got you at my ten o'clock high."

Sam peered down through the canopy of his aircraft. He picked up the little gray aircraft and pressed his mike switch. "Banjo Lead, this is Two. I've got him at our two, going three o'clock low."

"Yeah, I see him now. Good eyes, Sam."

"Lead, if you're through giving compliments to your wingman for actually spotting an aircraft that is exactly where I told you I'd be, I'll put in the first mark."

Stan was chuckling as he answered the feisty forward air controller. "Go ahead with your mark, Rash. I just wanted to give a little encouragement to one of your fellow FACs who's driving the second ship."

"Well," answered Rash Two Two, "I always knew it would come to this. We not only have to find and mark the damned targets, but now we're going to have to bomb them too. Probably just as well, if we want it done right. I'm in for the mark."

Sam was surprised at how tiny and vulnerable the Bird Dog looked from a fighter's cockpit. He watched the small airplane start a wingover and plummet toward the ground. For the first time Sam became aware of the dark green mass of trees. It was very different from the delta and looked more ominous than the highly populated flatland far to the south. Some of the taller emergents soared two to three hundred feet in their quest for sunlight. The canopy was virtually unbroken except for a few old bomb scars.

A rocket whipped away from the left wing of the O-1 and zipped for the ground. Quickly, a ball of white smoke rose from its impact point in the tree canopy. The smoke rose heavily in the windless air, standing out vividly against the verdant background.

"OK, Banjo Lead, this is Rash Two Two. We might as well start there. Hit my smoke."

"Rog. Lead is in from the east with the FAC and target in sight."

Sam watched the sun glint from the silver jet as it rolled into its dive toward the target. Quickly, he checked the switches on the arming panel and adjusted the mil setting on his bombsight. It had been months since Sam had dropped ordnance, but his hands remembered, prompted by years in different fighter-bombers. Red Morgan kept his peace in the rear cockpit. He would give advice only should Sam request it.

"Banjo Lead, this is Rash. You're cleared in hot."

"Roger. Cleared hot," Stan answered from the lead ship. Sam positioned his aircraft for a run-in from the north.

Twin explosions cleared matching holes in the rain forest vegetation. Sam had already started his roll into a dive toward the target when the lead ship called.

"Banjo Lead is off south," Stan reported, grunting against the 5-g forces he was pulling.

"Banjo Two is in from the north. Target and FAC in sight."

"Good bomb, Lead," the FAC said quickly. "Two, put yours about fifty west of Lead's craters. You're cleared in hot."

"Rog, cleared hot," said Sam, mentally adjusting the sight picture he wanted for the new aiming point. He rolled the fighter upright and checked his airspeed. Looking good. Thirty-degree dive. OK. The pipper in the lighted sight reticle on the windscreen stayed steady, so there should be little wind aloft to affect the flight of the bombs after release. He quickly squeezed the control stick and rudder to the right and as quickly stopped the movement. Altitude check. OK. Drop in a thousand feet. A quick peek at the airspeed indicator. Still OK. Dive angle OK. No pressure on the controls. Pickle! He punched the button on the control stick head.

Sam felt the two five-hundred-pound bombs leave the aircraft and started a steady pull on the stick. His body began to feel incredibly heavy as he moved on more g force. His eyes sought the accelerometer. Only 4 g's? Jesus, it felt like more than that. Then he remembered he wasn't wearing a g suit as he normally would have done when

delivering ordnance. Its pneumatic bladders would have inflated and
squeezed against his legs and abdomen to keep the blood flowing and
help prevent a blackout. He pulled harder on the stick and his vision
began to grow gray, losing all color perception. In another few moments he could expect his sight to begin tunneling under the constant
g forces. If the g's were sustained it would lead to a complete loss of
vision, then unconsciousness.

Through blurred vision he put the aircraft into a sixty-degree climbing
left turn and mumbled into the mike in the mask: "Two's off east."

"Nice bombing, Two," the FAC called as Sam released the back pressure on the stick to assume level flight in the bombing pattern. "Both
of you hold high and dry, Banjo Flight, while I do a quick look-see
down there."

Both fighter pilots acknowledged and watched the small aircraft dive
into the smoke rising from the bomb blasts. Sam lost sight of it just
as the Bird Dog bucked through the shock wave of the last set of bombs.
The FAC reappeared only to do a sharp 180-degree turn and dive back
into the smoke. Sam watched anxiously, knowing how vulnerable the
forward air controller and his small aircraft were during low-level
surveillance.

Rash Two Two suddenly popped out of the smoke unharmed. "Banjo
Flight, this is Rash. Talk about dumb luck! Two's bombs uncovered
the western corner of a bunker complex. I can see only the three or
four bunkers on the edge, so I don't know how big it is or if anybody's
home. Let's drop singles and see if we can't take this thing apart. Lead,
I want your next bomb about fifty meters north of Two's westernmost
crater. I'll re-mark for you when you're ready."

"Let her go, Rash. Lead's about ready for a roll-in from the south."

"Roger. Rash in for the mark."

Methodically, the FAC worked the fighters' weapons deeper into the
bunker complex. Sam was professionally impressed as Rash Two Two
wheeled and cajoled Banjo Flight into doing exactly what he wanted.
He ran the strike like a good traffic cop, and his little aircraft was always
in position to see both the target and the attacking fighters, a task easier
said than done.

"OK, Banjo Flight," the FAC called, "let's see if we can't spread
some nape under the tree line. I'll want it delivered in as low an angle
as you can get it. I still haven't seen any shooting, but let's don't get
careless. They could still be home and just playing it cagey. I'm in
for a new mark."

Sam had always enjoyed delivering napalm. The shallow dive just above the treetops was exhilarating. He watched the silver canisters tumble from beneath the wings of the lead ship and burst into flames as they struck the ground. The jellied gas mixture flowed like lava far beneath the trees.

"Banjo Two, this is Rash. Put your first napes about—Jesus!"

A huge explosion literally tore apart several acres of rain forest. Sam had been watching the Bird Dog so he had a fine spectator's seat as the shock wave nearly tossed the FAC aircraft onto its back. While he watched, the FAC managed to get his aircraft under control and up-right again. Sam switched his attention to the secondary explosions that almost incinerated the little aircraft. The pilots were silent as they circled the cauldron. Smaller explosions cooked off from the heat of the major blast, spreading the destruction. Tops of collapsed bunkers could be seen in the decimated forest. The heat was so intense that tree tops burst into flame as though they had been soaked in kerosene and torched.

Finally, Stan spoke from the cockpit of the lead fighter: "Jesus! Did I do *that*?"

"Sure did," said Rash Two Two. "I don't know what the hell they've got down there, but I want to tell you I've never seen a secondary like it. You folks stand by for a minute while I change frequencies. I *know* somebody's gonna want to put some people on the ground to check that out. You can amuse yourself by dreaming up a real good war story about this for your bar tonight. I'll be back in one."

The fighter pilots were silent, though, content to keep their orbit around the fire on the ground. Small explosions continued to erupt as the fire spread through the bunker complex. The Bird Dog, Sam saw, had dived to within a couple of hundred feet of the blaze and was crisscrossing back and forth across the area. Smoke reached the fighters' altitude and the air was bumpy and unstable with the rising heat.

"Banjo Flight, this is Rash Two Two, back with you. They're cranking up some ground troops for an insertion and I've got additional fight-ers on the way to cover it. Let's have each of you make one last pass and clear your racks. There's not much sense in laying down any cannon fire. I still haven't seen any ground fire. Put your remaining nape on the northern fringe, about fifty meters from where the fire has burned."

Sam was disappointed. He'd wanted to fire the guns. An attack pilot seldom got to see the explosions of his ordnance, unless it was a strafing run. It was a thrill to watch the 20mm slugs chewing up the brush and countryside. But it was not to be. He made his call and pulled into his last run. The g forces still had him pinned to the seat as Rash called.

"Banjo Lead, this is Rash Two Two with your BDA. Preliminary only. I'll pass any follow-up to your wing after the grunts let me know what they've found. But I'm giving your flight one hundred percent ordnance in the target area. Good bombing from both aircraft. I've counted thirty-six bunkers down; one major secondary explosion, and at least fourteen smaller secondaries; negative KBAs observed. Banjo Flight is cleared from the target area. Pleasure working with both of you; you're good bombers. If I ever get to Bien Hoa we'll have a drink and tell lies. So long. Rash. Out."

Sam banked hard to set an intercept course on Banjo Lead, who turned slowly southward toward Bien Hoa. In moments he was again tucked neatly behind the right wing of Banjo Leader. Stan spread him out again by fishtailing his aircraft.

"How about *that* shit?" Red Morgan said from the rear cockpit. Sam had almost forgotten he was there, for he hadn't spoken since early in the flight. "You could bomb here for two years and never see a secondary like that. Wonder what the hell it was to go up like that?"

Sam shook his head. "No telling. Have to be some kinda munitions, though. That's the only thing that could give that kind of bang."

"Did you have fun, kid?" asked Red.

Sam thought about it. It *was* great to be back in a fighter again, experiencing the pure joy of flying a sophisticated piece of hardware, and having the opportunity to bring all of his experience and skills to complete a complicated job. But there was a little something missing that he'd never noticed before. He had missed that feeling of control to which he'd become accustomed as a FAC. The bombing had been fun, but he'd felt as though he'd been on automatic pilot. Rash Two Two in his little puddle jumper had run the show, and Banjo Flight had followed his directions to the letter. It was comparable to a mahout and his elephant.

"It was great, Red. I really appreciate the chance to get back into it again."

"Beats those little Tinkertoys, doesn't it?"

"Yeah, it sure does." Hypocrite, he thought silently, and turned his attention back to the lead ship that was sharply dropping a wing, beckoning him into tight formation for the approach and landing at Bien Hoa air base.

*   *   *

Red Morgan had been right. Sam *did* seem to know almost half the pilots in the fighter squadron. As they walked into the sprawling wooden officers' club they almost collided with Peewee Schultz and Dutch Mueller, former squadron mates of Sam's at George Air Force Base in California. They headed for the bar in a group. Joining the pilots from the F-100 squadron at happy hour were the American A-1 fliers from the VNAF wing. A small group of B-57 aircrewmen sat alone at a pair of tables. Members of the Ranch Hand detachment, easily identified by their fatigues and bush hats, formed another group in the barroom. They could have been identified as easily by the strong smell of the defoliant they had sprayed on the jungle canopy. The odor was still emanating from their clothing. The groups tended to ignore each other. Solitary drinkers in khaki and fatigues filled the empty spaces along the bar's length.

Red Morgan strode purposefully to the bar and reached high to ring a small bell hanging above it. The noisy crowd became silent. "Let me have your attention," Red bellowed. "I'm buying the bar, even for you faggoty A-1 pukes." A chorus of boos and jeers quickly arose from the A-1 pilots. "I want you all to come meet Sam Brooks, who's a FAC down in the delta. But he's also one of the best damned fighter pilots I've ever known. We were flying together when most of you were still on mother's milk. That was back in the days when all a fighter pilot had for breakfast was a cigarette and a puke before he spent ten hours trying to pull the wings off an airplane. Not like you sissies who think you're overworked if you fly two sorties a day."

Jeers came from the entire crowd. Red held his hands up for quiet. "But the main reason I'm buying the bar is because me and Sam here, singlehandedly today, just about wiped the Viet Cong off the face of the earth. Stan," he gestured at his ops officer who was leaning against the bar, grinning, "helped a little. But it was really Sam and me who put the whipping on them. If any of you doubt it, trot outside and look north. You can still see the smoke rising."

"What d'ya do, Red," yelled a flight-suited lieutenant colonel from the A-1 squadron, "breathe on 'em? I know you couldn't hit 'em with a bomb."

"Never you mind, Freddy, just step on up here and get your free drink. I may not do this again until it's time for my DEROS."

"If I know your cheap ass," the light colonel retorted, "it probably won't even be then. You'll try to sneak out in the dead of night."

The crowd surged toward the bar, many of them stopping to cluster around Sam. Many he knew by name; others only by sight, though he'd been assigned somewhere with them. Many of the younger ones he didn't know. Their friendliness and acceptance was like a warm blanket that wrapped him in a sense of well-being. These were his people and this was where he belonged. Not stuck in the backwaters of the war with a herd of stiff-backed army officers. The thought suddenly hit him like a gunshot: These days would soon be over. What the hell did civilians do after work? The picture of himself in a business suit, slinking into a strange bar to furtively down a quick drink before the commute back to an empty apartment, depressed him. He motioned the bartender for another scotch.

Sam was unaware when he slipped from sobriety into drunkenness, but the change had undeniably occurred. He tried to focus on the face of the captain who stood before him trying to explain something Sam found very silly. It had to do with automobiles. Sam was fascinated by the captain's mustache. It was long and bushy and appeared to be alive. It seemed to be trying to escape from the young man's face, and Sam wondered if the man knew it or whether he should warn him. After all, mustaches didn't grow on trees. The captain paused to take a breath.

"Pardon me," said Sam, taking care to enunciate his words very clearly, "but I think your mustache is trying to get away." The captain stared at him, goggle-eyed. He probably didn't hear me, thought Sam. It *was* very noisy at the moment.

"I said," Sam repeated, "your mustache is trying to get away."

Understanding came into the captain's eyes and he clapped a hand over his mouth, face frozen in horror. Sam watched with a confirming smile. It wasn't every day that your facial hair tried to pull a fast one and leave without paying the rent. The captain sprang to the bar and, with only a little scrambling, hoisted himself onto it and peered into the mirror on the back wall. He turned his head to look at the offending hair from several different angles.

"Naw," he said, finally satisfied, "it's OK."

Sam noted, however, that he kept returning his fingers to his mouth to make sure. Good thinking.

A solid "thunk" followed by a cheer drew Sam's attention away from the captain and the errant mustache to a crowd circling the participants of the newest game craze to hit the fighter community. Stolen directly from the Australian fighter pilots, who were said to have purloined it from the British fighter messes, it was called, "Are You There, Moriarty?"

Two blindfolded players lay on their backs, head to toe with right hands clasped. The object was for one of them to scoot his body slowly around without the opposing player being aware of the new position. One would whisper the statement, "Are you there, Moriarty?" and the other had to answer, "Here." Using the whispered response as a guide, the questioner would then attempt to locate the other and beat his skull into pulp with a rolled copy of *Life* magazine. The players alternated being questioner and answerer. Sam joined the enthusiastic crowd just as another wild blow was launched by a gangly major at his opponent, a young first lieutenant. The magazine crashed into the lieutenant's shoulder, missing the head altogether. The crowd jeered.

The major, keeping his right arm and hand very still, inched his body in a direction he felt to be safe.

"Are you there, Moriarty?" asked the lieutenant, rolled magazine poised for the strike.

"Here," whispered the major, trying to duck his face from the coming blow.

The young pilot accurately analyzed the response, considered the wind effects and the probable escape route of his opponent, and sent a crashing blow to the bridge of the major's nose. There was a loud yell and the offended organ immediately geysered blood onto the major's flight suit. The crowd cheered lustily. Like an audience at a Roman circus, these men didn't want any safety-first entertainment; they wanted blood.

The game was stopped momentarily for first aid, and Sam wandered away from the crowd. He'd had too much to drink and he knew it. Red was leading a group of singers at the bar and Sam steered clear. There were suddenly too many people around him. He needed air.

At the end of the bar he motioned for another drink and glanced at the Mickey Mouse clock hanging on the wall behind the glasses. He was vaguely surprised to find that it was only 2100. He thought it was much later than that. Shoot, it was early. Still, he decided that this drink would be the last. He walked from the bar toward the front of the club and found himself in a large vestibule where there were several telephones on the walls. He had an inspiration. At this time of day he could probably get through to Can Tho! He might be able to talk to Lee if she were home, since he knew that her phone connected into the GI land line net. Why the hell not? This was suddenly a very important matter. He *had* to talk to Lee.

Sam fumbled in his wallet for her number, found it, and peered boozily at it. He picked up the phone and dialed the operator. Buzzing and crackling was the only response. Eventually, a harassed operator responded to his repeated clicking.

"Tiger!" the voice said, identifying the Tiger land line net.

"Can Tho," said Sam.

"Priority?"

Sam thought for a minute. "Two," he said.

"Verify," said the exasperated operator.

"Priority two. I'm Colonel Jackson Jones, deputy for ops, 2d Air Division." He turned his head and covered his mouth with his hand to suppress the giggles.

"I can get you to My Tho, Colonel," said the operator.

"Do it," replied Sam.

"Working?" An operator from another net broke in on the line.

"Working," said Sam, confirming that the line was in use.

"My Tho," said yet another harassed operator.

"Can Tho," said Sam, "priority two."

"Working?"

"Working," said Sam.

"Can Tho."

"Give me Tiger 543."

"Working?"

"Working."

"Call priority, please."

"Priority two."

"Tiger 543 is ringing, sir."

"Working?"

"Yes, goddamnit! Working!"

"Hello." Lee sounded very alert.

"Working?"

"Get off this goddamned line, you silly bastards. Of course I'm working, or trying to if you'd stop interrupting."

"Is that you, Sam?"

"Working?"

"Yes, you shithead! This line is working!"

"Sam! Why are you swearing at me?"

"I'm *not* swearing at you for Christ's sake!"

"Working?"

"Well, it certainly sounds like swearing to me!"

"Working?"

Sam gritted his teeth and tried to control himself. He spoke very gently. "This is General Westmoreland and if every operator on this net doesn't clear the line I'm going to have every one of you shot tomorrow morning."

"Working?"

"GET OFF THIS FUCKING PHONE!"

"Sam Brooks! If you think I'm going to listen to any more of this, then you're out of your mind! We'll talk about this when you're sober enough to carry on a sensible conversation. Good night!"

"No, Lee, listen—"

"Working?"

"No, Tiger. This is definitely not working," Sam said dejectedly. Replacing the receiver, he slumped into the chair, a beaten man.

CHAPTER 11

Sam had a problem. It was becoming worse with the passing minutes. He shoved his head into the slipstream and peered through the rain, searching for the interlocking barbwire and treeless minefields that surrounded the triangular Special Forces outpost of Tra Pho. The rain smeared on his helmet visor, making forward vision next to impossible. He shoved the visor back into the helmet slot and squinted against the stinging raindrops, trying to protect his face with a crooked arm. Holding his arm so that the rain didn't directly hit his face also blocked his vision. He pulled both his arm and face from the slipstream into the relative tranquility of the O-1 cockpit, then leaned forward to peer through the windscreen again, but the rain beat on it with such ferocity that forward visibility was less than a mile. Probably no more than half a mile.

"Blackjack Two One, this is Robin Two Echo. I can hear you but have no visual contact. The sound of your engine is on a bearing of zero four five from our position. Be advised that we've got people in the southeast wire at this time. Casualties are heavy and we're about outta beebees for the mortars. We're gonna need help from somebody and damned quick."

"Rog," Sam said, "I'm turning toward you. Let me know if you see me." Quickly, he added 180 degrees to the 045 bearing the sergeant had given him and turned southwest to a reciprocal heading of 225 degrees. First he had to find the outpost, a small detachment from a parent A-Team unit, then he'd try to figure out what he could do to help blunt the attack. In places, the visibility was no more than a quarter of a mile. A huge cyclonic system in the Gulf of Thailand had pushed the saturated air northeast onto the Cau Mau peninsula, where the heat of the land mass triggered gigantic thunderstorms rising to incredible proportions. The Viet Cong 18B battalion had been quick to take advantage of the inclement conditions to launch an attack at the small isolated Special Forces outpost sited almost on the Cambodian border. The defenders consisted of only two U.S. Special Forces sergeants and sixty Vietnamese strikers, duty that was rotated monthly from their permanent A-Team camp in Hau Doc province. Tra Pho had long been a thorn in the side of the Viet Cong infiltration net, sitting as it did squarely aside both the land and water routes used to bring men and supplies into South Vietnam.

One flight of F-100 SuperSabres had already departed the area for their home base, still carrying their ordnance, unable to find a way down through the turbulence. Sam glanced at the altimeter. He'd slipped down to four hundred feet trying to remain clear of the clouds. He leaned from the cockpit again to study the ragged bases of the cumulus above him—probably two hundred feet higher than he was flying, with irregular holes between storm cells through which he could see another higher cloud deck. The new flight of F-100s was flying between these decks, awaiting his determination as to whether they'd be able to bomb.

The stick shuddered in his gloved hand as the unstable air of a nearby storm cell shook the aircraft. He corrected without conscious thought. Shit! Where was the camp? He could have overflown it easily enough. No, the lone American sergeant still on his feet would have told him. He decided to hold the heading for another minute before reversing course.

Sam actually had several problems and damned few solutions. First, the camp's 105mm howitzer had been struck dead on by a VC mortar round that not only accounted for its demise but the severe wounds of one of the two SF NCOs. Now the defenders were quickly running out of ammo for their mortars. If that happened it would be only a matter of minutes before the superior forces of the VC would overwhelm the garrison. They needed the TACAIR badly. Getting it to them through the clouds was going to be dicey, since the fighters had shown up with five-hundred-pound slick bombs that some idiot had prescribed as the load for the alert birds. They'd need to release the slicks at a high enough altitude for them to arm before impact or they would not detonate. The fighters would need at least two thousand feet to pull out of their dive after release or they'd impact the ground alongside their bombs. Sam also had to consider that the bombs detonated by the M904 fuse would cause them to sling shrapnel at thirteen hundred feet per second in every direction until the air resistance slowed it. Nevertheless, within nine seconds of impact the hot metal could be up to nearly three thousand feet over the target. That was approximately the same distance as the current visibility, so he'd be lucky if he could visually clear their passes and not become a casualty himself. And that was forgetting about the normal 25 percent safety factor. It was going to be damned tricky, especially with the ground fire that was sure to come.

"Robin Two Echo, this is Blackjack Two One. Can you still hear me?"

"Two Echo. Affirm. Come south a little. I think you're heading straight for us. You gonna be able to help?"

"We're going to do our damnedest but you folks are going to have to dig deep. This is not the best bombing weather I've ever seen."

Sam could hear the man chuckle as though they were at a training exercise. He could also hear the small-arms fire and the crump of mortars landing as Two Echo keyed his mike on the PRC-10.

"You must be new to the area. There ain't no digging in down here. Groundwater starts about two inches below the surface. But we got bunkers and a concrete wall to get behind."

"I gotta be square with you, Two Echo. This is going to be damned close. The ordnance could just as easily fall on top of you as the dinks. Do you still want us to try?"

"Blackjack, this is Two Echo. It's not that we got all that much choice. They're in the wire and I'm down to about twenty-five effectives. Do what you gotta do. I'll approve it."

"OK, Two Echo. Is there too much rain to light your fire arrow?" Sam referred to a box built in the shape of an arrow and filled with sand, which was either saturated with gasoline or lined with individual buckets of fuel and lighted. The troops at the Special Forces camp could then rotate the burning arrow to point at the area outside the wire where they wanted attack aircraft to strike.

"I think we can get her cooked off. It'll be pointing toward our southeastern perimeter."

Sam didn't have the heart to tell him that directions would be virtually meaningless to any fighter pilot diving and squirming down through the heavy clouds. They'd have little chance to look at their instruments and remain free of the ground.

A brief flash of light caught his attention just as he was deciding he'd missed the beleaguered outpost. He could barely see the outlines of the camp below him. What he had seen was the impact of a Viet Cong mortar round close to the central bunker. He stared at the picture. It was like looking at something out of focus, blurry and lacking sharp detail. He thought he could see the first tendrils of fog stringing itself in the treetops like someone decorating a Christmas tree.

"I've got you in sight, Blackjack! Right over us."

"Rog. I've got you now. I'll try to orbit and keep you in sight."

"OK, but best watch your butt. They're starting to hammer at you."

Thanks very much, Sam thought, and heard the solid chunks of two rounds impacting on his aircraft. He heeled the Bird Dog over into a steep left turn and headed for the other end of the camp, a distance of only a hundred meters or so, but the crappy visibility should help hide him a bit.

"Two Echo, I've got your fire arrow. Confirm it's pointing in the direction of the dinks." He wanted to be positive, although he could see the dark figures prone in the southeastern wire. Most had gone to ground when he overflew the camp.

"That's correct, Blackjack. Lay it on 'em."

"OK, I'll be monitoring you but I'm going to have to talk to the fighters all the way in. If you want a correction, just sing out over the radio. I'll answer if I can. If not, we'll just have to soldier on. Understood?"

"Roger, I got ya."

Sam switched to his UHF radio, making sure that the toggle for the FM remained on so that he could hear the calls from the camp. He contacted the waiting fighters. "Rap Lead, this is Blackjack. How ya doing?"

"Well, we're getting pretty proficient in instrument flying again, Blackjack. We're down to fifteen minutes before bingo fuel."

The voice sounded familiar but Sam didn't have time to play games. "Stretch it all you can, Rap Flight. These people need help bad and it ain't going to be easy to get to 'em. Can you see the ground through the breaks in the overcast?"

"A little bit every now and then. But these storm cells are about to join hands up here."

"OK, let's give it a shot. I'm going to put two marking rockets on the wire to the southeast of the camp. It's fulla dinks. Maybe you'll be able to see one of the smokes. I'm gonna be right over the north edge of the camp. Anyplace in the wire or beyond it to the south is good hunting. For that matter, anyplace outside the wire will be OK. The camp is a triangular shape. Remember, anything to the south. Camp's fire arrow will be going and pointing in the direction to hit. The ceiling is about six hundred feet, with heavy rain showers all around. Your forward visibility is going to be piss poor, and you'll have only a second or two to find the target and drop. I don't have to tell you that you're gonna be damned close to your own weapon detonations, but we've got a real emergency down here. You're both cleared to drop."

There was a moment of shocked silence from the fighter lead, then: "You mean you're clearing us to drop before we even get into the run?"

Rap Lead was getting too concerned about the rules of engagement for Sam's liking. "That's correct, Rap Lead. You're both cleared in hot. It's my call and I'm making it. If you can't live with it, clear the area and I'll work with Two."

There was another moment of silence before Rap Leader transmitted: "I can live with it if you can, Blackjack." Sam knew that voice from somewhere.

"Right. Blackjack is in for the marks." Sam heeled the Bird Dog into a tight turn to the south, aligned himself with the dimly seen fire arrow, and overflew the camp at five hundred feet. He stuck his head from the cockpit into the rain again, trying to shield his eyes with an out-thrust hand. Directly over the burning arrow he began to make out the tangled wire outside the wall. He was helped by the AK-47 flashes directed at him from the forward VC unit. Jesus! At this altitude he could see the smoke from the muzzles of the enemy assault rifles. He pointed the nose of the aircraft at them and, without aiming, punched off two smoke rockets, then was in a hard climbing turn back to the north. He could feel the sweat dribbling from beneath his helmet onto his clammy forehead. His heart was pounding as he gained the sanctuary of the clouds.

Cruising in the safety of the clouds he tried to remember if he'd heard any rounds impacting on the aircraft. He'd been so frightened he couldn't be sure. He eased the aircraft down out of the clouds again, finding himself just passing the northern perimeter of Tra Pho. He turned the aircraft slowly back to the south and watched the two white balls of smoke rising from his rockets. One was in the tanglefoot wire, the other slightly outside. No problem.

"Rap Lead, smokes are away. Hit them or anywhere south. I'll be trying to stay outta your way—right on the deck at the northwest edge of the camp."

"Rog." The F-100 flight leader's voice sounded tight and a little high-pitched. It damned well should. He was about to stick his jet into the clouds in a thirty-degree dive, unable to see the ground except in brief snatches. A wrong drop could do as much damage as the VC attackers. A second's hesitation on the movement of the control stick could cause his aircraft to plow directly into the ground.

"Lead is in hot with bombs. FAC and target are *not* in sight."

Sam let his aircraft drift downward in a spiral until he had to cock his wing to avoid the tall radio antenna over the team bunker. He was anxiously scanning the base of the bulging clouds when the screaming jet almost took him broadside. It flashed by his four o'clock position so quickly that Sam didn't have time to react. Just as quickly its shaken pilot yanked it into a climb, barely avoiding the ground. No bombs had been dropped, but the sudden appearance of the jet had sent the attackers to the ground.

"Lead's off dry," the pilot said in a shaken voice. "Two," he continued, "the only way we're going to pull this thing off is to try to shallow the dive angle and drop before we can really see the ground. I damned near made a big hole in it myself that time."

"How about this," Sam broke in. "I know it sounds crazy but what if I overflew the target area and pulled up into a vertical climb and shot a rocket? You guys could see where it came through the clouds and use that as a target marker. You'd just have to make sure that your ordnance goes on it or south of it."

"Just how bad are these folks on the ground hurting?"

Sam glanced quickly toward the southern end of the camp before he answered. "Lead, the dinks are through the wire. The last time I talked to them the green beanie sergeant told me he had fewer than twenty-five effectives. Probably less than that now. He said they had no choice."

Rap Lead sighed audibly over the radio. "OK, but you'd better be pretty damned proficient in low-level, instrument-only aerobatics."

"Are we gonna try it?" Sam demanded.

"Just try to let us know before you shoot."

"OK, I'm in now. Remember, south of the rocket's smoke trail."

Trying not to think about what he'd talked himself into doing, Sam turned and carefully aligned the aircraft with the fire arrow. The rain was coming down harder as a fresh storm moved into the area. He was having difficulty keeping the small aircraft on course in the turbulence. Concentrating on the heading, he tried to ignore the outside distractions. His brain registered another clunk as an AK round tore somewhere into the aircraft's fuselage cavity. Over the fire arrow, he took another quick look at the southeastern wire around the camp. The enemy troops were up and moving. Green sparklers were directed toward him from the muzzles of the assault rifles. Some of them were coming toward him but most were aimed toward the camp proper. The Viet Cong must have decided that there was little danger from the air on this day. They're probably right, Sam thought. Maybe we're flogging a dead horse.

The wire was moving toward him quickly. Trying not to think he focused on the scant instrument panel before him. Another round whined off the strut. Sam didn't dare spare it a glance. Firmly, he pulled the stick straight back into his gut, compensating for the increased torque that came as the airspeed bled away with a booted foot on the rudder. Steadily the nose came up. Forty-five degrees. Sixty degrees. Airspeed down to seventy. Keep the nose coming! Seventy-five degrees of climb. Sam eased off some of the back pressure. The attitude indicator, his primary instrument for blind flying, suddenly tumbled. His heart felt as though it would burst from his chest before he remembered that it was a natural phenomenon as the aircraft approached the vertical position.

He punched a rocket and was immediately enveloped in the gray clouds. Nothing to it, he said aloud, trying to calm himself. Keep a nice steady back pressure on the stick and come right on through. Just bring it right around. The attitude indicator had again regained its sense and showed that he was on the backside of the loop. When the nose showed forty-five degrees above the horizon on the indicator, he began a steady roll to the left, uprighting the Bird Dog.

He popped below the clouds once more and was vaguely excited to find that he was back over the camp again. He leveled at four hundred feet and found that his hand was shaking on the stick. He also realized that he hadn't called the fighters that he'd launched the rocket. But they'd seen it.

"Blackjack, this is Rap Lead. A rocket just came bustin' ass through the clouds by us. Damned near hit Two. I assume that was yours but I didn't get a call about it." He was not a happy flight leader.

Sam, still shaking, didn't give a good shit whether he was happy or not. "That's the one for you, Rap. I got a little too busy to call. I suggest you go ahead and make a regular dive and just pretend that's your target. You can make your pullout at your regular altitude. You won't be able to see the ground but this should work. At least, the dinks won't be able to see you. You're cleared in hot. Remember, if you gotta miss, miss long."

"Rog. Lead's in hot. Nothin' in sight."

The pair of five hundred pounders seemed to come out of nowhere. Even Sam, who was expecting them, was startled. They detonated long on the southeastern wire, but they certainly got the full attention of the determined attackers. Sam was close enough to see some of them crouch and turn to see what the hell was going on behind them. The bombs had exploded in the thick trees to the south, flinging them about like so many toothpicks. Hopefully, the reserve VC troops had been squatting there, waiting their turn at the assault. The SF sergeant was yelling and whooping over the radio.

"That's the way to go, Blackjack! Whup their asses! Gimme all you've got. Do it! Do it!"

"Two's in from the north. I got your rocket smoke trail in sight."

"OK, Two. Cleared hot. Just try to do the same thing Lead did. Punch down through the soup as near as you can to the same place he did. Lead, those were two good bombs. A little long but damned good under the circumstances."

"Lead, Rog."

Rap Two's bombs were closer to the wire than the Lead's had been. Maybe the smoke trail of the rocket was drifting. It could be bad news if it was drifting back toward the camp.

"Lead, clear your racks on this pass if you can," Sam called quickly.

The fighter pilot responded with two clicks of his mike switch, the unofficial but generally used aviation signal for "acknowledge." Sam looked toward the attackers at the far end of the camp. They seemed to be undecided. Most were prone, looking back toward the wood line where the unexpected explosions had occurred. Doing so gave them a grand opportunity to witness an F-100 releasing a good part of its ordnance in one pass. Again, the aircraft was never visible and the detonations were well south of the wire, but they were spectacular nonetheless. The forest seemed to disintegrate as the six five-hundred-pound bombs tore into it.

The army sergeant on the ground was almost incoherent with joy. "Goddamn! Way to go! Damn, by God! Wahoo! Do 'em, do 'em, do 'em! Damn!"

"Good bombs, Lead," said Sam. "Two, can you still see the smoke trail?"

"Yeah, I can just make it out. I'd better dump everything on this pass unless you want to put another up."

The thought sent chills down Sam's spine. "Negative, just make this one last pass, but I'd appreciate it if you folks can hang around and maybe find a way under this crap. It's down to about five hundred feet or so now, but we could sure use some twenty millimeter in the wire."

"Let Two get rid of these damned bombs first. I don't know why they ever put us on the alert pads with slicks anyway," Rap Lead grumbled.

"You're cleared in hot, Two. Clean your racks."

"Rap Two. Rog."

There was another spectacular set of detonations—unfortunately almost a mile away from the embattled camp. Better than nothing, though. The increasing distance of the explosions seemed to spur on the VC attackers, for they were once more on their feet, threading their way through the broken wire and mud. Single-minded assholes, thought Sam.

"Rap Flight, are you two back together?" inquired Sam.

"Yeah, Blackjack, Two's joining up now."

"Listen, did you think about what I asked you before? Y'all think you can find a way under this crud and do a little workout with your cannons? It's really not so bad down here," Sam wheedled.

"That depends," said Rap Lead. "Are you going to insult me anymore?"

"Listen, I'm really sorry if I hurt your feelings. I apologize."

"Promise you'll buy me two, no, three drinks the next time you get to Bien Hoa?"

"Who the hell is this?" Sam demanded.

"Pete Lara," the lead pilot said with a laugh. They'd served together at Langley field in the late fifties and had been reunited at the party Sam attended at Bien Hoa.

"You're on, asshole. Where are you now?"

"Trying to find the bottom of this crap north of you. We were already coming down. I just wanted to have a witness to your promise. OK, here's what we're doing. I got a glimpse of that fire arrow and took us due north away from the camp. We're letting down through the clouds now. When and if we break out, we're going to do a ninety, two-seventy–degree procedure turn back to a reciprocal heading. That ought to put us within visual range of the camp. Sound OK?"

"Sounds real good, Pete. Let me know when you're procedure turn, inbound. I'm going over toward the wire and see if I can do anything to keep the dinks busy until you two can get back. When you're inbound I'll smoke the general area again. Remember, same rules as before. If you have to miss, miss long."

"Right, we're still descending. Through two thousand feet now and the gunk is as solid as ever. If anything, it's getting worse. It's raining like a bitch and right turbulent."

"Hang in there, Rap. These folks need help bad."

"Hell, I'm not going anywhere. Just giving you a running commentary."

"No sweat. I'm going off frequency to talk to the camp, but I'll be listening out so just call when you're inbound and I'll put out some smoke. Incidentally, for the record, you're both cleared to fire."

"Rog. Rap is cleared hot."

Sam banked toward the camp, which was rapidly becoming more indistinct in the heavier rain. Swirls of fog were definitely forming in the tops of the trees, he noticed with some alarm. Already some low-lying streambeds were obscured in the gray mist. If fog rolled in, there would be absolutely no way that anyone could give Tra Pho any sort of air support, helicopter or fixed wing. And they were located too far out on the limb for artillery support. Right now, the only option Sam could see for the defenders to stay alive through the night was the 20mm cannons of the F-100s.

Again, Sam used the burning fire arrow to orient himself to the southern wall and wire, although the fuel burning in the shank of the arrow had been extinguished, he noted as he moved closer. He let the Bird Dog drift down to stay out of the clouds. There was now no more than four hundred feet between the cloud base and the ground. He circled the radio antenna at the team house and peered in the gloom toward the southern end of the camp. Some of the attackers were all the way to the wall. As he watched, a flurry of grenades tumbled inside the wall to explode. South Vietnamese strikers answered with a flurry of their own.

Sam hurriedly switched to the FM radio. "Robin Five Echo, this is Blackjack. How y'all doing down there?" There was only an angry hiss from the radio. No nonchalant southern voice answered. He tried again. "Five Echo, Five Echo, this is Blackjack. How do you read?"

A voice answered this effort but it was not the one Sam wanted to hear. It spoke badly mutilated English, barely understandable over the static. "Airplene, airplene. Sarjunt hur' bad. Bery' bad. You help, OK?"

Shit! "Yes," Sam answered, "we're going to help. You help the sergeants and we'll attack the VC. Keep fighting! You understand?"

"Oui. We continues fight hard. You help, OK?"

"Yes, yes. We're going to help. Take care of the sergeant."

"Oui."

Sam switched back to the fighter frequency, since he could think of little more in the way of a pep talk. He'd be of more use talking to the fighters. "Rap Lead, where are you and how's it going?"

"We're through six hundred feet and I'm beginning to see the ground through breaks in the clouds. Sorry that it's taking so long, but I'm afraid to let down any quicker. We're not going to help anybody by running into the trees. Should be starting the procedure turn in about thirty seconds."

Sam acknowledged and continued watching the attack unfold. The VC inside the wire ignored his airplane, aware of its impotence. He knew what they were thinking. He was to be feared only if he was capable of directing the killer aircraft toward them. Obviously, this day he could not. After they gained control of the camp they could train their weapons against him, should he be so foolish as to stay above them. Maybe you're wrong assholes, thought Sam as he reached for his shotgun.

He positioned the Bird Dog to the west of the camp and began a power-on descent toward the heaviest of the fighting. Sam checked that the safety was in the off position on the pump gun and extended its barrel out the window into the rain. By twisting slightly he could hold the stock in his right armpit and the slide in his left hand. He let the aircraft sag to three hundred feet, then grasped the stick between his legs and moved his right hand to the trigger.

So intent were the Viet Cong attackers that they didn't spare him a glance as he wobbled in from the gloom. Directly above them, he twisted his legs sharply to the left to put the aircraft into a left bank and used his right rudder to keep the aircraft from turning. Jamming the muzzle of the shotgun in the direction of the massed enemy troops, he jerked the trigger, worked the slide furiously, and fired again. He continued until the magazine was empty, then dropped it to the cockpit floor and grabbed the stick with his right hand, setting the aircraft upright once more. He felt a grim satisfaction. He may not have killed anybody, but he stung some asses and got their attention, and maybe a little respite for the defenders.

"Rap Flight is procedure turn, inbound."

"Good deal, Rap. I'm putting in a Willie Pete and then moving west of the camp as far as I can get and still see it. Get some!" Sam turned his aircraft and aimed it in the general direction of the wire, squeezed off his rocket, staying as far as he could from the angry Viet Cong, then flew westward toward the Cambodian border until the camp began to blur in the rain. From that point he started a north to south race-track orbit, trying to keep the camp in sight. The two sleek jets materialized from the gloom like specters, and vanished as rapidly without firing a shot.

"Crap! Blackjack, Rap saw 'em too late to get anything off. We're bending back around to the left for another try."

"Rog, Rap Lead. At least your overflight got their attention. Be careful this time because they know you're coming. Work it right up to the wall if you can. I'm still about a klick west of the camp. You're cleared to shoot."

"Rog, we'll be inbound in thirty seconds."

Before Sam saw the two F-100s on the new attack, the high-explosive 20mm cannon rounds were tearing up the bodies in the wire. Some were thrown into the air; others seemed to disintegrate. Sam had never been so close to the actual detonation point of the aircraft's cannons. Line abreast, the two attack jets cut a swath of death before disappearing once more into the gloom. Each aircraft had fired for no more than two seconds, yet it was sufficient to blunt the attack. The psychological effect of their sudden and unexpected appearance had probably proven as valuable as the bullets they fired.

"We're coming around again, Blackjack. Want it in the same place?"

"They're moving back from the wall now, Rap. Try to start about fifty meters back from it and work it toward the tree line where the smoke from the bombs is rising."

"Rog, we're inbound now. This has gotta be the last pass. We're already past bingo fuel and God knows what the weather is back at home plate. If I splatter my ass all over the jungle for this, Sam, I'm never going to speak to you again."

"Understand, last pass. See if you can't empty your guns for me. You're cleared hot."

"Rap is cleared hot."

The savagery of the attack startled even Sam. Feeling more comfortable attacking under the lowering clouds, the pilots of the SuperSabres pressed farther than they had on the first pass. They also knew they would be leaving the area after the run. The twin explosive swaths walked into the tree line, blowing foliage asunder and chopping small trees into splinters. Branches flew high into the air. Sam turned quickly for the south wall of the camp as the jets disappeared, their workday over.

The workday also appeared to be over for the 18B Main Force Viet Cong Battalion. Survivors straggled toward the smoldering wood line. Others ran from one prone figure to another, assisting some, bypassing obvious dead who would be collected after dark. Several figures watched warily as the O-1 put-putted low over their heads, but none bothered to fire at it. An unscheduled truce appeared to have been declared. Sam turned back to the main camp lest he be the one to break it. He knew he'd never be able to get another set of fighters working beneath the lowering sky. A survivor from the camp crawled from a bunker and peered suspiciously over the wall at the enemy, then looked up and waved at Sam. Sam rocked his wings and continued his orbit, making a final call to Rap Flight.

"Rap Lead, this is Blackjack Two One. I can give you only an estimated BDA but I would like to pass along that you two saved any warm bodies that might still be down there in Tra Pho. I'm giving you a preliminary count of twenty-six KBA. All bombs in the target area. I'll pass on an eyewitness written report to your wing along with my recommendation for awards for both of you. I'm sure if either of the Americans survived they'll be glad to add their accounts to mine. I'll make sure those get to you as well. Good luck on getting back into Bien Hoa. I won't forget those drinks I owe you, Pete."

"Take care of yourself, Sam. Adios. Two, let's go company frequency."

Sam tried to raise the camp radio but had no luck. He deliberately steered over the trees to which the VC had retreated but received no ground fire, nor could he find evidence that they were still in the area. He knew they were, though. They'd hang around at least long enough to pick up their dead before heading back into their Cambodian sanctuary. Unless the strikers from the camp made a quick foray, no one would ever know how many of the enemy had been lost that day. If they were sensible, they'd forget about it, since it didn't really matter one way or the other. Sam had heard officers claim that the enemy always tried to retrieve their dead to deny that intelligence to the government forces. He figured such an idea was unadulterated crap. They brought back their dead for the same reason the Americans did—out of respect, as well as an innate primal fear everyone had of dying alone. For the Vietnamese, who worshipped their dead, there was even more of an incentive to recover the bodies.

Sam checked his fuel tanks and realized he would have to leave soon. He was a good half hour from the Bac Lieu airstrip. He tried the radio again and was rewarded by only a hiss of static. He slipped the Bird Dog down to one hundred feet and flew slowly over the center of the camp. It was a shambles, but a few figures were walking purposefully around. He decided he'd done everything he could do except make a radio call to the Special Forces A-Team camp and let them know what the situation was. He'd do that as soon as he was within radio range. He rocked his wings and turned away. Fog was filling the treetops, and the camp would probably be enveloped within another ten minutes.

The Bac Lieu airstrip had been turned into a duck pond. Sam considered calling the team TOC to see if anyone could tell him how deep the floodwaters were, but since Carl's departure for the States there wasn't another flier living in the compound. Damn! He really missed that redhead. Hopefully, he'd soon be replaced, and before Bill Robinson's own imminent DEROS. Without Bill to short-circuit the crap flowing toward him from Jackson Jones at 2d Air Division, Carl would probably be replaced with the worst kind of loser.

Sam had managed to climb to a giddy six hundred feet on the trip back from Tra Pho. He felt as though he should be on oxygen. He quickly ran through the landing check and nudged the left stick and rudder for a low pass down the submerged runway. He really needed some information. The water might be only an inch deep, or the runway could be covered to a depth of a foot or more. He had no idea how much rain the local area had received.

At the end of the runway he saw a figure standing by a jeep, waving his arms. He cocked the aircraft around to fly closer to the man. He was unidentifiable even at a hundred feet because of the poncho covering his head and torso, but he obviously knew what Sam needed and was trying to communicate the information. He stopped waving his arms, put his hands above his head like a referee signaling a touchdown, then slowly brought them together until they were inches apart. The man then dropped his arms, pointed to the runway, and gave a thumbs-up. Good enough!

Sam used power to drag the aircraft toward the runway, using full flaps and keeping the airspeed just above a stall. Just before he crossed the runway's edge he cut the throttle and pulled the stick back into his lap. The plane fell the last two feet in a three-point attitude and landed hard, just as Sam planned. The resistance of the water on the wheels made for a very short landing roll. His helper had been correct—it was only about three inches deep. He had to add power to get to the parking area, where the ponchoed figure waited again beside the jeep.

Quickly, Sam tied one wing and the tail of the aircraft to the large rocks brought in for just such a purpose while the ponchoed figure did the other wing. Sam grabbed his shotgun and map case, secured the door, and ran for the passenger side of the jeep. The other person took the driver's seat.

Seated, Sam took off his baseball cap and wiped the water from his face before he turned his head and met the flat, hard blue eyes of Col. Jackson Jones.

CHAPTER 12

Colonel Jones didn't speak a word to Sam on the short drive back to the advisory team's compound. The rain splashed the countryside in broad sheets now, reducing the visibility to only a few yards. The thirsty ground had already had its fill and could swallow no more. Standing water was beginning to pool in the carefully tilled paddies. Water boo lay content in the mud, almost purring under the scrubbing hands of their small herders. The Ruff-Puff gate guards had large smiles stretching their betel nut–stained mouths as they huddled together under a common poncho, sharing a cigarette. They waved the jeep through, although General Giap and Ho himself could have been lurking behind the fogged windscreen. It was incomprehensible to the guards that anyone except Saigon's soldiers and the Americans would have a jeep. Sam shook his head. Their laxness should be reported, but there was an unspoken agreement among the team members that it was useless to berate their guardians.

Jones pulled in front of the TOC, climbed wordlessly from the jeep, and walked into the building. Sam followed, wondering what the hell was going on. The province senior adviser (PSA) leaned against the counter talking to a tall, rotund figure in jungle fatigues. The man turned to face Jones and Sam as they entered. He had a silver eagle on his army baseball-style cap and on his shirt collars. He was the most unlikely looking candidate for an army colonel Sam had ever seen. His face was wide and florid and wore a petulant expression, although the corners of the small mouth turned up briefly as he made eye contact with Sam. A tiny automatic pistol was holstered on his right side, supported by a leather belt clasped in front by an ornate buckle. The buckle seemed to have an official seal on it. The ensemble emphasized the girth of the colonel's waist, in contrast to the slimness of the career soldiers in the room.

"Sam," Lieutenant Colonel Whitehead called in greeting, "come over here and tell me what's happening at Tra Pho. Our reports are still pretty sketchy. We're having to work through the Vietnamese comm net and it gets pretty bogged down when we do that."

The PSA listened intently as Sam described what he had seen happen in the camp. Colonel Whitehead drummed his fingers on the countertop after Sam had grown quiet. All eyes in the room were turned expectantly toward him. He ignored them and concentrated on the problem at hand.

"Charley," he said, turning to his ops officer, "we've got to get some arty sited to cover them. Try to get Colonel Tich to shake loose a couple of his 105s and reposition them at Tri Ton. He's not going to want to do it, but hint, very gently of course, that he might find his helicopter support considerably reduced if he doesn't go along with it. Then tell him I'm sending him a case of Black Label—make that two cases of Black Label—and a dozen cases of Salem for distribution to the survivors at Tra Pho in honor of their stand. They'll never get them, of course, but it'll help sweeten the pot. If he still won't go along with the idea of moving the tubes, as a last resort promise him a C and C slick—a real shiny one—for his personal use for a week. If that doesn't work," he turned to Sam with a grin, "tell him that I'm going to have Major Brooks put in an air strike on his sorry ass. No, don't tell him that. I think he'll move them.

"Next, get on the horn to the aviation battalion at Soc Trang and tell Jim Lusky that I want a heavy helicopter fire team within shooting distance of that camp all night or until the howitzers get moved. Tell him I know the weather is shitty, but if the air force can conduct operations under it then he should be able to. If I know him, that ought to be enough to get 'em all the coverage they need. Sam, do you think they'll have any problem operating over there?"

Sam thought a moment before answering. "It looked like there might be fog forming. It might serve as much use if you had them overfly the camp if they can, just to show the flag, then set down, maybe at Giang Thanh, to be available if they're needed. Night weather flying at low level can get nasty, and I really don't think the dinks are coming back except to get their dead and wounded. If they do, then the helicopters can launch. I would try to get a dust-off in for the wounded while there's still a little flying room."

"That's the way we'll do it, then. Tell them that," the PSA said to his ops officer. "I'll really be glad when they get off their asses in Saigon and appoint a new PSA over there. It's damned difficult to make judgment calls for an area you really don't know."

Sam nodded in agreement. The PSA of the province in question and most of his staff had been killed when this same 18B VC Battalion had overrun their compound two weeks prior. A new appointment had not yet been made, the nominee having to satisfy the Vietnamese as well as MACV headquarters. The forward air controller for the province had been among the casualties. Today had been Sam's day in the rotation of other FACs to cover this province while a new pilot was being brought in and processed.

The PSA turned to the plump colonel, who had walked over to stand quietly by Col. Jack Jones. Sam caught Jones's look of distaste as he surveyed the man. Lieutenant Colonel Whitehead made the introductions with a sober face.

"Colonel Wertz, this is Major Sam Brooks." Sam noted that he put a slight emphasis on the title *Colonel*.

A large pudgy hand rose indolently toward Sam. As they shook, Sam felt the small hard eyes boring into him, as though he was trying to read his mind. A little shiver rippled up his spine. This guy was *trouble*. There was no logical reason to feel that, but Sam knew it the instant their eyes met. The question was, trouble for whom?

The voice was deep and sonorous with just a touch of New England twang. The eyes locked onto Sam's with no hint of a blink. "How do you do, Major Brooks. I've heard a great deal about you." No shit! This guy was *real* trouble. "Perhaps you'd be gracious enough to meet me and Colonel Jones after the meal this evening. Providing, of course, that it's all right with Colonel Whitehead."

The eyes said that he didn't give a shit if it was or wasn't all right with Colonel Whitehead. Sam glanced at the PSA, who stared at the man with a wooden expression. He gave a curt nod and turned to the wall map with its myriad overlays, almost as though he was separating himself from whatever the Colonels Wertz and Jones were involved in. Without another word Wertz turned and walked from the room. After a moment's hesitation and a glance at Sam, Jones followed him. Sam stared after them into the slanting rain. He didn't realize that Colonel Whitehead had joined him until the PSA spoke quietly.

"Sam, I don't know what this is all about, but if that guy is an army O-6, I'll eat my silver leaves. To me, he looks, smells, and sounds spook all the way. Is there anything you think you'd better tell me? I don't care who he is, this is still my province until The Man himself tells me to clear out."

Sam shook his head slowly. "You know I've had problems before with Colonel Jones, but I've never seen this other guy. Have they been here long?"

"They were dropped here about half an hour after you left for Tra Pho. Showed me some pretty impressive paperwork and said they'd be leaving after they talked to you. Then the weather grounded their helicopter in Vi Thanh and Colonel Wertz said that it was just as well, that they might need more time with you anyway. What I can't figure out is that I know most of the people in the Studies and Observation Group—they do most of the covert work. Maybe this guy is just off the boat, but I've never seen him before. I asked this Wertz what he wanted with you and he put me in my place. Said it was on a need-to-know basis and I obviously didn't need to know. In other words, butt out. I don't like it, Sam."

"I don't think I care much for it either, Colonel. I don't have any idea what the hell's going on. I especially can't figure out why the director of operations for 2d AD is down here. I mean, here's the number-two man in the air division playing games out in the weeds. I don't know how it goes in the army, but it's damned unusual in the air force."

"It'd be damned unusual even in the Public Health Service, Sam," Colonel Whitehead said with a smile. "Let's let it ride for now. After you talk with them tonight, if you think there's anything I should know, tell me. If it's something that's none of my affair, keep it to yourself and I won't even question you about it. It's just that I can't imagine anything Colonel Wertz has in mind for you as being good. That man looks like *evil*."

Alone in his cubicle Sam sat in his baggy GI underwear and listened to the rain pounding on the metal roof, doing his best not to think about the coming meeting with Wertz and Jones. It had to be something bad if Jack Jones was connected with it. Lightning streaked the darkening sky, followed in seconds by a loud clap of thunder. Whatever they had planned couldn't be as bad as being aloft in an aircraft tonight. This weather could kill you in a moment. A thought chilled him. Whatever those two had in mind might be just as dangerous. He pushed these thoughts away. Maybe he should try to call Lee again.

He immediately recognized the futility in it—he'd tried to get through for a week now, ever since he'd made that stupid phone call from Bien Hoa. The lines had either been tied up, or she'd been out or else not taking calls from him.

Glumly, he wiped the sweat from his naked belly with his hand and flicked it to the rough concrete floor. A mosquito probed at his unprotected thigh and received a whack in return. Sam stared at the glob of blood where the insect had died. They seemed to be more tenacious in damp weather. The rain didn't really cool things off, but only made his clothing and bed constantly damp. Maybe he'd move to Arizona when they kicked him out of the air force. Maybe Santa Fe. Or anyplace where he didn't have to see or hear airplanes. He snorted aloud, knowing he was starting to feel sorry for himself again—he despised himself when he did that. He rose and pulled the chair to the tiny field desk and rummaged around until he found paper and pen. The paper was damp and the ballpoint smeared on it, but he owed those two fighter jocks for their work today. Laboriously, he began to compose his eyewitness account, which he would get Lieutenant Colonel Whitehead to endorse and then forward to their wing at Bien Hoa. It was the least he could do.

Sam preferred to eat alone that evening. Colonel Whitehead seemed to understand, for he only winked and waved as he entered with his staff from TOC. When the mess boy approached to take his order, Sam randomly pointed to selections on the card he offered, then sat back with his beer and stared moodily through the screen at the rain. The compound seemed to be underwater and he overheard someone in the PSA's party stating that there had already been more than seven inches recorded. Sam had heard that it wasn't unusual for the wet season to open with a bang.

Sam felt his muscles tighten as Wertz and Jones entered the mess room. Deliberately, he diverted his gaze back to the rain. Whatever they had would keep until after he'd eaten. He expected them to join the PSA and his staff but they isolated themselves at a table in the far corner of the room. The dining hut shook softly as the Vietnamese battery of 105 howitzers fired H and I (harassment and interdiction) rounds a mile down the road toward town. The rain muffled the sound until it was almost like thunder; its regular cadence was the only distinction between the two. Sam ordered another beer as the mess boy brought his plate of unidentifiable food.

Sam ate methodically, not tasting. Whatever was on the plate was fuel, no more than that. He considered driving to the small airstrip before it got too late and dangerous, concerned about his aircraft. He quickly dismissed that idea. If the Bird Dog hadn't blown away or become submerged by now, it should last the night. There was damned little he could do about it anyway. If it floated out into the South China Sea, the taxpayers would just get him another one.

He became aware of a figure behind him, blocking the light from the bare bulb. He glanced over his shoulder and found Colonel Wertz standing there like a stoic Pillsbury doughboy. Sam was briefly tempted to push his finger into the man's belly to see if he would giggle.

"Major Brooks," the doughboy said, exaggerating the vowels, "Colonel Jones and I would like you to join us in the team room if you've finished your dinner."

Sam looked at Wertz, then to Jackson Jones standing behind him. Neither man blinked. He nodded once and rose from the table to follow them into the rain. Wertz moved at a slow, steady pace, seemingly oblivious to the downpour. The true pecking order became evident as he barged through the door before Colonel Jones. Wertz pointed silently at a table, then seated himself. Rain dripped from his face but he made no effort to dry it. Sam watched with fascination as the water collected on the man's jaw, followed a crevice in the jowly cheek, then ran down somewhere beneath the collar of the fatigue blouse. With a start he became aware that Wertz was watching his inspection with unblinking eyes. He appeared content to wait until Sam had completed the task. Jones didn't sit but leaned against the wall to one side as though separating himself from whatever was coming.

"Brooks," Wertz began, dropping the military title, Sam noted. "You may or may not be surprised to find out that I am not a serving officer in the United States Army. The uniform is legitimate enough, but the source of my commission is from, ahh, let us say, an irregular source. The colonel's insignia is one of convenience. Had I needed it, it could have been two stars. Do you comprehend what I am telling you? There is ample power behind me for me to assume any role that is needed."

"Who *do* you represent?" asked Sam.

"That is not a matter for your concern. Let it be sufficient for you to know that I have the necessary backing to do the task assigned to me."

Sam decided to take the offense. "The fuck it's not my concern! It's pretty damned obvious that you want me for some spook shit. Maybe somebody forgot to tell you that there really ain't a club over my head anymore. Like the old saying goes, what are they going to do—send me to Vietnam? Not promote me? You'd better check with Colonel Jackson Jones before you start telling me what is or what isn't my concern. He and the air force have already pretty much decided my immediate future. So, if you're looking for a volunteer for any of your games, you can all stick it up your collective backsides unless you let me know who I'll be working for."

Wertz eyed Sam speculatively, unruffled by the outburst, for a long moment before replying. "I think you know very well who I work for, Major Brooks."

So, Sam thought with a little germ of satisfaction, the military title is back. He decided to press. "I don't want to think. I want to know for sure or we can just forget whatever proposition you have."

The doughboy sighed heavily. "Yes, Major Brooks, I do indeed work for the Central Intelligence Agency and, yes, we do have a, ahh, project in which we think you can be of some assistance. Be assured, however, you are *not* the only person who could accomplish this, ahh, task, for us. We find it convenient to use an asset such as yourself, but do not delude yourself into thinking we could not accomplish it without your assistance. Understood?"

Sam nodded and rose from his chair, starting for the door.

"Where do you think you're going?"

"Out of here. Get somebody else then," Sam retorted.

"Why?"

"You asked me if I understood. Well, I do, and I know I don't have to take this shit from some comic-opera spook who likes to play dress-up games."

Wertz turned to Colonel Jones, who nodded back toward the chair. Sam returned and sat.

The big man continued. "The fact is, we believe you will want very much to join us in this, ahh, enterprise. We checked with your air liaison officer, Lieutenant Colonel Robinson, in Can Tho, before coming here this morning, and he recommended you. He brought out your previous accomplishments, such as the rescue attempt of that unfortunate airman in the U Minh Forest and your part in the ambuscade of the remnants of the VC unit last month. Oh, there were several other glowing reports but we had already decided on you for several other reasons in addition to your deportment. I will go into that shortly."

"Do I have a say in this at all?" Sam turned to ask Jones.

Jones looked uncomfortable. "Yes, you can decline, but we'll talk more about that later."

"I will put the situation to you quite bluntly, Major Brooks," Wertz continued as though there had been no interruption. "Four days ago five U.S. personnel were forcibly taken, kidnapped if you will, from outside Cho Moi in the western delta. That's about twenty-five kilometers north of Long Xuyen, if you're familiar with the area." Sam was and he nodded his understanding.

"One of those, ahh, snatched was an American army major who was later found decapitated approximately five kilometers from the kidnap site. We have reasonably good intelligence that the remaining four, all civilians, have been taken intact by their captors into their Cambodian sanctuary. To put it bluntly, we intend to get them back."

Sam squinted at Wertz in the poor light. "Why? I mean, why are you so concerned about getting them back? I've never heard of you people getting that excited about a snatch before, unless . . . oh, yeah. They were your people, weren't they?"

"Close enough, Major. *One* of them is our, ahh, person. He was carried on the province advisory books as an agricultural expert. Of course, we had another of our men listed as the intelligence adviser; however, that was just to throw the dogs off the track, so to speak. The man they've taken is, I assure you, most, ahh, valuable to us."

"Colonel, or whatever you are, I don't want to burst your bubble but I'm really not the man for this job. I know I went into the U Minh but I was really more of a hindrance than a help to the green beanies. I have no training or—"

"Please don't take us for complete fools, Major. Of course we know what you are and are not capable of providing us. We have no intention of putting you in the, ahh, ground party. That group will, however, need an experienced aviator over them to act as radio relay and to provide navigational assistance should they require it. A major reason we have approached you is that the team leader has requested you. We are merely trying to honor that request. In addition, you know the area this side of the border."

It was then that Sam knew who the ground team leader was going to be. Wertz saw it in his face. "The leader will be Captain Christian, of course, as you undoubtedly deduced. There were several other reasons for your choice. First of all, you are a deniable asset, Major Brooks. As a forward air controller, your job is to roam the delta—specifically, your assigned province. The FAC assigned to the province from which the team shall, ahh, depart is known to have been killed along with several other staff members. Indeed, I understand it was that unfortunate's province in which you conducted today's activities. Look outside. The wet season is upon us. What could be more natural than a newly assigned forward air controller wandering across an ill-defined border, seemingly lost? A natural deniability should you be so unfortunate as to, ahh, fall into enemy hands. In any event, you could deny it plausibly, long enough for the ground team to, ahh, complete their assigned task."

"What does the air force have to say about all this?" Sam asked Jackson Jones.

"The 2d Air Division has been directed to provide complete cooperation with the agency in this matter. That direction comes from the very highest authority."

"Jesus!" Sam mumbled to himself. "They're even starting to talk alike."

"What was that?"

"Nothing, sir." Sam turned back to Wertz. "When are they going to sortie?"

"As soon as possible. Meteorology in Saigon expects extremely bad weather to continue for at least three days. Preliminary plans call for a briefing at Chau Phu at 0700 tomorrow. Ahh, jump-off will be anytime after that according to the schedule set by Captain Christian."

"If I decide I don't want to play in your little game, who takes my place?"

"I don't see that that would be any of your concern, Major," said Wertz. "However, Lieutenant Colonel Robinson has indicated that he would volunteer."

Sam shook his head wearily. The very last thing he wanted to do in his few remaining weeks in the air force was to screw around over the border in a neutral country where he had no business. "I suppose," he said finally, "that means there'll be no fighter support if the team needs it."

Wertz nodded his affirmation. "That's correct. Nor any artillery or helicopter support. If anyone is captured, we will attempt to deny you ever existed. If anyone is captured and brought into the public eye, we will give the press the provided cover stories. That is, a lost aviator or a ground team lost in the inclement weather."

"Do you think anyone will really believe that hogwash?" asked Sam.

Wertz shrugged his heavy shoulders. "Frankly, we don't really care. It's enough that we simply have a plausible story that will withstand scrutiny for a few days. The press has an incredibly short memory. It lasts as long as there is public interest in a story, which is even shorter. Within a week, it will be lucky to be on the back page of any paper."

Jones cleared his throat in his corner and Sam turned toward him. Jones took a step forward into the light. "Major Brooks," he said, clearing his throat once more, "I have been authorized, no damnit, I have been *ordered* to pass on to you that, should this operation be successful, and if you are a member of this team, the commander of 2d Air Division will personally convey an oral officer's effectiveness report to the lieutenant colonels' selection board. In it, he will ask for your immediate promotion to that grade. This request will be endorsed by COMUSMACV himself. In addition, my general has asked that I inform you that a squadron operations officer position will soon become available in the 209th Tactical Fighter Squadron, which is now deploying to the Republic of South Vietnam. Should you agree to participate in this operation and should it be successful, that slot is yours."

Sam stared at him in stunned disbelief, his mind working frantically. It was outright bribery, but what sweet bribery! Back to a fighter squadron! Promotion to light colonel and an ops officer slot in a squadron. The best job in the entire air force, short of commanding a squadron. Not to be a civilian after all. The enormity of the statement left him breathless.

Wertz was watching him with a slight sardonic smile on his moon face. "Yes," he said, "we thought that might be quite an enticement to one in your, ahh, position. I can only assume from the blissful look on your countenance that you have considered the offer and found it acceptable. Don't worry about the air force reneging on its promise. I assure you that we always make good on our promises, even if we have to sometimes bring subtle pressure to bear on some of our, ahh, associates."

Jones gave him a hard look but said nothing, retreating to his place in the darkened corner.

"I'm quite thrilled that you have decided to join our jolly group without further inducements, Major, for even I was a bit hesitant about using my hole card. Although I was never for a moment in doubt that it would have worked." Sam looked at him questioningly.

Wertz managed to look a bit embarrassed for a moment, but then it was gone and the small eyes bored into Sam's once again. "Yes, ahh, we did have a final trick up our sleeve if nothing else had moved you. It's only fair to tell you now, I suppose. Or, to be precise, to let you see for yourself." He handed a small piece of notebook paper to Sam. "These are the names of the missing personnel. I must have it back before you leave this room."

Second on the list was the name Lee M. Roget.

CHAPTER 13

For the first time in Sam's life he felt he *needed* a drink rather than just wanting one. Back in his cubicle after the meeting he stared through the grenade screen at the rain turning the compound into a quagmire. Lightning revealed the ragged cumulus bases of the thunderstorms charging in from the South China Sea, swollen with moisture and ready to calve over the rice fields. A plodding figure bundled up in a poncho walked slowly by, muttering half-heard curses against the drenching rain. Sam recognized the voice of the team intelligence sergeant, dutifully if not happily pulling his two-hour shift of guard supervision.

The news of Lee Roget's capture lay like a living thing in Sam's belly. He started from the chair for the door, sure that he was about to be physically sick as the bile rose into his lower throat. He stood under the covered walkway and mouthed deep breaths until the nausea passed. He reached for his cigarettes in the arm pocket of his flight suit and was momentarily puzzled not to find them. He shouldn't have been, since he hadn't smoked for six years. He thought about the drink, then calculated the time before he had to be airborne and decided against it. Anyway, he knew there was no solace for him at the bottom of a bottle.

Like a sleepwalker he returned to his damp room and, for lack of anything better to do, lowered himself onto his iron cot, moving slowly, like an old man. He forced his eyelids closed and willed himself to sleep but his brain refused to turn off, and his eyes continued to flicker rapidly. He could feel each microscopic movement against the clenched lids. With a sigh he allowed them to pop open and stare into the darkness of the room, broken only by a crack of light seeping from an ill-fitted joint of the hot locker. Inside it, a forty-watt bulb fought the greenish black mold and mildew that threatened the existence of anything made of leather or cloth. The heavy bass rumble and quickening timpani of rain on the metal roof was a harbinger of another phalanx of storms advancing inland. Sam wiped his face with his ever-present GI-issue towel and arose again to sit in the straight-backed chair. He switched on the small desk lamp and in its meager light rustled in his wallet until he found his only picture of Lee. It had been taken by an unknown photographer with a cheap camera, but it showed her facial features plainly. She had an arm clasped around the waist of her brother-in-law, Jim Christian.

Sam stared at the picture and felt the churning increase in his gut. Where was she right this moment? Wet and miserable in some log-covered bunker in Cambodia, as Wertz's intelligence sources had claimed? Beaten and raped by squads of Viet Cong soldiers? Perhaps she'd already been executed. He was driving himself crazy and he knew it, but like a tooth with a hole in it, he couldn't leave it alone. The worst was not knowing. No, that was pure crap. Perhaps not knowing was the only thing that kept his hopes alive. The truth could be worse than anything he could possibly imagine. Restless, he jerked from the chair and turned off the light again, then walked to the wall and leaned against it to stare at the rain once more. The mosquitoes seemed to become more aggressive as they hummed in his ear and stuck on the sodden flesh of his neck.

Sam turned back to the small desk and switched on the light to check the time. Almost 0200. Takeoff was scheduled for 0630. Wertz would accompany him in the backseat of the Bird Dog to monitor the briefing at Chi Lang, the deployment base for the ground team and Sam's support airstrip. The CIA man would remain there until the mission was completed, one way or another. Colonel Jackson Jones would return to his desk at 2d Air Division on Tan Son Nhut airfield, provided his helicopter could operate beneath the low clouds and rainstorms. Sam wasn't sure that *he* could stay clear of the weather sufficiently to get to Chi Lang but he was determined to try, for he was certain that Jim Christian would proceed without him should he and his aircraft not arrive on schedule. It was unthinkable not to be involved in the operation. Sam was certain that he would go completely insane unless he found an outlet for the excessive adrenaline flooding his system.

He opened the hot locker, finally admitting defeat. It was useless to try for sleep this night. He threw underwear and a couple of clean flight suits onto the bed and began to gather his flying gear. He took his shotgun from the locker and sat down on the bunk. Critically, he ran his eyes over the weapon. It appeared to have aged considerably since Jim Christian had given it to him. The rubber recoil pad was held onto the stock by fabric tape and showed evidence of rot. Scars grooved the stock and scratches marred the finish of the barrel. He worked the slide action and felt vaguely pleased by its well-oiled performance. He loaded five of the double-aught buckshot shells into the magazine and ensured that the safety catch was in the on position. He cast a critical eye at the shells in their individual pouches on the canvas bandolier and replaced several that were showing evidence of wear and weather. Finally, he stuffed his clean clothing into a small bag and looked around the cubicle. Except for his gear placed near the screen door, there was no evidence that he had ever even been in this room, much less lived here. That thought further depressed him, and he left the room in search of coffee and companionship.

Sam found the coffee easily enough. Day or night, it was always there in the team house. The pot of the black brew was nearing the end of its useful life, having obtained the consistency of road tar through constant heating. He poured himself a cup anyway, for there would be none fresher until the cook was allowed through the gate at 0530.

The companionship was more difficult to find, although the team intelligence sergeant was sitting by the coffeepot, leafing through a six-month-old copy of *Newsweek*, Far Eastern edition. He glanced up as Sam entered the room but other than a brusque nod gave no indication that he was in the mood for an early-morning conversation. Sam couldn't much blame him. The 0200 to 0400 guard shift was the worst on the schedule. Not only did it interrupt a night's sleep, but it was the shift in which it was most difficult keeping the guards awake. Coincidentally, it was also the time frame chosen by the Viet Cong for most of their probes and attacks. And, of course, tonight there was the rain.

Sam sank into one of the ratty armchairs, content just to have another person nearby. He sipped the vile coffee, decided it was undrinkable, and placed the mug on the floor. Leaning his head back, he shut his eyes against the glare of the naked bulb dangling from the ceiling. It was the last thing he remembered.

Sam was conscious that someone was shaking his shoulder but he seemed unable to open his eyes. The worry and fretting had taken their toll and his system had simply shut down in self-preservation. He lifted his fingers to his eyes and tried to ungum them, becoming aware that someone was trying to talk to him. He peered at the figure through slitted eyes, taking moments to realize that it was Colonel Wertz, or whatever rank he was using today.

"Major Brooks, it's getting rather close to our, ahh, takeoff time. I did not know whether you wanted breakfast or not. I assumed you would, so I woke you."

Sam stared at the doughboy. He looked even more sallow and pasty in the first pale light of the rainy dawn. Sam nodded, knowing it might be the last opportunity he'd have for food this day. He pried himself from the chair and rubbed his neck. It was stiff and sore from sleeping in the chair. His tongue felt furry, as if he were suffering from a horrible hangover. The thought of eggs made him want to puke.

Surprisingly, the buttered toast and bacon went down well and made Sam feel better. He even felt a little more benign about Colonels Wertz and Jones, again sitting together in the mess, heads bowed close together like two aging dowagers. He found himself considering the possibility that he just might be promoted and allowed to remain on active duty, and felt guilty at the thought. What the hell did that matter if he lost Lee? He refused to think about that possibility. Jim Christian would get her out, and she'd have exciting stories to tell their children. He realized with a start that this was the first conscious thought he'd ever had concerning children—his own children. Before, when confronted with the offspring of his married contemporaries, he'd found them to be irrational, ill-tempered, spiteful, and gluttonous.

Sam sipped his fresh coffee and looked toward Wertz. The stocky man was shaking hands with Jones and rising from the table. It was obviously time to get on with the war. A final drink of coffee and Sam rose, gathered his gear, and followed Wertz from the room.

Sam drained more than a gallon of liquid from each wing tank of the O-1 before the aviation fuel ran pure and free of water. Wertz sat huddled in the jeep as Sam completed the preflight check and unleashed the little aircraft from its rock anchors. Sam walked onto the flooded runway and stared suspiciously down its length. It looked like a pool designed for swimming laps. The rice paddies on either side of the strip were underwater, and a water buffalo lay in a drainage ditch, contentedly chewing its cud. The water boo's inevitable small watcher was nowhere in sight and had probably taken refuge in some nearby hootch where he could stay reasonably dry and still keep an eye on the family treasure.

Sam walked down the middle of the strip, checking the water's depth. Nowhere was it higher than his ankles. That would *appear* to be OK for takeoff, but he had nothing in his experience to guide him. For sure the takeoff roll would be longer, given the water resistance to the tires. He cocked his head back and peered at the sky. The base of the clouds appeared to be five to six hundred feet above the ground. It would be close. The rain had moderated for the moment, but a look toward the sea told him that heavier stuff was on the way. If they were going to do it, it would have to be now, before the fresh squalls reduced the visibility to nothing.

Wertz completely filled the rear cockpit, stretching the broad canvas lap belt to the limit. Fortunately, he had no gear, not even a weapon except for the ridiculous little handgun in its holster. The engine was balky with the dampness but eventually got the idea that Sam was not going to give in, so finally engaged. Sam carefully monitored the immediate rise in oil pressure and waited patiently for the needle on the cylinder head temperature gauge to creep into the green. While he waited he checked his armament panel and ensured that there was a full box of smoke grenades aboard. He spread his map, then folded it to the section he would be flying to Chi Lang. If the weather became too much of a problem he could always try for Vinh Tuy or Kien Hung. Each place had a landing strip and was fairly close to his planned flight route.

The needles on the cylinder head and oil temperature gauges finally nudged into the green arc of the normal range, and Sam made a careful check of the magnetos and prop cycling. He couldn't think of an adequate reason to delay any longer. Sticking his head out the window for a final quick check of the weather, he saw new squalls bearing down rapidly on Bac Lieu International Airport. He turned and silently inquired with raised brows if Wertz was ready. The CIA man nodded grimly. Sam noticed that his passenger's hands had a firm grip on the sides of the seat and that his knuckles were definitely white and tense. That made Sam feel a bit better.

The takeoff was rougher than Sam had imagined. The standing water not only resisted the aircraft wheels but caused the O-1 to veer from its proper path as each wheel entered varying depths. Sam was virtually blind, for the splashing and spraying eliminated forward visibility almost totally. Fortunately, he'd left the side panel open and by looking outboard he could judge the approximate ground path by his proximity to the edge of the strip. His breathing, he noted, had become quite irregular while trying to get the little aircraft airborne after an abnormally long ground run.

Sam set cruise power and initially concentrated on staying out of the clouds. His guess at their altitude had been close, for he lost sight of the ground at a little over six hundred feet. He eased the Bird Dog back into the clear and took up a compass course directly for Chi Lang. The first part of the trip should give him no undue navigational hardships since he knew the area intimately, although the surface of the ground appeared to be a new world, now that it was covered with water. Still, there were enough familiar sights to keep them easily on course. His problems could begin as he entered Chau Doc province and tried to find Chi Lang. Much of the province was only at sea level, with the Seven Mountains region rising up in the center like a spine to an elevation of two to three thousand feet. The mountaintops would almost certainly be obscured by clouds. And the Viet Cong owned all seven mountains.

A sudden rain shower obliterated his view of the ground and he was forced to rely on his instruments to maintain course and level flight. In two minutes they were through it. Sam estimated he had no more than two miles forward visibility even when clear of the showers. The sky appeared opalescent to their front. Its milkiness prevented him from focusing clearly on the details of the ground. A glance at his altimeter showed that he had descended to four hundred feet to stay beneath the cloud base, and the visibility didn't appear to be getting better. Just the opposite. He identified the Vinh Tuy airstrip as it passed beneath his left wing and lost it again in moments—also losing it as a landing option.

Staring through the gloom, Sam was heartened when he picked up the Kien Hung canal and then the road from Vi Thanh to Rach Gia. He was still on course, albeit much lower than he would have liked. Forward visibility was no more than a mile now. The aircraft lurched, steadied, and began to buck seriously. Shit! He'd blundered into the edge of one of the monster storms combing the countryside.

Sam fought to keep the wings level as the Bird Dog was tossed whimsically by unseen air currents. They bobbed up and down like a cork going through white water. Then the sky opened, and they seemed suspended in a solid waterfall. A glance at the airspeed indicator showed that the instrument's source of information, the Pitot tube on the wing, had apparently been overwhelmed by the deluge and had shut down.

Sam had expected that. What he had not expected was to enter a thunderstorm at only four hundred feet. The Bird Dog could easily be thrown to the ground at such a low altitude.

Diffused lightning seemed to surround them as millions of volts were suddenly released. Sam considered attempting a 180-degree turn and an exit from the storm in the direction they'd entered it. Common sense quickly prevailed, however. Training and experience had taught him that once he was in such an undesirable situation, the only rational course of action was to plunge straight ahead. Invariably it would be the shortest route out.

And so it was. The storm spat them from its bowels in an almost contemptuous fashion, Sam with both hands clenched around the stick, not so much flying as just hanging on. If there was a bright spot to the episode it was when he realized with odoriferous certainty that Colonel Wertz had been actively and gloriously sick. Sam turned his head to check his passenger and was thrilled to find the front of the CIA man's shirt covered with vomit. The pasty face now had a dead look and the little pig eyes were screwed tightly shut. Sam felt a glow of satisfaction and immediately developed an almost warm affection for the storm.

The flight smoothed as they moved northwest toward their destination. Sam was able to identify Rach Gia, a sizable harbor town situated on the Gulf of Thailand, and get a good fix for the last and most treacherous leg of their journey. He had been able to nurse the O-1 up to a dizzying nine hundred feet until the cloud base began to lower ominously once more, driving them back down. The rain began with gusto and Sam disgustedly opened a window to peer at the gloomy earth, hoping to find something to match against his map. The visibility could be no more than half a mile. Water poured into the cockpit through the opened hatch and soaked both of them. It couldn't be helped. They were fast approaching the Seven Mountains area.

Had the Viet Cong gunner not been eager, Sam would have driven the Bird Dog straight into the mid level of Nui Cam, one of the taller Seven Mountains, and put an abrupt end to the flight. However, the Viet Cong were virtually assured by the inclement weather that there would be no aerial response this day and thus felt free to try to down the foolish pilot who overflew their stronghold.

As it was, Sam had only to think briefly about the phenomenon of green tracer fire directed at him from a source well *above* his altitude and come to the conclusion that unless the VC had suddenly acquired all-weather interceptors, he was about to attempt the onerous task of chewing his way through a mountain.

Abruptly, he threw the stick to the left of the cockpit and trod heavily on the left rudder. The Bird Dog complained about the treatment by buffeting heavily and letting its nose shudder into a high-speed stall. Sam's immediate reaction had saved them from the mountain, but the aircraft's stall and consequent rapid drop to one hundred feet above the earth had saved them from the gunner. The tracers laced the gloom two hundred feet above them and then stuttered to a halt. Another burst searched the clouds but the gunner had his chance and lost it. A thoroughly shaken Sam was heading away from the danger as fast as his little aircraft could take them. The smell of fresh vomit from the rear seat spurred him on. Christ! One time had been amusing. Now the odor was starting to make him feel queasy.

They circled well away from the mountains, maintaining one hundred feet, while Sam stared at the mountains' dark shapes ascending into the gloom. At lower altitude the visibility seemed better and he was able to positively fix Nui Giai, Nui Coto, and the one he'd just missed, Nui Cam. More carefully now, he probed around the mountain bases, only tentatively sticking the nose of the aircraft into an area of poor visibility until he was sure that it wasn't a dead end or that it wouldn't bring the aircraft into the range of one of the mountain gunners.

Suddenly, the red scar that identified the Ba Xoai Special Forces camp was off his left wing; he knew that they had made it and that Chi Lang was just around the corner. And so it was.

The slimy mud sucked at the wheels of the O-1 as they touched down. Sam was forced to keep full back stick until they could taxi from the strip onto the pierced-steel planking of the parking area. He turned the aircraft until it was facing into the strong southerly wind and made for the refueling blivet. It looked like a large black cow patty surrounded by sandbags. He killed the engine and opened the door, anxious to get away from the redolent CIA man in the rear seat. His legs felt wobbly and he was wet clear to his GI undershorts. He turned and watched Wertz clamber gracelessly from the rear seat. Colonel Wertz decided to sit on one of the muddy wheels and hold his head in both hands. Sam felt better just looking at him.

An engine noise from the advisory compound made Sam look toward the small cluster of buildings, barely visible in the gloom. A jeep was careening from the gate, sliding from one side of the muddy road to the other but never slackening its speed. Sam checked his watch and was astounded to find that it was just past 0800. He would have guessed noon, at least. The racing jeep flung a spray of water and mud as it hit the holes in the road. The rain had begun to fall heavily again.

The jeep sloughed to a stop beside them. Even before its driver could dismount Sam recognized the face beneath the rain gear. There could be only one goofy grin like that in the entire delta. It had to be, and was, CWO2c. Donald "Stretch" Lyle.

"I got here this morning," Lyle explained as he helped Sam refuel and replenish the oil in his aircraft. He had completed the delivery of Colonel Wertz to the team house and returned. "They want me to fly backup for you on the snatch—you know, take over as airborne radio relay when you have to land to refuel and eat. Stuff like that. Captain Christian told me about the dinks grabbing your girlfriend and those other civilian guys. Don't you worry, Major Brooks. That snake eater up there and his bunch look like they could snatch old Ho himself if they wanted to. A mean-looking bunch of hombres for sure."

Sam gave the outsized warrant officer a sallow smile and turned his mind to the fuel he was putting into the wing tanks of the O-1. He shielded the opening with his baseball cap in an effort to keep the rain from entering with the fuel. Even so, he knew he'd have to be very careful and drain a lot of gas to get out the water that had inevitably seeped in.

"Girlfriend," Stretch Lyle had called Lee. She'd get a kick out of that phrase, seeing as she was in her mid-thirties. His mind was suddenly filled with a beautifully detailed picture of Lee. Sam ground his teeth in despair and frustration. The hazardous conditions of the flight from Bac Lieu had briefly cleared her from his thoughts while he coped with the more immediate dangers. Now, her being flooded his mind, encapsulating him with her presence. He looked up from his task toward the brooding rain forest of Cambodia. Somewhere out there Lee was trying to live with a situation for which she couldn't have been prepared. No one could have, for that matter, but at least those who expected to be in actual combat had steeled themselves to the possibility of death, wounds, or capture. Shaking his head to clear it, Sam carefully screwed the tank top into place.

"They'll get her, Stretch; they'll get all of them. And I appreciate having you to work with. Did they tell you what time we'd brief?"

"Naw, Captain Christian just asked me to tell you to make it as quick as you could. Guess they'll get started as soon as we get up there. Sure is shitty weather, isn't it?" Both pilots stared with distaste at the low, gray clouds. They were between heavy storms at the moment and the rain fell softly on their uptilted faces.

Sam suddenly had a worrisome thought. "Stretch, how many hours flying time you got now?"

Lyle looked slightly embarrassed. "Oh, I must have at least four hundred, maybe four fifty."

"How much instrument time? Actual weather flying, I mean. Not training time under a practice hood." Sam persisted.

"Not very much, I'm afraid."

"How much?" Sam insisted.

"Well, none, if you want to get really technical about it. I kinda flitted in and out of some clouds getting over here this morning but it really wasn't very far. Only twenty klicks or so."

"Hey! No problem. We all have to start somewhere. You'll be fine." Sam clapped him on the back.

Privately, Sam groaned with despair. Whoever was running the aerial support end of this thing really had his head completely up his ass. It looked as if they'd be operating under a two- to five-hundred-foot ceiling for the entire period of the snatch and one of the support pilots had never even been in a real cloud. Obviously, someone didn't understand the potential for danger here. Two hundred feet and one-half mile visibility were the *minimum* landing requirements for an airliner anywhere in the world. And that was where precision landing approaches were available, friendly radars provided guidance, and controllers issued clearances. Christ! If the maps were anywhere near accurate, he and Stretch Lyle could expect to be operating in an area where trees were higher than the landing requirements for airliners. They could expect to be in and out of the low-lying clouds, be subjected to enemy ground fire, and still support the ground team with navigational and radio assistance. What a lash-up!

The two pilots tied Sam's airplane to a couple of large rocks in case the winds became violent. Sam threw his gear into the rear of the jeep and gladly relinquished the driver's seat to Lyle. Both men swayed like wheat in a windstorm as the vehicle slipped from one side of the muddy road to the other.

The compound looked not unlike the one at Bac Lieu. Sam knew it to be a subsector with twelve American advisers assigned. Jim Christian stood under a roof overhang awaiting their arrival, throwing a languid salute as the two men climbed from the jeep. Sam ignored it and thrust out a hand. As their hands clasped his eyes examined the face of the Special Forces captain. Christian looked tired, but there was a determined thrust to his chin. There were little knots of tension behind each jaw and smudges under each eye which spoke of little sleep.

"Good to see you again, Jim."

"And you, Sam. Guess you know what this is all about."

Sam nodded, not trusting himself to speak for a moment. Then he said, his voice cracking, "Can we get her out, Jim? I need to know the chances."

Christian shrugged. "We're pretty sure we know where she is. If she's there, then there's a good chance we can do it. But they move prisoners around just to keep us from doing this sort of thing. I guess it depends mostly on how good our intelligence really is." He grinned suddenly. "In this case, I think it's pretty good." Sam punched his shoulder and they walked together into the team house, followed by Lyle. The rains came heavily once again.

The ground team sprawled around the room in casual attitudes, some in chairs, others on the floor. Two of them he recognized immediately. One, large and black, rose to his feet as Sam came in.

"Well, I'll be damned. If it ain't the killer pilot. Hey, Major. You bring that big ole scattergun with you this time? Man, you did; I want your ass on the ground with me again."

Sam pumped Dell Washington's hand. He hadn't seen him since the awards ceremony in Saigon and, before that, the day they'd left the U Minh Forest with the body of the dead American flier.

"Bac si, it's damned good to see you again. You're looking good. And yeah, I've got my old shotgun with me. Just don't make me have to come down there to pull your ass out of a jam with it."

"You oughta come with us, Major. We'd kick ass. Hey, Jesus! Look here. Our good luck done join us."

The dark Latin face turned from where he had been talking with another trooper and lit with unconcealed pleasure at the sight of Sam. Graceful as a cat he pulled himself to his feet and hurried to them. As they shook hands Washington beamed as though he had arranged the meeting himself.

"Anybody else from the old U Minh team along?" asked Sam.

Washington's face clouded before he spoke. "Don't guess you heard 'bout ole Jake Jacoby. Got his skinny white ass blew completely away las' week up by Moc Hoa. Got 'bushed coming back across the fence. Sad story."

"Everybody seems to be here, so why don't we get started." Christian's voice cut across the hum of conversation.

There was a general rustling as bodies rearranged to face the front of the room. The air was blue with cigarette smoke. Sam and Stretch Lyle joined Washington and Carrasco against the back wall. Christian stood before a detailed 1:50,000 map pinned to a map board. Colonel Wertz stood to one side. Sam saw that he'd either cleaned himself up or found a new fatigue shirt. The beady eyes were locked onto Christian's face.

"We all know why we're here," Christian began. "In approximately one hour a ground team composed of twelve SF personnel and commanded by myself will depart by helicopter for an LZ here." He turned and pointed to a small clearing approximately ten klicks across the border. Sam peered at the opened map Carrasco held in his lap and matched it to the spot on his own map.

"I'll ask you," Christian continued, "not to physically put any sort of markings on the charts you'll be using. Particularly you pilots," he said, looking at Sam and Lyle and then across the room to the helicopter pilots. "Should you decide to run into a tree over there we don't want Charley knowing exactly where to start looking for us." Sam and Stretch nodded their assent.

"After the insertion, which will not be covered by gunships I might add, the team will move overland to a position here." He indicated a spot approximately five kilometers from the landing zone.

"From there, the team will deploy for a snatch of any remaining survivors. I'm not going to go into the exact plan at this time for obvious reasons. The ground team will be briefed separately. Suffice it to say, we do not want aircraft over that area until the attack has gone off. If we're successful we'll plan to move in this direction. If we're chased, and I've no doubt we will be, we'll leave two-man ambush teams behind us while we try to make it either here or here for a pickup. The rain is going to help but hopefully we're going to have five civilians who are going to slow us down considerably. Particularly since we don't really know what shape they'll be in.

"If the pursuit gets too close, we might have to wing it and start off in another direction, even west, back into the Indian country to throw 'em off. That's where you pilots are going to come in handy. We're not going to have much time for the finer points of navigation and we'll be depending on you for proper directions. If we have to drop off the ambush teams they'll have to plan on making their way back across the fence independently. Major Brooks, will you or Mister Lyle have any problem working beneath this ceiling? I know it's damned low but the weather is good for us."

Sam thought briefly about the experience level of Stretch Lyle before he answered. No doubt Lyle would have problems. He'd just have to try to remain airborne himself as much as possible. "I don't think so," he replied, "unless you're planning on moving at night. There's no way we could cover then or we'd wrap around a tree within the first quarter hour."

"No night moves," Christian confirmed. "We'll hole up during the dark hours."

Sam shrugged. "Guess it'll be OK then, unless it gets worse."

"OK," Christian continued, "here's the way it'll go for you pilots. One of you will follow the two slicks with the team on board, trying to stay close enough to observe the insertion. As soon as you see we're on the ground, get away from us but stay within radio range. We'll pass a sitrep within thirty minutes of the time we're on the ground unless we've got troubles. In that case you'll hear us yelling. From then on, it'll be a sitrep an hour until we're in position. We'll tell you when we're going in and, as soon as possible, whether or not we were successful. From then on we're gonna be coming out as hard as our passengers can stand it. We'd like for you to have arty registered in at the border so that if we need it in a hurry we can get it. Try to fly as big a circle around us as you can so we don't get compromised by your engine noise. After you drop us off you chopper pilots are on twenty-four alert here until the main body is out. Understood?"

Sam nodded and looked across the room at the four helicopter pilots. Christ! They were young. Didn't the army have any aviators over eighteen? He glanced at Lyle and was rewarded by the large goofy grin that said, aren't we having fun? He turned back to Christian with an inward shudder.

"Questions, anyone, before we let the aviators get on with whatever it is they do and we brief the ground team? OK, we jump off in approximately one hour."

"Captain Christian, ahh, I have something to say if you are quite finished," Wertz said, stepping forward. Christian looked annoyed but made a slight gesture to indicate the ersatz colonel had the floor.

"Gentlemen, ahh, not to take up too much of your precious time but I feel compelled to point out the importance of this, ahh, operation. Specifically, I would stress the need to secure the, ahh, intelligence operative from his captors. This man is not only a valuable asset to us but has the information to compromise several productive intelligence-gathering nets within the delta. It is imperative that we either secure his return or else, ahh, neutralize him. He is to be your first priority in the target area. The other prisoners must be considered expendable should the situation come to that. You must—"

"No one is expendable on this operation," broke in Christian, his level stare locked onto Wertz. "Let's get this one straight, Colonel. This is a volunteer operation and if my ass comes out, so will *all* the prisoners. One is no more important than the others. If there's anyone who feels differently, then now's the time to get out."

Apparently no one did, for a pall of silence hung heavily over the room. Wertz turned abruptly and went back to his corner. Christian continued to glare at him for a long moment before turning to the group. "No questions? Let's move."

Sam and Stretch Lyle followed the helicopter pilots to the team mess hootch for coffee. A smiling Viet cook acted as though he was their personal host, showing them to a long table and quickly bringing a large aluminum pot of coffee and a tray of pastries. Lyle happily began shoveling the goodies into his mouth. Sam settled for coffee. One of the helicopter pilots entertained the others with a story of his amorous activities in Bangkok during a recent R and R.

Sam tuned him out and turned to Lyle. "Listen, here's the way I think we ought to work it. I'll take off with the choppers and take the first shift." Sam looked at his watch and did some quick calculations. "If we're off by, say, 1100, I'll be good on fuel until 1500. That'll give me a little reserve in case the weather really turns to doodoo and I have to head somewhere else to land and refuel. You plan on getting off by 1445. That'll give you plenty of time to get into the area and I can brief you on UHF 322.2. I should be back up by 1630 and can take it until they secure tonight. Make sure you pass on their sitreps to the TOC here as soon as you get 'em. OK?"

Lyle watched Sam as he spoke, pastry crumbs dribbling from his mouth. "You sure you don't want me to take 'em clear until dark? I ought to have enough fuel."

That was the very last thing Sam wanted. He could visualize the relatively inexperienced pilot bumbling his way through the dark trying to find the airstrip in poor weather. "Naw, let's do it my way. There's probably not going to be a hell of a lot going on today in any event. Either they'll get shot off both LZs and have to come back here to replan it, or they'll get in and spend most of the afternoon getting organized. When I get back tonight we'll plan for tomorrow. Main thing is to get refueled just as soon as you get down in case something does pop up. Like I get a cranky airplane or something. And don't wander too far from the TOC. When things start going to hell, they have a way of doing it in a hurry."

Lyle nodded his understanding and reached for another cruller. Sam thought of having another cup of coffee, but a four-hour flight was going to take his kidney capacity to the limit so he decided against it. Instead he wandered to the TOC, Lyle trailing along behind him, and found the advisory team's radio operator sitting before his equipment and frowning at a Bugs Bunny comic book. Bugs must have been in the act of playing a particularly devious trick on the irascible Elmer Fudd, for the radio operator's mouth stretched into a broad, happy grin as his eyes flickered across the page. Sam hated to disrupt this pursuit of knowledge but time was running short.

"Pardon me, Corporal, but I need to check out two of the special SOIs for me and Mister Lyle here." The SOI, or signal operating instructions, gave frequencies and call signs for various units during a twenty-four-hour period. A special document for the use of the snatch team and its supporting elements had been prepared.

The soldier reluctantly turned his eyes from the antics of that crazy rabbit and looked at the two pilots. He noticed Sam's dull golden leaf on the shoulder of his flight suit and quickly got to his feet. "You bet, Major. I'll have to check your name on this list that Captain Christian gave me. Just a moment, yeah, here it is. And what were your names, please?"

Silently, Sam pointed to the name tag on his chest. In a remarkable show of initiative the corporal managed to find Lyle's name tag without any help. The men signed the corporal's form and left him immersed in the world of Bugs and Elmer. Sam slipped the slim folder into the leg of his flight suit; Lyle placed his in an upper pocket of his fatigue blouse.

The two pilots checked and set their watches against the wall clock in the TOC, then walked to the map and figured coordinates to be called to the artillery units. Sam gave the job of calling them to Lyle. Stretch would have time to do the fine figuring after the team was airborne. There wouldn't be an opportunity to actually register the tubes against the chosen locations, but then no one really knew exactly where the team would reenter South Vietnam anyway. As they turned from the map, the door to the briefing room opened and Jim Christian led his team out.

"You zoomies 'bout ready to do it?"

Sam nodded. "I'll be first up. Mister Lyle will be relieving me about 1500. Arty coordinates are figured and he'll call them in once he gets word you're actually on the ground. We're ready."

Sam and Lyle followed the team into the rain and the waiting jeeps. The helicopter pilots spilled from the mess room to squeeze in their jeep, giggling and goosing each other like the Lamar Junior High basketball team. In the back of another jeep Sam watched Christian eyeballing the aviators closely. Jim noticed and he turned and grinned at Sam.

"Those little shits act more like your kids than pilots, but they've all got killer instincts and balls as big as a helmet liner. There's nothing that scares them."

Sam gave another inward shudder. There were *thousands* of things that frightened him. There seemed to be more all the time. He felt old.

Lyle helped Sam untie his aircraft, then leaned on the strut and bent to peer inside the cockpit as Sam buckled himself into the seat. Sam checked his switches and looked out at the lanky form. The familiar grin made him feel better. Lyle stuck a thumb into the air.

"Have a good one, Maj," he said, as if Sam was on the way to the office. In a way he was. He gave a little wave in return and watched until he was sure the tall man was well away from the prop.

"Clear!" he shouted through the opened window. The rain had already wet one shoulder completely; it was blowing almost horizontally under the wing as a fresh squall drenched the strip.

"Clear!" came Lyle's return call.

The engine responded immediately as Sam punched the starter button, for it was still warm and relatively moisture-free from the earlier flight.

A rapid scan of the instruments showed no apparent problems with any of the systems. He looked toward the two helicopters winding up a short distance away, the team sitting in the rain of the open hatches as nonchalant as commuters. Sam switched one radio to the interplane frequency and the other to the TOC. He double-checked the frequencies and call signs in the SOI, then placed the document back into his leg pocket and zipped it. Loss of the SOI into enemy hands could prove disastrous for everyone. They would be able to monitor all frequencies at will. Not that they didn't do that anyway, Sam thought with chagrin.

First the lead chopper, then its wingman pulled into a hover, turned slowly into the wind, tucked their noses, and began to accelerate down the runway. Sam gave a final check to his instruments and a wave to Stretch Lyle, still standing in the rain watching him. He advanced the throttle and taxied onto the muddy strip. Colonel Wertz also watched the departure from an enclosed jeep. The doughy face in the open window had a small smile on it.

CHAPTER 14

The bases of the clouds were five to six hundred feet above the ground. Visibility hovered around a mile. The speed of the Bird Dog was comparable to that of the Hueys, and Sam had no difficulty staying with the flight. The whirling rotor blades left small circles of vapor as they sliced through the moist air. Sam adjusted the throttle to maintain position and checked his map against the visible ground references, for they were nearing the border. In this particular sector there were no topographical features to delineate their passage into another country. Unbroken rain forest and thick jungle foliage were all Sam could see to their front—unbroken except for the bomb and artillery craters that pockmarked the verdant green. The craters stopped abruptly, almost in a straight line, which probably marked the border.

"Blackjack, this is Hobo Lead. Are you up this freq?" called the lead HU-1 helicopter.

"Rog. Blackjack is up," replied Sam.

"OK, Blackjack, this is Hobo Lead. Wanted to confirm that we're on course to the LZ. This viz is so shitty I just wanted a double-check."

"Near as I can tell we're dead on," said Sam. "Oughta be just about over the fence now."

"Yeah, that's what I figure too. OK, we'll be starting down now."

Sam watched the pair of Hueys descend and level off just above the treetops. He elected to maintain altitude just beneath the base of the clouds. For brief moments he lost sight of the helicopters as stray tendrils of cloud dribbled toward the ground, as though trying to escape the solid mass that birthed them. Hobo Lead called his wingman and told him to stop his rotating anticollision beacon. Sam did the same, then went back to map reading. Locating the small LZ would have been difficult in good weather; the poor visibility was going to make precision navigation mandatory.

Minutes passed and Sam was becoming concerned that they had missed the insertion point when a fortunate break in the clouds showed a small, irregularly shaped clearing a mile to their front. Quickly, Sam compared it to the chart and punched the transmit button of the radio. "Hobo Lead, Blackjack. Looks like the LZ just ahead at one o'clock. Suggest you come right about five degrees and slow to approach."

There was a pause as the helicopter pilot searched the murky horizon. At treetop altitude he didn't have Sam's loftier view. "Blackjack, this is Hobo Lead. Rog. I'm picking it up now. Hobo Flight will head directly in. If it's hot, we'll come out on the approach heading before turning right to zero niner five for the secondary."

"Rog," acknowledged Sam. He rotated his radio select switch to the TOC at Chi Lang. "Toad, this is Blackjack Two One."

"Blackjack, this is Toad. You're loud and clear. How me?" acknowledged the TOC.

"Got you five by five as well. Hobo is approaching the primary LZ. One mile to touchdown."

"Roger. Please keep us informed."

Sam didn't bother to respond to that stupidity. Of course he would keep them informed. That was, after all, why he was here flailing about in the Cambodian murk.

The helicopters approached the LZ as near to the northern tree line as they could comfortably get. The ground team stood on the helicopter skids as they neared the insertion point. Both ships flared together, hovering three feet over the sodden earth. They wouldn't risk miring their skids in the soft, wet ground. The twelve men leapt as one. Two fell as they hit the ground but rolled quickly and were only a few feet behind the main body of the team as it disappeared into the tree line. The two helicopters were lowering their noses and accelerating away before the first man's feet had touched Cambodian soil. They had cleared the LZ and pointed for the border before the lead ship called.

"Hobo Flight is away clean and team has been off-loaded. The LZ was cold. Repeat, cold LZ."

Sam acknowledged and called the TOC. "Toad, this is Blackjack. Cold LZ. Repeat, cold LZ. Mermaid is undercover. Negative contact as yet."

"Roger. Call us when you do have contact."

Sam flipped the TOC a mental finger and ignored the comment. Unless there was a problem, Mermaid—the ground team—would stay off the radio and listen for pursuit for half an hour. Sam decided to use the interval to establish checkpoints well away from the LZ on the four cardinal compass points so he could remain oriented without overflying the men on the ground.

It took only a few minutes to find ground reference points on all sides of the LZ from which he could take a heading and be over the insertion point within minutes. He orbited one of these, a large jungle emergent with its top fifty feet barren of green growth. It was at least three miles from the insertion point, yet to be certain he wasn't too close to the team he established an orbit that took him yet another five miles from the tree and the team.

He had no illusions that the Viet Cong battalion bivouacked beneath the heavy growth would not be aware of his presence. More than likely he was already being tracked by watchers huddled in some of the taller trees. He'd try to give them the impression that he was uncertain of his position—something not all that far from the truth, he thought as he tried to keep his tree in sight in suddenly worsening visibility. The challenge would be to keep up the deception for the remainder of the day. He had told Stretch Lyle that the team would spend most of the day getting organized before they started to move, but that was a long way from the truth. If he knew Christian and his hooligans they'd make every effort to be close to their attack positions before they ran out of light.

Now that he had established a routine and there was little for him to do, Sam began to feel uneasy. Overflying the strange countryside at low level gave him a vague squirmy feeling in his gut and made him twist about under his straps. He felt more vulnerable somehow than he did in the more familiar Vietnamese territory, though much of this terrain was identical in appearance. He changed headings and occasionally flew into the clouds, still playing his "lost aviator" charade for any ground observers, doing his best to simulate a pilot trying to find his way around a storm system. The little aircraft ran smoothly and Sam had leaned the fuel-to-air mixture back to the maximum extent possible to conserve fuel. In ten minutes he figured he must have stretched his credibility as a lost pilot to the breaking point, even playing to an unsophisticated audience. He banked sharply and headed to his eastern reference point, a fallen tree over a roiling jungle stream.

His radio cracked with static before he arrived at the stream and he had his first contact with the Americans hiding below. It was very brief. "Blackjack, Blackjack. Mermaid. Green, green. Moving now," the voice whispered.

Sam acknowledged, fighting the urge to whisper back. He keyed the radio set to the TOC frequency and repeated the message. So far, so good. Mermaid was down safely with no pursuit and they were moving. Get her out, Jim! he urged silently. Guiltily, he amended his plea. Get them all out! But, in all honesty, he knew that his primary concern lay with Lee Roget. He shook his head violently as though he could physically clear her from his thoughts. He had to remain objective or he'd end up running into a damned tree or doing something equally stupid.

Sam found his stream and watched the water flooding over the top of the huge tree that formed a natural bridge. The stream had already overflowed its banks and was slowly creeping back under the tree line. Suddenly Sam couldn't believe what he was seeing. Probably because he wasn't accustomed to seeing people at such a low altitude, his scan almost missed them.

Involuntarily, his hand jerked the stick and shoved on more power. His instincts had turned the aircraft away before conscious thought returned. At least a full squad of ten or twelve black-clad figures stood on the far bank watching him turn. The scene was frozen in his mind, complete with details. They made no attempt to hide but stood quietly, watching the small gray aircraft. Sam made a cautious ninety-degree turn to the left so he could see them from the window. As the figures began to blur in the low visibility he turned back toward them. They watched him approach, then as though on an unheard command, they took their strapped assault rifles from their shoulders and raised them toward him.

Sam didn't wait to see if they fired, but put the Bird Dog into a maximum, ninety-degree bank, pulling the stick hard back into his lap. He entered the clouds in the turn and quickly transitioned to instrument flight. He gave it a full minute before he warily lowered the nose and regained the clear air. He shivered convulsively as he reported the VC squad's location to the TOC. What the hell had he been thinking of? Unconsciously, he had expected them to bolt when they saw him, as enemy troops would have done across the border. But here, there was no reason for them to be wary of aircraft. This was their home turf. As fighting veterans they knew the power and limitations of air attacks better than most people who flew. They had been well aware that, international diplomacy aside, no attack aircraft would be launched on a day like this.

Sam spent the next fifteen minutes finding a new reference point, not knowing whether the VC squad he'd seen had just been passing through or was permanently assigned to that area. He had no desire to find out.

"Blackjack, this is Mermaid. Sitrep, green. Repeat, green. Out." The whispered transmission startled him but he acknowledged and passed the report along. He wondered what kind of progress they were making and also whether Christian would tell them. Immediately, he dismissed that thought. Jim had plenty to do without trying to satisfy the curiosity of the horseholders.

The ceiling seemed to be rising slightly as he monitored Stretch Lyle's takeoff call to the TOC. He climbed to check it and found he'd been correct. The cloud base had risen to more than eight hundred feet. Sam had been dodging trees for so long that he thought it a giddying height. He let himself sag back in the seat for the first time in almost four hours. He felt drained but knew he had another long sortie before dark. It had been only ten minutes since the last team sitrep, so Lyle would have plenty of time to get himself oriented.

Sam checked in with the warrant officer as he made his way across the border. "Tabby, this is Blackjack. How do you read?"

"Got you loud and clear, Blackjack. How me?"

"Five by five. I'll meet you five south of the LZ. There's a big tree there with a dead top. I'll maintain five hundred feet. You stay at seven hundred."

"Roger that," said the cheerful voice.

Sam picked him up easily, for the red rotating beacon still whirled away atop his green O-1. "Best kill that beacon, Tabby. I'm at your ten o'clock low."

The beacon immediately went dark. "Sorry 'bout that, Blackjack. What's going on?"

Sam briefed Lyle and led him to each of the ground reference points he'd used, giving him the heading from each back to the LZ. The team was no longer there, of course, but they had to have some place to use for a reference, and it was as visible as anything that existed in the unsullied rain forest. Sam checked his fuel and knew he'd have to start back. He waved a gloved hand at Lyle and, after getting one in return, wheeled abruptly and pointed the Bird Dog to the east.

The weather improved continuously on the return flight. Most of the squalls had cleared the area, although the clouds remained sullen and dark. The better weather cheered Sam until he remembered that it would make detection of the ground team easier.

His heading split the dirt runway at Chi Lang. As he turned from base leg to final Sam noted that the helicopters were still parked on the pierced-steel apron by the road to the advisory compound. The crews sat in the open hatches, feet dangling outside, and watched his approach. He didn't really care what they thought of his flying, he told himself, yet he made the extra effort to grease the little plane in and killed the engine thirty yards from the fuel blivet, letting the aircraft coast to a stop just in the right position. He pretended not to notice, but he clearly saw one of the chopper pilots nudge the other and say something out of the corner of his mouth. Probably something like "Hotdog."

One of the army pilots wandered over to help Sam refuel his aircraft from the rubber container. Sam added a quart of oil to the engine from the case he carried in the rear cockpit, then did a quick walk-around inspection. He couldn't find any new holes or other defects so he joined the helicopter crews.

"You guys pulling strip alert, huh?" questioned Sam.

"Yes, sir," answered one, who paused in the act of spooning in a mouthful of C ration pork and beans. "We asked them if we could come up, one crew at a time, and grab some hot chow but that colonel nixed it. Told us to 'ahh, please return to your, ahh, airships immediately and remain there until darkness or until you are relieved,'" the young pilot said in a reasonable imitation of Wertz.

"That peckerhead," grumbled another warrant officer who turned to Sam with a grin. "Want to join us for a late lunch, Major?" He rummaged in an opened case of C rations. "Let's see. We still got chopped ham, baby poo, or ham and mothas'."

Sam chose the fatty ham, knowing his stomach, already tight and roiling with tension, would have problems accepting either the canned scrambled eggs or the ham and lima bean mixture. It took a seasoned trencherman to deal with either of those. He munched the hardtack biscuit that came with the meal and tried to keep the ham from rising in his gorge. The helicopter crews drank instant coffee made by firing a piece of plastique explosive beneath a gallon can they obviously hauled along for just such situations. They reminded Sam of a high school football team after the game. No, he decided, watching them wrestle and throw mud balls at one another, the football team's demeanor would be much more sober. One offered him a canteen cup of the coffee.

After the meal and coffee Sam relaxed for a few moments. Thoughts of Lee tried to push into his mind and he stood quickly to stop them. He couldn't allow himself to think about her just now. Perhaps tonight, but not now. There was still too much work to be done. He checked the time and saw that it was just past 1600. It would be dark in about two hours and he'd been off station for more than an hour. He'd best get back up there and make sure everything was going smoothly. He trusted Lyle, but the younger man, any younger man, was liable to make mistakes in judgment. Not that his own had always been so damned great.

The Bird Dog started immediately and the needle indicators on the gauges swung into the appropriate areas. He taxied to the end of the strip, giving the chopper pilots a wave as he passed. The wheels left the muddy surface and Sam banked again toward Cambodia. He skidded the aircraft smoothly around a tall tree that grew close to the strip, then immediately regained his course, peeking back to see if the helicopter crews had seen him. OK, so maybe you are a hotdog, he thought.

Pipes of sunlight were beginning to force their way through the overcast, and the air rushing through the window felt crisper than it had in days. Sam loosened his shoulder straps and slumped comfortably back into the seat. Idly, he let his eyes wander the countryside a thousand feet below, drinking in the details as the sunbeams probed at the shadows beneath the trees. The dusty look was gone from the foliage and it appeared brighter, fresher, and incredibly green. A flock of parrots exploded from a tree at the noise of his engine. He thought he could almost pick up their garrulous scolding. Smoke from a tiny cluster of hootches drifted vertically into the air as someone prepared to cook an evening meal. Who were they? VC? Who cared. They probably didn't know themselves. More than likely they simply wished everyone would leave them alone to do whatever it was they did. Sam sighed heavily and pulled his shoulder straps tight. He was almost to the border.

"Tabby, this is Blackjack," he called.

"Go ahead, Blackjack. Tabby here."

"Rog. Crossing the fence now. Anything happening?"

"Not a thing, Blackjack. Weather seems to have improved considerably and we had a green sitrep about twenty minutes ago. That was a quick trip you took. Did you have a chance to chow down?"

Sam smiled. Sooner or later, all conversations with Donald Lyle seemed to drift back to food. "Yeah, I grabbed a bite. Why don't you head on in? I should be able to take it from here."

"OK, I'll do it. I'm over that big old tree you showed me, at nearly a thousand feet. The cloud deck is breaking up a lot quicker than they said it would."

"I'm heading toward you, going down to seven hundred. Have you seen any activity on the ground?"

"Not a thing. But with the growth down there they could be building a turnpike and I don't think anyone could see it. I think somebody might have taken a shot at me awhile back but I never heard another one and didn't see anything on the ground. Just that one crack, you know."

It sounded as though the Viet Cong might be getting tired of the constant presence of the observation aircraft. It shouldn't be a big problem, since darkness was only a couple of hours away. Sam planned to find a new orbit area, however, if the natives were getting annoyed enough to start shooting. His biggest concern was that the enemy commanders might decide that the wandering aircraft were doing exactly what they were doing—relaying radio messages from someone on the ground.

Sam pointed his aircraft to the north. In minutes the clearing of the LZ appeared off his left wing. He maintained course until the LZ was lost from view and began to look for another reference point. He found one quickly enough where the roots of one emergent had lost their loose grip on the forest floor and the tree had toppled over to rest against another, forming an A shape above the canopy. He orbited it while he took another green sitrep from the team and passed it to the TOC.

The sun was sliding down rapidly. Already, heavy shadows were hiding the few breaks in the trees. Jungle birds flew about in a frenzy trying to find suitable roosts for the night. A few flying foxes were already launching for their night patrol.

The hiss in his headset alerted him to an inbound call from the ground team. "Blackjack, this is Mermaid. Message follows," the whispered voice advised, then gave him a few moments to get his grease pencil ready to copy the message on the windscreen. It came in code since the ground team was not equipped with a secure radio, as were the aircraft and TOC.

He read the message back to the unseen voice to confirm its accuracy, then passed it to the TOC and turned for home. As he crossed the border Sam pulled his SOI from the leg pocket of his flight suit and began to decipher the message on his own. Primarily, it gave the position where the team would go to ground for the dark hours.

Sam's heart began to beat wildly as he plotted their position on his map. He replotted the coordinates to make certain there was no mistake. There wasn't. They were within a hundred meters of the location where the intelligence had reported the prisoners were held.

Sam ungummed his eyes and tried to figure out where he was. It was still dark and there was a musty smell to the poncho liner entwined about his body. The air mattress was slick beneath him; the other liner covering it had wormed off during his restless sleep. He could hear the gentle snoring of someone across the room as he sat and tried to clear the fuzz from his mind. It came back to him. He and Lyle had been billeted for the night in the main team bunker.

He groped until he felt the small travel alarm, which continued to buzz insistently until he found the button that turned it off. He peered into its luminous face—0430. He had an hour to get himself together, eat, and get his aircraft ready to fly. The remainder of Mermaid team's final message the previous evening had read that they were going in at first light. That should be about 0600.

Sam kicked Lyle awake and, clad only in his baggy GI boxer shorts and jungle boots, left the bunker for the wash hootch. There, he carefully scraped his beard with a dull razor, squinting in the only illumination, a sixty-watt bare bulb hanging from the ceiling. He splashed water on his face and scrubbed his teeth in the chemical-tasting water. Ablutions completed, he headed back to the bunker for a fresh flight suit. Lyle was sitting up scratching his head in a befuddled fashion. He looked like a six-foot seven-inch twelve-year-old.

"Mornin', Major. Sure was a short night, wasn't it?"

Sam grunted. Morning was not his best time. But, inside, he felt good about this one. Maybe things were going to go right. He remembered the deadly efficiency of Jim Christian and his men in the U Minh Forest. If anyone could make the snatch, they could. As he dressed and transferred items from the dirty flight suit to the clean one, he thought of the good things that could soon be realities. Promotion, a career that promised many more years doing what he liked best, a wonderful woman. Maybe even kids. He and Lee weren't *that* old. Lots of older couples were having kids these days. He thought about it some more. Well, maybe one kid. He was almost cheerful as he left the bunker for the team house.

Wertz and the advisory team operations officer stood before the situation map. The ground team's remain-overnight, their RON position, was marked with a small circle. Almost next to it was the army symbol for the Viet Cong Main Force Battalion headquarters. They were *very* close. Staring at the map Sam suddenly didn't feel nearly so cheerful. Jesus! If they could only provide artillery and air support.

He felt Wertz's little porcine eyes on him. Sam turned. "Good morning, Colonel."

"Major," Wertz responded, "will you be, ahh, aloft when the raid is scheduled to take place?"

"Yes, sir. I will."

"Excellent. No reflection on Mister Lyle but he is after all, ahh, rather young and inexperienced."

That didn't seem to require an answer so Sam turned and went searching for food. Lyle had beaten him to the mess hootch and was shoveling in bacon and toast. The helicopter crews arrived, looking like sleepy children whose mother had just gotten them up for school. They would go on strip alert just before daylight to be available quickly should the team need them. The chance of this was not rated very high since most of the TOC party expected a pursuit with little chance for a pickup. None of the army aircrew seemed particularly concerned about what could be in store for them this day. Sam quickly gulped two pieces of toast and a cup of coffee, then dragged a protesting Lyle from the table to run him down to the airstrip in a jeep.

Vietnamese troops were still sweeping the dirt landing strip for mines as they arrived. They didn't seem to be taking their jobs seriously enough for Sam, but there was little he could do about it, particularly since his grasp of the Vietnamese language was limited to ordering beer and swearing. Even the swearing must not have been very good, for there was no change in their expression when he tried it out on them—they continued in their nonchalant, easy way, working down the strip. All Sam could do was fume. He arranged his gear in the aircraft and went through the engine-start procedures, letting the aircraft engine warm slowly to full efficiency. By the time the gauges were solidly in the green, the Vietnamese had moved from the dirt strip and he taxied onto it.

Sam adjusted his power for cruise as he leveled at fifteen hundred feet. With the pale light of the early morning at his back the sky was cloudless and the visibility was as good as he'd ever seen it in Vietnam. The tropical depression had cleared the skies of the smoke and haze associated with the dry season, and it was too early in the day for thunderstorm buildup. He set his course for the team's RON position in the deep forest. He could smell, rather than see, early cooking fires. He ignored them. He had no quarrel with local Viet Cong this morning. Nervously, he fiddled with the throttle and prop levers, agitating the mixture control, all the time knowing that it was his own unsettled state rather than the aircraft's responses that were making him fretful.

One way or another, the waiting would be over within the hour, but Sam wasn't sure his nervous system could function properly for that long. He leaned his face into the slipstream and watched the pockmarked countryside glide away behind him. The unsullied rain forest of Cambodia was to his immediate front. He picked out the original LZ. He would use it for his final checkpoint to the team's attack position. First, however, he would use it as an orbit point and attempt contact with those on the ground. He glanced at the clock. If things were on schedule the assault would begin soon. He was assuming that it would be an assault; he'd never thought about them taking the POWs in any other fashion. They could have, however, infiltrated the camp at night. God! There were so many things that could go wrong. A premature sighting by a guard or a large guard force, or . . . He forced himself to stop speculating. He must keep his mind on the job if he was going to be of any use to Christian.

There were still a few spare minutes after he'd established his waiting orbit over the LZ, but Sam decided to try calling them anyway. Hell, maybe their plans had changed and they'd be glad to hear from him early. "Mermaid, this is Blackjack. How do you read?"

"Blackjack, this is Mermaid" came the immediate whispered response. "We're going in zero five. Get the choppers launched to the LZ we used. Have them orbit there in case we can try for an early pickup. Otherwise they'll have to head back to home plate and wait until we get to an LZ or across the fence. We're going to try to make this quick and get out before they can react. Do you copy?"

Sam acknowledged. He thought the whispered voice on the radio had been Christian's, but it was hard to tell. Quickly he selected his other radio and made sure that it was in the secure mode.

"Toad, this is Blackjack. Contact established with Mermaid. Jump-off in zero five. Mermaid requests immediate launch of Hobo Flight to original LZ. Repeat. Mermaid requests immediate chopper launch to original LZ. Suggest they orbit east of site at one thousand. Hobo should be prepared to depart the LZ for an early pickup if possible. Blackjack will be directly over the LZ at fifteen hundred."

"Blackjack, this is Toad. Copy all. Hobo Flight is scrambling at this time."

Sam did some rapid mental calculations. Even with good luck and no wounded to drag along, the team couldn't attack, regroup, and make their way to the LZ through five klicks of rain forest in less than five to six hours. If an early pickup wasn't possible, Lyle would have to relieve him at least once before the team's arrival at the LZ. Sam looked in the direction of the VC base camp. He couldn't see even a slight break in the tree canopy for five or more klicks and doubted they'd find a closer LZ. He wanted to be sure he would be on station for the extraction, so on the next contact with the TOC he'd pass the word for the army aviator to relieve him at 1000.

The minutes crawled by and Sam found his nerves settling. The raid was underway now and there was nothing he could do about it one way or the other. A calm descended upon him with the realization that he was, for the moment at least, a nonplayer. Everything was in Jim Christian's and his group's hands. And capable hands they were, he assured himself. He felt like one of the truly devout must feel when he surrendered himself to his god.

Sam's serenity vanished in an instant when he received the radio call. The voice was no longer whispered, just labored, as though the speaker was moving hurriedly or straining under a great burden.

"Blackjack, this is Mermaid. We've got 'em and we're moving. Heading zero eight five toward the LZ. Are the choppers en route?"

"Affirm, Mermaid. Choppers are en route and should be on station shortly. You want us to head your way?"

"Roger. The dinks are trying to get a pursuit organized and we're trying to make time while they do. All captives are in pretty good shape considering."

Sam's heart felt as if it would fly from his throat. She was alive! He felt tears seeping into his eyes and angrily wiped them away. Alive, yes. Out of danger? No. Still, he couldn't keep the grin from his face. "Mermaid, this is Blackjack. I'm going to Hobo's frequency but I'll be monitoring you. Any problem, just sing out. OK?"

"Roger" came the grunted reply.

Before notifying the helicopters he called TOC with the information and told them when he wanted Lyle airborne. He completed his turn around the jungle opening and faced his aircraft to the east, attempting to pick up the inbound helicopters. He tried to raise them. "Hobo Lead, this is Blackjack. Where are you?"

"Just crossing the border, Blackjack. We copied your report to Toad. Good deal!"

"Sure is." Sam wondered if they knew about his relationship with Lee. It was a pretty close-knit group in the delta so they probably did. "I'm over the original LZ at one point five altitude. OK, I've got you in sight now at my twelve o'clock, maybe three to four miles. Why don't you head for the target area and I'll fall in behind you."

"Roger that. You think we ought to go on down or just hang onto the altitude we've got?"

Sam pondered for a moment before answering. "I don't see what good it would do you or them to get down in the treetops. You might as well stay up high out of small-arms range until they need you."

"That's kinda what I thought too."

Sam swung the nose of his aircraft to fall in behind the two helicopters as they came abeam. The bright green canopy of trees looked serene in the first rays of morning sunlight. Then the god of war stepped in again. "Contact! Contact! Contact!" the unseen American barked into the radio.

Sam waited, the hairs prickling on the back of his neck. He wanted to scream questions but knew they'd never be answered. All he could do was wait. And hope.

"What do you want us to do, Blackjack?" asked the lead helicopter pilot.

Christ! How was he supposed to know? Who had suddenly elected Sam Brooks leader? He thought about it and decided he was a better one to assume the mantle than a teenager who had been playing in the mud yesterday. "Listen, Hobo, why don't you take your number-two man and return to the original LZ. I'll try to stay close to the people on the ground. If they find a way for you to get in for a pickup I'll

give you a call. And take over communications with Toad and let them
know what's going on. I'll monitor your frequency but I want to keep
my transmitter on Mermaid."

"You got it."

The helicopters circled away to the left while Sam kept the O-1 on
course for the RON site, the only coordinates he had that were close
to the team. It would be futile to call for their location now. His eyes
darted back and forth across the rain forest, hoping he would see something to confirm their position.

Sam had a notion he was in the proper area when he heard the crack
of bullets creating their tiny sonic booms outside his opened window.
Most of the VC battalion scattered beneath the trees probably didn't
know what the exact situation was at the moment, but they most as-
suredly connected it somehow to the small gray aircraft droning above
their heads. The order to fire on it had obviously been passed down
to individual units. He checked his altitude and decided that two thousand
feet would be healthier. The AK-47 rounds were reported to expend
their velocity quickly above a thousand feet, but Sam didn't like the
way they were sounding outside his window. They seemed to have plenty
of push left.

He raised the nose of the Bird Dog and quickly gained the additional five hundred feet. He forced himself to scan the ground and was
not surprised to see the twinkle of assault rifles well defined in the
early morning shadows of the trees. Thankfully, with such a thick canopy,
the riflemen could have only momentary glimpses of his aircraft as
he overflew them. That would reduce their tracking time. Nevertheless, he began a continuous corkscrew, jinking so that he was in a constant
turn or climb or both simultaneously. The ground fire was spread over
a very wide area and Sam concluded that the battalion must be dis-
persed so that if the Americans or VNAF decided to bomb their sanctuary the troops would not be caught in large bunches. Sam briefly
admired their commanders for such foresight.

He heard a close thudding sound and, checking the cockpit, found
that a copper-jacketed AK round had barely penetrated the side of the
fuselage, its nose protruding inside the aircraft skin a fourth of an inch.
He stared at the blunted shape. It looked like an ugly bug trying to
force its way out of the ground to complete its life cycle. With sufficient velocity it would have struck him in the left calf rather than being
trapped by the metal skin of the aircraft. Sam noticed he was beginning

to perspire heavily. He felt like something at the bottom of the food chain.

"Mermaid is turning north. Turning north," the radio cackled.

Helplessly, Sam could only acknowledge. He turned his map in his lap and tried to calculate the group's approximate location. They'd been running for more than half an hour toward the original LZ. If they were moving fast maybe they'd have covered, what, a klick? Two klicks? And why had they turned north? That would only take them farther away from the border and help. For sure, Jim Christian wouldn't do that on a whim. Five minutes later the question became academic and Sam knew more than he really wanted to know.

"Blackjack, this is Mermaid. We got problems." The voice was harsh. In the background of the transmission Sam could hear the popping of small-arms fire. His blood turned to ice. "We got hit." Sam recognized Christian's voice now. "One KIA and one wounded. Trying to get around them to the north. If that doesn't work I'll drop off a two-man ambush team to slow 'em down. We're taking a quick breather but plan on heading north for another klick or so, then break east again. The dinks are close but I'd like to pop a pencil flare and see if you can give us some help in finding an LZ. The WIA is bad."

"Roger, Mermaid. I think I know your general location and I'm faced in the right direction. Let it go." Inside, Sam was screaming for information. Who was the WIA? Now was not the time to ask, however.

"Flare's away" came the terse comment from Christian.

Frantically, Sam swept his eyes back and forth through the 180 degrees in front of his aircraft. He couldn't see anything. Christ! He was looking right into the rising sun. "Sorry, Mermaid. No joy on that one. If you can give me a minute I'm going to have to get the sun behind me."

"OK, but let's not screw around anymore than necessary. We're going to have to move."

Sam had already bent the throttle, prop lever, and mixture control as far forward as they would go. The little aircraft groaned at the maltreatment but responded like a quarterhorse out of the gate. He felt like beating its flanks to encourage it. He turned as soon as he thought he was by the ground unit. "OK, Mermaid. Let's try another one."

"Flare's away and we've got to move. Heading north again."

"Got it! Stand by."

Sam's heart fell. The flare was no more than a klick away at ten o'clock. North of the miniscule point of light stretched miles of unbroken rain forest. There wasn't even a tiny opening. He tried to make his voice casual. "Mermaid, it doesn't look too good in the direction you're heading. If there's any way to do it, I'd try to swing back to your right." Sam realized he'd have to be careful giving directions now, for the radio connecting him to the ground team was not secure and could possibly be monitored by the VC.

"Damnit, Sam. I know the direction we need to go. Do you understand we *cannot* move in that direction? We're completely cut off there and the way we just came. There are a lot of people down here. A *lot* more than anybody knows."

Sam was helpless. He didn't even know how to respond. The radio came to life again.

"Blackjack, Mermaid. We're moving november again. I've dropped off four troopers to try to slow the pursuit. They're good men and they'll give us some time. I know everybody's doing everything they can. It's just that we've got ourselves something of a situation developing down here. Our forward element says it sounds like they've got movement to our front as well. We'll continue in this direction until we get confirmation, but we may have to move toward the only open area we've got left."

The only open area they had was back to the west. Deeper into Cambodia and into the bivouac area of the VC battalion. Jesus! Sam's head was spinning with unrealistic schemes. Brought into the sunlight of reality for examination, they crumbled into dust. All he could do was swear and beat his fist against the window rail.

Sam was startled to hear Stretch Lyle calling on the interplane radio frequency. He checked his watch and was dumbfounded to find he'd been airborne for almost four hours. Quickly, checking his fuel gauges, he saw he was nearing the end of his flying schedule. He didn't want to leave but there was nothing else he could do. The engine would not run on his desires. As Sam was briefing the Army aviator, Christian broke in on the other radio to confirm that the enemy was in front of them. They would have to head west. Sam reluctantly turned for Chi Lang, keeping the little aircraft's airspeed indicator nudging the red line until the strip was in sight.

It wasn't until he flared for landing that he noticed the two Hueys sitting on the parking apron. The crews came to meet him as he cut the engine by the fuel blivet.

"How's it going up there, Major?" asked the lead aircraft commander. They were all somber now—no evidence of horseplay or games.

"Crappy," Sam muttered. "They've had to turn west. Could you guys help me get—"

"You bet," the warrant officer responded and motioned his crew toward Sam's airplane. A gunner grabbed the fuel hose and the helicopter copilot checked the oil. Sam watched them until it became apparent that they knew what they were doing, then wandered to the side to relieve himself. He was zipping up when the copilot from the second helicopter shouted from his open door. He was wearing his helmet, obviously monitoring the TOC radio.

"Lyle is down! TOC just got a mayday call that he'd been hit and was going in. They say . . ."

Sam was running for his aircraft before hearing the remainder of the message. He'd heard all he needed to know. Cursing, he coaxed the still-hot engine into a reluctant start and made a running takeoff, ignoring the before-flight checks. He was at a thousand feet before he realized he hadn't fastened his shoulder and lap belt. The TOC was trying to talk to him and he forced himself to focus on their words.

"Blackjack, this is Toad. Do you read?"

"Blackjack. Go ahead."

"Roger. Tabby radioed that he had taken hits from a heavy-caliber gun. Probably a quad fifty. We can't reach the team without him so their status is unknown. Let us know what's going on as soon as you find out."

Screw you, Sam thought. He didn't bother to answer but concentrated on making his best time to the team's last known location. The aircraft seemed to be dragging, but a glance at the indicator showed that the airspeed was almost at the red line. Some minutes out he tried to raise the ground team. "Mermaid, this is Blackjack."

"Hello there, Blackjack. This is Mermaid."

Sam was alarmed at the calm, casual voice of Christian. Gone was the raspy urgency of earlier transmissions. "Toad says that Tabby is down. You know anything about it? And could you pass your situation?"

"Well, ole Tabby is sitting about five meters away from me complaining that he's hungry. He damned near crashed through the trees on top of us when those guns took him out. We had to walk a few yards and pull his lanky ass outta this mighty bent-up little bird. You ought to see it. The damned thing is sitting about twenty-five meters up in the air, resting in the crotch of a tree. Luckily, us elite troops are good at shinnying up trees, although from the length of this guy he could have damned near stepped down without any help. He's OK, except for a broken nose and a few scratches."

"How are y'all doing?" Sam persisted.

"Well, if you get right down to it, we've had better days. They've blocked us to the whiskey as well. In fact, I'd say we've done a pretty good job of getting ourselves surrounded."

A chill of fear ran up Sam's back. This couldn't be! Those guys could get themselves out of anything. He couldn't find words to speak to Christian.

As if reading his thoughts Christian continued. "Our biggest problem is that we've got two more WIAs we're having to carry, and most of the civilians are so exhausted that if we move we have to carry them as well. We sounded like a herd of Thai elephants tromping through the woods. No wonder they caught up with us."

Sam finally got his tongue working. "What do you plan to do, Jim?"

There was a long moment of silence before Christian answered. "I don't really have many options, Sam. The Forces types could probably get away, but we're not leaving the civilians and we'll never make it with them. They'd nail us before we got half a klick. I guess we'll just have to sit tight and keep our backs together as long as we can. We all knew it might come to this."

"Shit, Jim!"

"Exactly, old buddy."

Sam orbited the general area. A volley of heavy-caliber tracers burst from the trees. Quickly, he slammed the stick to the right and dived to a lower altitude. Away from the gun he raised the nose and scanned the treetops. The entrance hole made by Lyle's aircraft was readily visible in the otherwise unbroken green. The team was only a short distance from it.

Sam switched to the TOC radio. "Toad, this is Blackjack. Here's the situation. The team has recovered Tabby with only minor injuries but they're completely surrounded, with several WIAs. The POWs are unable to move and Mermaid will not move without them. I don't think they've got a prayer without gunships or TACAIR. I'm requesting that you release these assets to me at this time."

"Negative, Blackjack." It was Wertz himself on the radio, his voice unmistakable. "U.S. or Vietnamese government assets will not be allowed over the border, as you very well know. I suggest you inform Mermaid to, ahh, take any necessary action to see that our man does not fall into enemy hands, abandon the remainder of the civilians, disband, and individually find their way back across the border. I repeat, additional assets will not be, ahh, forthcoming. Do you understand?"

Sam's head was whirling. This was impossible. Those were Americans down there, and he could no more relay such an order than Jim Christian could carry it out. Besides, Lee Roget was still there. He felt helpless but knew he had to do something. He might be able to get the Hobo chopper team to assist, but they carried only door guns that would probably be useless in the heavy foliage. To get a heavy-fire team of helicopter gunships he'd have to put a request in through sector, and Wertz would immediately kill it. TACAIR was the only thing his fevered brain could grab onto, for he knew that the ARVN would never fire arty across the border, no matter who was down there. So, TACAIR it would have to be. But how? Wertz would be sure to kill any request that went through channels.

There might be one chance. If Sam could get his Bird Dog up to seven or eight thousand feet, in this flat countryside he'd probably have line-of-sight communications directly with the IV DASC at Can Tho. He could request fighters from them. They might question why he was going outside regular channels, but if told there were Americans on the ground who needed help, they'd give him all he could handle from the U.S. air units, bypassing the Vietnamese altogether.

He'd have to be canny about it. No American duty officer would send aircraft over the border, regardless of circumstances. That could be overcome, though. He'd rendezvous with them over Chi Lang and lead them over himself. That would also cover the fighter pilots' asses in the inevitable investigation that would follow. His hands had already taken over and the aircraft was climbing as his mind sorted through the ramifications of what he was about to do. It would mean not only no promotion and no operations job, he'd be damned lucky to escape without a general court-martial. He could be looking at some serious time in a federal prison. The main thing he had to do was keep everyone else involved out of trouble.

Sam quickly looked up the IV DASC frequency in his SOI and found that Razor Control was on 314.4. He switched his UHF radio to that setting. "Razor Control, this is Blackjack Two One with a request."

There was only silence on the radio. He tried once more, with no response. He almost wept with frustration. He couldn't leave the team on the ground with no one over them but he was just too far from Can Tho to reach IV DASC.

Suddenly, an unknown voice came through his headset with startling clarity. "Blackjack Two One, this is Red Rider Three Three. Can I be of assistance? I'm in contact with Razor Control. Be glad to relay."

This time Sam almost wept with relief. "You sure can, Red Rider. Please pass to Razor Control that I need all the U.S. flights they have available, as well as anything they have on alert. Rendezvous them over Chi Lang at fifteen-minute intervals. I'll brief and direct them from there."

"Rog, Blackjack. Can you give me target coordinates and nature of the target? You know old Razor is going to ask for it."

This is where it gets tricky, thought Sam. "Negative, Red Rider. Just tell 'em we've got a tactical emergency and I've got twelve-plus U.S. types on the ground who are in great danger of being overrun. I don't have time to screw around with coordinates."

"Roger, Blackjack. I'll pass that along. Look, sounds like you're going to be pretty busy. If you need some help I'll be glad to do what I can. Anything at all."

Sam felt a surge of gratitude toward the unknown FAC. The guy knew something was going on and was willing to step into it with his eyes open. Sam couldn't do that to him. "Naw, just act as a relay for me if you would."

"Roger, I'll pass your requests now. Stand by."

There was a lengthy pause before Red Rider returned to the radio. "Blackjack Two One, this is Red Rider Three Three. Expect first set of fighters in zero five. They're diverts from the Rach Gia area. Two F-100s with snake and nape. Call sign is Sword. They'll be up Blackjack company frequency shortly. Razor Control advises that they'll be diverting other U.S. flights to you as per your request. In addition, Razor Zero One wants to know, let's see, how did he put it? Something like 'What the fuck's going on?' He wants a description and location of target."

Bill Robinson was suspicious. And he should be! Bill knew about the cross-border operation. He'd been briefed on it by Wertz. He must think that they were back on the sunny side of the fence however, or he'd never have approved diverting the strike birds. Or would he? Sam knew that here was another ass he was going to have to cover.

"Ah, Red Rider, this is Blackjack. I'm having trouble reading you. You're breaking up badly."

Sam could almost hear the smile in the voice of the other FAC. "Right, Blackjack. Understand you can't read me. I'll stand by on the off chance your radio comes back to life. And I'll keep the relay open and keep shuttling the fighters to Chi Lang."

Sam couldn't risk a thank you but he did squeeze the radio mike button twice, then decided he'd better let the folks on the ground know what was happening. "Mermaid, Blackjack here."

"Go ahead, Sam. This is Mermaid."

"OK, Jim. Some good news. We've got TACAIR inbound. We can be working your area within ten minutes maximum. Where do you want it?"

"God! I can't believe it! They released TACAIR? Sam, that's great . . . wait a minute. Did they release it or did you?"

"Doesn't matter. It's on the way. You'd better be getting your people under cover."

"Aw, hell, Sam. The dinks are completely around us and I've taken another KIA and two WIAs since we talked last. Let me know when you want smoke. It doesn't matter if Charley sees it or not 'cause he sure as hell knows where we are anyway. You have your flyboys put it anywhere they want, at least fifty meters from the smoke."

Sam could hear the rapid popping of automatic weapons as Christian keyed his radio mike. While they were talking he had turned to Chi Lang and was watching the camp slide into sight on the horizon. He thought furiously. Hobo helicopter flight had returned to base to refuel and await developments. He could launch them now and have them orbit east of the team while he worked the strike aircraft, keeping them available for a pickup. As soon as the immediate pressure was off the team, he could use succeeding sets of fighters to blast a way out of the entrapment, and when they were clear of the attackers, Hobo Flight could snatch them. First, a quick call to Hobo Flight.

"Hobo Lead, this is Blackjack."

"Hobo Lead, go ahead."

"Rog. Get 'em airborne. Orbit the southern edge of the original LZ at fifteen hundred. We'll be putting TACAIR around Mermaid's position."

"Atta boy, Maj! We're cranking. How'd you ever get 'em to release the fighters?"

"Don't ask."

Wertz's voice broke onto the communication net. Sam had all but forgotten him. "Blackjack, this is Toad. Cancel those fighter strikes immediately. Do you copy?"

"Sorry, Toad. I've got some comm problems. I can't read you. I'll talk to you when I get on the ground."

"Blackjack, return immediately. Don't give me that faulty communications crap. Hobo Lead, cancel that request to launch from Blackjack."

"Was somebody calling Hobo Lead? Two, did you hear anything?"

"Just some kinda scratchy noises. Sounds like somebody has radio problems."

"Yeah, that's what I thought. Let's do it, Two."

"Right on your ass, Lead."

"This is Toad. Land immediately! Repeat, land immediately!"

"Hobo Two, this is Lead. Let's change to Blackjack's strike frequency and listen to how the fast movers do it. The static on this freq is getting awful."

Sam smiled and switched to the frequency on which he would work the fighters. "Sword Flight, this is Blackjack Two One."

"Rog, Blackjack, this is Sword Lead. A flight of two Huns with a mixed load of snake and nape plus the usual twenty mike mike. Approaching Chi Lang now at ten grand. Where are you and what's the target? Understand we got a TAC E in progress with round eyes involved."

"That's correct, Sword Lead. Figure sea level for the target elevation. Best bailout will be as far to the east as you can get. Friendlies are in a small grouping and will smoke for us. I'm right over the Chi Lang camp. Do you have me in sight?"

"Rock your wings." Sam rolled up on one wing, then the other. "Yeah, Blackjack, Sword has you. Which way is the target?"

"Just follow me and keep me in sight. It's not far." Sam turned to the west, dreading the inevitable inquiry from the fighter lead.

"Hey, Blackjack. We're getting awful close to the fence line, aren't we? Just what are the target coordinates?"

"Sword Lead, just for the record, it's my call. OK? If we stray it's on my head. You guys just do like you're briefed. We've got some of our own in trouble and we're going to help 'em. We're well inside Vietnam in case anyone is listening up this frequency. I've got to leave you for two to talk to the folks on the ground."

Sam had a few minutes before he had to contact Christian, but he also wanted to have an excuse not to answer Sword Lead in the event the fighter pilot felt particularly pugnacious about his orders. Sam doubted he would. Experience had shown that most of the fighter pilots put their complete trust in the FAC's judgment. He was, after all, the one who had to bite the bullet if a bomb was misdirected. He flew westward until he heard Hobo Flight call that they were orbiting the opening in the jungle, then he took up a heading for the team's position.

"Mermaid, this is Blackjack. How's it going?"

"Well, Sam. About how you'd expect. Those little devils have made two assaults. I don't think they'll try that again for a while, but we're starting to run short of ammo and we've got another WIA. Were you able to do any good?"

"Rog. I've got the cavalry right behind me. Give me a smoke anytime."

Christian didn't answer but within seconds Sam saw bright yellow smoke begin to seep through the tops of the tall trees. It hung above the green as though reluctant to rise in the cooler morning air. No more than fifty meters from the smoke the green tracers of a VC weapon lifted lazily toward him. Sam banked away from the ground fire and called, "Mermaid, I've got yellow."

"That's us, ole buddy. Like I said, you can pretty much take your choice of where to hit. They've got the noose drawn pretty tight."

"OK, Jim, here's the way we'll work it. I'll start to the west, then work the north and south flanks, and finally the east. That's the way we'd like you to go. After we try to rattle their brains a little so they won't be too interested in pursuit, we'll start blasting a corridor toward the fence." Sam was not worried that the VC would intercept his messages and thwart their plan. There would be no way to coordinate an intercept with five-hundred-pound bombs falling on their heads. His major concern was that, should anything happen to him, there would be no one to direct the extraction. He'd just have to stay out of harm's way.

He flipped his radio console switch back to the fighters. "Sword Lead, there's yellow smoke on the treetops at my twelve o'clock, maybe a klick out. Do you have it?"

"Roger. Sword has the smoke."

"OK, those are the friendlies. They're bunched close together and have requested three hundred sixty degree coverage at fifty meters.

But that's too close. We're going to try for a hundred meters. I'll want your bombs first, then nape. I want the first run to be north to south; break is your choice. I'll be over the target at one point five. There's plenty of ground fire. I'd like to warn you again that you're going to be working very close to the friendlies. If you're not sure of a pass, then go through dry. Any questions?"

"Lead, negative. You going to mark?"

"Negative, not on the first pass. I'm trying to conserve my rockets. If you've got the smoke you're cleared hot."

"Rog. Lead will be in from the north in thirty seconds."

The bombs looked beautiful. Sam acted as guide and cheerleader as Sword Flight expended the remainder of its ordnance, including the cannon load. By that time another flight was on station over Chi Lang, demanding to know why no one was there to greet them. Sam directed them to fly west toward the smoke from Sword Flight's weapons. There was some initial reluctance, but they did so after Sam told them he would take full responsibility.

A pair of A-1 Skyraiders was up next, but Sam had them continue their orbit. Their accuracy and loiter time could be put to good use on the breakout. In their place, Golden Flight, three F-100s, completed the destruction on the third side of the beleaguered Americans.

Only once did Christian call Sam during the attacks. "Blackjack," he complained, "I know we told you fifty meters, but that last pair of bombs damned near took us out as well. You might want to move them back just a tad. Fragments just cut down a tree as big as your waist about ten meters from us."

Sam acknowledged with a smile. The destruction pattern of a large bomb was often not appreciated by those near it. Had he actually been placing the bombs fifty meters from the group, the Americans would have been blown away long before.

Sam took a deep breath. It was now or never. "Spad Flight, this is Blackjack," he called to the A-1s orbiting Chi Lang. "If you've been monitoring you know what we've got going on. Head for the smoke and I'll tell you what I've got in mind."

"Spad Lead. Roger. On our way."

"OK. I want a series of passes from north to south on the east side of the smoke. I'll be marking for you on each run with either a rocket or a smoke grenade. We're going to walk your ordnance from the smoke you can see, eastward toward the bor . . . 'er, toward the east at about a hundred or a hundred and fifty meter intervals. When we've used up your external stores I'll want gun passes in front of the friendlies, who'll be moving that way. I'm going to try to work 'em toward one of your bomb craters. There are a couple of army slicks orbiting southeast who'll go in for the pickup. I'll need you to conserve enough beebees to cover that. OK?"

"We'll give it our best shot. I've got you in sight. Let me know when you're going to mark."

"Blackjack is in for the first mark now." Sam tried to conserve his rockets and use smoke grenades, but initially there was still enough ground fire to make this option impractical. After several passes, however, he found he could overfly the area with no opposition. There was nothing like a dozen or so snake-eye bombs to make a person lose interest in anything other than keeping his head down.

It had to be now. "Jim," he yelled into the mike, as though that would give them more impetus, "get 'em moving. Head zero seven five. There's a bomb crater about a hundred meters from your location. I'll get the choppers started toward it."

"No reason to yell," Christian said reasonably. "I can hear you perfectly well."

Sam's nerves were taut enough to reflect gamma rays. "Move, you square-headed sonofabitch!" he yelled and switched hurriedly to the helicopter frequency, not sure whether they had continued to monitor the interplane talk between him and the fighters. He knew that they would be monitoring their primary frequency.

"Hobo Lead, Blackjack. Get moving toward the first bomb crater east of the main body of smoke."

"Roger. We've been listening. We'll be there in about five."

Sam circled the still-smoldering bomb crater and realized that he had three fingers of his left hand in his mouth, nervously chewing through the leather flight glove. He removed it in disgust. The minutes dragged, then suddenly he saw the small group stumble into the crater, some of them immediately taking up defensive positions. He could hardly breathe as he tried to pick out Lee, but they all looked the same from his altitude.

"Hobo Lead is half a klick out."

Sam didn't trust his voice to answer. He wanted to fly lower but he had their only protection—the A-1s circling their position—under his control. He had to be prepared to mark for them if opposition closed in.

Slowly the first helicopter dragged itself over the lip of the crater

and hovered. Flying debris kept Sam from witnessing the loading
operation, but the aircraft was quickly away and the other replaced
it. The perimeter guards pulled back from the lip and stumbled toward
the open hatches. Then the two helicopters were away, climbing together into the cloudless sky. Sam felt tears rush into his eyes, then
he broke into uncontrollable racking sobs. It was a full minute before
he could speak to the escorting Skyraiders.

"Spad Lead, this is Blackjack Two One. Damned good work. I'll
forward your BDA along with my recommendations and eyewitness
account for DFCs for both of you. I expect the team leader will be
doing the same."

"I just hope it ain't an eyewitness account for our court-martial,"
grumbled Spad Lead.

"I'll make sure the responsibility rests with me. I appreciate what
you've done and you're cleared from the area. Good day to both of
you. Blackjack, out."

The helicopters were aiming for Can Tho rather than Chi Lang, and
Sam made the decision to accompany them. He had to find out about
Lee, besides having no stomach for a confrontation with Colonel Wertz.
He was too damned tired for that. He shoved the power forward and
was just able to creep ahead of the Hueys carrying their heavy loads.
He slumped back into the seat and numbly waited for the Can Tho airfield
to appear. He'd gotten them out but he'd jettisoned any chance of
promotion or staying in the air force. In addition, the possibility of a
general court-martial loomed over his head, depending on how pissed
they were topside. But, all things considered, he didn't feel too bad.
In fact, he felt pretty damned good. He sat straighter in the seat. He'd
pulled off a feat that, although technically illegal, was also the right
thing to do. He could live with himself, no matter what happened.

Sam waited at the helicopter revetments as the two Hueys of Hobo
Flight made their approach. He'd beat them in by only moments.
Ambulances stood by, having been requested as soon as the flight cleared
the border. Sam made a conscious effort to stop hyperventilating as
the ships flared together and settled gently to the PSP ramp. The medics
crowded around the hatchways and he watched them place the wounded
on stretchers and rush them to the ambulances. Weary soldiers stumbled
from the open doorways.

Then, the unmistakable form of Jim Christian clambered down with a small figure clasped in his arms. Sam began walking rapidly toward them, then broke into a run. He skidded to a halt in front of them before he saw Jim's wide grin.

"Hello, Sam. She's going to be fine. A teeny little break in her arm, but mostly just exhaustion. She's OK."

Sam couldn't speak but reached out a hand still covered by the leather flying glove and stroked her hair. A small face, burrowed in Christian's chest, turned to him.

"Hi, Sam," Lee Roget said in a low, hoarse voice. "Did you miss me?"

CHAPTER 15

". . . On that day Lieutenant Colonel Brooks, then Major, did successfully plan and execute the rescue of the United States ground element deep in hostile territory. The ground team had . . ." The adjutant droned on and Sam let his eyes drift slightly from the tall general officer standing at attention in front of him to Lee Roget just to the COMUSMACV's right. Her left arm was in a cast supported by a camouflage sling that had a 5th Special Forces flash attached to it. When the general saw the flash he had immediately dispatched a lieutenant to find a similar metal MACV badge to join it. To Lee's right was Maj. Gen. Franklin Rogers, commanding officer, 2d Air Division. Bill Robinson stood languidly behind them, a half-smile on his face. Why shouldn't he smile, thought Sam. It was the large man's last day in the Republic of Vietnam. He'd depart before sunrise for thirty days' leave in the States, then on to Nellis Air Force Base for upgrade transition into the F-4 Phantom before assuming command of a fighter squadron at MacDill Air Force Base.

As the adjutant continued reading the citation for the Silver Star, second Oak-Leaf Cluster, Sam's mind drifted away. It had been a very close call. There was as much evidence for a general court-martial as for an award. In the end it had come down to a matter of convenience: It was simply more expedient to promote and decorate Sam than send him to trial, with its possible ensuing publicity. There were now nearly as many newsmen in Vietnam as there were advisers, and it wouldn't have taken long for one of those hungry young men to discern something out of the ordinary in what happened that day. Even so, the military might have pushed for punishment, feeling as they did about disobeying orders, until cooler heads prevailed, pointing out that if Sam

287

were no longer in the service, few constraints could be placed on him to ensure his silence. And, technically, a serving air force officer was not sworn to obey Central Intelligence officers wearing ranks of convenience.

The four-starred figure standing in front of Sam had been completely briefed, and he was far from happy with any of the participants. His displeasure was, however, well concealed behind the veneer of his good southern breeding. An outsider would have never guessed that the kindly appearing general had threatened underlings with loss of jobs and promotions should such decisions be made again without his knowledge. Few knew the knife edge of politics the general walked in leading his convoluted command, which seemed to double monthly.

". . . brought great honor upon himself, the United States Air Force, and the Military Assistance Command, Vietnam." The adjutant concluded the narrative accompanying the award and stepped forward to hand the commander the medal.

"Well done, Colonel," the soft voice said as deft fingers pinned the medal to Sam's sodden khaki shirt. "Three awards of this citation are extraordinary by any standards." The smile hardened slightly. "We sincerely hope we don't see you in here again for a while. As I think I told you on the last occasion, gallantry is a necessary virtue for any fighting man. However, when one is in an advisory capacity to another man's army, discretionary valor is of prime importance and damned foolishness should be avoided at all costs."

The general finished attaching the medal to Sam's shirt and stepped back to study the newly anointed lieutenant colonel. "I understand you will be given the opportunity to return to an all-U.S. squadron, Colonel Brooks. That's good because we need experienced combat pilots and planners for the new units your government has seen fit to send us. I must confess, however, that I shall dislike seeing you leave your post in the delta. I have had excellent reports on your conduct by senior officers within IV Corps, and I have personally commended your gallantry and fortitude on three occasions in this very room. We do hate to lose your expertise and knowledge of one of our more demanding areas, but I understand a promise was made to you and I will honor that."

The aristocratic features softened into a genuine smile. "If you ever need a job, son, give us a call." He shook Sam's hand once and stepped back. Sam took the hint, executed a left face, and moved briskly from the room followed by General Rogers, Bill Robinson, and Lee Roget.

In the small vestibule, an odd assortment awaited Sam. Colonel Jackson Jones looked on stony-faced; Jim Christian, fresh from his own awards ceremony with the COMUSMACV, grinned like a large pixie. True to his spook training, Colonel Wertz succeeded in looking like a fat potted palm in one corner of the room. He was out of uniform and wearing a tan safari suit that would have covered a reinforced platoon. Sam turned to Lee, who smiled and put her good arm around his waist.

"You're going to look pretty silly," Sam said, "wearing that stupid camouflage sling in San Francisco." Lee only smiled and held him tighter. She was leaving Saigon for good, boarding a Pan Am flight that departed in less than three hours.

It took Sam a moment to realize that General Rogers was talking to him. After all, he thought, I've been a lieutenant colonel for only forty-five minutes and I was a major for . . . well, a long time. It might take awhile to get used to being called by the new rank. He turned to the general.

"Colonel Brooks, we have some things we need to discuss about your new posting. Advance elements of the new squadron will commence arrival in the Republic of South Vietnam within two weeks. As you know, this war is heating up and we'll have to change to meet its new demands. You have been in a rather unique position of seeing the war from all sides and I would value your input. Would you be available tomorrow afternoon for a couple of hours?"

"Of course, sir. At your convenience."

General Rogers swung to face his director of operations. "How about 1400, Jack? Are we clear then?"

"Yes, sir. That should be no problem," said Col. Jackson Jones.

"That's it, then. See you tomorrow, Sam. And I'm truly sorry about having to downgrade your award recommendation from the Air Force Cross to the Silver Star. We all know you deserved the Cross but an award like that just brings too much publicity. And the operation doesn't need anything like that right now. Until tomorrow. Good-bye, Mrs. Roget. I hope that arm isn't too painful. You're a very lucky young lady."

Lee hugged Sam tighter. "Isn't that the truth, General."

He smiled at her. "That wasn't what I meant but it'll do. Have a good trip home. We'll try to get Colonel Brooks back to you in one piece."

General Rogers turned to leave as Bill Robinson ran a quick intercept on him. "Sir," the large black man said, "I wonder if I might have a moment before you leave?" The air division commander looked puzzled but nodded his assent, and they withdrew into a corner.

Colonel Jackson Jones stepped in front of Sam and Lee. "Well, *Colonel* Brooks," he said quietly, emphasizing the new rank, "it appears you won another round, at least temporarily. But it's going to be a long war, and I'll be around watching you."

"Jack," said Sam with a hard smile, using the man's nickname for the first time ever, "you might want to rethink your position on that. It's been too long since you've had to check your six, and you ain't got a wingman to cover your ass anymore. You'd better look out 'cause I might decide I want your job one of these days."

Colonel Jones's only reply was a tight smile. Lee looked worriedly from one man to the other until Jones turned and left the room.

"Is all that *ever* going to end?" she asked, a crease of concern furrowing her brow.

"Who cares?" Sam answered. "I'll just do my job and let old Jack get the ulcer. He can do the worrying for a while."

"But couldn't he still make trouble for you?" Lee persisted. "Won't he keep trying to get you thrown out of the air force?"

Sam patted her cheek gently. "Honey, if what the Big Man in there said is true—and just looking around Saigon, I believe him—they're going to be throwing people *into* the service, not out." He glanced at his watch. "Come on. Let's collect Bill and Jim and get moving. We don't want you to be late for your flight." As Sam turned to leave he found the doughboy man in his path.

"Ahh, Colonel Brooks. I merely wanted to convey my congratulations on a job well done. If you should ever be interested in employment suitable to your, ahh, temperament, please let me know. I'm sure something could be arranged."

Sam stared as the overweight man walked in his oddly graceful manner toward the stairs.

The civilian terminal of Saigon's Tan Son Nhut airport was crowded with military and civilians either just arriving in country or getting ready to leave. It was easy to tell who was doing what. The new arrivals, thrown into a combat zone and not knowing what to expect, had that lost, close-to-panic look. Some obviously thought that the Viet Cong might suddenly start flinging grenades, for they tried to keep one eye on their luggage and the other on the myriad Vietnamese wandering about. Sam saw the gut-heavy sergeant who had met him on his first day in country and smiled at the memory. A lot of water under the bridge since then, and still several months left on his tour.

Lee was saying good-bye to Bill Robinson and Jim Christian as Sam watched the melange of people waiting, scurrying, and generally looking confused. Lee hugged Bill Robinson and kissed his cheek, promising to call his wife the moment she arrived in San Francisco and tell her to get the champagne iced for her husband's arrival only hours behind her. She clung fiercely to Jim Christian's neck. Lee would be staying with Jim's wife, her sister, until Jim DEROSed later in the month.

"You'd better be careful, doofus," Sam overheard her telling the Special Forces officer. "You mean a lot to both of us girls. And promise you'll take care of that one for me," she said, cutting her eyes in Sam's direction. "I've decided he's a keeper."

Christian hugged her hard, and turned away grinning. Sam was not surprised to see that the burly man had glistening eyes. His own began to moisten as she stepped in front of him.

"Sam Brooks," she said softly, "you know where I'll be. If you still want me when you finish over here, I'll be waiting. If you don't, well . . . I'll still be waiting."

Sam wrapped his arms around her and held her tight, hardly able to speak from the sudden constriction in his throat. He squeezed her until he felt her wince, then stepped back, held her at arm's length, and let his eyes roam over her face, trying to memorize every detail. She stared back silently.

"Lee," he faltered, "you know I'm not very good with words. Especially talking with women. But I want you to know that you've shown me a piece of life that I never knew existed. I was pretty soured on the world when I came over here, until you showed me . . . well, that things could be different. I think I loved you the first time I saw you and I can't think of a thing that could ever change that. I can't promise you that I'm ever going to make a good yard-mowing civilian, but if you'll marry me I'll do my damnedest to be the best fighter pilot husband there's ever been. The only thing I can say in my defense is that what you see is what you'll get. There'll be no surprises."

Lee's eyes crinkled at the corners but her mouth stayed straight, no hint of a smile. With her good hand she gently grabbed the front of his shirt and shook it gently.

"Listen, you bozo. I don't want a pet dog. I've had plenty of those sniffing after me for the last few years. I had a good man once and I lost him. I don't want to lose another, but I know that if I tried to leash you and turn you into a 'yard-mowing civilian,' as you put it, you wouldn't be the same person I was attracted to in the first place. I want *this* Sam Brooks." For emphasis, Lee jabbed her finger firmly into his chest. "Bark and bluster, egocentric and caring, selfless and selfish—the whole bundle of contradictions that make up people like you and Li'l Abner over there." She nodded her head toward Jim Christian.

"You do your job over here," she continued, "and try not to get your fool self killed. When you're through, you know where to find me."

Lee grabbed his neck and pulled his head down. Her lips pressed fiercely to his, then she abruptly pulled away and walked without looking back to the boarding gate where the outgoing passengers were being checked aboard. Sam stared after her, vaguely aware he had been joined by Bill and Jim. The three men watched as she marched straight-backed across the tarmac and up the ladder to the Boeing 707. She never once turned to look back.

It was early afternoon and the three men sat glumly around a shaded table in the outside bar at the Rex Hotel, sipping iced San Miguel beer. Bill Robinson was having trouble maintaining his sober countenance as he thought of his steadily approaching departure time. In truth, even Sam had started feeling better. After all, Lee's departure put her out of danger and they'd be together in only a few months. Then, there was the fighter squadron that would soon be arriving and his new job in it. His fingers actually twitched as he imagined holding the control stick of an F-100 once again.

Bill Robinson nudged him out of his reverie. "Uh, Sam, you probably saw me have a word with General Rogers before he left COMUSMACV's office today," he began.

Sam looked at him questioningly. "Sure, I saw you giving him last-minute advice on how to run his air war. So what? You tell everyone how to run their business."

"Well, the fact is," Robinson said, clearly uncomfortable, "we sorta discussed my replacement. You know, they haven't named a new ALO for IV Corps."

"So?" Sam asked, beginning to feel the itch he'd developed over the years when a bogie was trying to slide unnoticed into his six o'clock position.

"Well, you see the Table of Organization calls for a light colonel, and we were sort of wondering that since you'd been promoted and had all this experience down there in the delta if—"

"Oh, no you don't! They promised me the ops job in a fighter squadron and I'm going to damned well hold 'em to it. By God, if they think—"

"Easy, easy. It was just an idea. I mean, we thought that since they were getting all these new FACs in country, and there's damned few people who know shit from shinola about the war down there, it would really mean a lot to get everybody started off on the right foot. You know, there's plans for American units to be assigned to the northern part of the delta and they're going to be real handicapped if they don't have some experienced people to look after 'em."

Sam stared at him in disbelief, then turned to find Christian grinning at him like an idiot.

"I mean, you don't have to do it, of course. The general assured me that they'd honor the promise they gave you about the fighter squadron. It's just that . . ." His voice trailed off.

Sam stared at one, then the other, his mouth sagging open. They both looked at him with expectant smiles. Slowly he shook his head, then lowered it until his face was resting in both palms. "Aw, crap!" he mumbled.

Bill Robinson patted him gently on the shoulder, then sat back with a satisfied smile. He looked at the grinning Christian. "Pretty day, isn't it? Just makes a man glad to be alive and kicking."

Praise for Marshall Harrison's previous books:

A Lonely Kind of War: Forward Air Controller, Vietnam

"An instant classic—the best book about the air war over Vietnam in more than a decade."
—Topeka Capital-Journal

"A vivid slice of combat life . . . an outstanding first-person experience. Air-to-ground war stories don't get much better than this one."
—Airpower Journal

"One of the best personal narratives to come out of the Vietnam era. Harrison is a storyteller and a good one."
—Marine Corps Gazette

"A tough, stirring account. . . . Very good writing indeed.
—The Book Reader

Cadillac Flight: A Novel

"A real fireball of a book. Take a ride with *Cadillac Flight* for a trip you won't soon forget."
—Rocky Mountain News

"Taut and realistic war fiction . . . *Cadillac Flight* is to Hollywoodized warfare as prime rib is to cotton candy."
—Amarillo Globe-News

"A realistic military adventure . . . supports a lot of first-rate flying scenes."
—The Kirkus Reviews

"War as she is lived. Powerful."
—The Book Reader

"Authentic and thrilling."
—Times Record News

About the author

Marshall Harrison, a retired Air Force officer, served three combat tours in Vietnam. His last active duty assignment was as an intelligence officer with the Defense Intelligence Agency. Harrison's previous books are *A Lonely Kind of War*, the critically acclaimed account of his experiences as a forward air controller, and *Cadillac Flight*, his first novel. He now lives in Lubbock, Texas.